BURN FOR HER

THE REFLECTION SERIES
BOOK 1

BY BRIANA MICHAELS

COPYRIGHT

OTHER BOOKS BY THIS AUTHOR

DEDICATION

To all the vampires I've loved—The Lost Boys, Dracula, the Black Dagger Brotherhood, and Lestat—cheers to sinking your teeth in and swallowing.

PROLOGUE

Nearly three hundred years ago...

Thunder cracked and lightning shredded the sky as the boy staggered through the woods, bloody and broken. Wheezing, he pressed his trembling hand against the most painful of his many wounds. Blood flowed freely from between his fingers. His lungs ached, caught between frozen and burning. A fresh wave of panic and terror propelled him forward. Unbalanced, his bare feet slipped in mud causing him to slide down a small ravine and crash into the river.

The harsh chill of the water attacked his burns, both soothing and searing them at the same time. The current was too strong for his weak body to fight. He let it drag him under and smack his brittle bones against the large rocks. Instinct demanded he kick his legs harder, faster, while his arms pinwheeled and clawed at the water. Finally, his head broke through the surface and he gasped for air.

The current sucked him down again.

In this darkness, he saw nothing. The chill of his terror combined with the frigid water, froze the marrow in his bones. He was tired. So tired.

Should he continue to let the river drag him down to the bottom, or should he crawl his way out? More than anything, he just wanted it to be over. *Please let this be over... by death or by miracle, please someone end this nightmare.*

The whispering, taunting, seductive voice of death tried to

lure him into a watery grave. His ears filled with the rushing current of the river. His eyes blinded to all rock, felled tree, and whatever else lay ahead of him. His back slammed against something hard and sharp. It forced the rest of the air to leave his lungs while blinding white agony shot stars in his vision.

He was going to throw up.

He was going to drown.

He wasn't ready yet. Not ready to give up. Not ready to relent to death's peaceful embrace. He needed air. He needed help. The next boulder he crashed into, he clutched the sharp edges and pulled upwards. Squeezing his eyes shut, his head broke through the surface again. His grip slipped and the current swept him away.

But this time he fought it.

Snagging a low hanging branch whipping through the wind and rain, he clung to it with both hands. Using it as a lifeline, he painstakingly pulled himself up and out of the water.

Every bone in his body ached with exhaustion from over a decade of brutality.

It's over, he told himself. *It's over.*

He was losing too much blood, which made him slow and disoriented. He couldn't afford either weakness right now. Wolves would scent him. If he didn't get moving, he'd be dinner.

And there were worse things than wolves out there...

Trudging through the woods to get away from the river, he stumbled, fell, and dragged himself across the ground, leaving a bloody trail in his wake. There was a light ahead. Small and blurry, that tiny glow was all the hope this dark forest offered, so he locked his gaze on it and forced himself to keep going.

It took forever to reach the light source. His eyes kept shutting and legs kept wobbling. He vomited twice, but his empty belly cramped with nothing except dry heaves. He didn't care. He ignored the pain, dismissed his fear, bit back his next whimper, and banged on the solid wooden door of the cabin shining the single light like a beacon calling him to safety.

The door swung open.

His eyes widened a fraction with panic. Danger stood before him, staring down at him with a growl. *Lycan.* As if some piece of his soul recognized what this beast was by instinct, he knew it was a

Lycan. A powerful one. A dangerous one.

But he had no strength left to run away from the beast staring down at him.

The Lycan's fierce gaze shot fear through the boy's veins. They stared at one another, neither moving.

"Who is it?" A woman peered from around the large Lycan's shoulder. She held a hand protectively over her swollen belly. "Alistair, who's at the door? Move so I can see."

"Get back, Marie. It's a vampire."

She didn't listen. "He looks like he's been half eaten alive!"

"Get. Back. Marie." The shifter's hulking body took up every square inch of the doorway. "What is your name, boy? What House are you from?"

"Dorian." He slowly blinked and swayed with the effort to keep upright. "No House." He so badly wanted to be stronger than he was but had nothing left in him except terror and starvation. "I... have... no other place... to go."

At the threshold of his sworn enemy's doorstep, he collapsed in the shifter's arms.

CHAPTER 1

Present Day

"There's not enough room to fuck inside a coffin and don't let anyone tell you otherwise."

Dorian grimaced as he clenched his teeth. He didn't want to know how Lucian knew that.

"It's true." Lucian kept yammering. "Unless the lid has a sizeable bump out." The vampire tapped his chin, thoughtfully. "Then *maybe*. I'm considering having one special ordered for the club just to test it out."

Not surprising. Lucian was willing to try anything at least once. Dorian gave him the side-eye and kept walking. Lucian couldn't help his constant chatting any more than Dorian could contain his anger most days.

"I had the best sex ever last night."

"You went to the club?" Dorian highly doubted that.

"Hell no."

"Then who'd you fuck?"

"Myself." Lucian shrugged. "I know just how I like it. Therefore, I'm never disappointed."

Holy Hell. "Please stop talking."

"Jealous? Because if you ever—"

"Hard pass."

"You can be top."

There was no universe where Dorian *wasn't* a top. "Pass."

"You don't know what you're missing." Lucian had the nerve to waggle his eyebrows.

"I'm good."

"You're not good, Dorian. You're miserable just like the rest of us."

Lucian wasn't wrong. Between the never-ending war with the *Savag-Ri*, last week's catastrophe, and the blood curse acting as a constant reminder of how strong their misery flowed, vampires like Dorian and Lucian were more than miserable. They were tortured.

Dorian locked his jaw and kept walking. Even now, his rage burned hot in his veins. Unrest was dangerous for a vampire.

But after what happened last week with Luke, no one blamed him or anyone else for being on edge. Dorian just needed to get through tonight, then maybe this constant angst riding his ass like a jockey at the derby would ease up. He also seriously needed to feed. Accustomed to going weeks or even months without tapping a vein, he might have let it go a little too long this time. Groaning, he massaged the back of his neck while keeping a steady pace down the hallway and immediately fell into a rabbit hole of dark thoughts. Like always.

Lucian grabbed his shoulder and the sudden, unwanted contact sparked Dorian's aggression. He whirled around and slammed his friend against the wall and hissed. It took him a full three seconds to put a lid on his temper and shove it down where it belonged. "Don't grab me like that."

Lucian put his hands up and got serious. "Shit, sorry. I was trying to get your attention. You checked out on me, and I forgot you don't like contact on your shoulder."

"It's fine."

"It's not fine," Lucian said just as hostile as Dorian. "I'm up to my ass with this shit and haven't slept in five days. I've grown careless. I didn't mean to set you off or show disrespect."

"It's fine." Christ, was that all he could say tonight?

Lucian didn't talk again until they nearly reached the inner sanctum of the Kill Box.

Now Dorian felt like an asshole for snapping. Lucian shouldn't have to apologize for anything. Of the two of them, Lucian suffered far worse than Dorian right now. He needed to cut his friend some slack.

"Hey." Dorian paused with his hand on the doorknob. "I'm sorry for losing my temper."

2

"Stop talking and go to work, Reaper."

Just like that, Lucian was no longer the smiling, outrageously wild and funny guy. He was back to his tense, sullen, bad attitude.

That was Dorian's fault. He should have been more present for Lucian and less holed up in his own darkness lately. Especially after what happened last week. He glared at Lucian for a hot second, his hand still clutching the door handle.

"Let's just get this over with," Lucian growled. "I'm sick of death and want to get out of this Hell."

This, he said, to the Reaper. Dorian's heart remained quiet in its cage, but the pain in Lucian's tone applied a good amount of pressure on his sternum. "I'm sorry about—"

"Go, Reaper. Everyone is waiting."

Dorian swung open the door, shut down his mind, and went into kill-mode.

The prisoner's laughter died out the second Dorian entered the room.

"You know who I am." It wasn't a question. Everyone knew who Dorian was. He rolled his sleeves up to avoid any stains on his crisp, white Armani dress shirt. "Let's not waste anyone's time with bullshit."

Without saying a word, the *Savag-Ri* spat in Dorian's face.

He'd pay for that in a minute.

With an eerie calmness, Dorian reached into his back pocket. He loved how the *Savag-Ri's* eyes went from defiant to scared shitless in a blink. Pulling out a red handkerchief, Dorian cleaned the spit from between his eyes and calmly asked, "Where's Stryx?"

"Don't know what you're talking about."

He hated foreplay like this. It was boring and made the clean up barely worth it. "Let's see if this jogs your memory." Dorian slammed the *Savag-Ri's* stomach with a well-placed punch, then held him with one hand on the nape of the fucker's neck, the other grabbing his balls and squeezing. Dorian felt those twin danglies burst when he crushed them in his palm. "Is your memory working yet or should I crack that swizzle stick you call a cock in half to help you remember things more clearly?"

The *Savag-Ri* shrieked and fell to his knees, panting with pain. "I don't know where he is."

Dorian glanced over at Lucian and the other vampires watching. He didn't like voyeurism. Death was personal. So was torture. Bending low, he snarled, "When did you last see Stryx?"

"A month ago, at least," the *Savag-Ri* sung in soprano. "Swear it. And I didn't touch him—it got me two weeks in the hole for my mercy."

Typically, vampires didn't take a *Savag-Ri's* word for shit. They were liars, cheats, and killers. Guess they shared that in common with their mortal enemy, huh? But *Savag-Ri* have hunted vampires for thousands of years. Since vampires were better as predators than prey, they enjoyed hunting those motherfuckers right back. It was a glorious, endless, and dangerous game of cat and mouse.

Some, like this piece of shit, were too easy and no fun to play with. Time to see if it was game over for this sniveling soprano. Glancing over at Lucian—who was basically a living lie detector—Dorian waited for him to make the call. The vampire's eye twitched. The others in the room wouldn't notice the small gesture, but Dorian never missed it. The gesture meant the fun was over and there was nothing else to work towards. The prisoner was telling the truth.

Dorian figured as much.

This *Savag-Ri* was useless to them, so playing with him only wasted precious time. Dorian took a second to glance around the archaic room. The Kill Box reeked of old blood, rust, curses, and defeat. Every layer of grime, piss, and body fluid added another level of dangerous oaths—promises of revenge and justice. Dirty deeds and corruption. Bargains and lies.

As dark and depraved as Dorian was, this disgusting place was home to him. Not that he'd ever admit it to anyone. Chains, shackles, hooks, and an impressive collection of tools, the Kill Box was more a workshop than an execution room. This was his domain. No vampire judged his methods of getting information out of *Savag-Ri*, or the forms of execution he chose. However twisted the carnage, however long Dorian dragged the punishment out, no one insulted his use of imagination.

Sometimes they paid double.

4

Vampires had iron stomachs and a bloodthirst that went beyond the nourishment of their bodies. They were all sadists in one manner or another.

Royalty and aristocrats wouldn't dream of showing their gruesome sides in public. They were too pure-blooded for it. There were exceptions, of course, but none came close to Dorian's level of unrepentant savagery. That is why he served as the House of Death's Reaper.

"You're not good, Dorian. You're miserable just like the rest of us." Yeah, Lucian's words hit a little too close to home. Calmly walking over to a wall of goodies, he grabbed a short-handled scythe. He'd be a liar to say this wasn't his favorite toy. The weight of the steel and well-worn handle grounded him in a surreal fashion he'd grown dependent on.

"Any last words?"

The *Savag-Ri* leaned back on his haunches, wheezing. "You'll never—"

While the bastard was halfway into his wasted remark, Dorian sliced through the air. The cut was quick and clean. The *Savag-Ri's* mouth was fixed and open, his stare cold, body paralyzed. Then, in slow motion, blood welled across his neck. His head slipped off and rolled onto the floor with a thud. Right on cue, the body slackened and slumped to the side, pulling his chains taut.

One less piece of shit prowling the earth.

Glancing at the audience, Dorian cocked his eyebrow and asked, "Want me to piece him out or did you have something else in mind for this sack of shit?"

The King of the House of Bone rose from his seat with a scowl. "You delivered him *mercy*," Marius hissed. "Why?"

"I delivered him nothing but his fate." Dorian stepped back before the blood touched his shoes. "He knew nothing and I'm not wasting my time, or anyone else's, with petty cuts and breaks. We'll use his bones for dust. That's all he's good for."

Marius's eyes blackened with rage. "We paid you for torture."

"His or yours, Marius?" Dorian's aggression rose to the surface again. "Because I assure you, I never disappoint a paying client." To make his message clear, Dorian licked the blood from the scythe and grinned. "Your call."

Marius shuffled as if he was actually going to do something to make Dorian's day, but Lucian stopped the stupid prick from advancing. With a cool tone, Lucian said, "I'm sure the House of Bone appreciates your swift delivery of justice, Dorian. Had there been any hope of getting more information, we trust you would have sensed it and gotten it out of the *Savag-Ri* one way or another. Your time is valuable, as I'm sure Marius is well aware."

Marius looked like he'd just sucked on a lemon dipped in battery acid. "I want to know where my son is!"

"He's not in this room, so I suggest you keep looking elsewhere." Dorian sucked at being nice. He didn't have patience for assholes like Marius who thought because he was a pure-blooded royal, he could boss lesser vampires like Dorian around.

Lucian held the door open for the other vampires who came to watch, as they exited in hushed tones of disappointment and frustration. They wanted a bloodbath and Dorian hadn't given them one.

Well tough fucking shit. If they wanted gore, they should learn to make it themselves instead of constantly looking at Dorian to fulfill their depraved desires.

Now he felt dirty and used. Again.

"Clean this up, Marius," Lucian barked, "and take the body back to the House of Bone with you. There are coffins in there," he said, pointing at a chipped wooden door with ornate iron hinges, "for you to transport this carcass in."

"I am to clean this mess up myself?" The pampered king looked appalled, which added a few centuries worth of wrinkles to his prissy, sharp features. "This is beyond disgraceful. How dare you treat me in such a way."

"You wanted this done, Marius." Dorian did the King of the House of Bone a favor and wiped the scythe clean before hanging it back on its proper hook. "Which means *you* have to deal with the aftermath. That's non-negotiable and not at all new."

When Dorian took the job as executioner, he made rules about what he wanted in return. Vampires who hired him to do their dirty work still needed to get their hands filthy. There was a price to everything, both during and after death. The House of Death didn't see a problem with that, so the rule stuck.

"There's a hose and towels in the storage closet," Dorian pointed in the general direction for him.

6

Marius's face turned crimson with rage. "But my son is still not found! This was all for nothing!"

Dorian was on him in a flash. Grabbing the pompous bastard by the throat, he growled, "Then I suggest you hurry and clean this place up so you can keep looking for him. I did you a favor by not wasting time. The more you whine, the more time you waste here when you could be looking for your son."

Marius slapped Dorian's arm away. "This isn't over, Dorian. We paid you for torture. For answers and you've given us *nothing*."

"I gave you all that *Savag-Ri* had to offer." Dorian backed up nice and slow before he got tempted to snatch the scythe again and do something he might later regret. The Houses weren't necessarily friendly with one another anymore and to start a war with the House of Bone, when their own House was in disarray, wasn't ideal. "Dust his bones and place chunks of his flesh around all the hot spots you know your son favored. A *Savag-Ri* will smell the rotten meat and recognize it. They'll retaliate. When they do, call me. Until then, keep your money and get out of my fucking face."

"This is unacceptable," Marius sneered and put great effort into not making eye contact with the entourage he brought to the Kill Box. "You can't dismiss us like this."

Dorian flashed him a predatory smile. "Watch me." Then he growled low in his throat, reminding Marius exactly who and what he was up against. Dorian reveled in how the king took two chicken-shit steps backwards.

With a chuckle, Dorian swung open the heavy metal door and stepped out of the Kill Box feeling more murderous than he had five minutes ago. When Lucian caught up with him halfway down the tunnel, Dorian was breathing deep to calm the hell down.

Jesus, why was he so angry? This was a routine execution, and a quick one. He literally had no reason to feel so set off.

"You good?"

"Fine," Dorian lied. "That little shit didn't know anything. Marius's son is likely still out there."

"Think Stryx went Rogue?"

"Maybe."

"Shit, if that's the case then this just got a thousand times more complicated."

"I'll take care of it."

"You'll start a war if you do."

Dorian whirled on Lucian and got all in his face. "You want bloodshed then you want peace. You can't have both, Lucian. If Marius's son has gone Rogue, he *must* be put down. It's law."

"I know." Lucian didn't even flinch. "I also know that Marius is influential with the House of Blood, which could bring other problems to our doorstep. If you deliver his son's ashes, he'll think you did it out of spite, not justice."

"I don't give a flying fuck about his son or what Marius thinks."

"That's exactly my point." Lucian pushed back with a firm hand on Dorian's arm.

Dorian stopped dead in his tracks because he needed to give Lucian a margin of grace. He looked down at where Lucian's firm grip had a hold on him, then flicked his gaze to the vampire. "I fail to see your goddamn point."

Lucian released his grip. "You're a cold-hearted killer. The Reaper, Dorian. Your reputation has an extremely long reach for someone who's only three-hundred years old."

He didn't know what to say to that. The vampire society made him the monster he is. Well... not entirely, but they certainly helped his dark side flourish. Dorian ground his molars together and let his fangs pierce the inside of his bottom lip. The sting and burn were swiftly quelled by the heady taste of his own blood in his mouth. He swallowed before saying, "My job is to execute our enemies. By law, a Rogue is an enemy."

Rogues were vampires who broke away from one of the three vampire Houses to be on their own. Most vampires indulged in drinking from humans, but it was more for fun than nutrition. Without powerful vampire blood to sustain them, which was always supplied in the Houses, they eventually lost their minds and control. Once that happened, they bit, maimed, and killed anything that breathed. If a Rogue turned a human into a vampire during this manic state, that person would also need to be put down due to their instability and tainted blood. Otherwise, a toxic turn like that ate their mind and they became a threat to all societies — vampire, human, Lycan, even the vile *Savag-Ri*.

It was a vicious cycle and one of the many reasons why vampires had a specific code they lived by. Rogues needed to be executed. End of story.

"*If* Stryx has gone Rogue," Lucian warned, jabbing his finger at Dorian, "and that's a big fucking if, then he'll need to be captured and brought to judgment first. Marius will need irrefutable proof that his son is beyond saving. Even then, this could get incredibly messy. I doubt Stryx has gone in that direction though. Rogues are sloppy and mindless. By now he'd have been seen and captured if that was the case."

Hence why they snatched a *Savag-Ri* to question instead. Those pricks were a tight-knit crew with a well-oiled communication system. Not to mention they were insufferable braggers. Always comparing kills. Always wanting credit for taking another of Dorian's kind down.

Vampires weren't that way. They killed quietly. Secretively. Selectively. Passionately and possessively. Death was a personal thing, and they didn't take it lightly. The only time a vampire craved mercy was when one of their own was facing a death sentence. That's why executions were always brought to a deliberation first, which was a waste of time in Dorian's opinion.

But that's what all immortals had, right? Time and insurmountable patience.

Only one thing made both those commodities run out fast—*alakhai*. Their fated mate.

Dorian never bothered to put effort into searching for his because he'd never drag a soulmate into Hell with him. Some lives were best spent alone. Others filled their time by hunting *Savag-Ri*, fucking each other, playing with human minds, and throwing parties.

And when it came to hunting down their enemies, a vampire's predator instincts were satisfied, and the thrill of the slaughter never got old. Dorian was no exception. He lived for that shit.

Vampires were like cats with a world full of mice. How brutally they behaved depended on how bored they were. That was the lifestyle Dorian thrived in. That was all he knew. All he wanted. All he fucking deserved.

"Relax. Stryx could be dead already." Dorian pulled his keys out of his pocket. "Or maybe he ran away because he was tired of living under his father's thumb and following the House of Bone's rules. Either way, it's not my problem." He turned to head towards his car. He needed to get away from this place and clear his mind.

Lucian's tone cut through the gathering darkness in Dorian's head. "Meet me at the mansion in twenty."

Dorian froze. Turned. Frowned. "Why?"

"Someone's waiting there for you."

"Who?"

"I think you know the answer."

Shit, if his girl was there, something must be very, very wrong.

CHAPTER 2

Dorian pulled up to the House of Death's mansion and parked on the pad out back. Trudging up the steps to the main door, he saw Lucian already waiting for him, which was frustrating as hell. That vampire was a fast one. Faster than most, which was why he remained at the top of the food chain. Dorian was nearly equal to him in rank, but only because of his brutal, merciless kill streak.

"She's been here a while," Lucian shut and locked the front door behind them.

"You didn't want to tell me this *before* the execution?"

"Business first," Lucian said, clearly not giving two shits about how cruel that sounded. "I needed you to keep your focus in the Kill Box. Marius is looking for reasons to have our House infested and dominated. I'm not going to let that happen."

Dorian couldn't argue with the judgment call. His pace quickened to get to his girl. *His girl.* Shit, no one better hear that slip from his tongue in this House. "Where is she?"

"In the library."

Dorian walked the rest of the way, alone. Ignoring the dagger-like gazes of the vampires living in the House of Death, he set his jaw and kept moving forward. They might not like her being here, but they knew better than to get too close to her.

Vampires and Lycan weren't mortal enemies, but they weren't exactly on the same side either. History and curses were wedged between their species, and one blamed the other for everything they've been forced to suffer.

He practically raced to get to her. Each beat of his heart,

pound of his step, and exhale of air fueled his speed and aggression. By the time Dorian reached the library, he nearly kicked the door down.

The library was stacked with shelves of books, mix-matched furniture, and at least ten mirrors varying in sizes. A blue Persian rug stretched across in the center of the room, faded from the sunlight pouring in through the large windows. In the center of the rug, was his girl, and a vicious vampire.

"Victoria, get away from her." Dorian stormed inside.

Victoria was a vampire who spent her existence alternating between the thrills of tease, tempt, and take. She was older than Dorian by at least fifty years, yet her adventurous lifestyle made her seem younger. "I was only consoling her." She stood up and brushed her dress to smooth the wrinkles. "Relax, Reaper."

She moved out of Dorian's way so he could see his girl wasn't hurt by Victoria's hands or fangs. His eyes locked on Emily, who sat on the floor with a box of tissues in her lap. The tip of her nose was red, her eyes swollen, her face gaunt.

How long had she been here crying? Why was she crying? Who made her upset?

Because Dorian was going to fucking kill them.

"Em." He dropped to his knees and crawled over to her, even though his insides screamed to get up off the dirty floor. But his needs were secondary to Emily today. He'd suck it up and scrub clean later.

"Better not let the others see," Victoria hissed from behind him.

"Leave," Dorian growled, not taking his eyes off Emily. "*Now*, Victoria, before I rip your throat out."

"A vampire crawling like a dog to get to a sobbing pup will *ruin* your reputation, Reaper."

Growling, he turned to give Victoria her final warning. She was a hunting partner of his, but that didn't mean he wouldn't rip her heart out and make her watch while he ate it.

"Okay, okay, I'm going." She left in a huff and closed the door.

Dorian heard the lock click into place and finally exhaled. Now he was able to put all his attention back where it belonged. "Are you hurt?"

Emily hiccupped and grabbed another tissue from the box in her lap. "No."

Then why was she all emotional like this? Shit. "Is someone else hurt?" His heart slammed into his ribs with worry. "Talk to me, Em. I can't fix it if you don't tell me what's wrong."

"They don't see me. Not like you." Emily dropped her tissues.

Ahh crap, not this again.

"Don't," he warned. "You can't do this, Emily. It's not fair to either of us."

Emily was like a sister to him and that was all. He'd been raised by her pack and when he reached his final transition to full vampire, things hadn't gone well between the House he chose, and the pack he left behind. It took the better part of two centuries for them to be friendly with each other for Dorian's sake.

To make it worse, a year ago, one of Emily's brothers had turned. As in shifted to his wolf form and remained an animal with no chance of ever shifting back. He was lost to his beast because he hadn't found his mate in time.

Emily tried to reach out to cup his face, but he dodged her. "I said *don't*."

Emily bristled, half-hurt, half-pissed off. "You're the only one for me, Dorian. You have to be."

"Stop," he hissed. Her words cut too deep because they were lies she kept feeding herself to avoid her fate. It was starting to poke too many holes in his heart. "I'm not the one for you, and you know it." When she tried to grab him again, he clutched her wrists and held her still. "Stop it, Emily."

She was too good for him. No matter how much she wished it, they weren't soul mates. No god would be so cruel as to tie a sick fuck like Dorian to a sweetheart like Emily. This wasn't the first time she'd gone down this hole, either. Falling in love and mating were two very different things in their worlds. Besides, crossing the line between Lycan and vampires was a huge no-no. Dorian hated that she was back to the idea of them being together because it meant she was turning desperate. Damn, just look at her sunken cheeks and her sallow skin. And the way her t-shit hung off her bony shoulders, it was obvious she'd lost weight recently.

Dorian's brow pinched and he made sure to keep his tone softer than normal. "When was the last time you ate?"

Emily turned nasty on that note. "Screw you, Dorian."

"You can't starve yourself, Em. You know what that'll do. It's already happening." He gripped her chin and tilted her head towards the light. "Your eyes are already bloodshot."

"From *crying.*" She smacked his hand away. "Not starvation."

"You know better than to lie to me."

She wouldn't make eye contact with him now. A Lycan's way of admission and submission.

Something horrible stirred in Dorian's veins. A hunger that nearly drove him to do the unthinkable. Biting down on his bottom lip, he pierced his flesh and licked the blood dripping down the corners of his mouth.

Emily watched him do it, and she paled with disgust.

Dorian laughed through his hurt pride. "You say we're meant to be, yet you can't stand to look at my fangs. Or the blood they draw so effortlessly."

Emily leaned back until her head and spine smacked the floor. Rubbing her face, she sighed. "I feel crazy, Dorian."

And that's why you say I'm the only one who can see you, he thought bitterly.

They were two peas in a pod. Always had been. No romance, lust, or emotion bound them together. Yet, in her worst moments, Emily always sought Dorian out and damned if he didn't come crawling to her aid every single time.

"Why now?" He laid on his back, next to her on the floor. "What's happened in the pack I haven't heard about yet?"

"There's going to be another ceremony soon. Dad's making this one really big and has invited *everyone.*" She looked over at him, her eyes red-rimmed from crying. "He asked if I'd participate."

Dorian's heart wedged into his throat. "And... will you?"

"Would *you*?" She glowered.

"You know the answer." He scrubbed his face and stared up at the ceiling because he couldn't stand the look of agony on her face.

"Better to live a half-life alone than chase after destiny and be killed by fate," Emily said, throwing the words he'd said to her, more than a hundred times growing up, back in his face.

"That's right." Dorian avoided mirrors for the same reason Emily wanted to avoid the Lycan ceremony. Once they caught a

14

glimpse of their true soulmate, their lives would be over.

But damned if something thorny didn't pierce his heart hearing her say those words now. He wanted Emily happy. He wanted the best of everything for her, and that included a mate. Sure, she could fuck anyone and have a relationship with whomever she wished — *just not him* — but if a Lycan found their true soul mate, it was a complete gamechanger in the best of ways.

Or worst.

Dorian hated that she was even contemplating it, almost as much as he loathed the idea of her actually going through with it.

When a Lycan drank liquid silver during a ceremony, they dreamt of their mate at some point before the full moon. It could be that night, or three weeks later. There was no way to guess when the vision would arise. But once it did, the Lycan had until the next full moon to hunt down and find their mate. If they didn't, they were forced into their animal form and trapped in it. Lost. Alone. Tortured to howl for a mate who would never answer. They eventually went insane and would need to be killed before they returned and devoured their pack or anyone else who crossed their path, including humans.

It was even worse for vampires. Contrary to the age-old myth about vampires not being able to see their reflections, they most definitely could. It was their goddamn kryptonite. They saw their mate in reflections. Once they caught the first glimpse of their soulmate — their *alakhai* — the clock started ticking. If they didn't find, bond, and turn their mate in time, the vampire weakened, went mad, and ultimately burned to ash.

Unlike Lycan, who knew their time ran out at the next full moon, vampires had no way of knowing how long they had physically. But mental deterioration began almost immediately upon the first glimpse of seeing their soul mate. They became more violent, possessive, and uncontrolled until they drank from their fated mate's vein and ultimately turned them into vampires too.

In both instances, a vampire and Lycan became ticking time bombs as they searched for the one cure to ease their suffering and rarely did they find it. So yeah, you bet your ass it was better to live a half-life alone than chase after destiny and be killed by fate. Dorian avoided all reflections because of this. So long as he didn't see his fated mate in a reflection, his blood curse would remain as is—putting him in a constant state of longing. But if he saw his *alakhai*, it was game over. The curse would kick into the next phase and slowly kill him unless he found his mate and turned her in time.

The curse sucked for both Lycan and vampire.

As much as Dorian wanted to protect Emily from ever risking her life, he had to make sure her decision to drink or not drink the liquid silver was entirely hers and wasn't tainted by *his* insecurities. "I'll stand by you," he said. "If you want to drink it, I'll go to the ceremony and be there for you. I'll one-hundred percent support you." It had been a long time since he stepped foot on pack land, but she was worth it.

"You're serious?"

"Dead serious." He looked over at her again, his emotions ebbing away so he could deal with this better. "And if you want to reject the ceremony, we can go out for the night and get sloshed. How's that sound?"

"Like heaven," she said. "Both options do, actually."

Oh fuck, her chin was quivering and her eyes started leaking again. Damnit, he was shit at consoling people. Emily rolled onto her side and Dorian just froze on the floor. He knew he should hold her, but that would be like holding a grenade with the pin out. No thank you.

She started bawling her eyes out again. It gutted him. He could never take her tears and now he no longer cared about the fallout of his actions. "Fuck, Em, come here."

He hooked his arm around her waist and dragged her against his chest. If a vampire ever saw how he behaved with Emily, they would never let him hear the end of it. His reputation for being a terrifying killer would be questioned or challenged. But he didn't give a rat's ass about his reputation right now. All he cared about was being there for his girl like her family had been there for him so long ago.

"I get it," he said against her ear. "I completely get it, Emily, and I'm right there with you."

She was afraid to have the same fate as her brother, Killian. Dorian was too. Being creatures like them meant it was a damned if you do, damned if you don't, situation when it came to their endgame. Kissing the back of Emily's head, he held her tight until she finally put a muzzle and choke collar on her anxiety and pulled away from him. Her hair was tangled. Jeans ripped. T-shirt wrinkled. The woman looked like she always did — adorably messy.

"Shit, I'm sorry." Emily stood up. "I hate it when I get like this."

Dorian kept his mouth shut. There was no need for her to apologize, but she wouldn't see it that way.

"What time is it?" she said asked, looking around the room for a clock.

He glanced at his watch. "Two-sixteen."

"In the *morning*?" Emily's eyes widened. "Shit! Emerick's going to *kill* me!"

"What time were you to meet him?"

"We're heading home at three am. I'm to be there at 2:30 because he knows I always run late."

"Where?"

"Café DuMonde."

"You didn't tell him you were coming to see me?"

"No." Emily cringed in shame. "I took an Uber halfway and walked the other six blocks to get here."

Unprotected. In vampire territory. But Dorian knew better than most that Emily could handle herself in a fight. He'd taught her how to protect herself.

"Why didn't you have him drop you off?"

"I don't want him to know I'm upset about the ceremony. He'll worry too much, and he's got enough on his plate as it is."

"I'll drive you."

"No, I'll just make him come pick me up here. I feel like a shit for sneaking over anyway. And now I smell like vampire. He'll know exactly where I went." Her cell went off. She frowned and pulled it out of her pocket, "Shit, it's him." Hitting the button, she rolled her eyes. "I'm not late, asshole. Give me a min — oh. Okay. Yeah, fine. Yeah, I will." She hung up and withered, "He's out front."

"He knew you'd come here."

Emily rolled her eyes. "He said to tell you '*Hi*'."

Dorian chuckled and made a note to text Emerick later.

Grumbling about overbearing brothers, Emily stormed across the room and went to the wrong door. She swung it open, then

17

slammed it shut. "I hate this damn Mad House. How do you get out of this place?"

"In a body bag."

"Ha ha, very funny." She opened another door, identical to the last, and it was also the wrong choice. "Damnit!" She slammed that one too. There were several doors and two secret passageways in the library, so it was a little confusing.

"To your left," he said, lightly chuckling.

While Dorian stood up and brushed off his pants, Emily beelined to the exit, then doubled back and tackled him in a hug. "Thanks for putting up with my shit. I love you." She kissed his cheek and shoved off him again. "I'll let you know my decision when I make it."

His fat tongue clogged his mouth, and he didn't say a word. Nodding, he watched her race out of the library, nearly running Victoria over in the process. "Sorry, Vic!"

"Well," Victoria said from the doorway. "I believe your girl just broke a record for speeding out of the Mad House, Dorian."

He straightened his shirt and tugged the sleeves down. He despised wrinkles in his clothing and now he was covered in them.

Victoria strolled in and got a little too close for comfort. "Will she be okay?"

"I have no idea." He rubbed the back of his neck, eager to get the fuck out of this mirrored mansion and home where he belonged.

"Will you stay the night?" Her words offered a proposal. Though she didn't touch him, it was obvious she wanted to.

"Can't." He kept his gaze locked on the doorway and headed for it. Slipping past Victoria, he knew she wouldn't dare try to stop him, and thank fuck for that. For being the loneliest sonofabitch in the world, women were drawn to him like magnets. He questioned their sanity because of it. No woman in her right mind should be drawn to a dangerous monster like Dorian. It bent reason.

However, Victoria was a willing lover for many. She craved touch the way Dorian craved violence.

Before he was delayed by anyone else, Dorian quickened his pace and headed to the east wing. In his peripheral vision, he noticed other vampires leaning against the walls and whispering to one another, along with several large paintings hung with elaborate frames, and mirrors stretched from the floor to the motherfucking

18

ceiling.

It made him feel as though the mansion was closing in on him. Avoiding each mirror and reflective surface took tremendous navigational skill to get through the house and a focus that remained more on the floor and furniture than looking eye-level at anything. It was enough to drive him batshit crazy.

He walked faster and got halfway down the steps when someone called out to him.

"Dorian."

He stopped on a dime. *Fuck, fuck, fuuuuck.*

There was only one vampire with such a commanding tone. Dorian slowed his roll on the stairs. His brain checked out as he went into an autopilot state-of-mind. It wasn't compulsion, it was conditioning that made him so obedient. Once his feet hit the first floor, he swiftly crossed the vestibule and entered the only room this particularly powerful vampire dwelled in. "Yes, sire?"

"What news have you?"

Dorian wasn't sure how to answer. Was the Mad King asking about the *Savag-Ri* he'd executed, Emily's appearance, or Stryx's disappearance?

"All is well, my lord." Dorian came closer to the master of the House of Death. There was a reason this place was also dubbed the Mad House, but Dorian would never make light of the king's ailment.

"Approach."

Rolling his shoulders back, Dorian slapped on his cold-hearted gaze and came towards the king. All he could see from this position was the back of Malachi's head. His long, thick, tangled hair was like a nest of unrefined waves. His broad shoulders made the enormous chair he sat in look almost dainty.

Malachi didn't budge from his seat, nor blink to break his stare from the gold-gilded floor-length mirror set before him, even when Dorian stood between him and the silvered glass. Dorian made sure to give the mirror his back when he addressed his master. "My lord, what do you need from me?"

"Marius means to usurp me," Malachi said in a deep, rough tone. "Do not allow it."

"Never."

"Do not play into his hand, Reaper. Give him *nothing* to use

19

against you."

"I won't."

"Maybe you already have." Malachi's stare remained fixated on the mirror behind Dorian. The king's color was so pale, even with the constant string of veins he fed upon night after night.

Yet Malachi's power was undeniable.

And mentally crushing.

Dorian needed to get the hell out of here. "I gave Marius exactly what he paid for. Nothing more and nothing less."

The Mad King's lips quirked upwards into a half-smile. "Be sure it stays that way, Reaper, or I'll tear your throat out with my teeth and feed you to that wolf you're so hellbent on coddling."

Dorian's hiss ripped from between his teeth before he could stop it.

Malachi was on him in an instant. The power, speed, and force with which he spun Dorian around and slammed his face against the mirror was mind-blowing. And even then, that crazy son-of-a-bitch didn't break his stare from the mirror.

That's why Malachi, even in his maddened state, was still king after all this time. It was also why Dorian chose this House to serve. This king was too strong to take down and gave zero fucks. Though Malachi's gaze remained locked on the mirror and his mind was in constant unrest, he still ran the House of Death with a viciousness unmatched by any other of their kind.

"Be careful, Reaper. If I see your weakness, then others do as well."

"I have none to hide," he gritted out.

Malachi pressed his weight against Dorian's back and grabbed a handful of his hair. Pulling by the roots, he managed to tip Dorian's head back only because Dorian didn't fight him. Submission was non-negotiable with Malachi. Even the Reaper bowed to him. "Do *not* let this House fall."

"Never."

"Look at me," Malachi growled against his ear. "Look me in the eyes and swear it."

Dorian tried to turn his head, but the Mad King wouldn't allow him to move an inch. It was either deny the king's request or face his fear and look in the mirror at his king.

Damn you, Dorian silently cursed. But what was the big deal?

Vampires used mirrors all the time, and right now, a reflection was the least of his goddamn worries.

"Swear it, Reaper."

Dorian dragged his gaze across the looking glass and deadlocked on his king's reflection. "I fucking swear it."

Malachi released his hold and dropped back down in his chair. "Call Lucian in here before you leave." The king waved him off and didn't say another word.

Damnit. Damn the king. Damn the Houses. Damn everything. Dorian stormed out of the room and headed towards the mansion's front door as he dialed Lucian's cell.

"Miss me already?"

"The King wants to see you."

"Shit." Lucian hung up on him immediately.

Dorian made it to the exit, hand on the doorknob, and he jerked it. It didn't budge, and there was no mechanism to unlock it. "Let me out!"

He whirled around to find someone to unlock the damn door. "Hey!" Dorian stormed towards the sound of people talking down the hall. "Someone better let me the fuck out of this house!" He caught movement to his right and turned to order whoever it was to get that front motherfucking door unlocked.

Suddenly, he was staring at a six-foot tall, black framed mirror mounted on the wall. The air whooshed out of his lungs. His body locked. The floor dropped out from beneath his feet. A savage beast awoke inside his bones and his vision tunneled.

In a daze, he cautiously came closer to the mirror. Heart pounding, mouthwatering, lungs burning, Dorian pressed his hands against the silvered glass, praying this was some kind of twisted trick Lucian was playing on him.

It wasn't.

Dorian's palms hit cold silver and flattened against what was on the other side, completely untouchable.

Staring back at him was the prettiest woman he'd ever seen in his life.

And she was covered in blood.

CHAPTER 3

Lena grabbed more paper towels and held them to her face as she assessed the damage. "I don't think I'm missing any teeth." It was hard to tell though because the mirror she was using was a filthy, cracked mess.

"Let me see." Bane tipped her face up to the low light and frowned. "I think you're gonna be okay. All teeth accounted for. But the rest of you is a mess, girl. And you bit your tongue pretty good."

She spat more blood into the sink. "It'll heal." Lena ducked out of Bane's arms. "I'm good. I want to go back in."

"No."

"You don't get to tell me *no*." No one did. She was a solo fighter for a reason. "I want a rematch."

"He's not your level, Lena! Jesus Christ woman, you got a death wish or what?"

She licked her busted lip and winced because it hurt like hell. She knew Bane meant well, but she didn't come to these underground fights for a slap and tickle. She came for the pain, violence, and adrenaline. The rush. The victory.

"Rematch or I'm out for good."

Bane narrowed his gaze at her threat. "You don't mean that."

"Try me."

It would kill her to walk away from this perfectly suitable money maker, but there were other outlets she could immerse herself in to burn her aggression. Lena held a wad of bloodied paper towels in her hand and ignored the sting and ache across her face. It didn't hurt nearly as bad as her back. But that was her own damned fault. She'd been too slow to protect her soft parts.

"I can't stand by and let you go another round against that guy, Lena." Bane gripped her shoulders as his intensity levels went through the roof. "Trust me on this. He's. Not. A. Fair. Match."

"I'm not here for fair. I'm here to win and walk away with bank." That's why she took on the opponents she did. Even after two years of fighting with the fools who stepped into the ring with her, she was still considered the underdog because of her size and sex. It pissed her off, but she'd learned to use it as a leg up.

And she won more than she lost.

That meant all those new guys who came and took one look at her, thinking she was an easy win, paid out and most of it went into her back pocket. She even challenged men who looked like they could take her down in one hit because it made her ego inflate when she was the last one standing.

Tonight, however, she might have bitten off more than she could chew. A mistake she wouldn't make again. "Fine, let him have the bragging rights. *This time.*"

Not that there was much to it since that fucker was twice her size and moved like the Flash. Hand-to-God, she had no idea if he struck her too many times in the head, or if she just lost the ability to keep track of his movements, but that guy — known as the Jackhammer — moved like lightning and struck as hard as his name insinuated.

It was unreal.

She wanted a rematch, and she'd get one. Just not tonight. Lena had more training to do before she challenged that prick again. She was a fool to think, all because he looked unraveled earlier, she could take him on. "Put me in with Nekko instead."

"No fucking way."

"I'm not asking, Bane." She punched him in the chest with her bloodied, busted fist. "If I go home now, after having my ass handed to me, I'll *never* get into a good fight again. My profits will plummet."

"It would serve you right!" Bane roared. "You were *reckless* with this one, Lena. What would you have done if I hadn't come tonight?"

Damnit, she didn't want to think about that. But he was right, this was a totally fucked up decision on her part. It's just that she was desperate, which, okay fine... might have made her stupid and careless. Reckless, like Bane said.

"I made a mistake," she whispered. "It won't happen again."

"He could have killed you."

She winced. Again, Bane was right. There were no rules down here. Well, except the obvious one... The Jackhammer could have beaten her to a pulp and left her for dead out there. She had no one except Bane to watch her back. He was the only one who kept a close watch on her at these meet ups.

"You don't need the money, Lena. We both know that." Bane handed her a fresh wad of paper towels. "Everyone here knows that."

"What? How?" They never used real names. Besides Bane, who she sometimes confided in, how could anyone possibly know who she was?

"No matter how busted you get, you're still fire. Every man with a pulse can see the beauty past your bruises. I think some went a little overboard and did a little digging on you. They know exactly who you are."

Lena rolled her eyes. "Fuck it, I don't even care."

"Reckless." He wagged his finger in her face. "Seriously, what's gotten into you lately?"

He was right. Again. Damn him. "I'm sorry," she said and looked down at the stained, filthy floor. "I honestly don't know what's come over me. And tonight, I just took one look at that guy and wanted to ring his motherfucking church bells."

Ironic how she chose him because he was a cocky sonofabitch, when the truth was, Lena was the pot to his kettle. What she wasn't willing to admit about her derailment lately? Nothing satisfied her—not food, not fights, and she hadn't orgasmed in so long, a good dick-down wouldn't even touch the itch she needed scratched at this point.

Life was losing its color. Her "fair-matched fights" had lost their thrill.

Tonight, she chose an opponent she had no chance of winning against. Lena just wanted to go down swinging, if only to feel the burn and rush of adrenaline while she fought for her life. If there was only a slight chance of being victorious, it would make the win so much sweeter and exciting.

Soooooo maybe she did have a death wish.

If Bane hadn't showed up and kept track of when things went from bad to worse, no one else would have pulled her out of that ring in time. The Jackhammer would have drilled her sorry ass into the ground and left her there for dead.

That was the bad part of this underground ring. It was cutthroat, ruthless, and savage.

Holy Hell, how had she gotten to this point? Lena couldn't even bring herself to connect the dots that brought her down to this level of finding meaning in life by letting it slowly get beaten out of her. She was the only woman in this circuit. No others had ever returned for a second chance at victory. That meant the men Lena fought against were always bigger and stronger than her. At five foot six and a buck thirty soaking wet, she was a joke to them.

A legend too.

It also meant she had to train harder and fight dirtier than most.

"Please," she said. "Match me with Nekko."

"He's not going to like it."

Lena sighed in relief when she realized Bane was giving in to her request. "He doesn't have to like it. Just ask him to give me a chance to turn this night around for myself."

She didn't want him to throw the fight, but she also knew Nekko was exhausted too. He'd gone against five other men so far this evening. Lena had only fought two. There was a good chance she could beat him.

Bane cupped her face. She could only see him out of one eye because the other was swelling at an impressive rate. "Let me see what I can do."

Lena grinned and her lip split open more.

"Damnit, woman, don't look at me like this a good thing. I feel like I'm sending you into an early grave."

"Well, at least I'll die swinging, instead of sleeping."

"Not funny," he growled. "Not. Fucking. Funny."

"Still true, though," Lena called out before heading into the sound of roaring men, the stink of sweat, and the promise of blood that never ceased to fill her soul with fire.

She was a depraved woman with a savage side no man could

tolerate except those in this pit.

A loud whistle ripped through the air and everyone scattered as Nekko roared, "Cops!"

Men ran, climbing out the back way. Bane pushed through the crowd and grabbed Lena's arm. "Go! Go! Shit!" He shoved her forward towards the exit door.

Lena slipped on spilled beer and tried to catch herself. Arms pinwheeling, she pitched forward. A set of strong hands caught her. "Got you," Nekko growled. "Come on, Bane's not far behind."

She nodded and found her footing with his help. Guess she had two friends in this dark life. "Thanks," she wheezed as they made it to the exit.

"Thank me by never taking a fight like that again," Nekko's deep voice rumbled while he pushed her through the opening. "You scared the piss out of everyone with that stunt tonight, Lena."

"Thanks for not leaving me back there," she said after climbing out of the tunnel. When she turned around, Nekko and Bane weren't behind her. Lena hauled ass.

CHAPTER 4

Dorian was vaguely aware he'd cracked the edges of the mirror with his grip. The black frame was crushed as well. In his dazed and mesmerized state, he tried to reel in his terror and think straight.

Holy fuck, the blood. Her face.

Her mouth.

Dorian couldn't pull his gaze away from her swollen lips and the blood that dripped from her chin. Whoever hurt her would pay dearly and slowly. His glimpse of his mate didn't last more than a few seconds, but time stopped the instant he saw her. Dorian couldn't tell if he'd been standing in front of that damned mirror for a minute or a year.

And what had he done with that time? Wasted it. Instead of trying to piece together where she might be, so he had a shot of finding her, he gawked, snarled, and smashed the mirror instead. His rage was on a tight leash on a normal day, and now this glimpse of that woman pulled the trigger on his control.

"Dorian," someone spoke behind him.

He didn't turn around. Keeping his gaze focused on the silvered glass, he practically tried summoning her with his sheer will and fury.

It didn't work.

The woman was lost to him until she went in front of another mirror again and who knew how long that might take. What could happen to her between now and then? What danger was she in? Dorian couldn't get the image of her bloodied face out of his mind.

He both loathed and lusted for it.

Sick. Fuck.

He was a twisted, depraved monster to have such a hard-on right now. His woman was out there, bleeding and hurt, and he was standing like a statue with an erection hard as stone, gawking at himself in a mirror that was no longer being helpful.

"Dorian."

Someone's hand rested on his shoulder and it set him off. No one. *No. One.* Was allowed to come behind him and grab his shoulder like that. Everyone in this House knew it. Dorian grabbed that hand, pitched forward, flipped the motherfucker over his head, and slammed them against the mirror. The looking glass shattered and fell off its mount. Bits of plaster crumbled down with it.

A vampire named Xin stared up at him with a furious expression. "The fuck, Dorian!"

Too late to stop his momentum, Dorian snatched Xin by the throat and picked him up again. Slamming him against the wall, Dorian snarled in his face. He couldn't even make a word come out of his mouth. All he was capable of was snarling. Hissing.

And killing.

"Christ, he's gone mad!" someone else said behind him. "Get Lucian!"

If one more person tried to grab him right now, he was going to raze this motherfucking mansion and bury everyone in it. His mate was out there bleeding, whoever hit her was out there still breathing, and he was stuck without a clue on how to find her.

That would be enough to make anyone — vampire or not — go insane.

"Dorian!" Victoria tried prying his hands off Xin's neck. Took her three attempts, but after she said his name again, and clipped him in the side of the head with her elbow, his hands relaxed.

Easing up on Xin, but still keeping him pinned, Dorian looked around like he wasn't sure where he even was. His instincts swarmed him, spiraling into a funnel of chaos. He felt out of control. Out of his element. It caused him to tense and gasp for air.

Victoria's eyebrows knit together with concern. "Dorian, did you see someone in that mirror?"

He didn't want to say. As fast as it happened, maybe he hadn't seen her at all. He hadn't slept much lately. Hadn't fed in forever. And with all the stress he was under, this could very well have been a trick of the eye. A figment of his dark and monstrous imagination. It would certainly explain all the blood on her.

No sooner had Dorian allowed the possibility of that woman's image being nothing but a twist of his mind, a terrible roar ripped from his throat. He dropped Xin like a sack of potatoes and stumbled backwards.

She was real. Not even his warped imagination could conjure such a bloodied beauty.

He had to get out of there. Had to find her. Had to put space between himself and everyone here before he hurt someone else.

Lucian dashed into the scene, took one look at Dorian's face and the shattered mirror, immediately piecing the mystery together. "Aww shit, come on." He rushed forward and steered Dorian towards the door, leaving Victoria to help Xin up. "Let's get you out of here."

Dorian, for once, matched Lucian's phenomenal speed.

"What does she look like?" Lucian asked in low tones.

"Bloody."

With a flick of his wrist, Lucian unlocked the front door and didn't lift his grip from Dorian's arm. Not even after they made it all the way to his car. "Get in. I'll drive."

"I'm capable of driving my own car."

"You seem to be capable of a lot right now, Dorian. You just knocked three vampires unconscious."

Wait. What?

"I..." Dorian's brow furrowed. "I only slammed Xin. He grabbed my shoulder and I snapped." Xin knew the rules with Dorian, so he had little regret for his actions back there.

"You also knocked out Kai and Reys."

Shit, had he? Dorian didn't remember that part at all. Shaking his head, like he could rattle it back into proper working order, Dorian knew which battles to fight and which to surrender. He opened the passenger side door and slid in.

Handing the keys to Lucian, he went numb. He hadn't felt this lost in a long time.

Desperate, Dorian flipped his visor down—thank fuck he hadn't gotten rid of the mirror over here—and prayed to catch another glimpse of her. *This is how Malachi feels*, he realized.

Knowing it and experiencing it were entirely different horrors. Mere knowledge of fate's existence didn't come with fear. This though? This need, this desperation for another glimpse? It was downright terrifying. Knowledge didn't devastate the mind as well as experience could.

What if he never got another look at her? What if he couldn't figure out where she was and she got hurt again? Had someone attacked her? Would they attack again? Was she dead already? A thousand screaming questions barreled out of him, robbing Dorian of breath and sanity.

"What does she look like, besides bloody?" Lucian flew out of the mansion's private driveway, heading towards Dorian's house.

"She—" His tongue was like sandpaper in his mouth. "She has brown hair. Brown eyes." No, that didn't do her justice. Her eyes were the color of tiger eye stones with specs of honey gold. Her hair wasn't just brown, it was chestnut.

"Brown hair and brown eyes. Good, that narrows it down to like five gazillion women."

Dorian didn't laugh because it wasn't funny. It was too true to be funny. He tried again. "She's..." He thought hard about everything he saw. "About five-five, five-six, maybe." He gauged that on where the sink of the public bathroom hit her waist in the reflection. "No tattoos that I could see." *Just blood and skin and welts.*

He saw red and he tensed with a vicious need to protector her. A low growl rumbled out of his throat.

"Focus, Dorian. What else did you see?"

"I..." He had nothing else to go on. Too enthralled by her reflection, he forgot to look beyond her face for details of her whereabouts. "She's the most beautiful creature I've ever seen on this cruel earth."

Lucian huffed a small laugh, but Dorian caught how his friend practically choked the steering wheel while driving. They drove in silence the rest of the way.

He frowned at the tiny vanity mirror—the lone survivor of his futile fight against fate. Dorian ripped all other mirrors out of his car the day he bought it but somehow forgot this one. The oversight was a miracle. He couldn't stand the thought of missing another glimpse of that woman. Gritting his teeth, he ripped the damned mirror off the visor and hated the compulsion to not let go of it.

He caressed the mirror without even realizing what he was doing. The urge to somehow put her in his pocket and keep her was maddening.

Lucian didn't seem surprised at Dorian's behavior. Then again, he lived with Mad King Malachi and knew damn well what happened between a vampire and a mirror. Not to mention what Lucian went through with Luke.

Holy shit. Dorian was going to be sick.

As they pulled onto his street, he actually had to breathe through his nose and out his mouth to keep his panic in check.

"Home, sweet home," Lucian announced as he cruised down the narrow street.

Dorian lived in Treme, just outside the French Quarter. The nine-hundred square foot residence was home to the vampire who chose to live alone, secluded from others of his kind. Six houses down, a man sat on his stoop, playing a trumpet. Trash cans awaited on the curbs. A roach skittered across the uneven pavement.

No one fucked with Dorian here. No one fucked with *anyone* here. He made sure of it.

Across the street, a screen door slammed shut. His neighbor stood on their porch and lit up a cigarette, not saying a word.

Dorian didn't look at his neighbor. He barely looked at his own front door. With a wave of his hand, he unlocked the thing without the use of a key. Some perks came with being a vampire. Keyless entry to their own houses was one of them. It's why he couldn't unlock the mansion to leave earlier. He didn't live there, so he couldn't magically unlock the doors and get the hell out without an escort.

Swinging open the front door, Dorian was proud that he hadn't just mindlessly kicked the damned thing down. He stepped inside and Lucian followed.

Dorian kept silent and headed straight forward—through the living room, kitchen, and to the back room. This narrow house boasted two bedrooms, but the back one was a gym and laundry area. He stripped out of his clothes and headed into his bedroom next, not giving two shits about walking around naked with company over. Lucian stayed out in the main area, quiet and patient as ever.

Kicking the bathroom door shut, Dorian's hands trembled when he tried propping the vanity mirror onto the ledge of the sink so he could keep an eye on it while splashing cold water on his face.

How the hell was he going to do this? He couldn't hunt her down and keep an eye on her at the same time. This was pure hell and it had only been less than a day. No! Less than an hour.

"Fuuuuck," he groaned and then buried his face in a towel. This was going to be impossible.

Snatching a fresh set of clothes from his closet, he got dressed, grabbed the vanity mirror, and headed back to the living room.

Lucian sat on the couch, pitched forward, elbows on his knees with a scowl. "You're such a minimalist."

"When you come from nothing, you learn to not need much." His house was triple the size of the shack he grew up in. The biggest difference? He was the only monster that lived here, and the place was clean. Impeccably so.

It was also barely decorated. He didn't have paintings on his walls and festive pillows on his couch. There was a leather sofa, and a small media center with a flatscreen he probably turned on twice in three years. The living room bled right into the kitchen, which boasted one cupboard filled with cooking appliances, a drawer for dishtowels, and some cleaning supplies under the sink. The four dishes were stacked neatly on a shelf, beside two coffee mugs. The rest of the cabinets and space was empty.

"You've added to your collection." Lucian fingered a set of blades laid out on the tiny kitchen table. "These are impressive."

By impressive, Dorian knew he meant terrifying. Lucian might be a cutthroat, dangerous vampire, but he wasn't at Dorian's caliber of bloodletting.

"Impressive or not, they do the job. I can target specific arteries with that one." He pointed at a thin blade that looked like an oversized needle. "I had it specifically made by someone up north."

Lucian sucked in a breath as he picked up the delicate blade. He didn't say a word, but then again, he didn't have to. Dorian knew what he was thinking, *Monster*, and he was right. Dorian stopped apologizing a long time ago for what he was.

"The lengths you go to for our House." Lucian let out a strangled exhale before glancing around the rest of the room to see what Dorian did or, more accurately, did not have. "You should hang some pictures. Make it homey."

"It's homey enough."

Monsters didn't need homes. They just needed a place to rest. But he understood Lucian's lack of understanding. Lucian was an aristocrat... or had been once. His family turned their backs on him when he decided to serve the House of Death instead of the House they chose. But before he came to New Orleans, Lucian had grown up with lavish rooms, the finest quality of everything, and dined in extravagance. Hell, the mansion he lived in now with the King and the others was just as huge and luxurious as the estate he left centuries ago. He'd traded one luxury for another, albeit the Mad House was in need of some repair.

Dorian's house looked more like a prison than a home. It was cold and unfeeling, but at least it was clean, and it was *his*. All his. That was worth more to Dorian than any grand suite the mansion could ever offer.

His grip tightened around the visor mirror. How could he ever invite a woman into this space? It was nothing more than a lair.

Wait. Was he actually considering going after her?

His protective instincts set off and he wasn't sure why.

"Let's go through this again." Lucian tapped his thumb on the table. "Five-six, brown hair, brown eyes." Lucian pulled a chair out from the dining table and dropped his ass down into it. "If she's been beaten, maybe we can ask Reys to go through the database of hospitals? It's a long shot but, we gotta start somewhere. How bad was she hurt you think?"

Badly. Dorian couldn't bring himself to say the word. The thought alone had his veins boiling. He slumped into the chair opposite Lucian and clutched the sides of his head. There were a million monsters out there—a potential threat around every corner. His mate was already in danger and he hadn't been there to stop it.

"I can't do this." His voice was ragged and warped with pain. "I can't fucking do any of this."

"The House of Death needs you, Reaper."

Dorian swallowed around the tension in his throat.

Lucian toyed with one of the blades on the table. "And if you're distracted with finding your mate, that means *Savag-Ri*, or one of the Lycan packs, or even someone from one of the other

Houses, could see it as an opportunity to come for us."

"The pack would never—"

"You only speak for *one* Lycan clan, Dorian. Don't presume all shifters are the same. You know firsthand they're not friendly to our kind."

Dorian bit the inside of his cheek. "Your point?"

"I'm going to do all I can to help you find your mate."

Fuck if Dorian didn't growl at that offer. He didn't want Lucian anywhere near his mate until he could find, drink, and turn her himself. Bind her to him for all eternity. A savage possessiveness outshined all his other instincts, and it presented itself with his next growl.

Lucian cocked an eyebrow. "You don't have a choice in this. I stay close to you until it's over."

Until it's over.

"You can't leave the King unguarded."

"Malachi will understand."

"This can't be happening." Dorian stared at the visor and hated what glared back at him. He wasn't ready to die... *What if I hurt her? What if I hurt others in my pursuit to find her? What if I never make it?* The what ifs were going to break him at this rate. "I can't do this."

"Yes, you can. I'm going to help you—"

"No," Dorian voice strained. "I can't do this to you, not after Luke." That vampire's death was still too fresh, and Lucian hadn't had any time to grieve his loss. "And I can't do this to *her*. She deserves better than a monster like me."

Lucian's gaze darkened. "She deserves to make that choice herself."

"I can't..." Aw shit, now he couldn't breathe. His heart raced a mile a minute. "I'm unraveling already."

"Then stop wasting time."

Fury surged in his veins. "You think I don't know what every second is going to fucking cost me?"

"Then think harder of what you saw, Dorian. Give me more to go on."

"I HAVE NOTHING!" Dorian gripped his head and started rocking. The fear of finding her was just as suffocating as the terror of something else. "What if I go Rogue during this?"

34

"You're too good for that level of cruelty, Dorian. You won't go that far."

You have no idea the depths I will go to in order to find that woman... Too far isn't far enough.

Urges, foreign and frightening, overrode Dorian's better behavior and he slammed his fist down on the table. "You need to get back to the King."

He didn't want Lucian to see him this way. Didn't want him to suffer watching another person in his life ash out.

"I'm with you until it's over."

"It's already over!" Dorian roared. "It's done! *I'm* done!"

Lucian screamed right back in his face. "I'll be damned if you're gonna suffer the same fate Luke did! I *will* help you find your mate or, so help me God, I'll die trying."

The air whooshed out of Dorian, and he sagged where he stood. Last week, Luke burned to ashes because he hadn't found his mate in time. Lucian was there to see it happen.

He didn't want his friend to go through that pain again. Dorian would rather die alone than let Lucian suffer something so horrific twice.

"I can't lose you, too," Lucian whispered. Then he shoved Dorian in the chest and caused him to stumble backwards. "So, fuck off with that 'I gotta do everything by myself because that's all I ever do' *bullshit* and let me help you do this."

Damn his heart for having the capability of feeling hope and gratitude. And damn his voice for cracking when he asked, "What if we can't find her?"

What if, what if, what if...

"What if we do?"

The weight of that question was so heavy, Dorian's walls began to crumble.

CHAPTER 5

Five days passed and still nothing. Not a hint, glimpse, or indication that Dorian's mate was even still alive. In those five days, Dorian convinced himself the curse would be his downfall and ultimate ruin. Food was losing its taste. Sleep never came. His temper burned holes in his conscience, making him even more volatile than usual. Case in point: He'd been called to do another execution this morning and didn't spare a glance nor word when he stormed into the Kill Box, snagged the prisoner, and decapitated him with his bare hands in one swift wrench.

Oh, and Dorian hadn't stopped there.

He also ripped off the bastard's limbs, punched a hole through his torso, and ripped out his heart. Then Dorian ate it while everyone watched.

Normally the blood of a *Savag-Ri* tasted like the foulest toxin one could swallow, which was why most vampires didn't bother to bite them, but Dorian wasn't most vampires. Shit got real though when he ate the heart and couldn't taste the signature sour flavor.

His tastebuds were on strike.

For five days, he kept his business-as-usual routine, because if he didn't stay busy, he'd go crazy. And he feared if anyone else knew about him seeing his mate in the mirror, they might use it against him somehow. If a strong enough enemy got wind of Dorian's current situation, they might attempt to detain or restrain him long enough for the clock to run out and *poof*, Dorian was ashes. Then the House of Death would be one step closer to ruination.

He made a promise to Malachi long ago and had every intention of keeping it for as long as possible. The House of Death would remain under Malachi's rule so long as Dorian drew breath. Now here he was, day five without hope or prayer of finding his mate, and fate's grip was choking him as much as the weight of his responsibility to the king was crushing him.

He wasn't going to survive this. It was impossible.

After annihilating that *Savag-Ri* prisoner, he dismissed everyone from the chamber and cleaned the mess himself. On hands and knees, he scrubbed every square inch of the stone floor and wiped down all the walls. Decades of grime and filth turned to mud beneath his scrub brush. The hose flushed it all down a drain in the center of the room. By the time he left, it looked brand-new and never used.

Oh, if only it were so easy to erase what monsters did...

Dorian managed to drive himself home and not run off the road as he checked the vanity mirror a thousand times. He showered and cleaned up, but still nothing except his angry gaze stared back at him in the new mirrors he installed in the house. They were everywhere now.

Dressed and waiting for Lucian to return to him, Dorian paced in his tiny living room.

"Damnit." He hooked his fingers into the collar of his shirt and yanked his tie loose. He still couldn't breathe right, so he popped the first three buttons of his shirt.

Still not better.

Shrugging out of his suit jacket, Dorian pulled the tie off his neck and ignored the tremble in his deft fingers as he unbuttoned his dress shirt and shrugged it off. It was - Dorian glanced at his watch - three o'clock in the afternoon. Pacing made him feel like a caged animal, but it was safer to stay in than be set loose again today. He was no longer in his right mind. Too aggressive. Too dangerous.

He might not care for humans, but he didn't want to hurt them either. The aggression riding his ass right now brought him to nuclear levels of violence. He wanted to shred things. Tear, rip, crush things.

Holy fuck, he couldn't stand this!

Dorian stormed into the bathroom for the tenth time that day and splashed cold water on his face. Droplets hit the floor, wall, and new mirror he installed over his sink. Dorian snagged a hand towel and gently wiped the mirror clean.

Funny, he lived his whole life avoiding mirrors. Didn't have a single possession with a reflection in his house. All windows were blacked out. All surfaces sanded down. Anything he couldn't alter to save his soul, he ignored with fervor. Now, he craved reflections more than he craved blood.

"One glimpse," he whispered darkly. "Show yourself one more time so I have *some* hope of finding you."

All that stared back was his green eyes with dark circles under them. He looked worn down and filthy. Christ, just look at the scruff on his face.

That was another no-no for him. Dorian had lived in poverty growing up, with a monster he was convinced the devil himself had spat out of Hell because he was too vile for even demons to harbor. When Dorian finally freed himself of that beast, he'd vowed to never be so dirty or live so wretchedly ever again. He kept his clothes clean and blades sharp. Hair washed, face shaved, nails trimmed, and suits pressed.

Staring at his reflection, he forgot how much he looked like his father until now. Maybe that was one more reason why he always kept away from mirrors—so he didn't have to see a killer's predatory gaze looking at him all the time. At least he inherited his mother's toffee-colored curls instead of his father's jet black, stick straight hair. Dorian kept his at chin's length and made sure it stayed clean and finger combed.

His father would have hated this hair style and hacked it off with a blunt blade or likely ripped it out by the roots until Dorian's scalp bled and he begged for the monster to stop.

Wait, why was he thinking about any of this right now?

"Snap out of it," Dorian growled at himself. Turning away from the mirror was harder than he ever expected. But he managed to make his way over to the shower and start the hot water. Again. He needed to wash this misery off so he could begin with a clear mind.

Again.

Jesus, he was a wreck. A stir-crazy, overthinking, ball of chaos.

Stepping under the spray, he braced his hands on the tiled wall and groaned with the heat steaming around him as scorching hot water cascaded down his back. Closing his eyes, he gritted his teeth as a memory assaulted him...

"Get over here, son."

Dorian's heart clogged his throat, making it impossible to swallow the saliva building in his mouth. "Yes, father?"

"Did you cover the wood to keep it dry?"

"Yes, father."

"Good. Bring me the water bucket."

Dorian ran outside in the pouring rain and retrieved the bucket they used to collect river water. Looking back at the light flickering in the window of their one-room shack, his feet seemed bolted to the ground.

"Now, Dorian!"

His father's booming voice snapped him back into action. Head down, he focused on the pricks of evergreen needles piercing the bottoms of his bare feet instead of the sounds coming from father's newest victim. He ran back into their shack as fast as he could. The water sloshed out of the bucket, splashing his legs. "Here!"

Dorian was cracked across his face so fast and so hard he saw stars. The shock of the attack caused him to drop the bucket.

"That's for making me wait." His father snagged the bucket from the ground. "I swear the best part of you slipped between your mother's legs the day you were conceived. Waste of spunk, you are."

Dorian kept his mouth shut and gaze fixed on the ground. Gritting his teeth, he fought the instinct to act out and retaliate. He knew better than to run. He knew better than to help.

Drenched from the rain, all he could do was shrink into his shell and wait for it to be over. He couldn't cover his ears to muffle the screams. He couldn't close his eyes, or his father would likely cut his eyelids off if he did. He couldn't budge or run and hide because that would make things a thousand times worse for everyone in the room.

"Watch carefully, son." His father pulled a blade from his belt and ran his thumb across the dulled edge.

His victim screamed as she tried to yank free from her restraints where she lay on the dirt covered floor. The human was no match for a fully matured vampire like Dorian's father. She was no match for a scrawny malnourished child like Dorian, either. Especially with how starved he'd been lately.

The woman cried out again. It was shrill and icy, filled with terror. Dorian's panic set in. He hated screaming. Hated what his father did to make screams come out of the mouths of his victims too. Never once did he show mercy because in his opinion, fear made the blood sweeter. More powerful.

Dorian thought it ruined the blood.

Their one, small taper candle flickered, causing dim light to dance around the room. The movement of shadows and light only made the act of violence worse. As if the flame itself struggled to escape the fate awaiting that human woman, it trembled and flickered and made Dorian dizzy.

This woman hadn't been given the chance others had to escape. His father brought her home naught more than an hour ago and did unspeakable things to her.

Dorian swayed when he heard a gurgling sound. His cheeks tingled when he smelled fresh blood permeate the air. Outside, the rain pelted the roof, and sounded like an applause all around them. Dorian focused on that sound. The rain.

Wash it away. Wash it away. Wash it away.

If he had the strength to destroy the walls and roof of this house, Dorian would do it in a heartbeat. He'd welcome the thunder and lightning to crash down upon him and his father if only to put them out of the misery they were stuck in. He'd beg for the rain to rise, flood, and sweep them away so they may drown.

"Dorian, get over here."

Trembling more with anger than fear, he obeyed his father. Stepping up to the female, he first noticed a wetness between his toes. He didn't need to look down to know that he'd stepped in her blood, so he kept his gaze on her eyes. They were kind eyes. Round like a doe. Scared like a doe, too.

"Get on your knees like the animal you are."

Dorian's knees buckled and down he went. Years of this made the act automatic.

"Drink, son." His father grabbed him by the nape of the neck and forced Dorian to bend over. He shoved Dorian's face into her mangled neck. "I said drink.*"*

The woman didn't move, using all her might to hang onto her last breath, she didn't even blink. His father took everything from her — had done so much carnage to her body, blood drained from various wounds, leaving nothing but a small sip for Dorian to take.

But he didn't even want that. He'd rather starve than take that woman's last drop.

He hated this. Hated what he was. Hated what he'd mature into. Hated his father. Hated his house. Hated his life.

"Drink," his father commanded.

Dorian knew if he didn't obey, his father would go out and find another victim and waste her life too, if only to force Dorian down on his knees, yet again, and make him take the last of their life.

It wasn't fair. Why was he left being the one to clean up his father's mess? Why was he the one who had to be the final act that would ultimately snuff out an innocent life?

His hesitation earned him another crack upside his head. Dorian lost balance and threw his hands out to catch himself before falling face-first into the woman's stomach cavity.

"DRINK!"

With a furious hiss, Dorian opened his mouth wide and attacked the woman's throat. Instead of nourishment and strength, he pulled malice from her vein and swallowed it with all the fervor a starved wolf would its hard-earned meal...

The water ran cold as Dorian remained braced against the shower wall, struggling to yank himself out of his past. Once he succeeded, he swiftly dried off and froze in front of the mirror again. It had fogged over, making him look like a faded blur. Unwrapping the towel from his waist, Dorian used it to clean the mirror in order to see the reflection, uncompromised.

What a beast Dorian had turned into. His hair dripped onto his shoulders, already curling into tight coils. His eyes were darker than they'd been a week ago—a sign of starvation and other things he refused to acknowledge. He ran a hand across his chest. He worked out every day and his constant dedication paid off. Sometimes he forgot he was a vampire and not something else. He wasn't built to impress. He was built to kill.

Kill.

Dorian leaned over the sink and gripped the counter. "I'm built to kill."

Not love. Not protect. *Kill.*

Running his fingers through his hair angrily, he slicked it back, shut his eyes and let the truth sink in. How was he going to be a good mate to a woman when all he could bring to the table was death and torture? He was a monster. No matter how far he'd come in life, at the core, he was still his father's son. Dorian didn't deserve sweet, pretty, innocent things. He'd ruin them. Break and destroy them. Tear them apart, chew them up, and spit them out.

He sure as shit didn't deserve love or the honor of having a woman who loved him back. No one should be so unfortunate to be tied to someone like him for all eternity.

When Dorian popped his eyes back open, his vision blurred, and he no longer saw himself in the mirror anymore. He saw his father glaring back at him instead.

Angry, scared, withdrawn, and cold, he screamed, "I'm not like you." But even his words were weak and unconvincing. Heart hammering, he roared again, *"I'm not like you!"*

Furious to be stuck in this position with no way out but death or damnation, Dorian smashed his fist against the mirror and shattered the goddamned thing to pieces.

CHAPTER 6

Lena caught up with Bane after a couple days of radio silence. Relief washed over her when she saw Bane's number light up her phone with a text: *All good. Lay low. Be in touch soon.* Phew. She worried they might have been arrested. The cops were getting smarter and faster, which meant the fight club was running out of spots to meet in. There wouldn't be any fights until a new spot was designated. Once that happened, Bane would text her with the location so they could resume the fun.

Lena bit her lip and smiled at the thought. She liked it when they switched meeting places. It made things more exciting.

Man, if her parents could see her now. They were probably rolling over in their graves.

Good.

Okay, that was harsh. But... well... damnit, she was a shitshow and refused to be shamed back into a box and put on a shelf ever again. She always loved her parents but didn't know why. They had only loved themselves and money. Not her. Never her. She was a tool for them. A bargaining chip.

Now? She was a weapon for herself.

A weapon with no use since there were no fights happening for a while.

Damnit! That left her with nothing to do. Her stomach grumbled. Today was as good a day as any to grab tacos. It was also a good day to make someone else's day a little brighter. Grabbing her keys, she slid her flats on and hopped in the car for a drive.

Before leaving, she texted: *Where are you today?*

Carmen texted back: *South and Main.*

Sweet! Fifteen minutes later, Lena pulled into a vacant spot and headed straight towards the food truck, Count Tacola. That name was never going to not be hilarious, and Lena had a good amount of pride in having come up with it when Carmen asked her for a loan to get her business started.

"Holy shit, what happened to your face?" Carmen gawked from the order window.

"You should see the other guy."

Carmen cringed. She never asked Lena about her bruises and Lena never offered answers. Besides, it wasn't a secret that Lena trained in boxing, judo, and a few other martial arts, so Carmen most likely assumed this was from one of her lessons.

"Business is doing well, I see." Lena stuffed her hands in her pockets, her fingers brushing the folded envelope tucked away.

"Well enough to have you paid off sooner than I expected."

Lena grinned with pride. "I'm not surprised. But you know there's no rush."

Two years ago, Lena lent Carmen all she needed to start up her business—from the truck, licenses, supplies and advertising. Carmen promised to have her loan paid off in ten years, but Lena would bet it took half that time. Carmen was a driven woman who built her business and ran it like it was all she lived for. Passion was in her food. Pride was served with every order, too. Count Tacola had become a tourist sensation and local favorite fast. Hell, customers drove up to three hours away to get her street corn alone.

Crazy right? But good for her. Carmen had a vision and was making her dreams come true. Lena was still trying to figure hers out.

"Street corn and a lunch combo number 6. Heavy on the heat, please."

Carmen grinned. "Coming right up."

Lena glanced behind her at the line forming. "I'm so proud of you, girl."

"Not gonna lie, I'm proud of me too." Carmen scooped the street corn into a paper to-go bowl. "That magazine article really helped. People are coming from all over the place now."

Yeah, she figured that write-up would boost Carmen's

exposure to a new level. That was the point of Lena's recent interview with a small business magazine for a piece on legacies. Her tragic backstory, coupled with a string of happy endings, gave the magazine piece a "pay it forward" gold star in popularity. Lena, however, kept the focus targeted on her pride and joy: top picks of local businesses. Carmen's, especially. Next time, it would be the florist on the other end of town.

"What do I owe you?" Lena asked while grabbing her lunch sack.

"Your money's no good here and you know it. I'm just so glad you came!"

Lena didn't argue about the bill. Instead of paying for her lunch, she tucked more than enough money into the tip jar and stuck her tongue out when Carmen made a noise about it. She also stuffed the jar with the folded envelope with Carmen's name scrolled across the front. She'd get it at the end of the night—and would find out her loan with Lena was forgiven and no longer existed. She owed Lena nothing.

Smiling to herself, Lena headed back to her car with a sack full of *oh hells yes*. Taking the first bite, she winced when the hot corn hit her damaged tongue. Looking in her rearview, she checked her tongue out and was impressed it healed so fast. Not fast enough to not hurt like hell from the hot sauce, but it was way better than it had been. Her face was still a lovely collage of bruises—some blue and black, others greenish yellow. At least the swelling around her eye had gone down, considerably, and it wasn't so bloodshot anymore. She avoided her reflection for five days now because the reminder of her loss in that fight really pissed her off. Her pride was way more bruised than her face, honestly.

Idiocy wasn't a good look for her.

Her cell rang and she glanced at the screen. Unknown number. Not helpful, considering the circles she ran in.

"Hello?"

"Lena McKay?"

"Yeah?"

"A trusted colleague has made us aware that you're looking for certain entertainment at our establishment."

She clutched her cell and dropped the taco she was about to crush into her lap. "Yes," she said steadily, praying like hell her tone remained calm even while the rest of her screamed with excitement. "I'm interested to see what you have to offer."

"We have an opening tomorrow for a tour."

Tomorrow? How the hell was she going to get to New Orleans by *tomorrow*? And shit! Her face! She was going to look like a disaster during the one time she wanted to look perfect. Oh well. "What time?"

"There will be an envelope waiting for you at the front desk of the hotel."

She didn't have a hotel reserved yet. "I don't—"

"Room reservations have been sent to your email."

Wow, that was... uhhh...

"Do you accept our invitation?"

Like she had a choice? This was a once in a lifetime shot. Lena looked into her rearview mirror and smiled. "I'll be there."

Dorian ignored his cell phone ringing while he got dressed. But after the damned thing wouldn't shut the fuck up, he grabbed his phone, ready to crush the thing for having the sheer audacity to not stop ringing. Lucian's number lit up the screen. Then there was a knock at the door.

Pulling his shirt down, Dorian marched to his front door and swung it open without looking through the peephole first. In his current mood, any unwanted guests would be sure to never come back. As it was, however, Lucian scowled at him from the other side of the threshold. "Answer your fucking phone!"

"I was in the shower."

Reading Lucian's vibes, he'd probably thought Dorian had burst into flames already. Lucian barreled past him and came inside. "Marius has demanded retribution."

"For what?"

"The House of Bone said you didn't execute their last prisoner according to plan."

"I did them one better." He annihilated the *Savag-Ri* and ate his heart. After dismembering the bastard, of course. "That was a complete waste of time." It also happened to be the second prisoner this week Marius threw to the monster for execution. That tiny detail hadn't slipped Dorian's mind, no matter how dark it was growing lately. "Our job is to take out the *Savag-Ri* before they do the same to us. He needs to remember what kind of creature he is in this war."

"Fangs or not, Marius is an opportunist. He does nothing without an agenda."

"Then why do we always entertain him and the House of Bone?"

"You know why," Lucian seethed. "And Marius insists you didn't question that *Savag-Ri* before taking him out."

Dorian was about to reject that accusation but stopped himself. Had he questioned the guy? Nope. He'd gone overboard. A mistake he might apologize for eventually. "I'll give him back his money."

"That payment went to the House."

"I'll pay him out of my personal account, then."

Lucian got all in Dorian's face. "He doesn't want money, you asshole. He wants *you*."

Dorian ignored how his vision dimmed for a few seconds. He also refused to hear how ludicrous Lucian sounded just now. "My loyalties are to Malachi and the House of Death. Nothing will ever change that. Marius can suck my cock."

"He's going to force your hand."

"There's nothing he can do to persuade me to tilt my allegiance towards his House." Dorian gripped Lucian's shoulders and shook him. "Relax. I'm not leaving."

For the life of him, Dorian couldn't understand why Lucian was being so distraught about this. Minor politics never unraveled him before, but lately, Lucian was just as unhinged as Dorian.

Then again, losing Luke was a blow Lucian might never recover from. They were brothers, and Dorian couldn't imagine what it must have been like to see a family member burn to ashes right before his eyes.

Oh wait… yes, he could. Only Dorian relished that moment and Lucian's personal experience left him heartbroken and lost. There'd been no time to mourn Luke's death.

Dorian tilted Lucian's chin, forcing the vampire to look at him. "I'm not going anywhere." He made sure to keep his gaze locked on Lucian. "Not to the House of Bone, and not to find my mate."

Lucian stumbled back as if Dorian sucker punched him. "What?"

"I'm not going to find her. So, whatever you need me to do on behalf of the House of Death, let's see it done in the time I have left."

"The fuck, Dorian?"

He slashed his hand through the air. "I can't." Dorian swallowed around the lump growing in his throat. "I can't chain a perfect creature like her to a savage monster like me. I refuse to put anyone in that kind of Hell."

Lucian's face reddened with fury. "This is about your father, isn't it?" When Dorian didn't respond Lucian shouted, "You're not him! Damnit, Dorian, how many times must we go through this?"

"Soon, you'll never have to say that lie to me ever again."

Lucian cold-cocked him in the jaw hard enough to knock Dorian off his feet. "You are a fucking idiot!" Lucian attacked, slamming Dorian to the ground. They threw punches, bit, kicked, and gouged each other any way they could. The only issue was, they were both damned good fighters. The brawl could have gone on for days if they wished it.

But Dorian felt too much like a ticking time bomb and he didn't want to waste the last of his precious time on earth beating the piss out of his best friend. "Enough!" he roared.

Lucian's eyes were pitch black, and he hissed before reeling in his temper. Sucking in air, his chest heaved as he stared at Dorian with saliva dripping from his fangs.

"You need to feed," Dorian snarled. "And you need to fuck."

"Says the pot to the kettle."

"Only one of us has hope of staying sane, Lucian. And it's not me." Dorian gracefully stood and tried to smooth away the wrinkles in his clothing. Looking down and seeing all the blood on his freshly pressed shirt, he scowled and tore the threads from his body and tossed it onto the floor. Turning to grab a fresh shirt from his closet, he ignored the feeling of Lucian's gaze boring into his back.

He knew what it looked like — a mess just like the rest of him.

Storming into his bathroom, he washed the blood from his hands. As warm water ran over his busted knuckles, Dorian glowered at the shards of mirror scattered across the counter and piled in the sink. He would clean this shit up later, now wasn't the time.

Scowling, Dorian focused on the sting of his cuts. Damn, Lucian had a hard head, and his teeth were razor sharp. Dorian half-smiled at the bite mark on his arm from his friend.

Movement caught his attention, and at first, his mind couldn't get with the program at all. He stared at a shard of mirror laying face up on the counter. The woman's reflection was distorted…

Dorian blinked. Then he blinked two more times, hoping his vision would clear up. Then he realized it wasn't his vision that was the problem. It was the reflection.

Snatching the shard, he held his breath and stared at his mate. Holy Hell, she was a knockout, and that smile? Never saw a brighter one in all his life. Her face was a mess of cuts and bruises, but her eyes crinkled with delight. It just about knocked Dorian over. His black, tarnished soul filled with fire and relief.

She's alive.

This was his chance. The compulsion to find her overrode all his other hardwired instincts and overrode his declarations of not looking for her. Fuck that. He *needed* to find her. That need drove him deeper into a special kind of madness called *desperation.*

"Give me something," he pleaded. "*Anything.*"

Her reflection became more vivid with each beat of his panicked heart. Before long, he saw every crisp detail of her lovely face. The bruising. The arch of her perfectly shaped eyebrows. The deep black fans of lashes. The flecks of amber in her brown eyes. Then he saw —

Dorian leaned into the mirror, desperate to make it out.

Count Tacola. What the fuck was a Count Tacola? Whatever it was, she was eating something out of a cup with its logo on it while she was driving. He could only make out the black leather headrest from her driver's seat, and nothing more to even suggest what make and model car she was in.

"Count Tacola." What was that, a food chain? Only one way to find out.

CHAPTER 7

"Blah, blah, blah, he blah blah."

Storming past a chattering Lucian, Dorian was already searching his phone for what and where this Count Tacola place was located.

"Did you hear what I said?"

"Hmm?" If he could at least narrow it down to what country it was in, that would be a major win. A state would be too much to hope for, but...

"Holy shit." He stopped dead in his tracks and stared at the picture of the food truck. A. Food. Truck. All stainless steel, making it look like one of those airstream camper things. A sign stretched across the side of it in splashes of bright colors that had the name *Count Tacola* on it. Was this a goddamn joke? The Ts in Count and Tacola were elongated to look like a set of fangs with... Jesus Christ was that supposed to be hot sauce dripping off of them?

He didn't know if he should laugh or cry.

"Dorian?"

Ignoring Lucian, he stared at the picture under the Facebook page he'd opened. The business was run by a woman named Carmen Lopez. The pinned post at the top was a link to an article showcasing a picture of Carmen and... Dorian's fated mate.

His ass dropped into a chair. His jaw clenched and his entire body tensed as he stared at the picture.

How could it have been so easy? One simple online search and *boom*, there she was. This picture didn't do her justice though. No camera could capture the beauty he saw in her reflections—and that was saying something considering her condition both times he saw her. In this picture, however, she was dressed in a blue sundress.

Holy shit, she was a stunner.

How… how could she be so goddamn decadent? It was a hard truth to swallow — a perfect creature like her fated to be tied to a wreck like him. Why would the universe ever be that cruel to an innocent person?

He knew why and it made his heart shrivel. The curse. This was part of the blood curse put on his kind.

Paralyzed, his gaze locked on her picture. Now he back-peddled again because seeing her happiness, her smile? A life with him would ruin all of that.

I shouldn't go after her.

Deep down, he knew it. Better to leave her alone so she could live her life without the trouble that follows a vampire. But deep, deep, waaaayyy deep down, buried under a shit-ton of shadows and misery, Dorian desperately wanted to find her if only to see her with his own eyes, just once. He wouldn't even approach her. Wouldn't make his presence known. But to see her before him, before fate killed him, would be…

As close to heaven as I'll ever get.

And that would be enough for him. More than he deserved, really.

"Dorian, are you listening to me at all?"

No, he wasn't. All Dorian heard was the swishing of his blood pounding in his ears. His throat was working overtime to swallow the amount of saliva building in his mouth. Sweat bloomed across his brow. His hands trembled as he stared at the picture of his mate. He couldn't read the article below it because the words were too blurry.

"I can't read it," he said quietly to himself. "Why can't I read what this says?"

"What?" Lucian leaned over. "What *what* says?"

Oh, hey, he completely forgot Lucian was in the room. Dorian looked up at him and all words failed. Already, his health was downward spiraling. Colors dulled. There was this awful high-pitched ringing in his ears. His chest ached as if a vice was compressing his ribcage. His vision was no longer perfect.

"Something's wrong," Dorian said slowly. "I'm losing my

sight and hearing."

"Fuck," Lucian snagged the phone from him and looked at what was on the screen.

Dorian watched Lucian's blurry face drain of color completely and when he stared at Dorian, he couldn't even tell what color Lucian's eyes were. Shit, was he going color blind?

"You're changing because your body's gone into survival mode, Dorian."

"And it's deteriorating." He really hated this. To crumble and weaken so fast wasn't something he'd truly been prepared for.

"No," Lucian handed back the cell phone. "Your body and mind know exactly what it needs to survive. This was how it was with Luke too."

Damn, but Dorian's hearing could still pick up the heartbreak in his friend's tone even if he couldn't hear the street noises outside anymore.

"Can you see her?" Lucian tapped the phone screen to light it up again.

Dorian looked down and his heart slammed against his rib cage the second he saw her. "Y—" He cleared his throat. "Yeah. She's crystal clear. But the words beneath her picture are too blurry."

"But her face isn't?" Lucian pushed.

"No, she's..." *perfect, gorgeous, breathtaking.* "She's crystal clear and vibrant."

Lucian nodded. "It's because she's your chance at survival. Your body is caught in the crosshairs between the curse and the cure. Soon, your sense of smell will go too. You'll be able to see nothing, hear nothing, sense nothing but her. And that's only if she's close enough to you."

Dorian scrubbed his face with both hands. "I... I wasn't prepared for this. I didn't realize what it meant." He was okay dying. Just like he was okay living without ever having seen her. But this in-between life and death shit wasn't something he thought he had the capacity to handle. "I can't chase her down and bind her to me. She deserves better." Dorian dropped his hands into his lap and glared at Lucian. "But I don't think I have the strength to stay away from her either."

Hunting her down was suddenly all he could think of.

"I'm not losing you," Lucian growled. "And it's not up to you who she spends eternity with, Dorian. Fate has already set her up to be your destiny."

"I don't want her forced to be with me."

"Then don't force her. But give her the chance to decide. Find her, woo her, and then let her choose what she wants. An eternity with you, or a lifetime without you."

It seemed so simple, didn't it? Just court her, spoil her, worship her, annnnnd then leave the ultimate decision up to her on how she wanted to spend her days and nights.

All that was perfectly fine, except for one thing...

"What if I kill her?" If he died before she made her decision, there was nothing he could do about that. His fate was sealed the second her reflection was shown to him. But if he lost his mind — as all vampires in his position did once death drew near — he might accidentally kill her in a mindless rage, and that... was insufferable.

A shot at love wasn't worth the risk of her death.

"You won't hurt her," Lucian growled.

"You can't know that."

"I can and do know that," Lucian said, pressing his forehead against Dorian's. "You would *never* hurt her, even if you go completely mad before she makes her decision."

"I don't trust myself." This didn't feel like a desperate need to survive, it was worse than that. More dangerous. "I feel obsessed with her already."

An obsession, as he'd learned from his father, was a toxic and deadly disease.

"Let's find her and see how far you can get with her." Lucian backed away. "I think I have a plan."

CHAPTER 8

As far as plans went, this might be the worst one Dorian had ever been part of.

"I'm going to stall Marius as much as possible while you go get your girl. When you come back, call me and I'll buffer you."

Buffer really meant monitor. Lucian was only being nice about his word choice. Eventually Dorian would need monitoring, whether he liked it or not.

"I may not make it back in time. You realize that, right?"

Lucian ran his hand through his dirty blond hair and kept his gaze cast to the ground. "You will," he said solemnly. "You've been on the brink of death before and survived. No reason to think you can't do it again."

"You can only cheat death so many times before he wins." The irony, right? Considering Dorian was the motherfucking *Reaper*.

"Pack your shit and let's hurry. The faster you find her, the better... for all our sakes."

Dorian couldn't argue with that, but even with how eager he was to reach his mate the dread of this entire thing slowed his movements. "I keep thinking I shouldn't do this."

"Stop thinking then." Lucian began to pace. "And hurry up. Airport traffic's a bitch to get in and out of."

For the vampire who always had control of everything in his life, Dorian was completely out of his element now. He hated his curse more today than he ever dreamed possible. As he stuffed a bunch of clothes into a duffel and grabbed three stacks of cash from his safe, he didn't even realize how messy he was getting. No folding. No carefulness. No regard for cleanliness. He packed in three minutes.

I'm doing this. I'm off to do the one thing I swore I'd never do. And the craziest part? It was compulsive. If he couldn't control his desires and actions now, how much worse was he going to get?

He couldn't bring himself to answer that.

"Ready?" Lucian asked at the door.

Dorian locked his jaw, bit down on the inside of his lip, and let the blood flow into his mouth while he slipped past Lucian and headed for the car. Walking out into the sunlight, the bright light of day made his eyes water. Damnit, he needed sunglasses and his were in his car.

"Here," Lucian smacked a pair of shades against Dorian's chest. "Wear mine."

It must have been obvious that light sensitivity was becoming an issue already. Normally vampires were fine in sunlight. Great. Just great. Dorian was one big weakness after another since seeing his mate's reflection. If their enemy found out, about any of this, he'd have a harder time in a fight with a *Savag-Ri* and they might actually have a chance at taking him out before he found his girl.

The thought of that happening made him tense. At some point, his speed would slow down and his strength would deteriorate too. Could he still kill an enemy in his current condition? Yes. But every day he would get worse. If fate didn't kill him first, a *Savag-Ri* had a damned good shot.

Shit.

Sliding into the driver's side of Lucian's car, he said, "I need control of something." Driving would have to be it, even if his eyesight wasn't the best right now.

"It's fine. That'll give me more time to look your girl up."

My girl. Dorian had only ever called Emily that until now. Shit, Em... "Hey, I need you to do me another favor."

"Well now I'm starting to feel used," Lucian teased. "What is it?"

"If..." He couldn't stand this. "If I don't make it back, please take care of Emily for me. Whatever she needs, make sure she gets it, okay? And leave my assets to my mate. Just be discreet and anonymous, okay?"

Lucian looked up from his phone, face grave. "Absolutely."

Relief settled in Dorian's chest with a sigh. Lucian would never back out of his promises. He was one of the few vampires welcome on pack land because of Dorian. Lucian would have no trouble carrying out Dorian's final wishes.

He blew past the red light and hung a left. It was like driving with plastic goggles—everything looked slightly warped and dull. He glanced over to see Lucian intently staring at his phone, his fingers flying along the touchpad. "Also, Emily might be attending the full moon ceremony for her pack. If that's the case, and I'm not able to, please be there for her on my behalf. If she decides to not go, take her out to keep her mind off things for the night, okay?"

"Consider it done."

That was the thing about a vampire like Lucian, his word was golden. No other was more trustworthy than him, which was one more reason why King Malachi chose Lucian to lead and protect their House as high guard.

"I feel like I'm leaving you to clean up my mess," Dorian confessed. "This isn't right."

"This is all that's right. Damnit, man, if ever there was a time to do something for yourself, it's now."

Dorian didn't see it that way. With the House of Death in jeopardy, Stryx missing, the war against the *Savag-Ri* becoming more devastating, now seemed like the worst possible time for Dorian to buy a flight and head out of his territory to find his mate. This was beyond selfish, it was....

All his mind, body, and soul were hellbent on doing.

Holy Hell. How had he become so desperately fixated so fast?

"You need to take care of yourself so you can take care of the House, Dorian. The King is dependent on you."

"He's dependent on you, too."

"Then don't leave me hanging. Find her and be done with this. It's time to put yourself first for just a minute, and if anyone can understand that it's Malachi. Just look at what happened to *him*."

Yeah, they still hadn't figured out how Malachi managed to stay alive. Regardless of how insane vampires thought him, he was still powerful and breathing—even after all of his suffering. Dorian couldn't imagine what must be going through the king's mind all day and night but seeing how often Malachi stayed fixated on his massive mirror, Dorian could relate to the compulsive obsessiveness. It wasn't fun. It was taxing.

Necessary.

"This still feels wrong, somehow," he grumbled, even as he sped faster down the road.

"It's because you're not used to putting yourself first."

"I've been selfish before." Dorian clenched his teeth. "And it didn't end well."

Lucian stuffed his phone in his pocket and scrubbed his face. "I won't go through this with you again. That wasn't selfishness, it was survival. Same concept applies now. Besides, you were doing our society a favor when you did what you did, and no one will say otherwise."

Except me, he thought. "Survival looks a lot like murder then."

"Can't argue there. But back then, would you have rather been on the other end of that blade?"

I was... many times. But Dorian didn't say it because conjuring those memories made him sick. Pulling into the airport drop off zone, he slammed the car in park and hopped out.

"You should take the private jet," Lucian argued.

"It would only raise flags. Everyone knows I'd never use the jet unless it was a dire situation." They both knew Dorian handled everything with an eerie level of calmness. Going against his personality and taking the jet would only lead to suspicion and plotting among the other Houses while Dorian's back was turned. "My circumstance and sudden disappearance could easily put the King in great danger while I'm gone."

"Shit, you're right," Lucian groused. "I can't believe I hadn't thought of that." The lapse in judgment was excusable — Lucian was going through his own horrible shit lately.

"You can't let anyone know. Understand me? If word gets out that I'm weakened and preoccupied, our enemies will move on the House, and once I find her, I can't protect myself from *Savag-Ri* while also concealing what I truly am to her. So, getting attacked isn't going to help me and will also put my mate in danger."

"Her name is Lena." Lucian walked around his car to get in the driver's seat. "And I've got your ass covered, Dorian. Don't worry. Now go."

Dorian numbly held his duffel while Lucian drove off and left him at the airport with nothing but a prayer and a name.

Lena. How fucking beautiful was that?

Lena. Her name was like a satin ribbon twirling in his mind, binding his thoughts and keeping him from completely unraveling.

Lena.

His phone buzzed in his pocket. Pulling it out, Dorian stared at the screen and enlarged the screenshots so he could see the words better, something he should have tried earlier had he any sense in him. Finally able to read the big ass text on his screen, a smile crept across his face.

Lucian just sent him everything he needed to find his mate.

CHAPTER 9

Dorian thought he knew torture. Considered himself an expert on the matter. Dare he say, a master. Torture was a constant, aching, biting hunger which had no hope of being satisfied.

That was nothing compared to this fresh Hell he found himself in now.

His plane wasn't due to take off for another six hours due to a mechanical malfunction. He barely got here by the skin of his teeth, trying to make the flight in time, only to be grounded on the runway. Great. Just fucking great.

The miracle of getting a ticket hadn't been a miracle at all. With the excuse of "running an errand," Reys hacked the system for him and overrode the airlines database, getting Dorian a seat on the first plane to Savannah, Georgia. Reys most likely thought it was an errand for the king. Dorian never corrected him. He felt guilty but not guilty enough to come clean. At least not yet.

Now karma was biting him in the ass.

Damnit, he should have taken the House of Death's private jet. He could land in Georgia and hunt down his woman in the same amount of time it was going to take for this hunk of metal to get fixed and take flight.

Damnit, these seats were too narrow. No leg space either. He was confined and trapped.

A baby started crying behind him.

Closing his eyes didn't help cool his nerves. He fumbled with the air vent which did nothing at all. Jesus, he couldn't breathe in here. Yanking his tie, he ripped the fabric clean off his neck.

"Nervous flyer?"

Don't talk to me. "Just impatient."

"I got ya. This shit is annoying. Better to be safe than sorry though, right?"

Please. Stop. Talking. "Yeah."

Better safe than sorry—what a joke. Was Lena safe or would she be sorry? How was he going to introduce himself to her? Did he go to her address and knock? What if she wasn't home? Did he wait by her door or come back later?

"Fuck." He sounded like a sick stalker. But that's basically what he was. Sick. Annnnd a stalker.

And a killer.

This wasn't going to go well. Already, he could feel this overpowering drive to tear the world apart to reach her. His mouth started watering again. Opening his eyes, Dorian looked out the window and frowned at how blurry everything looked. His vision was getting worse. Soon he might be blind. Then what?

Holy Hell, was he even going to be able to drive after this? He might not even be able to see the airport gate much less anything else once they landed. Then what? How fast was he going to deteriorate? How the hell was he going to woo Lena and convince her to be his mate all before he turned to dust?

This was an impossible task. The lucky strike of finding her fast was quickly doused with the reality of *finding* her only being the *first* hurdle of the curse laid upon his kind.

The true issue wasn't that he couldn't find her or make her fall for him. The challenge would be not killing everything under the sun as his hunger worsened and his sanity unraveled in the process of convincing her to be with him.

How does a beast get a beauty to fall in love with him?

Spend a life with him? Love was too much to ask for. But friendship? Was it too selfish to pray for that? Wait… did he really expect her to be with him?

Yes, damnit. Yes, he fucking did. How deranged was that? He wanted her to choose to stay with him. Allow him to sink his teeth in her vein and *suck*.

SUCK. DRINK. SWALLOW. CLAIM. TURN.

He'd cherish her. Spoil her. Kill for her.

Dorian clenched his jaw and let the familiar sting of his fangs piercing his inner lip pull him down a few notches. He didn't deserve a happy ending. He didn't deserve the kind of love that came with having an *alakhai*. He deserved only what he was now suffering from — a deterioration of all his senses and the madness that would soon follow.

He didn't know Lena. Didn't even want to acknowledge the possibility of her existence until now. And all because fate said this was the one for him. It still shouldn't be possible for him to feel this obsessive over a creature he'd never even met.

But here he was. On a plane. Biting his lip to keep from sinking his fangs in the neck of the human sitting next to him who was still flapping their gums.

Pressing his head back into the headrest, he fought the urge to puke. His duty was to be the King's Reaper. His purpose was to slay the fuckers — the *Savag-Ri* — who threatened their race. He shouldn't be on this plane. He shouldn't be selfishly thinking of his own survival, but instead remain patrolling the streets of New Orleans and saving the House of Death from threats until he combusted.

That was the honorable thing to do.

He almost got up. Hand-to-the-Creator, he was just about to stand when he caught a glimpse in the reflection of his window. It was like Lena was on the other side of the pane, her head pressed against the same window, looking right into his blackened, tainted, doomed soul.

Lena. Of its own accord, Dorian ran a featherlight touch across the tiny windowpane. Was that a sign? To see her just before he was about to walk away from this endeavor? Maybe.

Or maybe his brain was already starting to melt. Honestly, it was hard to say at this point. But then the little *ding-ding* over the intercom chimed and the pilot said, "Good news, ladies and gents. We're back on track and will be taxiing out of here in ten minutes. Please remain seated."

Too late, Dorian thought. He was strapped in and committed to seeing this through.

61

Lena almost missed her flight. The problem with booking things last minute was yeah, the tickets might be cheaper, but it also left little to no time to get packed and to the airport. Staring out the window, she watched buildings and trees and cars come closer and closer as her plane prepared to land. She pressed her face to the pane and smiled down at New Orleans.

For the first time in a long while, Lena was excited and hopeful. Her heart pounded with anticipation in her chest. This beat any underground fight she'd ever been in. With those, there was anticipation, but also an aggression that kept her excitement on a tight leash. Here, however, she was unchained and out for a good time.

Pulling her cell out, Lena checked it for the one thousandth time to make sure her email with the room reservation was still there. It was weird to have it all set up this way, but the club was beyond exclusive and bordered on illusion. The leg work and strings it took to pull this off was going to be worth it though. It had to be.

The Wicked Garden was a fleeting opportunity and Lena didn't let those go to waste. Ever.

As the plane skidded to a stop, her stomach flip flopped. She hated flying and not having control—even though she wasn't a pilot, some survival instinct insisted if she was in the pilot's seat, she'd be safer. Which was strange considering she wanted to have someone else take the reins from her for a little while.

That was exactly what she was after—and Lena needed to be bound in a safe space so she could unravel. With a professional supporting her.

Except Lena didn't want to just be tied up and given an outlet to come undone. She wanted other things too…

The plane stopped and the door opened. Ahead of her, travelers stood and stretched before grabbing their bags from the overhead departments. She waited until the other two people next to her went down the aisle before she snagged her bag and moved off the plane.

Once she made it outside to the Uber line, Lena breathed in the hot air and scanned the airport. She had a few hours before hitting The Wicked Garden for a tour and hopefully, soon after, would be able to scratch the itch that had plagued her for so long, it was starting to drive her batshit crazy…

Mother. Fucking. Finally! Dorian leaned forward in the backseat of his Uber and gawked at the scenery. Georgia was nothing like New Orleans. Not in vibe, at least. The House of Bone had a little territory across the South Carolina border, and he knew for a fact a rebel pack of werewolves claimed territory in Florida's northern region, which was too close to Lena for his liking. He needed to make this visit fast and not catch anyone's attention.

It was nearly two in the morning when the driver pulled up to the Airbnb Dorian rented. "Thanks." He tossed him a hundred-dollar cash tip. Getting out of the car, he grabbed his duffel and headed for the door.

Thank fuck for keyless entries and seclusion. The flight here nearly broke his self-control and endangering humans wasn't something Dorian had interest in adding to his list of sins.

The sooner he got to Lena, the better.

Flicking the lights on, he scanned the house for trespassers out of habit. Dorian lived a life where threats were around not only every corner, but also draped in satin sheets, and sometimes served pancakes at the local diner. Between the *Savag-Ri*, Rogues, and the occasional assassin from another House, it was a miracle the vampire race hadn't been killed off long before now.

Once he was sure the place was secure, he unpacked his outfit for tomorrow and was almost grateful he couldn't see the number of wrinkles on his clothes in his poorly packed bag. Damnit, he was going to roll up to her house as wrinkled as a Shar-pei.

Growling, he snatched a hanger from the closet and made a half-assed attempt at shaking the wrinkles out of his shirt and pants. Then he groaned because he had no idea why the state of his clothes bothered him so much. Oh wait. Yes, he did.

"Damnit."

Dropping the duffel bag onto the floor, he marched into the bathroom and splashed water on his face. Catching his reflection, Dorian gawked at the blurry man staring back at him. Though his eyesight was poor, he could still see the darkness of his reflection. It wasn't only in the color of his irises. It ran deeper. Blood deep. Soul deep.

"Fuck."

He turned away from the mirror and sat on the edge of the bed with his head buried in his hands. There he remained until he gathered the courage to find his mate...

CHAPTER 10

Lena cruised down Bourbon Street with a pep in her step, drink in one hand and a killer po' boy in the other. So far, she'd hit an absinthe bar, a gothic boutique, and three voodoo shops. Already, she was making a mental list of the souvenirs she would go back later to buy after hitting Jackson Square tomorrow. Today, however, she was making a total pig of herself.

It couldn't be helped. The food was insane. The gumbo, beignets, oysters... hell, even their pancakes were mind-blowing.

The streets were packed. Everyone was in a good mood.

Jazz music pumped out of bars and local musicians set up buckets and chairs at the corners of each intersection. Never had she been so enraptured with a city before. Talk about love at first sight. It was more like love at first *bite*. Something about this place was a perfect mix of happy and successful, artistic and creative, dark and sensual.

Sucking back the rest of her drink, she dumped her cup in the nearest trash can and pulled out her map again. She was looking for another shop - a boutique which sold authentic shrunken heads. Why that fascinated her, she'd never know, but it sounded cool.

Aha! One block to the left and two over. Lena shoved the street map back into her pocket and took another huge bite of her po' boy while she walked. This one was grilled shrimp. The next one would be fried oyster.

Was it bad she was already planning out the one after that one too?

For all the money she had, she really needed to invest some of it here. She had a million ideas already.

Crossing the street, a sudden dizzy spell attacked her, and she tripped on the curb and nearly went ass over elbow on the sidewalk.

A man caught her before she faceplanted. His hands were strong and hot on her skin. "Easy," he said with a crooked smile. "Don't go busting that pretty face any more than it already is."

She backed away from him. "Sorry about that."

"No problem."

After the man tossed her another smile and kept walking, Lena stood on the sidewalk and stared straight ahead without really seeing anything. Not the stores, the signs, the cars, or people. Not the trash, the dogs, the mardis gras beads on the ground, or the jazz funeral making its way closer to her. Everything became a muted, colorless blur.

Squeezing her eyes shut, Lena took in several deep breaths. This wasn't the first time she had a spell like this. Probably wouldn't be the last either. She was a mess and getting worse. It wasn't vertigo or fatigue. No, it was this unholy gripping, domineering combination of aggression and lust which assaulted her randomly and without warning.

That phone call saying she could take a tour of The Wicked Garden couldn't have come at a more perfect time.

Lately her thirst for the most unsavory of lusts ruled her mind, her self-control, and quite frankly, her sense of honor. The more she wanted it, the more her body derailed.

It was foolish to think what she was here for would be a cure, but she'd run out of other ideas, and the amount of effort to get this far had cost her a small fortune. The Wicked Garden was an elite kink club that wasn't open for everyone. Hell, it sounded more like a myth than an actual place. But she put in the work, handed off the information, and waited for the game-changing phone call to one day come through.

Her patience had paid off. That had to be a sign, right?

Rolling her shoulders back, Lena was going to carpe the fuck out of this diem until she ran out of money, blood, and morals.

Dorian glared out the window as the Uber pulled up to a modest looking home. No car in the driveway, but that didn't mean there wasn't one in the garage. He liked that it was attached to the house. That was safer. She could close herself in and be locked up and untouchable that way.

"Stay," he growled at the driver.

Slamming the door shut, he shoved his hands back into his pockets and made his way to the front door.

He had no idea what he was going to say to her. If she was even home.

The thrum of the Uber's engine was a nuisance, setting Dorian on edge. The buzzing of bugs added another layer of tension. Even the sunshine pissed him off. Gritting his teeth, he tried to calm his nerves, pace his heart rate so he didn't feel swept up in a current of chaos. The engine noise died down... the bugs quieted... the sun was warm on his already hot brow.

Dorian climbed the three measly steps to her front porch. Flower baskets filled with ferns, flowers and vines hung on both sides of the front porch. A wicker swing swayed gently to his left. Only one person could fit and there were no other seats out here. Did that mean she was single? Not interested? Divorced? Widowed?

Was he about to wreck a woman's beautiful life with someone else?

Yeah, well, tough shit. She belonged to him and no other.

Exhaling a long, shaky breath, he dragged his gaze away from the swing, and glowered at her red door. Shit. His moral compass was going haywire. He hadn't thought this through. Hadn't prepared nearly enough. What the fuck was he doing stalking her online, hopping on a plane, and showing up at her doorstep like this? He was out of his goddamn mind if he thought this was okay. She'd take one look at him and run.

As well she should.

He stared at the little brass knocker on her door. He lifted it with his middle finger, poised to gently tap, tap, tap it to get her attention. His other fist tightened, ready to pound the damn door down and storm inside.

Dorian went crazy with random thoughts. He stared at the doorknob. How would she open her door? With a tight grip? Would she crack it open, or swing it wide fucking open? Jesus, the image of gripping and thrusting tore through him with a primal need. All that from just staring at her door.

This was madness.

He swallowed his lust and blew out another calming breath. Inhaling, his nostrils flared. His body hardened even more. Dorian picked up the slightest hint of sweet cherries, which was the first thing he'd been able to smell in three fucking days.

Lena... She smelled like cherry blossoms. *Lena...* He chanted her name in his mind just so he had something to latch onto as the rest of him unraveled into more and more of an unpredictable, dying beast. Running his finger across the peephole, he wasn't sure what to do. Knock or—

He needed to leave. This wasn't right. He couldn't just bang down her door and demand she become his mate. And there was still the little detail about turning her into a vampire to contend with.

No. She was too young and vibrant and had her whole life ahead of her. Even if she was miserable with her life, that was still a better situation than becoming an immortal bound to a piece of shit like him.

It was simple, quiet, and peaceful here. This was her home.

Dorian's world was cutthroat, vindictive and depraved.

He couldn't force her into that—not with his charm, his desperation, or his depressing curse. He refused to do that to her. It wasn't fair. Numbly, he took a step back. Then another. Aaannnd another.

Even her house looked like heaven. All sweet flowers and bright, cheery colors. His house was like a cell block—grey, white, black. Cold. Bet she had fifteen throw pillows on her bed, and ten more on her couch. Probably had a bowl of perfectly ripe fruit on her kitchen counter.

He had blades on his.

Yeah... this was a really bad fucking idea. His lungs tightened with shame and regret. His body tensed, fighting itself. This was wrong... *so fucking wrong.*

Holding his breath to keep from smelling her sweet, fruity scent again—a torture he couldn't stand any longer—Dorian backed off the porch and stumbled on the petunia-lined walkway. Biting his lip hard, he let the blood well and swallowed it as he slid back into the Uber and asked to be brought back to his Airbnb.

For the rest of the day and night, Dorian laid on his bed debating on whether or not he should try to catch a glimpse of her with his own eyes before he died or if he should go home and defend his king's territory until fate put him out of his bloody misery.

Staying here wasn't the safer option. Not for Lena and she was most important. The longer he went without her, the more deadly and uncontrollable he would become. Space between them was paramount. His death, unavoidable.

Pulling out his cell, he called Lucian. "Send the jet. I've got to get home as fast as fucking possible."

Damn the consequences.

CHAPTER 11

Lena walked every inch of the French Quarter before heading back up to her hotel room to get ready for her night. With every step down each street, every sip of every drink, every bite of food, every note played on an instrument, she fell deeper in love with New Orleans. But, holy shit, her feet were killing her. Sitting back on her bed, she ignored the fluttery feeling in her belly. She hated excitement like that. She much preferred the full blast of an adrenaline rush where chaos swirled around her until she bucked up and owned it, possessed it, mastered and controlled it. This fluttery bubbly bullshit was for the birds.

Give her intensity. That's how she went into fights and that's how she intended to go into The Wicked Garden, damnit.

Sinking into her pillows, she sighed and closed her eyes to refocus and slam down her nerves. A weird mix of red and black sensual ribbons twirled behind her eyelids. It was the strangest thing to see. Her body tensed, even as heat pooled between her thighs. She had no idea what this was, but the vision had haunted her lately. It made no sense, but the way her body responded to it made it almost addicting. The ribbons coiled and slipped, lashed out and twirled—almost like it was trying to pull her in to lure her somewhere.

Slipping her hands down to her waist, she opened her fly and shimmied out of her shorts. Maybe... maybe if she took the edge off just a little, she wouldn't feel so twisted right now.

Lena slipped one hand between her thighs and found herself already slickened. Her panties were wet from it. This had been her constant state for months… her lust was a dangerous thing. Always hungry. Always front and center.

The ribbons in her mind coiled and twisted into a tight rope. It thickened. Pulsed. Slithered and zipped behind her eyelids as her fingers delved into her pussy. Lena worked herself into a frenzy, heels digging into her bed, back arching, head digging into her pillow as she rub, rub, rubbed her clit with one hand and fingered herself with the other. Her heart slammed in her throat like a wild thing. She was close… so close she could almost—

Lena lost it.

That fast, she lost her fucking orgasm—just like every time she tried to take care of her needs. This, too, had been going on for months.

The Wicked Garden was her last hope. Her only hope.

Each time she reached that cliff of pleasure, everything frayed, including the ribbons in her mind. It was enough to drive her batshit crazy. Going into the bathroom, she splashed water on her face and glared at herself in the mirror. "Snap out of your shit and carpe this fucking diem." Orrrrr noctem. It was nine o'clock already.

Shit! Lena grabbed a dress and struggled to pull the zipper closed, then snagged her cell from the dresser. Following the instructions on her email, Lena waited outside her hotel for the car service, which had been lined up for her by the staff at The Wicked Garden, and at precisely nine-thirty, a black Mercedes pulled up just like the email said it would.

A large man stepped out of the driver's seat and opened the back door for her. "Good evening."

Her words caught on her tongue. The sheer size of this guy was intimidating, but his voice purred. *Whoa*. Lena flashed him a smile and slid in.

The driver didn't even look at her in the rearview as they headed down the crowded street at a snail's pace to give pedestrians the right of way. Lena ran her hands down her simple, black cocktail dress, smoothing the non-existent wrinkles, impatience snaking into her system. As they left the French Quarter and headed into the Garden District, Lena looked out the window at each of the homes they passed.

She came from money. Lived in a mansion once.

No more though.

Lena bit her bottom lip and tried to get out of her own damn head. "How long have you lived here?"

"Long time."

She got the feeling he wasn't much of a talker, so she didn't ask more questions. Or maybe that was the introvert coming out in her. To busy herself, she studied the way the driver worked the steering wheel, calculated the width of his shoulders, his height. The thickness of his neck, the size of his hands. He was big. Real big. Too big for her to win a fight with.

That almost disappointed her. She loved dangerous challenges.

Speaking of dangerous...

What would The Wicked Garden offer? Was it going to give her the very things she craved so desperately? First, Lena had to get through a tour and interview. This place wasn't just elite, it was almost impossible to find and become a member of.

She bit her bottom lip. If this place gave her what she needed, she was moving here. Hands down, no question. She was already madly in love with New Orleans, and if this kink club satisfied her ungodly itch, she would pack her shit and move next week.

She looked at a few condos online this afternoon when the idea struck her.

Classical music played softly on the radio. While she fantasized about life in Louisiana, the driver remained quiet. Lena's ears started ringing. She lost track of her thoughts.

Blink. Blink, blink. Blink.

The car stopped in front of a large home and her door swung open. The driver leaned down with a frown. "Are you feeling okay?"

"I'm fine." She cleared her throat and touched her neck. "Just... nervous."

He tossed her a killer smile and held his hand out. "The heat doesn't help."

"Neither does two bags of beignets and three po'boys in one day."

He whistled, impressed. "A woman with an appetite is enough to make a man fall to his knees." He kissed the back of her hand. He nodded towards the big house. "You know what you're getting into there, sugar?" He genuinely looked worried for her.

"It's a kink club."

The driver cocked his eyebrow, a slight smile slithering across his face. "You better be careful in there."

Lena tensed. "Why?"

"This city? This place? Once they sink their teeth in, they don't let go."

Lena's body melted at the thought. "You say that like it's a bad thing."

He rocked back and clutched his heart. "You're gonna be a dangerous one."

She winked at him and headed towards the estate, aka, her potential salvation.

After smoothing her dress one last time, Lena gripped the tips of the wrought iron gate, molded into an elaborate French door style, and noticed white dust scattered across the threshold and lawn. *Weird.* Pushing the iron gate open, she sauntered up the walkway, climbed six wide concrete steps, and stopped under a gas lit chandelier. Lena raised her hand to ring the bell, but the door opened before she had the chance.

"Welcome to The Wicked Garden."

The man talking to her had fangs. Actual fangs. Were they clip-ons? Veneers? Did it even matter?

"Your name, please?"

Lena swallowed through the tightness in her throat and gawked at the doorman. Dressed in head-to-toe black, he was something out of a dark fantasy — sharp jaw line, brown eyes, dark skin, broad shoulders. He tipped his head to the side. "Name, please."

Oh whoops. "Cherry," she said in a heavily sexual voice. Rules were, no one used real names here, so she went with her favorite fruit. So dumb right? But it didn't feel dumb when he flashed her a killer smile and said, "Right this way, Cherry." It felt decadent and sinful.

She'd been to sex clubs before but hadn't stayed long enough to participate. None of them hit the mark. And none of them looked like this.

"This is the mingling area. We encourage our guests to relax but getting intoxicated is forbidden. As is drug use of any kind. We pride ourselves in hosting parties where our guests always remain clear-headed, for consensual purposes. If, at any time, you are feeling uncomfortable with another guest here, just gesture like this," the man swiftly tapped the tip of his nose, "and one of our staff will escort you to a safe area and deal with the one offending or threatening you."

"Good to know."

"The safety of our guests is of utmost importance to us."

Lena's gaze sailed around the first room—a parlor decked in creams and golds. A large painting of a woman was mounted on a heavy frame, positioned between two massive windows adorned with heavy drapes. There was an intimate sitting area by the fireplace. Several extra chairs with high backs and cream cushions sat along the perimeter of the room, and there was a large piece of furniture that looked like three settees smashed with their backs together in the center. Off to the side sat a round table with seating for eight.

"Voyeurism and exhibitionism are both welcomed, as long as all parties are in agreement," the man said. "Through these doors is a dancefloor." He took her into the cleared room that only boasted hardwood floors and a few paintings. It was... boring. "However," he continued, "this space requires clothing. Rooms with windows for an audience can be reserved upstairs, and chairs can be placed in the room as well, to make all parties comfortable. Just ask a staff member to fetch whatever you require, even if you decide halfway through the evening to change things."

"What if... you don't have a room reservation?"

The guy smiled and his brown eyes twinkled, "Then you can go to our pool." He swept his arm in the direction of the back door, but first, they passed six more large rooms—a musical room set with grand piano and string instruments. A painting room, with canvases on easels, and four other sitting rooms.

"No kitchen?"

"Meals are not offered, only drinks." His full lips twitched with a hint of a smile. "The kitchen was pulled out and replaced with a bar."

"That doesn't serve alcohol," she confirmed.

"You'll find our establishment is heady enough to be drunk on lust alone, Cherry. Alcohol dulls the senses. We endeavor to heighten them."

With this boring ass place? She doubted it.

Still, her curiosity was piqued, and she was in it to win it. No way could an establishment this difficult to get into not be worth the trouble. Or maybe it was overhyped?

Only one way to find out.

"This is the pool area." The man opened the double doors and Lena's breath hitched as she stepped into an elaborate and well-designed garden. A fountain with naked women touching each other was the first sculpture she passed by. The pool sat nestled in a jungle of large greenery, making it perfect to conceal dirty deeds.

"All surfaces, linens, and bodies of water are purged and sanitized after each evening."

Impressive. And probably necessary if this pool was eventually filled with naked bodies, semen, and who knows what else.

Okay, now she was starting to feel a little bit of ick factor. You know how they show you orgies in the Greek baths? All the steam and skin and oil and candles? That's what she pictured, but now she considered the logistics and Lena figured Hollywood romanticized too much. This seemed more like taking a dip in funky ass water, enjoying a few short bursts of pleasure, followed by jellyfish-like blobs floating around in the pool afterwards.

Yuck.

"Would you like to see the upstairs now?"

His voice was velvet. Lena steeled herself, once again questioning if this was the right place or not for her. It was nothing like she expected. Where were the chains? The paddles? Hot wax? Leather and cuffs? Rods? Something!

This place looked like her great aunt Mildred's house who Lena was forced to spend Easter with for ten horrible years until the old bird croaked and her estate filtered into Lena's father's name.

"Sure." She smiled tightly. "I'd love to see the bedrooms." She might as well keep going since she was here. Besides, looks could be deceiving. For instance, folks once looked at her and thought she was a doll.

How wrong they were.

"Our private rooms require reservations in advance. Each guest is assigned a host to spend their evening with." His tone was calm and deep, and his gait was long as he climbed the enormous staircase to the second floor. "You can specify anything you'd like, and we will match you with a host who can fulfill those needs. This is a no-judgment club, Cherry. We pride ourselves in fulfilling your every desire… no matter how depraved you think it may be." He pressed his mouth to her ear and added, "I assure you we've done worse and enjoyed every second of it."

Lena's knees almost buckled.

Holy shit, she hadn't noticed him move so close until he was suddenly there. His quiet, sultry laugh shot a chill down her limbs.

Next, they toured seven different bedrooms. None of which screamed kink club. All were decorated in hues of cream, gold, and fucking beige. She was underwhelmed and it must have showed.

"Is this your first time in a place like this?" he asked.

"I've toured other clubs. None like this."

"Then you've noted the difference."

The corners of her mouth fought between curling up and curling down. "It's noticeable."

Shit, she didn't even know his name. Just like she never caught her driver's name.

"The French Quarter looks entirely different depending on the hour with which you walk it. Same for our club. Looks, Cherry, are deceiving."

Hadn't she told herself that like five minutes ago.

"But if you wish to relinquish your spot, we understand. This isn't for everyone. If you feel it's not in your best interests to join us, by all means, say the word and we'll close your account immediately."

"No," she said in a rush. "I'm… I'm just processing. I definitely want to stay."

"Excellent." He flashed her another killer grin, giving her another glimpse of his impressive fangs again. "Every guest must have an examination to ensure there are no health issues before staying their first evening. Like I said, safety is of utmost importance for everyone here."

"How long does that take?" Her heart plummeted at the thought of having to come back in a few weeks or months. She didn't think she'd last that long with the need biting and chomping at her like it was…

"Only a few minutes." He headed towards the grand

staircase, and she followed him back down to the first floor. "We can take care of that before you leave this evening."

Lena's cheeks heated. If she had to take the test before leaving tonight, that meant she wasn't going to be able to stay to enjoy anything this visit. Damnit. "If I get tested tonight, can I stay the evening?"

"Unfortunately, tonight our rooms and hosts are completely engaged."

Where? It was nighttime and she was the only person in the entire house. This must be a damn joke.

"You get three visits into The Wicked Garden, Cherry. This tour doesn't count as one of them."

Only *three*? Holy shit, there was a restriction on how many times she could come here? So much for moving and being a regular customer. If... of course... this place even did what the rumors promised. "What happens after three?"

"You leave and never think of us again."

Lena frowned at him. "I find it hard to believe anyone could leave here and never think of it again. If it offers what you imply."

"You'd be surprised what some are willing to forget... and what the mind can suppress."

Lena couldn't argue with that one. The way he talked, it sounded like depraved and dirty things happened in this club. She, for one, was all over that. No way would she want to forget anything she did. Nothing Lena did was regrettable in her life.

"Follow me," he crooked his finger and headed into another hallway, away from the main house. "Like I said earlier, some rooms have designated toys and arrangements made to accommodate certain appetites. All rooms and structures are sanitized after each session. Any toys, enhancers, or products are destroyed and replaced for each new session. Once you pass our health tests, you'll need to fill out a file of what you'd like for your first time with us. Don't worry about adding everything at once. Lust, like life, should be savored one pleasure at a time. No need to rush."

"No need to rush?" She sighed in disgruntlement. "Three visits to make all a girl's fantasies come true? That would be a pretty packed three nights."

"What one wants and what they think they want aren't

always in line. Go slow and let us spoil you. You can always beg for more as the evening progresses."

Her pussy swelled and became drenched when she heard those words. She was going to walk out of here with a stain on her black satin dress, damnit.

"What's the cost for this?" Because she knew damned well it wasn't free.

"We take payment in a variety of ways. Depends on what the guest is willing to give."

"First born? Piece of my soul? Credit card?"

"Clever, but terribly unoriginal."

She couldn't argue with that. "What's your name?"

"Pain." His brow arched, and it made Lena smile. Okay, maybe she was in the right place to get what she'd been dying for. Pain licked his bottom lip playfully. "We require our guests to wear a specific outfit during their first visit."

"The red dress?"

He nodded. "It allows all hosts an opportunity to sway your mind and gain your favor."

Lena's cheeks grew hot again. All arrangements from the hotel room, the driver here, and even her wardrobe was assigned and arranged ahead of time by The Wicked Garden. All Lena had to do—besides find and get an invitation to the club—was fly here and follow orders. Now a tour and simple test. They thought of everything and were insanely thorough. It gave her hope that they applied that level of commitment to all their services. If so, she planned to not be able to walk out of here after her first visit. "You go through a lot to keep your guests happy and feeling special."

"We are rewarded, I assure you."

I bet, she thought. Biting her bottom lip, she followed him into a small sterile room with a counter, desk and two chairs. "Now, Cherry, let's conduct our health test and you can fill out the necessary waivers."

In less than a half hour, her insta-blood test and background check came back clean. Pain also scanned her ID. "What about anonymity?"

"Cherry is your name between staff and guests. Your true name is only for legal purposes. We require true identities which will be kept in an encrypted file until you are no longer a guest with us."

"Lots of paperwork for a three-visit max."

"You're worth it." He flashed her another grin and she practically groaned while glaring at his fang tips.

"You stay in character all the time, Pain?"

"I'm never... out of character." He grabbed her hand and kissed the back of it again. A shot of electric heat zipped up her arm. Damn... he was good.

"So, it's official? I'm in?"

"I presume you'd like to return tomorrow evening?"

"Correct."

"I'll reserve a room for you." He handed her a black envelope. "Here's a list of suggestions for your first evening. Fill it out and hand it to the front desk of your hotel. We'll take care of the rest. A car will pick you up tomorrow evening at eleven."

No mention of a fee was made tonight. Something in her gut said this was going to cost her more than money, which should concern her. But the bottom line was, Lena was willing to pay any price to get what she craved. Lena had three visits, three chances, to hopefully get whatever this was riding her so hard out of her damn system. She was going to make those three visits count. Big time.

Pain escorted Lena out of the mansion and her driver was at the curb, waiting for her. The instant she was in the backseat, she began poring over the options The Wicked Garden offered. So many "standard services" as well as a variety of "a la carte" options she could request of her host.

Shouldn't she be at least a little bit scared about what she was getting into? Fuck it. She had zero fear. Plus, Pain made her feel confident, safe, and welcome... which was entirely opposite of that Dom she tried to hook up with a few months ago.

As the car drove off, she vibrated with anticipation.

Tomorrow she'd be back and ready to play.

CHAPTER 12

The flight back was so hard on him, Dorian was grateful he sent for the jet, if only to spare humans from his unraveling. He was chained to his seat. So fucked up and necessary.

As well as agonizing.

Leaving Lena alone went against his survival instincts and was the hardest thing Dorian had done to date.

It felt like he was being torn in half. He projectile vomited, strained to the point of bending the metal links of his chains, and managed to pop the blood vessels in his eyes with the roars he let out as the jet took to the skies and put distance between him and his best chances of meeting his mate.

It killed him to leave her.

He should have never chased his fate like this. What a tremendous waste of the precious time he had left.

"I can't believe you got so close and didn't at least *try*," Lucian fumed. "The fuck is wrong with you, Dorian?"

"I can't do it. I can't subject her to this life." *Or to me.*

This conversation lasted for an hour until they fell into a thick silence of regret and resentment.

When they landed in New Orleans, Dorian wheezed through the eye-watering pain in his chest the whole way back to the House of Death. Had someone driven a stake through his heart? He couldn't breathe at all. They walked into the mansion together and all Dorian wanted was to go home and be alone.

Lucian wasn't having it though. "I'm not leaving your side until you can stand upright without stumbling."

Dorian now had a goal for the night.

They headed into Lucian's bedroom. On the way, Lucian grabbed a decanter of wine and two glasses from a service cart at the top of the steps.

In the mansion, food, wine, music, blood, and sex were a mere arm's length away.

"This life isn't all that bad." Lucian leaned back, taking a sip from his wine glass. "Stop acting like it sucks to be one of us. We've got a good fucking life."

Lucian was just as edgy as Dorian. It made him feel even worse because the endgame was Dorian's death, and Lucian would have to mourn another loss in his life.

He didn't expect Lucian to understand why he'd deny himself the chance at happiness.

"I remember the day I met your scrawny, feral ass." Lucian drained his glass and slammed it on the table.

Dorian cringed at the accuracy of that description.

"You legit had a bounty on your fucking head. Remember that?"

Dorian remembered well. "And you told the Houses to fuck off with that price tag."

"Do you know why? Because I saw in you the same thing the pack that took you in did. You aren't a broken monster, Dorian. You're just... different. And thank fuck for that."

Different or deranged? Dorian didn't bother asking, he knew the truth.

The more accurate answer was the execution order was dropped after a stiff interrogation happened between King Malachi and Dorian when he was younger. Dorian didn't utter one single lie to the king that day. He told him everything his father did and what he forced Dorian to do.

Any questions the king asked about Dorian's mother or anyone else was harder to answer because Dorian honestly didn't know much about her, and he knew nothing, at the time, of any other vampires. Back then, he only had intimate knowledge of the monster who raised him and the innocents they killed.

It turned out his father murdered more humans than the vampire community had been made aware of. Unbeknownst to Dorian at the time, the search for his father had been going on for decades. They suspected the bastard had an accomplice but since Dorian was never allowed off his father's property, there was essentially no trace of him to pick up on. Dorian was a dirty secret, a caged animal for his father to abuse behind closed doors.

During the massive Q and A he had with the king, Dorian worried he'd be accused of being a rat for spilling all his dead father's secrets, but he didn't tell the king everything to gain favor. He did it because when Malachi offered solace under the House of Death's roof, among others of his kind, Dorian didn't want to accept it without everyone knowing exactly who, and what, they were inviting into their House. It earned him respect.

And constant judgement.

"I'm a monster, Lucian."

"Even monsters deserve love."

"Monsters don't even know the meaning of the word." It had certainly been a foreign concept for his father.

"I'm tired of this conversation," Lucian ran a hand down his face. "If you're going to die, let's party hard until you burn."

Fuck that. Partying was the last thing he should be doing, regardless of whether Lucian wanted to make some last-minute memories with him. "I'd rather spend the last of my days serving the House of Death." He stood and shoved his hands in his pockets. "I've got to talk with Malachi before I lose any more of my senses." They kept going in and out—his hearing, vision, energy—he was constantly teetering, and it sucked.

Lucian glared up at him for a moment then blew a puff of air out. "Fine."

He knew Lucian would never see it his way because they came from very different upbringings. Lucian was an aristocrat who literally had servants brush his fucking fangs when he was younger. Meanwhile, Dorian was glad he still had all his teeth by the time he was a teenager.

Lucian took on being a guard for the House of Death as his big rebellious move against his parents—they were from the House of Blood and were furious he chose the savage House instead of the sophisticated one. Lucian took on protecting the House of Death like it was his only purpose for drawing breath and became the youngest guard when he pledged fealty here. He climbed the ranks so fast it made vampire's heads spin and corroded their arteries with jealousy.

Meanwhile, Dorian came from nothing and stayed that way. He lived because others took pity on his mentally warped ass. They used him so their hands stayed clean and his remained bloody. He killed for pleasure *and* for business. He did it to protect his kind. He did it because he wanted to eliminate those who threatened the House of Death, as well as all the vampires affiliated with the House of Bone and House of Blood. Otherwise, he might as well have stayed the weak little boy under his father's blade and never tried to be anything better than a feral animal.

But years of being a hunter and executioner did unkind things to his morals. Though he never killed an innocent, somewhere along the way Dorian lost his ability to feel remorse for any of his actions. Good people felt bad when they killed. Dorian felt nothing when he took a life.

"Oh good, you're back." Victoria said from Lucian's bedroom doorway. "The King wants to see you."

"Thanks." Lucian speared a hand through his thick wavy, blond hair and blew out an exasperated breath. "Damnit, Dorian, how the hell are you going to be able to do anything if you can't see, hear, or move right anymore?"

"I'm better," he half-lied.

"You're stable. That's not better. Jesus, how are you going to function as executioner?"

Dorian clutched his jaw and didn't answer. "I refuse to lay around and wait to die."

"I can't stand this." Lucian grabbed Dorian's arm to help him get to the damn door.

Silently, they made it into Malachi's chamber.

"My lord," Dorian's tone was exhausted and gravelly.

"Leave us, Lucian." The king never broke his gaze from the mirror. "Come over here, Reaper."

Dorian swayed as he obeyed the king's orders and slammed down on his knees before his king. "I wish to spend the last of my time on this earth serving you."

"And how best do you think you can do that? You can't even stand."

There was no callousness in his tone. Only sympathy. And that made Dorian feel like he was a child found by the wolves again. At a loss, he relinquished his pride, "Shut me in a room and throw *Savag-Ri* in with me." He'd gladly burn with the blood of his enemies coating his body. It was a fitting way for him to leave this world.

Malachi's eyes narrowed and his lips thinned. Dorian's blurry vision was still good enough to see the tic in his king's jaw. "You think I should cage you?"

"I think you should use me. I'm already deteriorating. I can't hunt on my own—I'll likely hurt someone who doesn't deserve it. Lock me in the Kill Box and have the hunters bring me anyone they find. I'll kill on your behalf until I turn to ash."

Malachi's chin thrust out. "I'm not ready to lose you, boy."

"It's already done."

"You won't find her? You refuse fate's offer?"

Dorian didn't want to have this conversation again. "I won't force her into this life, and I have no control left."

"You had enough control to leave her and send for the jet, did you not?"

"And the act ate more of my strength."

Malachi broke his gaze with the mirror and stared directly at Dorian. The piercing intensity of the Mad King's glare almost made Dorian shrink back, but he wasn't so easily spooked.

"You're a miraculous vampire, Dorian. The battles you've fought. The nightmares you've lived. No other in this House would challenge you."

Because they knew better than to try a bastard like him. "They only respect me because you force them to."

"You are like a son to me, Dorian." Malachi ran a rough finger down Dorian's jawline and he fought the urge to not jerk away from the touch. Malachi's eyes hardened as he said, "I'll not let you go easily. And the respect you have was earned by your fealty to this House. You are willing to give the last drop of yourself to protect those in my territory. That is why they respect you."

"That is why they fear me."

"You still have much to learn, boy."

"Lock me up," Dorian begged again. "Let me be of service to you the only way I know how."

Malachi went back to staring at the mirror and didn't say anything for a few heartbeats. Dorian was just about to stand and walk away when the king grumbled, "Monsters are capable of love. Or are you saying I do not deserve it?"

What? Dorian stiffened.

"I know what they say about me," Malachi's tone was laced with venom. "I know what I did to get the crown I wear. I know still, what I'd do to keep my seat, even if I'm the only one left standing when I'm through."

"You'd never hurt your people, Malachi."

"You don't know what I would or wouldn't do, Dorian. Monsters are unpredictable." He ran a thumb across his mouth, thoughtfully. "One can love a monster… and it can love back… but it's still a fucking animal, Dorian. We are all made this way, some are just better at hiding their true nature, where you and I live our truths openly and without regret, son."

Dorian shriveled a little. "You're a far better father to me than mine ever was."

"He should have never gotten as far as he had," Malachi said softly. "For that, I will forever be sorry."

It wasn't your fault. That's what Dorian wanted to say, but it would have been a waste of breath. Malachi always took blame for things that made no sense.

"Had he not abused and treated you so poorly, perhaps you'd not be so willing to sacrifice yourself for the one you'll never get a chance to love."

Dorian shook his head, unable to argue with that logic but not willing to accept it either. "She deserves better than me, sire. I can't bond a woman to me, knowing what I am. What I'm capable of."

"How do you know she's not the same as you?" Again, his eyes were deadlocked on the mirror, even though it was obvious the king only saw his own reflection staring back at him. "If she's your fated mate there must be a purity to her soul that will cleanse yours, and vice versa. No *alakhai* is without power of their own. Even if that power is to bring out the best of the beast they're bound to."

Dorian bit his lip and began to second guess himself. Then he shook it off because taking advice from a mad vampire wasn't going to solve anything.

"Here." Malachi brought his arm up and bit the inside of his wrist, tearing his skin and piercing his vein. Blood poured all over his lap and spilled to the floor as he held his wrist out for Dorian. "Drink from me."

He didn't want to. No one fed from the king. *Ever.* But he couldn't reject the offer, either. Fuck!

"*Now*," Malachi growled. "Before I lose even more of my patience with you."

Dorian sealed his mouth over the king's wound and pulled. The blood burned down Dorian's throat and shot adrenaline through his veins. His eyes peeled wide as he guzzled faster and faster. His hunger had ridden him hard lately. This wasn't a feeding. It was a feast. Tightening his grip on Malachi's arm, Dorian groaned and swallowed even more.

He knew it was risky. Knew it was wrong. Knew it was dangerous. But his survival instincts kicked in and the instant royal blood hit his tongue, Dorian could no longer deny what he needed. He was too far gone in bloodlust. His body hardened. Fangs throbbed. Tightening his grip on Malachi's arm, he drew hard enough to solicit a hiss from his majesty's mouth.

"*Enough.*"

Dorian forced himself to unlatch. Rocking back on his heels, he gasped for breath and fell on his ass. Shit, his heart pounded like a wild stallion kicking and bucking in its stall. His lungs froze with his next inhale. Thousands of invisible bugs bit him all at once. Then a burst of energy ripped down his spine and Dorian doubled over, gasping.

"Rise," Malachi ordered.

Panting and still hungry, Dorian rose to his feet without swaying.

"Serve me well, Dorian." Malachi licked his wound closed and dismissed the Reaper with a flick of his hand. "Do *not* waste this gift bestowed upon you."

CHAPTER 13

Standing at the corner of Bourbon and Dumaine, Dorian scoured the streets looking for *Savag-Ri* and vampire Rogues. Until he was finally locked in the Kill Box and put out of his misery, he would hunt and kill all enemies in the French Quarter.

This felt right. To die this way, with a little bit of clarity and fucking dignity left in his dying heart.

Once he left the king's company, Dorian found Lucian and didn't tell him what happened. He just said he was going out hunting and left. Dorian took the opportunity to get out of the mansion and back on the streets.

Lucian could yell at him later for it.

The rush of strength pulsing through Dorian's veins made it painfully obvious that Malachi was, hands down, the strongest vampire to still draw breath. As far as Dorian knew, Malachi never offered his vein to anyone. Whatever caused the king to make such an offer, Dorian was secretly grateful. He wasn't conceited enough to think he was special.

Though his sense of smell wasn't completely back, it was better than it had been earlier today. Dorian scented the air, eager for a hit. Sometimes, older *Savag-Ri* had a strange tinge of bitterness to them, similar to moldy citrus. It was too faint for a human to detect, but for a skilled vampire like Dorian, the scent was traceable.

For a werewolf, it was an automatic trail to follow.

Dorian smiled at the memory of when he first came to his full, mature power and the pack who'd taken him in rallied together to celebrate by letting Dorian lead his first hunt. He got his first hard-on playing that deadly game of hide and seek. Fuck, he still got hard every time he became a predator in search of prey.

Monster. He was such a monster.

Biting his tongue, he let the blood well into his mouth and prowled the French Quarter. At this time of night, the place was popping with people and other creatures of the night. *Savag-Ri* couldn't stay away from an open market like that. They were too righteous for their own damn good. Always trying to protect the humans from vampires and werewolves, when, in reality, they didn't need protecting at all. Vampires policed their own kind. Lycan were the same.

The history of this centuries-long war became more muddled the longer it went on. But so long as a *Savag-Ri* lived to raise their guns and blades at a vampire, Dorian refused to see them as just another creature born with a curse in their blood. In fact, they were the reason vampires and Lycan were cursed to begin with.

What goes around, comes around, assholes.

Palming a small blade in his right hand, he stayed discreet and scoured the streets. The scents of puke, alcohol, cologne, cigarettes, and fried dough mingled in his nose. Leaning against a building, Dorian watched people pass by him and he tried to get a hit. He knew every vampire in town. Lycan rarely came into New Orleans because it was the House of Death's territory, and they didn't like crossing lines. Humans were too oblivious about what crept around them all the time, so they did their own thing without much concern. *Savag-Ri*, however, walked with purpose, no matter how discreet they tried to be. The one thing that marked them was their eyes. A curse was etched into their irises in the shape of a cross.

But unless they were face-to-face with you, you'd never notice. In the daylight, they could hide the mark with sunglasses. It was annoying.

Dorian remained still and observant while the world passed by. Jazz blasted out of bars. Street performers put on shows. Laughter, loudness, and life buzzed as bright as the neon lights glowing in front of shops.

There.

Dorian stiffened as he saw a *Savag-Ri* cross the street. He was heading into a café. A wolfish grin locked into place and Dorian made his way closer, careful to not bump into anyone as he neared his target.

A plan formed in his mind of how to lure the fucker out, kill him, and where to dump the body for another vampire to pick it up and take it to one of the House of Bone's properties to be dusted.

He made it all the way to the café entrance before stopping dead in his tracks.

His body locked. Mind fritzed. Nostrils flared.

No.

Dorian's knees nearly buckled when he smelled a distinct cherry scent. This... this couldn't be real. He must be going in-fucking-sane because no way on this cruel earth would that be his mate who just dropped her empty paper coffee cup into an overflowing trash bin and slipped by him, paying no mind to the vampire with the throbbing hard-on in the middle of the doorway.

This... this wasn't possible.

For a solid thirty seconds, Dorian stared at the back of her head, her bare back, and her luscious ass until she disappeared around a corner. His feet moved without him being aware that he was closing in on her. He tucked his blade back in its holder at the small of his back as he prowled. All light and sound faded until it was just the woman in the red dress.

His woman.

His *mate.*

Whatever cruel miracle this was, he couldn't stop himself from getting closer to her. She stopped at an intersection and stared at her phone. Her long, delicate fingers danced along her cell screen and then she looked up and jogged across the street in a set of killer heels.

How did she move so fast in those things?

She looked beyond incredible. No picture online did this woman justice.

Dorian's lips peeled back as a hiss slipped between his teeth. Where the fuck was she going, dripped in sinful promises like that? If she had a dinner date, Dorian would kill her companion before appetizers were served. If she was here for business, he wanted know what kind warranted a dress so stunning. If she was here for a girl's weekend, he'd make sure she stayed safe, and no one came close to touching what was his.

It took tremendous control to keep his distance and follow her, but when she stopped in front of a specific vampire owned hotel and a particular car was already waiting for her, Dorian's possessive instinct ripped out of him like a Lycan turning wolf.

Oh. Fuck. No. She better not be going where he thought she was going.

It took tremendous effort to not chase that goddamn car down and rip her out of the back seat. Instead, he swallowed his panic and ran, with inhuman speed, back to his own car. He knew where that driver was headed. He just couldn't fathom that Lena would be going there.

It twisted his insides up.

Part of him demanded he blow every red light and beat her there. The other part of him thought he deserved to watch her go in and disappear behind the heavily guarded gate of that place. He'd given her up… walked away from his chances with her. Lena was doing exactly what he wished for. She was living her life.

But here? Now?

Fuck that. He couldn't stand the thought. And if chasing after her made him a dumbass or hypocrite or jealous monster with venom in his veins, so fucking be it.

That dress. She was in a red dress. The signature color of a new guest at The Wicked Garden. Red wasn't the color of passion and sinful pleasures. It was the color of dinner.

Dorian slammed down on the gas pedal and flew down the street.

As requested of her first visit, Lena wore a red dress and entered The Wicked Garden with a little more nervousness than she'd anticipated. Call her paranoid, but she swore someone was watching her.

Probably the ghost of her parents, disapproving of her life choices.

Shaking off the heebie-jeebies, she focused on her endgame. This was it. This was her chance to finally find someone to give her what she craved.

"Good evening, Cherry." Pain smiled from the door.

"Welcome back to The Wicked Garden."

Her heart beat wildly in her throat as she stepped across the threshold.

"I'll take this," Pain said while taking her small purse.

Lena looked down as she smoothed her dress and noticed she'd accidentally kicked some of that damned white powder by the front gate onto her shoe.

"Allow me." Pain kneeled with an unearthly grace, and gently held her ankle while rubbing his thumb across the dust, brushing it away. "Perfect," he purred, while gazing up at her and running his large, warm hand up the back of her calf.

"Thank you."

"Allow me to escort you to your private room."

She'd debated on one with a window to allow for voyeurism but wasn't up for that just yet. She wasn't sure if she'd ever be ready to be the star of a peepshow, and until she knew exactly what she was getting into and what all she wanted to try, privacy was the better option for now.

Pain grabbed a black folder from a small table against the wall and discreetly skimmed its contents before escorting Lena to her room. "Your room is just this way."

Music, not classical, but edgy with dark tones, pumped through the speakers.

The entire house was completely different. All the white, cream, gold had been replaced with black, purple, reds, and steel. She'd fallen into a rabbit hole. A dark, sensual, sexy rabbit hole where the Mad Hatter fucked your throat and Alice hung from chains, her nipples pinched with clamps.

Wait... what? Lena shook her head and swallowed. Shit, she couldn't think straight again.

Loud mewling noises ripped through the hall. A growl, ferocious and earth-shattering followed. The bass of the music vibrated Lena's ribcage. She held onto the banister as she climbed the steps. Everything smelled like sex and spice and secrets. "This is different than before."

"Didn't believe me?" Pain flashed her a big, hungry smile. "You've asked for some very fun services, Cherry. I took the liberty of setting you up with one of our finest, and most sought-after, hosts."

91

Her heart was practically cartwheeling by the time they reached the top of the grand staircase.

Someone cried out in ecstasy. The crack of a whip tore through the air. More moans. The sound of skin slapping skin.

She could see none of the people, but it sounded like they were everywhere—on the floor, in the rooms against the walls, on the ceiling even.

Lena broke out in a lust-induced sweat. She slowed her roll and looked down at the first floor. Black lights and candles danced everywhere. The chandeliers glowed in reds and purples. The furniture was rearranged. There was movement but... she couldn't see anyone.

Strange.

"This way." Pain lured her to the room at the end of the hall. "He's not usually here, and even so, rarely takes guests. I think you'll enjoy him." Pain practically purred those words, then grabbed her hand, kissed her knuckles, and said, "You look good enough to eat."

That's the plan, she thought. Her cheeks instantly growing hotter at the thought.

Pain chuckled. "And don't worry, your host will be gentle until you beg him to be otherwise."

Lena's breath rushed out of her when Pain opened the door and ushered her inside the bedroom. "Welcome to your paradise, Cherry."

As Pain placed her folder on a small table then walked over to a set of closet doors, Lena gawked at the rich textures of reds, blacks, silk, and velvet. The room dripped in plush fabrics and cushions. A bed with a large, black frame sat against the wall to her left. Candelabras were lit all over the place. There was a bath in the right corner with red rose petals floating on top. A chandelier bigger than a Buick hung from the ceiling, along with ropes, chains, silks, and...

Holy shit. Red ribbons.

Nothing like this was here yesterday. Nothing.

Red ribbons.

Lena's gaze locked on those things and she froze. Solidified in the fact that she was absolutely meant to be here, her skin pebbled and cheeks tingled.

"If you don't mind," Pain ran a hand across her waist. "I must place this blindfold on you now."

"Why?" Her voice trembled from a toxic mix of trepidation and anticipation.

"Rules are rules. Your host will take it off only when he deems the time is right." Pain winked. "It's only temporary, Cherry. Don't be afraid."

"I'm not afraid." She was annoyed. "That's not on my list."

Pain wasn't deterred. "To take away your sight will enhance the sensations of what you've signed up for. Don't fight it, enjoy it."

She swallowed hard.

"Come." He grabbed her hands and walked her over to a small, circular platform. The red silk ribbons dangled directly above her now. "Stay just like this for me, Cherry." Pain gently tied the blindfold over her eyes.

Her breath caught when his hot hands slipped down her arms to grab her wrists, raising them above her head.

"Reach out until you feel the satin," he said against the shell of her ear.

Lena let out a small groan of desire.

"So eager and ready," Pain purred against her neck. "You're so ripe for sucking, Cherry."

Oh fuuuuuck.

She was so in the right place. Winding the ribbons around her palms brought her a little more confidence because it was similar to when she wrapped her hands before a fight.

"Good girl," he purred. "Enjoy The Wicked Garden, Cherry. Your host will be arriving soon."

Lena bit her bottom lip and waited for her host to walk through the door.

CHAPTER 14

Dorian was too late. She walked into The Wicked Garden just as he parked the car.

Damnit!

The only reason he didn't kick the door down and snatch her was because his protective nature had taken over his possessive one. He'd likely kill everyone who stood between him and her, as well as anyone within sight just for being in his goddamn way.

There were vampires in there. Innocents too.

So, like a rabid dog chained to a light post, he was forced to remain at a safe distance until he could think straight again.

Fate really hated him. That's the only reason she would somehow be in his territory—among his kind—just after he came to terms with the fact that he couldn't have her as a mate. He'd been desperate to save her from this world and what had she done? Walked right into it, dressed for supper.

He shook with unholy rage. His fangs had a fucking pulse to them.

Pacing his breathing, he stalked up the steps and didn't knock. He glared at the security camera hidden discreetly to the left and the doors opened immediately.

Victoria, of all vampires, was the one to greet him. Perhaps that, too, was a joke made by fate. That bitch was going to witness Dorian lose his shit over a woman. And enjoy every second of it too.

"Dorian, what are you doing here?"

He pushed past her and picked up Lena's scent immediately. Following it through the mansion, his vision reddened as blood rushed to his ears. Climbing the steps, he was vaguely aware of the movement around him. Reys passed by, his eyes widening with terror. Dorian shoved a finger in his face but didn't say a word. His glare said it all. If anyone tried to stop him, he'd eat their face off.

Lena. All he cared about was getting to Lena and dismembering any vampire foolish enough to try and touch her.

His heart slammed in his chest, raging. His veins burned with poisonous fire. He had tunnel vision. The door ahead of him was all he could see.

Dorian was vaguely aware security had gone on high alert. He also didn't give a rat's ass. Victoria and the others were most likely trying to protect those in this building from Dorian's wrath, and they were right to do so. But—so help him—if one of these vampires tried to lay a hand on him right now, he'd kill them. Friend or not, if they tried to stop him from going through that door and reaching his mate, they were fucking dead.

His hand landed on the doorknob. With a twist and shove, he swung that heavy door open wide.

The world fell off its axis. His lungs slammed down and tightened.

Lena stood on a dais in the center of the bedroom, still dressed. Her back was to him, her toned arms raised above her head and hands wrapped around red satin ribbons strung from the ceiling.

A fierce need to possess every inch of her ripped through Dorian. He stepped into the room and shut the door.

By some miracle, no one interfered.

Damn, look at her. His mouth parted as he tried to suck in more air. Panting, his chest was too tight, his muscles too tense. He was going to snap in half. The only thing keeping him from jumping her was the fact that Lena's scent had changed.

There was a slight tang to it now.... *Fear.*

He couldn't bear the thought of her being afraid of him—even if she very well should be. No woman in her right mind would volunteer to be locked in a room with an animal like him. But there was no stopping this now. If fate wanted something to happen, it happened.

Dorian's fate was literally wrapped in red and tied with a bow.

She was a gift.

He could only hope he didn't break it.

Lena had tensed when she heard a sudden burst of commotion outside her room about thirty seconds ago. It sounded like people shouting but she couldn't hear what they were saying. Then her bedroom door opened, a rush of energy blasted in, then the door clicked shut again, silencing the outside noise. Now all she could hear was her heart pounding in her ears.

Her host had arrived.

Was he staring at her? Going through her file? She remained still and focused on the embarrassing fact that her palms had started sweating. The air felt electrified—same as when she made the first swing in a fight. Perhaps that's why she was suddenly so nervous. For once, Lena wasn't going to make the first swing.

But that didn't mean she liked dangling like a punching bag either.

Seriously, part of her felt like a slab of meat hanging there. But she was also exposed and vulnerable, which she secretly liked too.

"Are you there?" She hoped her voice didn't give away how excited she was.

Pain was right, now that she couldn't see, her other senses were trying to make up for it. Lena heard soft footfalls come closer to her. She inhaled and smelled the most amazing cologne. "What's your name?"

Should she be talking? Fuck it, she paid for this experience so she could do what she wanted so long as it wasn't against the rules. "I know you can't tell me your real name, but I want to call you something. Master? Sir?" Her head turned when she heard his approaching footfalls land on her right. "Alpha?"

"Reaper."

Holy. Shit. Her host's voice was pure seduction. Lust shot straight down her belly and pooled between her thighs. "Reaper," she purred with a smile.

Here's hoping he lived up to that name. She needed someone to slay the beast inside her...

Lena came to New Orleans looking for danger. Here's hoping

she finally found it.

"What's your name?"

Dorian didn't want to give her his real name. Not here. Not like this. And he knew the rules of the club were no real identities, so he went with "Reaper."

It wasn't a lie.

"*Reaper*," Lena purred as if his name alone made her wet.

Sweet mother of all that was unholy, he nearly dropped to his knees and begged forgiveness for what he wanted to do to her to make her scream his name until the Devil himself woke and shuddered.

He walked around her. Admired every angle. Breathed through the rising, thunderous need clawing its way out of his soul.

"What are you here for?" His voice dropped to an ungodly level. His fangs pierced his lips with each syllable. He was thankful for the pain and the reminder of what he was right now. It helped keep him in check.

"My file is—"

"I don't give a *fuck* about your paperwork. Tell me yourself."

What did his mate crave so fiercely she'd step into a warzone for? This wasn't a paradise. It was a buffet. Thank fuck she was dressed in red. That meant no other had tasted her yet. The fact that she was dangling alone in here before he arrived meant her assigned host hadn't seen her.

Another miracle.

"I want to be edged." She straightened as much as she could in her position, and he admired her attempt to have some confidence.

His dick strained against his zipper. Edging was only the beginning of his plans for her. He ran a thumb across his bottom lip—the urge to take her and mark her was so strong he wasn't sure how much longer he could hold back. "Go on."

Tell me everything I can do to you...

Dorian had gone from denying himself this exact opportunity to refusing to give it up. He wasn't leaving here without her. He couldn't. Not now. One glimpse of her in the flesh and she was under his skin. Every atom he possessed set off like a billion little flint sticks, sparking to life. Heating his veins. Melting his control.

A terrible sensation brushed his other senses. Dorian didn't want a tiny taste or nibble. He wanted to gobble her up whole.

Flexing his hand, he ached to spank her ass just to see his handprint mark what was his. Instead, Dorian curled his hand into a fist, bought it to his mouth, and bit it. The pain brought him back to reality… for a minute.

"Tell me what else you want."

"I want to be railed hard enough that I go into some kind of subspace," Lena's chin thrust out and a brow arched over her blindfold. "I want to float and fly apart. Scream, cry, sweat, and lose myself."

Dorian shook his head. No. That wasn't enough. "You didn't need to come here for that." Didn't mean he wouldn't oblige her with that tiny, mild request. "What else?"

No guests of The Wicked Garden came for a slap and tickle like she was talking about. They came for other things. Darker things. He wanted to hear her say it. Admit it. *Own* it.

Lena bit her bottom lip and a groan tried to tear out of Dorian's throat when he saw it. He no longer smelled the tang of fear. Her lust overpowered every other emotion rocking her right now.

He desperately wanted to hear her say what she really wanted out of this night. "What else did you request, Lena?"

She sucked in a sharp breath and frowned. The woman looked as though she was staring right through his soul, even with the blindfold on. "I… why are you using my real name?"

Fuck! Shit, fuck, shit, fuck! Dorian slipped up. Time for damage control.

"I can use anything I want in this room." His voice dripped with seduction as he walked around her again. "Including your name." He stroked his finger down her spine, making her back arch in response. "Your body." His hand sailed further down to caress her ass. Finally, Dorian climbed onto the dais and ran his thumb across her red stained lips. "And that pretty little mouth of yours."

He smeared her lipstick and loved how her cheeks were starting to match her outfit.

"Your voice is incredible, Reaper."

Her breathlessness made him ache to fuck her pretty, red stained mouth. Dorian clenched his teeth as a barrage of sensations tore through him at once. His body burned with a fierce hunger, his lust matched hers by the smell of things. All his careful plans quickly disintegrated with each panting breath they took together.

Did she feel what he was feeling? This need? This ungodly starvation?

"Reaper?" Her dark brow arched playfully above her little blindfold again. "Are you going to stand there all night or give me what I came for?"

Fuck. Him. Senseless. Dorian rocked back on his heels, unable to speak for a solid ten seconds. This wasn't supposed to happen. He left her alone so she could be safe from him. If he was a good guy, he'd leave right this minute and never look back. But he wasn't a good guy.

And he wasn't leaving this room without her.

Dorian was going to Hell anyway, might as well go to his grave with the taste of his mate still lingering on his lips.

CHAPTER 15

Lena wanted nothing more than to rip her blindfold off and get a good look at her host, Reaper. As far as kink club identities go, that was a pretty scary one. It also turned her on way more than she'd ever admit.

The only thing that made her wetter than his name was the sound of his goddamn voice. He should do narrations for romance books. Women would cream themselves before the first paragraph was finished.

Reaper's voice was deep and delicious. Each syllable punctuated with a dark tone that ramped her lust meter to new levels of heat.

This was the host who was their finest and most sought after? Her lips peeled back as she hissed at the thought of anyone else getting to hear Reaper's voice, feel his touch... get fucked with his dick.

Oh shit, oh shit. Why was she this possessive over a guy she didn't know? Hell, she hadn't even seen him yet! This place was messing with her head, and her mind was damaged enough before she came here.

Still... the thought of Reaper being in this room tomorrow night, or any other, with someone else, made her furious. She wanted to punch something.

"What's the sudden aggression for?"

She refused to admit what she was thinking. It was too preposterous and embarrassing.

"Answer me."

"No."

"No?"

The dais trembled as he stepped back on it, and she wondered how big her host was. How powerful. How skilled. If she kept on like this, would he try to tame her? Spank her? *Bite* her? Whoa, now her imagination started getting way too colorful.

Reaper collared her throat with his hand.

She'd never been turned on so fast in her goddamn life. An undignified moan rumbled in her chest. Her pussy swelled with need. Her nipples hardened.

He chuckled and — no lie — Lena could feel the vibration in the air between their bodies.

"Take my blindfold off," she demanded.

Silence grew into a loud roar in her ears.

"Take. It. Off. I want to see you, Reaper." She could just untwirl the ribbons around her wrists and take the damned thing off herself, but she liked the comfort the bindings brought her. And the restraint. She didn't trust herself to behave if her hands were free.

The Reaper made an animalistic noise that set her loins ablaze. Goosebumps burst along her arms. The hair on the back of her neck prickled in a delicious way.

He slipped behind her soundlessly. His fingers making fast work untying the knot of her blindfold, he pulled it away like an unveiling. Lena swallowed the lump of anticipation clogging her throat and turned her head just enough to catch part of his arm. Then she started to twirl herself to face him, but he stopped her with a firm grip on her hips.

"Are you sure you want to see what you're locked in here with, Lena?"

Her heart fluttered like a moth in a jar. "Absolutely."

"What if you don't like what you see?"

"Only one way to find out." Really, even if the guy was a Quasimodo look-a-like, she highly doubted it would matter. Something about his presence, his voice, even his scent drove her wild. She never had another person affect her in such a way. It seemed downright suspicious.

What were they doing? Pumping pheromones or drugs in the room?

What happened to clear minds and all that jazz? Her head was a lust-induced fog, and she was still fully clothed. This was…

Damnit, she didn't know what this was. "I want to see you."

He lifted his hands off her hips and allowed Lena to turn around and see him for the first time.

She started at his shoes and moved up from there. Black boots, buffed. Fitted, black slacks. Dark grey shirt, tucked and buttoned with the sleeves rolled up to showoff really sexy forearms. Dear God, why were forearms such a thing? Lena made sure to keep her perusal nice and slow to savor this moment. She counted one, two, three, four-five-six-seven buttons on his crisp shirt. His chest heaved as if he was struggling to catch his breath. He wasn't massive like a pro-wrestler but definitely built with solid muscle and probably zero body fat under his designer clothing. Her eyes lingered a little on the tattoo on his right forearm. A Reaper holding a scythe.

Yesterday she would have called that cliché. Today, she'd argue it was the sexiest thing she'd ever seen. His ink was so well done, it was like the Reaper could rise off his skin to reach out and seduce her. Shred her dress with his blade. Cloak her in darkness and do unspeakably dirty and glorious things to her body and soul.

Okay, seriously, what were they pumping into this room to make everything so hot and provocative, some kind of magical aphrodisiac? Whatever it was, that shit was working magnificently. Lena was so turned on she was starting to sweat.

Drawing in a ragged breath, Lena allowed her gaze to finally work past his collar, up his throat, to his chin, jawline — geez, was it sharp — and across his face to his nose. She could choose his mouth or eyes next, and she didn't know which would be the lesser of two evils.

She chose mouth.

Bad choice. Such a bad, delicious, full-bodied choice. His bottom lip was a little fuller than his top one. Both looked like she should taste them. As if seeing how enthralled she was with his mouth, Reaper sucked in his bottom lip, then dragged it back out, letting his teeth scrape all that sensual flesh.

She caught a glimpse of his fangs.

They were huge. Way bigger than Pain's.

What did it say about her that she wanted to feel those on her skin? Could he pierce her with them? Would he if she begged? It was in her file. Had he looked at what she wanted or come in here blind and purely winging it?

She wanted those veneers to clamp down on her body. Rip her skin. Break her limits. Tear her open.

To break her bloody fantasy off before it went further, Lena dragged her gaze away from his mouth and sailed to his eyes.

Well fuck her six ways to Sunday, Reaper's eyes were the color of sage and held such fierce intensity, he burned holes in her soul with them.

Dramatic? Yes. Accurate? Also, yes.

She couldn't breathe with how he glared at her. Couldn't focus. Couldn't—

"Does it hurt that much to see what you're locked in here with?"

"What?"

"You look like you've just seen the fucking Devil."

"If the Devil actually looked like you, I'd have crawled my way into Hell years ago."

Her retort caught him off guard and his response lit her insides up. Reaper ducked his head and flashed a smile that made Lena tug at her restraints because she wanted to lift his chin back up and see his eyes again.

He pulled on the cuffs of his sleeves and bit his lip again. "I didn't expect that."

"I didn't expect *you*," she shot back. Lena untwirled her wrists and unbound herself. "You're supposed to be in charge of me tonight," she said with a little ire. "But you aren't being very aggressive." She rubbed her wrists and took a step down, to come closer to him. "I wanted someone to take control of me."

He didn't move away. But he hardened. His eyes darkened a few shades and his shoulders tensed. "You might want to be a little more careful about what you wish for, Lena. Control is a dangerous gift to give me."

Reaper said it like a warning, not a tease.

"Then should I call for another host?"

What he did next had her regretting that threat immediately.

Dorian snapped. It was too late to take back his actions once he drove Lena backwards and slammed her against the wall, pinning her with one hand on her throat, the other on her hip. "You will not be requesting another host." He didn't compel her, but he wished he was asshole enough to do so. "*I'm* all you need."

Lena's pulse fluttered wildly under his thumb. He wasn't choking her, but his grip remained firm enough to assert dominance.

And she fucking loved it. Her lust filled the room. She liked this, he realized. Liked that she could make him snap. He studied her perfect rosy cheeks, smeared lipstick, bright brown eyes. She made him ten kinds of twisted up. And that fucking dress fit her like a second skin, leaving too little for his imagination.

"I could break you," he warned.

"I hope you do."

He almost laughed, except she was being serious. That was dangerous for a creature like Dorian. Too dangerous for a human like her.

The bruises all over her face were still fresh. The vision from her first reflection was still very vivid in his mind. She'd gone somewhere and gotten hurt.

On purpose? With intent?

Was she a fighter or a pain junky? A masochist?

That was going to take time to find out. Time he might now have... Dorian slammed his aggression down a few notches and pulled out his sensuality. "You like it rough," he purred against the shell of her ear, his thumb caressing the throbbing vein in her neck. "But I wonder how far you'd push me to get what you want and aren't willing to say."

"I..." She exhaled a shaky breath. "I... don't even know." Her confession came with reluctance.

Dorian grazed her hip with his fingers and slid his hand up her ribcage towards her face, carefully watching her reaction. She both winced and sighed.

"Who put these marks on you?" Because Dorian was going to return the favor ten-fold.

"That's... none of your business."

He positioned himself so he could see her full gaze before

saying, "You are my *only* business, Lena. Everything about you is my responsibility."

She pressed her hands on his chest and pushed him a little. He eased off and gave her a tiny bit of space. "I understand that The Wicked Garden strives to make sure the safety of their guests is top priority, but I didn't get these marks here if that's what you're worried about."

"Then where?" He was painfully aware of the fact that his voice became razor sharp. Her safety, and the marks on her sweet body and face, were his top priority. To not have a direct answer from her about who did this was utterly unacceptable. As her mate, he needed to know. As her mate, he demanded retribution. As her mate, he—

Fuck, what was he doing? He wasn't her mate. Never would be. This was just a one-night miracle and would go no further. He needed to back the fuck off before he ruined his only night in heaven before he spent eternity in Hell.

"I don't like to see bruises on you." He backed off a little more. "My instincts are to punish—" He needed to shut the fuck up. Right. Now.

"Then punish me," she purred as if this whole thing was some kind of fantasy role play. "These bruises mean nothing. I earned and asked for them."

Dorian stiffened. What the fuck did that mean?

"Replace them with a few more," she tempted. "I've got a high pain tolerance and I'm not fragile."

Holy Hell, his dick hardened to the point of blinding pain. "I'm not going to put bruises on you." He couldn't, even if it was life or death. There was no way. He might go too far. "I won't use violence," he said, but it was more a reminder to his monstrous side than a promise to her.

"Then bite me." She moved forward, unphased, and forced him to hold his ground or back up.

He backed the fuck up.

Jesus Christ, who was this woman? Dorian backed down from no one, especially not a human. Holy shit, he needed to put some space between himself and this creature shrouded in red. The things she was tempting him with were beyond his wildest fantasies and she couldn't possibly mean what she was hinting at.

When she tipped her head to expose her throat, a guttural growl clawed out of him. His fangs ached to pierce her flesh. His tongue tingled with anticipation over what her blood would taste like. His cock wanted in on the action too, and he could imagine how hot her pussy would feel wrapped around his dick while he drank from her vein. As for marring her skin? He wanted to devour every fucking inch of her. Slap her ass until it glowed red. Grip her hard enough to leave finger bruises on her inner thighs while he fucked her brains out.

His world started rocking. His mind glitched. His mouth watered.

"I paid for seduction, yet I'm doing all the work." Lena brushed her hand against his cock through his pants and he clenched his jaw. He had mere seconds to decide before things went too far.

Three... two...

Dorian bolted.

CHAPTER 16

"Dorian!"

He ignored Lucian's commanding voice, painfully aware of everyone staring at him right now. He rushed down the steps, hell-bent to get out of The Wicked Garden and leave Lena alone. His pride and instincts bowed down to the priority of Lena's safety. Sweat poured down his temples and trickled down his spine.

His lungs slammed together, trapping air and suffocating him.

"Dorian, stop!" Lucian grabbed his shoulder.

Getting grabbed like that was a tripwire for him, which Lucian knew well. Wracked with tension, Dorian snapped and swung. Lucian caught his fist, mid-strike. The two vampires snarled and hissed at each other, their bodies dangerously close. Eye-to-eye, they locked onto each other—both waiting to see what the other would do next.

Dorian didn't want to attack anyone here, especially Lena or Lucian. He had to go. Now!

"I've got to get out of here," he pleaded.

"You're going to just leave her up there? *Abandon* her?"

Dorian's vision wavered and everything turned red. "I'm not abandoning her. I'm sparing her."

"You're sparing yourself," Lucian hissed.

Maybe he was. "I thought I could do it," he whispered. "When I saw her, smelled her... followed her here..." Holy Hell, why did the universe hate him so much? "Why would she be here?"

Lucian wouldn't know the answer, but Dorian didn't expect

him to. Coincidence, fate, rotten fucking luck - there were plenty of reasons why Lena would be in this club tonight.

"You can't deny your destiny," Lucian pressed.

"I can't bear the idea of me being her fate." She deserved better than him. Way better.

"That's *her* choice. Right now, you just *left* her. In a very vulnerable position, might I add. If she leaves, she's not going to come back. Is that really what you want?"

Dorian didn't want Lena here to begin with. She needed to get out of this club, because if someone else became her host and dared look at her sweet body, much less touch it, Dorian would tear them to pieces.

He closed his eyes and immediately saw her face. Those purple and green bruises on her. The hunger in her gaze. The snap of her teeth. Sharpness of her wit...

Maybe that's another reason he panicked. No way would she be turned on by the same things he was. He'd never be that lucky. Her confidence alone made his blood roar. She didn't have an ounce of fear in her.

Lena was the perfect package for a creature like him. A gift.

Don't waste this gift...

He wasn't wasting it. He was *saving* it. Why didn't anyone else understand that?

"No one touches her," Dorian's grip tightened on Lucian's shirt. "Do you understand me? She cannot have another host."

"Then you better get back up there." Lucian shoved him backwards. Or attempted to. But Dorian's feet remained planted firmly on the ground at the base of the steps and his aggression throttled into overdrive.

Suddenly, the hair rose on the back of his neck. He felt Lena approach.

Don't turn around and look at her. Don't do it.

All eyes locked on her, the commotion dying immediately. Shit, even Lucian gawked as everyone watched Lena come down the steps.

"Pain, give me my personal items," she commanded.

Pain, who was actually Reys, complied. His eyebrows shot up into his hairline as he turned to collect her belongings.

The air in Dorian's lungs became thick and suffocating. He

gripped the banister to keep from reaching out to her. Lena walked through the throng of vampires, grabbed her things from Pain, and stormed out of the club. The door shut with a loud thud. Dorian thought he might burst into ashes on the stairs.

He heard whispering all around him and didn't know how to handle it. He didn't like being talking about. He hated being the focus of attention, even when he was executing someone. And he sure as shit didn't want any of them staring at his mate or following her back to her hotel.

His protective instincts went haywire. The second he couldn't see, hear, or smell her, every molecule in his body demanded he hunt her down and possess her. Mark her.

Keep. Her. With. Him.

A roar ripped from his throat. His body engaged, poised to chase.

A blaze burned down the marrow in his bones. His vision hazed red. Dorian was vaguely aware of what was happening. His focus was solely on getting through the front door and to his mate.

"Dorian, stop!"

He took a step. Then another.

"We're losing him!" Lucian yelled.

Dorian looked down at his arms, convinced they were on fire. Instead, he couldn't find them at all. Lucian had pinned them behind Dorian's back and started moving him away at a fast pace.

The world flipped and he was suddenly staring at the ceiling, everything a blur of motion and sound until it all went black.

Lena had never done a walk of shame before, and she sure as hell wasn't going to start tonight. When Reaper left her in that bedroom, a hurricane of emotions tore through her, which made zero sense. Intrigue, lust, anger, resentment, hunger—they spun in her mind, demolishing her common sense completely. But disappointment was the biggest emotion, and she used it to fuel her footsteps out of the room, down the steps, and out the door.

Everyone in the club seemed to be positioned somewhere between her and the exit, all watching with strange looks on their faces.

Maybe she was the first guest to leave without satisfaction. Maybe her host was going to get fired for leaving her hanging high and dry.

Her skin crawled when she looked at some of the staff when she passed by. Their fangs were out, some held anger in their gaze. Others looked bewildered. Most looked scared shitless. Or confused? Or... hungry? She didn't care. She just wanted to get out of there as fast as possible.

The worse part about this night wasn't that it ended so fast... it was that it ended with her assigned host so fast.

Reaper.

How could a man elicit so many volatile emotions out of her in a matter of minutes?

Talk about hot and cold. One minute he looked like he wanted to eat her up, the next, he looked disgusted and terrified.

Maybe that's why they insisted on the blindfold. Didn't Pain say the host takes that off when they deemed the guest ready? Had she prematurely unveiled herself and tipped the balance of their night?

Tough shit.

She hadn't done anything to warrant Reaper's sudden bolt out the door. And you know what? If he couldn't handle her heat, he didn't deserve it. Pain said he was the best one... what a load of bullshit.

Yet, even as she slammed the door shut and marched towards the gate, Lena could still feel Reaper's lingering touch where he'd swept his fingers down her back. It was nutty to be so warped and enthralled over a single touch. No, it was *desperate*. Lena didn't do desperate. Now she was pissed off.

Could she have insisted on being assigned another host for the night? Fuck yes. But she didn't want to. How sad was that? She was so close to getting her wildest fantasies and now poof!

Gone.

Over.

The. End.

She didn't want another host. That sonofabitch Reaper ruined her for all other experiences there too. She was never going back. How could she?

And what's worse? Lena had this ridiculous feeling that no

one could compare to Reaper. No one had before tonight and she sure as shit wasn't going to hunt down someone else to satisfy her fetishes now.

Reaper.

Damn that sonofabitch straight to Hell.

Lena never experienced a more electrified chemistry with another man in her entire life as she had while being tied to that dais, fully clothed, and blindfolded. If her body responded so intensely to just his voice and a few touches...

"Holy Hell." She wrapped her hands around the gate and tried to take in a few breaths. Whatever pheromones they pumped into that room must still be rocking her system. She needed to cleanse her lungs. Shit, she needed to cleanse her soul! With the cravings she had, she was going to rot in Hell.

Worth it though. Damnit, if she had just *one night* to live out her wildest fantasy, she'd chose Reaper as her partner, and if going to Hell was the price for playing with danger, she didn't care.

Reaper seemed like a man who could fuck a woman boneless. His big, sharp fangs practically taunted her in that room. Lena closed her eyes and imagined what they felt like scraping along her skin... piercing her.

She leaned into the closed gate and let the iron bars cool down her cheek. This was her one shot and she was blowing it because her pride demanded she leave this club. No... not her pride. Something else.

"Damnit." Pushing the iron gate, she grunted when it didn't budge. "Hey!" She waved her hand in front of the little security camera over on the light post. "Let me out! Unlock this thing."

Nothing happened.

"Hey! Unlock this right now! I want to leave."

"You alright, Miss? Need some help?"

Lena looked up to see a man in jeans and a black leather jacket with a hoodie cross the street, heading straight towards her.

"Is the lock stuck or something? The gate is usually wide open."

"It's fine," she said, and let go of the iron bars. Her gut said to back up, so she did. The man made no move to come closer. "I just have to run back in to tell them to unlock it."

"Oh... okay." He pulled the hood over his head, stuffed his

111

hands in his pockets, and walked down the road just after saying, "Have a good one."

Lena didn't bother responding. She was too busy heading back in to give the manager of this place an earful. Furious and fed up, she shoved open the front door to the club and —

"You need to come with me," a woman said.

"Yeah, no, you need to let me out. Unlock the front gate."

"No." The blonde crossed her arms over her chest. She reminded Lena of a cheetah, smooth lines, lanky limbs, probably fast on her feet. Her hair was pulled back in a tight, high ponytail and she was dressed in a latex outfit and combat boots.

"Lookie here, cat woman. I'm not going to ask you again. Let me out of here or I'll knock you out and unlock the damn thing myself."

The woman arched a perfectly manicured brow. Lena thrust her chin out, ready to rock and roll with this bitch.

"We can't let you out. We've gone into lockdown. All guests are hidden safely in their rooms with their hosts. The pool is secured and heavily guarded. The gate will remain locked until the threat we're facing is over. You need to come with me. Now."

What the hell? "Am I the threat?" Because that was just laughable. Lena turned when she heard someone come up behind her.

Then she was knocked out cold.

Dorian came to, chained to a wall in the back room of the club, with dried blood smeared all over his face and neck. He looked up at the sound of someone else entering the room.

"Your woman is a fearless one," Victoria said as she carried Lena in. "Can't say the irony's lost there."

He strained against his shackles, desperate to get to her. "What have you done?"

"Lay her down gently or he's going to lose it again," Lucian said from Dorian's right.

Dorian couldn't remember how he got here, or what he'd done to warrant being chained, but at this rate nothing would surprise him. And he didn't care. All that mattered was Lena. He didn't want her in this club, around him, or the other vampires here. This club wasn't just for the House of Death. It was open to all vampires who needed to release their tensions. Or feed. "Get her out of here."

"Not a chance," Victoria wiped her hands over her latex pants. "She stays with you until you turn her."

"What? No!"

"*Yes*," Lucian shoved his face in Dorian's. "We're not willing to lose you. And the fact that you're unraveling this quickly only convinces us more that this is the right thing to do."

"I'm unraveling as is my *fate*."

"Bind her! Turn her, damnit!"

"No!" Dorian jerked against his chains. "I can't curse her like that! I refuse to bring her into our Hell."

He saw stars when Victoria slapped him with all the strength she had. He was pretty sure she knocked a tooth loose. "Get over yourself, Dorian."

Good thing he didn't have use of his hands because he would strangle her. "Get Lena out of here."

"Fine," Victoria grabbed Lena's ankles and started dragging her back towards the door.

Dorian roared in fury.

"You're fighting your nature, Dorian. Stop." Lucian walked over to Lena.

Dorian couldn't stand the idea of her laying on this filthy, dirty, *nasty* fucking floor. His voice cracked when he said, "Pick her up." Dorian shook with rage and disgust when no one obeyed. "Damnit, Lucian, pick her the fuck up!"

But when Lucian bent down to scoop her into his arms, Dorian went ballistic for a whole new reason. "Get off her!"

"Damned if you do, damned if you don't," Victoria grumbled. "Which is it, Dorian? Want Lucian to hold her close, take her away from you, and watch over her until you turn to ashes? Or should he let her just lay here unconscious on the grimy floor where you can keep an eye on her from your shackles?"

He... he didn't have an answer. Dorian wanted to gag. "Please get her off the floor. She deserves better."

"Then show her better. Give her exactly what she deserves, Reaper." Victoria walked out of the room, stepping right over Lena like she was trash.

"I'm going to unlock your cuffs," Lucian warned. "Don't chew my fucking throat out, Dorian. This is all for your own good."

"It's for *yours*," Dorian snarled. So betrayed and furious with his best friend, he almost didn't want to be unchained for fear of popping Lucian's head clean off. "You just don't want to lose the only animal you have left to protect the House."

"Dorian!" Victoria castigated from the doorway.

"It's true," Lucian admitted. "I don't want to lose you. None of us do. But you're not our only source of force, you cocky sonofabitch." He took a cheap shot and punched Dorian in the gut before unchaining him. "I care about you, man. If you weren't already so unraveled, I'd wipe this filthy floor with your face." Lucian unlocked the shackles and Dorian slammed to his knees like deadweight.

Crawling over to Lena without even thinking, his every action was instinct driven. His fangs pulsed with the need to bite her. His body roared to make her his so no one else would come near her again.

"Take her home," Lucian swung the door open.

Dorian's arms slipped under Lena's warm body of their own accord. He picked her up as if she weighed no more than a pillow. He turned to look at Lucian, pleading with his best friend. "I don't know how I can do this."

Lucian looked like Dorian stabbed him in the chest with a stake. "I can't lose you," he whispered. "And neither can she."

Lena would be fine without him, Dorian was convinced of it. She'd gotten this far, hadn't she? And holy shit, just look how strong and confident she was.

But those bruises. Her busted face…

"I'm pretty sure a *Savag-Ri* was on the other side of the gate," Victoria said. "I locked it before she could break through the barrier and he had a chance to get to her."

Lucian rubbed the back of his neck. "They'll hunt her, Dorian. They know her scent and her face now. That's all they need, and you know it."

A vicious hiss ripped from his lips as he held her closer to his chest. They were right. Lena hadn't been scrubbed before she left, and no precautions were taken to escort her out of the club safely, as protocol dictated, because she'd left before her time was up. If a *Savag-Ri* happened to be waiting on the other side of the gate, she could have easily walked right into his arms and waiting dagger. That vile piece of shit would have taken her to one of their hidey-holes and tortured her for information about vampires, and most likely done worse, before killing her.

Dorian trembled in fury at the mere thought of someone laying another angry hand on his woman. His next sound was a strangled one. *I won't let them hurt you.* The bruises on her face mocked him... warned him... gave him a peek at what her fate was if he didn't protect her at all costs.

And just like that, the idea of Lena no longer being with him for all eternity became the one thing Dorian could no longer tolerate. If he died, that *Savag-Ri* still knew what she looked like. What she smelled like. He could track her. And whether she was bound to Dorian or not, whether Dorian died or not, they'd kill her out of spite because she was a fated *alakhai*.

"I can't lose her," he whispered.

Lucian's voice dropped to a deep whisper, "Then you know what you must do."

CHAPTER 17

Lena blinked and tried to figure out what the hell just happened.

"Easy," a familiar deep voice said. "You're going to feel a little fuzzy at first."

Reaper was with her.

Lena hated how her body lit up at the sound of his sexy voice because now wasn't the time for her lust to take charge. Her anger needed to grab the reins. "What happened?" She couldn't piece things together as fast as she wanted. Reaper touching her. Reaper leaving. Her leaving. The locked gate. Her coming back inside to demand they unlock it. Then... nothing.

"What did you pump into the vents?" She rolled over, surprised she was still dressed.

"What?"

"I can't repeat myself. I can't—" Nauseous, she curled into a ball.

"Nothing's pumped into the rooms."

"Then why can't I think straight?" Her head became a dense fog.

"You're out of your element."

Lena would roll her eyes if she thought it wouldn't make her hurl. "I'm going to be sick."

"Here." Reaper moved closer and held out a glass of water. "Drink this."

She knocked the glass out of his hand. No way was she accepting anything from anyone here. Not after she just blacked out for no good reason. Had that woman hit her? No... definitely not. This wasn't that kind of knockout. It was more like she'd crashed and gone into a deep sleep. The idea unnerved her.

"I want to leave. Let me out of here." Lena sat up and damn, she couldn't pull her gaze away from Reaper. He looked rattled and furious. Lena went into fight or flight mode and for the first time ever, she chose flight. Maybe she could take this guy down if she was at her best, but she wasn't right now, so flight it was.

They were no longer in the foyer of The Wicked Garden, but back in the bedroom she'd started in. Fuck this. She was getting out of here.

Lena rolled off the bed, and her knees buckled.

Reaper caught her before she slammed to the ground.

How... how did he move that fast?

"Breathe," he commanded.

Like an obedient submissive, she inhaled and an inexplicable physical response to his scent made her so confused, she shoved away from him. He put his hands up in surrender. "I'm not here to hurt you. I'm here to protect you."

Lena stiffened. "Protect me from what?" Now she didn't trust anything including herself or the one who told her about this place to begin with. "Does this have to do with Bane?"

Reaper remained frozen where he stood. He didn't even look like he was breathing anymore.

"Are you in it, too?" That was all the clue she could give without breaking code.

Reaper still didn't move. Nor did he speak.

"Hello." She waved her hands in his face. What the hell, had he gone catatonic? "Hey!" She snapped her fingers in his face.

He caught her hand and firmly, slowly, gracefully brought it back down to her side. Then he captured her other arm and pinned that one too. "Listen to me very carefully," his voice was deep and rubbed along the inside of her skull. "I'm never going to lie to you."

"Aww sweet." She tried wriggling out of his grip, but it was a no go. "Get off me," she warned.

"I will once I say this." He rubbed the pulse points on the inside of her wrists. "I'm your mate."

Lena tipped her head back and laughed so hard, she almost pissed herself. "Oh, come on. That is..." She sucked in a deep breath and kept laughing before she finished with, "That's the worst line I've ever heard in my life. Did you pluck that out of a cheesy paranormal romance novel?"

Reaper looked like she slugged him right in the gut. "It's the truth."

"Okay. Sure. Why not."

"There are people who will hunt you because of this. They'll kill you, Lena. Do you understand me?" His grip tightened but didn't hurt her.

"I'm pretty sure I didn't have ravish fantasy, nor did I have kidnapping/rescue role play in my file for tonight. You can stop this bullshit now." She wanted to leave and never come back. What she thought was a chance of a lifetime now seemed like a huge mistake. "I'm leaving."

"You're not hearing what I'm saying to you, Lena." Reaper shook her. His face contorted and the veins in his neck stuck out. He let go of her wrists, only to cradle her face and press his forehead to hers, "I can't leave you unprotected. Ever. You're my mate."

"Buddy, you gotta get a grip." Why was it always the pretty, sexy ones who were delusional?

And why was she such a sucker for it now?

Probably because she was off her rocker too.

Reaper hissed in frustration and backed off. Lena took the window of opportunity and dashed towards the door.

He beat her to it.

Holy. Shit. "H-h-how did you do that so fast?"

Reaper remained between her and the only exit. His chest heaved with each ragged breath. His pupils blew wide, swallowing his sage green eyes in darkness. The guy looked like a terrifying serial killer.

"Look," she said, backing away nice and slow. "I have money. Tons of it. Just… just let me go and you can have it all. Swear it. I won't call the cops. I won't tell anyone about this place. I'll do whatever you want, just…"

"You aren't hearing what I'm saying, Lena." Reaper ran a hand through his curly hair and closed his eyes for a moment. When he opened them again, his eyes were back to their beautiful sage green and just a little red around the rims. That small detail made his lashes stand out, which downright mesmerized her.

She... completely forgot... what she was doing...

Reaper turned around and slammed his fists against the door. "Stop it!" he roared.

"Just trying to help, asshole!" said a woman's voice from the other side.

"Who's that?" Lena pointed at the door. "And what's she doing?"

"That's Victoria. She thrives in making a bad situation worse."

Lena didn't care anymore. She just wanted out of this madhouse. If she couldn't bribe him, maybe she could sweet talk herself out of here. "I want to go, Reaper. Please." She approached him with little aggression and lots of doe-eyed innocence. Pressing her hand on his chest, she ignored how her body warmed with the contact, and instead let her eyes fill with tears. "Please, let me go..." she cry-whispered.

"Oh, you're good," Victoria said from the other side of the door. "I like her."

Reaper kicked backwards and almost put his foot through the heavy wood-carved door.

"Reaper..." Lena's brow knit together, and she pressed her hand against his chest, hoping her gaze was pleading enough. "*Please...*"

"My name is Dorian," he said, unmoved by her act. "And I can smell your lust, Lena. It's overpowering your other emotions." He placed his hand over hers and removed it from his chest.

"Okay, I don't get this." Now she was straight up pissed off. "Let me out. *Now.*"

"I told you, you're not leaving my side. My enemy has you on their radar now." He walked closer to her, forcing Lena to back up or get slammed by him.

"I know you all pride yourselves in making sure the guests of The Wicked Garden remain safe at all times, but this is overkill," she snarled back. "I'm *leaving.*"

She tried to dodge him. He blocked her every time. After her fourth attempt, she was no longer lusty or angry.

Lena swung out, he blocked her effortlessly. She tried again. He thwarted each one. Calculating her next attempt, Lena went all out with everything she had, only to get pinned and hadn't hit him once.

"You're incredible," he said with awe.

She wasn't incredible. And she wasn't pissed anymore either. Lena was scared. "Reaper... Dorian... whatever your name is. Please let me go."

"I can't," he whisper-screamed at her. "Just let me explain, Lena, then you can walk out that door and no one will stop you."

"Because I'll be in a body bag?"

"What?"

"No one will stop me because I'll be dead anyway, is that it?"

The man looked like she just dumped boiling oil over his head. His face turned crimson, and his eyes darkened as if in agony. "No, never." Holy moly, even how he said those two words sounded painful.

"Then tell me what's going on because nothing's making sense. And," she jabbed a shaky finger at him, "come up with a better hook than 'you're my mate' and 'my enemy is coming for you' okay? Be more creative when you lie to me before you slaughter me."

"I'd never hurt you."

She hated that part of her believed him. It made no sense. "Go on. *Dexter*. Tell me why this is happening."

"It's Dorian and I'm telling you the truth. My kind has enemies. Those who will strip away every chance we have of survival. Including taking our mates."

"Which is me."

"Yes." He stepped closer. Then his gaze flicked to something else and in less than two seconds, he'd retrieved the folder that had been left on the small table. On the other side of the big ass room. "I won't ask you how you found this place. For now, tell me exactly what you came here hoping to get?"

"I assume you're not illiterate. Read my waivers and requests yourself."

"No, Lena." He waved the black folder in the air, "What's on here is bullshit. You knew it but you requested it anyway because you're too scared to admit what you really want."

Her facial expression betrayed her. Instead of looking impassive, her cheeks heated. Damnit. "I don't know what you're talking about."

"You don't?" He swaggered over to her. "Lately you've

developed cravings... your body is reacting to things in ways it shouldn't."

"We all have phases," she shrugged.

"This isn't a phase. It's the cusp of a transition." He got within inches of her and tipped her chin up with his finger. "You crave being bitten."

"Lots of folks have that kink. Hence the veneers you all wear to make bank with people like me."

"You didn't pay a dime to get in here, did you?" He licked one of his canines, keeping her attention on his mouth. "Did you know what it was going to cost you to be here?"

She didn't answer.

"It's more than I'm willing to allow you to pay," he whisper-growled against her ear as he tilted her head. "My teeth are real, Lena. As real as the danger you're now in."

He sealed his mouth over the side of her throat, and she groaned when his fangs grazed her skin. They were like two needles scratching down her throat column.

Did she pull away or stay put? Fight, fly, or freeze?

He didn't give her time to pick. Dorian moved away, and she touched where his mouth had been. "I didn't bite," he said. "And I won't until you give me permission. But you feel it don't you?"

Lena's mouth dried up. She didn't answer.

"You feel that heat in your belly? That hunger for something you've never had? You want to run out that door, but your mind and body are at complete odds with each other." He turned her around slowly and gripped her hips. Then leaned down and breathed heat along the shell of her ear as he said, "You came here for something else, didn't you? You might want to be edged, fucked, tied and spent, but that's not what you truly hoped to get from a night in this place."

Her lungs sawed to take in air.

Dorian moved her across the floor in a graceful glide that was so fast, she couldn't keep up. Suddenly, they stood in front of a floor-length mirror together. Dorian stood behind her, his head pressed against the side of hers, his hard cock pushing against her ass. He stared at her reflection in the mirror as he said, "Tell me what you crave, Lena. Admit it."

"I..." Her body betrayed her and leaned into his. "I..."

121

"Say it."

Her eyes fluttered when the echo of his voice bounced down her spine. *Say it. Say it. Say it.* "I..."

"Dorian!" Some guy banged on the door. "We gotta move out, now!"

Whatever just built up between her and the man pressed to her back shattered. The spell broke. The intensity fizzled. Dorian backed away, cursing and shaking his head. He looked absolutely gutted.

"I tried to spare you," he said while frowning. "I tried to save you from this world, but you just had to walk right into it." Dorian ushered her outside and Lena saw the woman from earlier—Victoria—and a blond man who must have been the one to bang on the door.

"We've got to hurry," said the blond guy. "Fuck, this is a goddamned mess."

"Can we bring her to the House?" Dorian asked.

"We're going to have to." The blond replied. He and Victoria hopped into the front of a car parked in the back of the property and once Dorian and Lena were secured in the backseat, they sped out of there.

"I'm so sorry," Dorian said as they flew down the road. "I didn't mean for any of this to happen."

"I believe you," she mumbled, unwilling to admit anything more.

Lena wanted to tell him he didn't have anything to apologize for. This wasn't his fault. It was hers. She'd been warned this was a dangerous step in the direction she was hellbent on going in. Lena hadn't believed the guy who warned her and came here anyway.

For years Lena was drawn to danger, to pain, to violence. She came here seeking answers... and she found Dorian.

CHAPTER 18

Lena kept her shit together as they pulled up to another sprawling mansion. This one was triple the size of the kink club they just fled. As impressive as it was, the columns and balconies needed some repair. Vines crawled along the base of the foundation, spreading and choking out the bushes and crept along the right, front corner of the mansion. Oaks lined the drive, but there was no color, nothing that welcomed guests. It dripped gothic melodrama. Spanish moss had made it a mission to drape dramatically across everything it could. The fountain out front wasn't turned on and the statue of the angel in the middle was missing a wing.

They pulled around back. Several cars were parked along a pad to the left, all of them high end. A centuries old oak tree bumped up against the detached garage to the point where most of the branches had formed around the roof. Trellises out back were covered in dead vines and brown leaves. Iron chairs and tables lay strewn about, abandoned.

It looked haunted and romantic at the same time.

Jesus, she needed to get a grip. The blond guy pulled into a vacant parking spot and everyone hopped out. Dorian hadn't said a word the entire trip, but she noticed he was vibrating with tremors. She didn't know what was wrong with him but decided to keep a little distance between them until she figured it out.

For all the gentle curls of his light brown hair, designer clothing, and his soft, green eyes, Dorian exuded aggression and intensity which never wavered. This guy was going to be trouble.

She could feel it in her damn bones. Dorian was a well-designed trap.

And she wanted to take the bait and be caught.

Lena's fists tightened in her lap and she closed her eyes, mentally shedding that idea. She didn't need to be caught, she needed to be careful. *You're my mate.* Why'd he have to say that bullshit with such sincerity? Why'd he have to hold her like she was a precious treasure in danger of being pilfered by someone else?

Why was she even in this damn car?

"Welcome to Maison de la Morts, Lena." The blond smiled.

The House of Death. How perfectly named, she thought. Dorian slipped his hand around her bicep and she jerked away from his touch. "I'm not going to run off," she growled. "No need to manhandle me."

"I'm not manhandling you." His gaze never wavered. "I'm escorting you in."

The blond grabbed her other arm, and the two men looked serious. Dead serious. Like the kind of serious you saw on a cop's face when they arrested you for fighting in an illegal ring and didn't want to hear your excuses. Not that she'd ever seen that look. *Ahem.*

"I'm Lucian, by the way," the blond said as they went up the steps.

"Lena." She didn't know what else to say right now. Her heart kept fluttering in her throat, and her palms were sweaty. She had zero desire to fight or fly and that worried her. She was literally walking into a house, restrained by two men, and was going willingly.

There was something deranged about her. This proved it. She was in worse shape than she thought, damnit.

"Lena McKay. Twenty-eight. Heir to the McKay resort fortune, with two prior arrests, a knack for spotting good investments, and you have an allergy to strawberries."

She halted and glared at Lucian. "H-how do you know all that about me? None of that's in my file at the club."

"I never looked at your file, sweetheart. I looked online and found everything I needed to know about you so Dorian could find you."

Her instinct to run rushed her. "What do you mean *so Dorian could find me?*"

"You're his mate. We covered this already," Victoria snipped as she swung open the door and held it for them to go through. "Want me to take her so you can talk to the King?"

"She's not leaving my sight." Dorian's grip tightened on her arm.

"I'll go," Lucian said. "Victoria, you contain the others. Keep them away until we can sort this shit out."

"Fine."

Lena had no clue what was going on, but when she refused to budge, Dorian's aggression got worse, and he ended up carrying her up to a room. He moved so fast Lena barely saw anything in the house that wasn't a blur. When he set her down and slammed the door shut, he dropped to his knees, gasping for air.

Part of her wanted to run while he was weak enough to not chase after her. But she wasn't a runner. She stayed where she was because something about this entire situation felt strangely right to be in. Lena had the same reaction when she joined her little fight club too.

Her tone remained soft as she asked, "What's wrong with you?"

"Nothing."

Lena bent down to put her hand on his shoulder. He swiftly caught it, "Never touch my shoulder from the side or behind."

"Oooookay."

When she tried to pull back, Dorian wouldn't let go of her hand. "I'm a little undone, Lena. When one of my kind sees their mate for the first time, it... does things to us."

"Yeah, about that, I'm still confused. I'm telling you right now, that cliché doesn't fly with me. Whatever this is, be a little more creative with it because mates and veneer fangs and gothic mansions are great for tourists, but—"

Dorian let go of her hand and rocked back on his ass. He looked pale, his eyes bloodshot.

"Should I call a doctor or something for you? Tell me what I'm supposed to do. You're scaring me."

He cringed and licked his chapped lips. "Everyone's scared of me... should have known you'd be no different."

"I'm not scared of you." She squatted down as best she could in her dress. "I'm scared *for* you. Your face is pale, and your eyes

125

keep doing weird things. And the fact that I even care is scary too. I don't know you."

"You do." The register of his voice dropped. "Deep down... you do know me." He reached out and cupped the side of her face. "I wish I could explain all this in a way that won't make me sound crazy."

"Try." She pulled away from him again. Every time he touched her, Lena's body blazed, and her mind got fuzzier. It was messing with her head, big time, and she needed her wits to be sharp to get out of this mess.

Dorian knew she was calculating her next move. He found himself enthralled with her ability to roll with the punches until she found a weak spot to strike, which was exactly what she could have done the instant he dropped to his knees and gasped for breath a few moments ago.

But she hadn't run. She stayed. He hated how it made his heart swell.

Dorian teetered between right and wrong. Sanity and surrender. He was deteriorating in strange ways. There was no sequence he could figure out. First his senses, then his mind, now his body. His bones ached as if turning brittle under his skin. On the car ride here, he was freezing, and his fingernails had turned blue. But the instant he touched Lena, Dorian's ailments weren't as agonizing. He warmed again. Could think and move with coordination.

If he bit her, drank her, would he be completely cured? Or would he have to turn her in order to completely heal from the curse of the damned?

Lena looked like a sunset - draped in warm colors. She sank down on the floor with him, her hands in her lap. As if she was the sun itself, Lena was too beautiful to look at directly. He felt as if her image would burn into his retinas if he made eye contact right now.

His body burned for her. Hardened and sizzled for one graze of her fingertip. His fangs throbbed to pierce her veins—and he particularly wanted to taste the one on her inner thigh. He needed to get her to understand this wasn't some elaborate joke. It wasn't a tourist trap either. He was going to fucking die without her.

How could he say that without sounding completely insane?

"My kind," he said, clearing his throat and rising to his feet. He couldn't say this from the ground like a wounded animal. He needed a show of strength or she'd never consider him a good match. Pulling her up to stand with him, he loved how steady she was. "My kind are cursed, Lena. We can survive without a mate, only if we haven't seen them."

"You don't miss what you never had."

"Something like that." He wiped his mouth and rolled his shoulders back. "Once we see our mate, we start to darken. That's part of the curse as well." He staggered closer to her and hated how she backed up. It was smart on her part but made his admission harder. "I saw you last week, and Lucian helped me gather information on you."

"Hence why golden boy knew my family's name and way too many other things about me."

"I didn't know any of that," he said quickly. "I only knew your name and address." The instant those words left his big, fat mouth, he knew he was in trouble.

"You... you've been to my *house*?" Lena took several steps back now. "What the hell is this, Dorian?"

"I just told you!" His voice rose with desperation. "Things change for us once we see our mate. I—" A knock at the door cut off his next words. Whoever it was better back the fuck up if they valued their lives. "Leave us!" he roared.

Lucian popped his head in. "The King wants to see her."

Fuck, shit, damnit! "Fine." He went to grab her hand, because there was no way he was going to let her waltz down the hall and into the king's mirrored room without him as her shield. The vampires of this House didn't all get along with Dorian.

Jealousy was a nasty animal—hungry all the time, always searching for its next meal. Some of the vampires here might try to attack her, if only to get at Dorian to make him lose his shit and ultimately die. Few in this House liked him. He might be one of King Malachi's favored ones, but he didn't have that status with everyone. Most would love to see him dead or gone—all because he was sired by a psychopath and then raised by wolves. In their eyes, he was dirty. A stain upon vampire society.

"I'll take her," Lucian offered.

"You lay one hand on her, and I'll bite it off."

"I'll take myself. How about that?" Lena rushed out of their reach and headed for the door.

Dorian noticed Victoria leaning against the railing in the hallway, a wry smile across her porcelain face. He snarled at her. She blew him a kiss and walked with Lena.

Damnit. He stumbled towards the door to catch up and swallowed down the vomit rising in his throat. Holy Hell, he was a mess.

Lucian tried to help, but he shoved a hand up. "I can make it on my own."

"I know you can." Lucian's voice dropped with a hint of sorrow. "But I don't know if anyone here will survive your wake as you follow your *alakhai* down this fucking hall. Do me a favor and let me guard you, and ultimately spare anyone here your fury, because it's going to get worse long before it gets better. You're taking forever to turn her."

"You don't know," Dorian struggled to take in air, "how hard it is to stop myself. I think," he sucked in another lung-full, "I could possibly rip her throat out by accident if I attempt to bite her. I tested it once already… nearly killed me just letting her skin touch my tongue."

Lucian groaned. "At the risk of sounding like a complete shithead, I'm glad I'm not in your shoes, man."

Dorian was glad too. He never wanted Lucian to feel this level of agony. At least Dorian had built up a tolerance to this kind of anguish.

But when Lena disappeared behind the door with the king, Dorian realized he only *thought* he knew what agony felt like. The instant the door locked, keeping him out, Dorian was overcome with a fresh wave of unimaginable pain.

His knees buckled, he slammed down on the ground and screamed.

CHAPTER 19

Lena tensed at the sound of an animal screaming outside the room she'd just entered. It couldn't be Dorian. No way could a grown man sound like that. But deep down, she knew it was him, and it hurt her heart when his voice died out as he ran out of air. Part of her wanted to rush out and see what was wrong with him, but another part of her was fixated on the thick-haired giant sitting in a chair, facing a huge ornate mirror. His reflection was menacing as he glared at her.

"Come forward."

Her feet moved even though she swore she was trying to stay back. The room was filled with mirrors and it made her dizzy.

"Stand before me and face the mirror so I may gaze upon you."

She didn't want to give this guy her back. Nope, nope, nope. But even when she tried to keep facing him, her body slowly spun around anyway. "Holy shit," she whispered under her breath.

"You are a stunning creature," he said into the mirror. "I'm sure Dorian wasn't expecting you to be cut into perfection."

"I'm far from perfect."

"He'd argue otherwise."

Lena hated how her cheeks heated. This was embarrassing and stupid. "What's going on? Why am I here?"

"I'm sure Dorian told you those answers already. He's an open creature, no secrets or lies. It's one of the many admirable things I treasure about the Reaper." The big man tilted his head and let his gaze roam over her reflection. "I'm Malachi, the Mad King, ruler of the House of Death."

She wasn't sure how to respond to that. Another loud roar reverberated from the other side of the door, followed by two big thumps, as if someone was using a battering ram to get inside. Lena jumped at the noise and broke her gaze from the mirror to spin around.

Malachi stopped her somehow. She couldn't budge.

"Remain focused on the mirror, Lena. Dorian's aggression will get worse until you're willing to soothe it."

"What's that mean?" Another loud bang. More shouting. Lena gulped as she remained deadlocked on Malachi's reflection.

"He's dying, Lena. The instant he saw you, his biological clock began ticking. He tried to spare you. He's willing to die just so you aren't tied to him for eternity."

Her heart plummeted. "What?"

Malachi, without breaking eye contact in the mirror, reached over and grabbed a wine glass from the large table. Whatever was in it looked blood red and was thick enough to coat the sides of the glass. He took a large swig and winced, "I hate it when it cools to room temperature." He set the glass back down. "But I drink it because I refuse to give up just yet."

"Give up what?"

"My seat." Malachi shifted in his chair.

Lena noticed his nails were longer than most men's. His hair was completely unkempt and frizzy, thick and dark. It didn't look awful, it just didn't look fitting for someone who claimed the title of "King".

Malachi licked his lips, and she saw his huge fangs. They were even bigger than Dorian's.

"Who told you of The Wicked Garden?" Malachi's dark brow arched.

"I'm... not saying. When something is told to me in confidence, I keep it."

His mouth twitched. "Where did you get those bruises?"

"Not from Dorian."

"I know that, girl. He'd die before laying a violent hand on you."

"And according to you, he'd rather die than be with me too, is that it?" Why did that bug her so much? She didn't know Dorian.

Hell, she didn't know anyone here!

Another scream tore from the other side of the door. Sweat trickled down her back.

Malachi ran a thumb across his bottom lip. "Vampires are possessive creatures. Even after they find, bind, and turn their mate, this virtue remains steadfast. They don't like others playing with their things."

"I'm not a thing. And you're not playing with me."

"Agreed and yes, I am."

Lena grew flustered and tried to walk away. Her feet wouldn't budge. *What the hell!*

"You will move when I dismiss you, girl."

"How are you doing this?" She tried jerking her feet, but they might as well have been bolted to the floor.

"Vampires as old and powerful as I am are capable of many terrible things, including compelling the soul to do my bidding. This is me... playing with you."

Her hips rotated in a circle, big and slow. *Oh my God. Ohmygod, OHMYGOD!* "Was I hypnotized or something? Is that how—"

Another roar ripped through the air. Lena gulped. *Dorian.*

The king chuckled.

Okay, these guys really took this vamp thing to a whole new level. As he took another sip from his glass, Lena really didn't like the fact that it looked exactly like blood. Between that, her inability to move, and the noises coming from outside, her fight or flight response kicked into high gear.

"You must stay." Malachi ordered. "My house is your home for however long it is necessary."

"And if I want to go to *my* home?"

"That's not possible right now. Our enemies would eat you alive and leave your corpse as a gift for Dorian if you do."

"Who's your enemy?"

"Creatures who are just as cursed as we are."

"And... what lifts the curse?"

"Our *alakhai*," Malachi said, keeping his gaze locked on hers in the mirror. "A mate makes life more tolerable than torturous."

"What about this ticking time clock thing? How's that work?"

"It ends when either the vampire burns to ash, or their mate

131

binds to them and is turned."

She hated herself for the way her body immediately reacted to that statement. "Why are you telling me all this and not Dorian?"

"He'd likely think you'd pity him, and he'd rather die than have one more person feel sorry for him. He's... complicated."

"How so?"

Malachi smiled, and it was big, broad, and predatory. "I like that you want to know more about him."

Lena bit her lip.

"Dorian's past haunts him. It shaped him into who he is today. Our kind looks down on him for it."

"Same could be said for anyone. We're all shaped by our past."

"Dorian was carved from it, Lena. I won't say more. That's up to him to share if he dares to have the balls to open up to you."

She arched her brow. "And if he doesn't?"

"Then he dies, and it will no longer matter."

She didn't want him to die. This seemed entirely too theatrical, not to mention, overkill. "What's the cusp of transition?" Dorian used that phrase with her earlier, and she latched on to it because it struck a chord.

"As an *alakhai*, you're matched perfectly for one of us. It means things you didn't crave before you'll now desire with a longing so fierce it could make you shatter with want. There are..." his gaze narrowed, "personality changes sometimes. A docile person could become increasingly aggressive. Someone patient may turn into a hair-trigger. A vegetarian could suddenly crave raw steak."

Lena chewed her lip. She'd always been violent. Always been impatient. Always liked meat. But... there was something she never craved before and a few months ago the desire to go down the deep end of fetishes had led her here. Was that enough of a clue? Was it a clue or a coincidence? Was she suddenly trying to make herself fit in this situation for Dorian's sake, or was she exactly who and what they said she was... a *mate*.

"Healing tends to be faster—physically speaking." Malachi tapped his temple. "The mind is another beast entirely."

He was staring at her bruises.

"Dorian thinks he's a monster." Malachi leaned forward. "Do

you agree?"

"I don't know him." She hated how her voice trembled.

"You were locked in a room with him. Dressed in the color of our favorite meal. Tied like a slab of meat ready to be served."

Lena swayed. Holy shit, was that why they demanded she wear red? To signal the hosts that she was fresh meat? No. No way. Her friend wouldn't have suggested that place if people died there.

Malachi's voice rumbled as he said, "You were blindfolded, were you not?"

"Yes."

"Your senses are heightened by now, Lena. Your body knows when you're in danger and will act accordingly. Tell me." He leaned in, his gaze intensifying in the mirror. "Did you wish to flee when you felt his presence? Whimper at the sound of his voice? Cringe at his touch?"

"N-n-no."

"I thought not." He leaned back with a satisfied grin. "Fighting one's fate is futile. Dorian's learning that lesson now."

"This is real," she whispered more to herself than him.

"As real as the heart beating like a jackrabbit in your chest." He took another sip of his drink. "Dorian's incredibly special to me. I can't afford to lose him. No one here can, though half would never admit it."

"Why?"

"He's willing to do what most are not."

Lena rolled her shoulders back. "What does he do here? Is he your right-hand man or something? And what is this place?"

"Vampires are separated into Houses according to laws, bloodlines, and *honor*. Dorian is the executioner for the House of Death."

"Exe... cutioner?" She said it slowly to let the word roll off her tongue in hopes it sounded less terrifying. It didn't work. In fact, it backfired.

Malachi's nostrils flared and a true smile spread across his handsome face. "Go to your mate, Lena. Allow him to prove his worth."

"He doesn't have to prove anything to me."

"You're right. He must prove it to himself."

The tension snapped, and Lena could finally move her feet

again. She headed for the door and was almost there when Malachi said, "Don't let him die, Lena. I cannot bear to lose one as pure as him."

She swallowed the lump in her throat and beelined for the exit.

"Dorian! Lucian! Get in here." Malachi's voice boomed. Lena's chest rumbled with it. The door swung open.

Lucian and Dorian staggered into the room. Murderous thoughts rocked Lena to the core. Dorian looked worse than he had five minutes ago. Now he was covered in blood and welts. Lena ran to him on instinct. "What happened to him?"

"Easy, Lena. Give him a second to calm down." Lucian strained to hold Dorian back.

Holy motherfucking Hell. Dorian looked positively insane. His eyes were wide and completely black. His fangs dripped with blood and saliva. He hissed, the tendons in his neck straining as he dragged Lucian across the room. With as big as Lucian was, Dorian was stronger. His torso bulged with a crazy amount of muscle as he pitched forward, hellbent to get into the room. To get to Lena.

"She's not hurt, Dorian. Can you see her?" Lucian moved forward cautiously, keeping Dorian restrained. "Smell her. Read her body and know she's unharmed."

Dorian let out a painful groan. His voice cracked as he said her name. "Lena." He swayed once Lucian let go of him. "*Lena.*"

No man had ever said her name so soulfully before. She closed the space between them and almost touched his shoulder but remembered him warning her about that. Instead, she ran her hand through his thick, curly hair and tipped his head back to inspect him. His eyes deadlocked on hers. His gaze begged her… cherished her.

Oh God, what was she going to do?

"Dorian, Lucian, get over here," Malachi said from his chair.

If the king was pissed about Dorian's outburst, it didn't show. In fact, he seemed to have expected it. That set Lena off. Had Malachi done this to push Dorian's buttons? Make him look weak? Make him unravel just so Lena could see it?

Now she wanted to throat-punch Malachi.

"I said get over here, Reaper."

Dorian shook off whatever had been riding his system and

staggered forward. Lena let him go and turned her gaze to Lucian. He stared at her with a mix of *I'm sorry* and *please help.* "Yes, my King?"

"Marius has demanded a bloodletting. Two from his House were attacked in the French Quarter."

Should Lena be listening to any of this conversation? Maybe she should leave?

Lucian hissed angrily. "This is bullshit. He's trying to stir drama up when there's nothing."

Dorian agreed. "He's trying to prove this territory is no longer safe."

"All so he can attain it himself and do better?" Lucian scowled. "Fuck that. This is a low blow, Malachi, even for Marius."

"Some will stop at nothing to get what they want," the king said.

Lena immediately looked over at Dorian. He was staring at her with a blank expression. "He likely paid for an attack, hired thugs to make it look like we aren't patrolling and keeping the streets safe."

"Most likely, yes."

"Why?" Lena cringed the second she inserted herself into the conversation.

Malachi smiled but wasn't looking at her. His gaze, just like earlier, remained fixed on the mirror behind her. What was it with all the damn mirrors? Weren't vampires supposed to not see their reflections? Wasn't that a rule or something?

"Marius wants this House," Malachi explained calmly. "He wants the power that comes with it—and that includes our Dorian."

Our Dorian...

"Why's he so hellbent on targeting Dorian, Malachi?" Lucian fumed. "Marius's fixation makes no sense."

"It does when you understand Dorian." The king grabbed his glass and took another sip. He cringed as he swallowed.

"Too old now?" Lucian asked in a low tone.

"I fear its potency is lacking."

Lena tried hard to keep up, but it wasn't going well anymore.

When Lucian said, "Dorian, grab your girl and hold her tight for a minute." Lena had zero time to brace for impact. Dorian wrapped his arms around her like an anaconda and nuzzled his face into her neck. His entire body was hard, including the giant dick in his pants that now pressed against the top of her ass.

Heat radiated off his body, melting her into him.

But Lena wasn't sidetracked by the dangerous man in possession of her. She was enthralled with the view up front. Lucian dropped down on one knee and rolled his sleeve up, presenting the king his forearm. "It would be an honor, sire."

That's all Lucian said. And all Malachi needed to hear.

The king's mouth opened wide, and, like a viper striking, he bit down on Lucian's wrist. Then he latched on and started swallowing.

Lena shuddered. Dorian's grip tightened around her. Lucian's gaze snapped to her and his nostrils flared. Malachi's gaze drifted away from the mirror and locked onto her as he drank from Lucian.

She nearly fainted.

Maybe her legs would have given out on her if Dorian wasn't holding her up. And how pathetic was that? Her lust was a deranged beast to want this so badly. Malachi's gaze flicked back and locked, once again, on the mirror behind her. He continued to drink from Lucian's vein until Lucian began listing. Then the king pulled back and licked his lips, dragging his tongue across his massive canines.

Lena groaned.

"Dorian," Malachi purred. "Do not waste this gift."

"No sire."

Ohhh shiiit. Those two words rumbled out of Dorian's mouth and straight down Lena's spine. Heat pooled between her legs and her thighs quivered.

This was downright embarrassing.

"Take her home." Malachi ordered. "The distractions of House business will be tended to by someone else. For now, go home and finish this, Dorian."

Finish this? Finish *what*?

"They're safer here, Malachi," Lucian argued as he stood, licking the two puncture wounds on his arms. They sealed and disappeared immediately. "I prefer them to be here, sire."

"They may be safer here," the king growled back, "But no one else will be until he finishes this. The aggression and possessiveness are going to get worse for him. I'll not risk the House. He goes home where he's most comfortable."

"Then I wish to go with them," Lucian pushed. "He can't be unchaperoned."

"I'm standing right here," Dorian growled.

Lucian scowled at Dorian. "You can't be unchaperoned. We already discussed and agreed to this, or don't you remember?"

"I remember," Dorian said against Lena's cheek. His breath tickled her shoulder and she'd be a liar if she said this whole thing didn't crank her up six different ways. "Malachi's right. We can't risk the House and I'm clearly unstable. We'll go home."

"And if things escalate?" Lucian's brow furrowed. "What then?"

There was something the two of them were saying but unwilling to spell out. Whatever it was, Lena wanted to know. She didn't like being left clueless about something she was supposed to be part of.

"I'll be taken care of," Dorian finally said.

"Wait, whoa." Lena's brow cinched. "What are you two saying?"

"Nothing," Dorian and Lucian told her at the same time.

Nothing her ass. If Lena was supposed to stick with this guy, and he was too unsafe for a bunch of big, grown ass men to be around, what did that say about her safety with him? On that note, why on earth was she eagerly entertaining any of this?

You know why, Lena thought to herself.

"The House needs it's Reaper." Malachi eased back in his chair, his gaze remaining fixed on his reflection. "We depend on you. Clean yourself up and finish this."

The three of them were dismissed that fast. Lena still had a ton of questions. But with Dorian in need of help, and Lucian now looking like he was going to puke, she had no choice but to roll with the punches for now and save her questions for later.

They left the room, staggered down the steps, and headed outside. Lena remained strangely calm. Some things were explainable with special effect tricks—like fake fangs and red-dyed corn syrup in a wine glass. Other things, however, were inexplicable yet completely undeniable.

What she saw upstairs between Lucian and Malachi was no act. What she experienced when Malachi made it so she couldn't budge wasn't a drug-induced hallucination. The way her body responded to Dorian's voice, touch, and smell wasn't role play. Not even the promise of threats and attacks phased her. In fact, she secretly felt protective of Dorian and almost wished someone would try to attack just so she could burn a little energy and kick their ass.

For the first time in her entire life, Lena wasn't out of her element — she was smack dab in the middle of it. The fact that it was amidst violence and danger didn't shock her at all.

Lena belonged here.

CHAPTER 20

Dorian's raging headache made it impossible to open his eyes, but if he kept them closed, he grew nauseous, so he was pulling a one-eyed willy as Lucian and Lena practically dragged him inside his house. "I'm so sorry."

He didn't know what else to say at this point. He was embarrassed, infuriated, and getting so much worse. The highs and lows were steep. At least he was back in his own home now, and away from everyone's prying eyes. "I should have never—"

"Can you shut the fuck up and put one foot in front of the other and get in the shower?" Lucian manhandled him into the bathroom.

Dorian almost laughed at how pathetic this was. It had been lifetimes since he was this weak and unfocused. For Lucian to shove him around was a first. It was usually the other way around.

Lucian turned on the shower and sprayed him in the face with cold water.

"Fuck!" Dorian jolted. "That's freezing!"

"Well at least you're not numb yet. That's a good sign."

The water slowly warmed and the tension in his shoulders started melting. He had no clue how long he sat on the floor of his shower, still dressed and in boots, but the world kind of fell away for a little bit. It was foggy but cozy. Peaceful. The light scent of cherries tickled his nose making him sink deeper into calmness. He both liked and hated that Lena was also in the bathroom. Maybe he needed to use this moment to fess up a little.

"It's nice to have hot, running water," he thought out loud.

"No buckets to fill up anymore."

He cracked his eyes open and saw water funnel down the drain. It made him feel hollow inside. The past crept up behind him. "It never washed away... not even in the river." He fanned his hands out. "I should have never left that place. None of this would be happening if I hadn't left."

"What do you mean?" Lena asked quietly.

He buried his head in his hands, swept away in memories...

"Dorian, fetch me the cleaver." His father held out his meaty palm, skin cracked from the cold. Dried blood coated him up to his elbows. "Now, boy!"

It was always the same — this hell cycled over and over again. Dorian was supposed to be used to it by now, right? His father promised.

Stars burst in his vision when his father backhanded him for not budging. Dorian flew back, his spindly limbs no match for the massive arms of his father. While Dorian remained scrawny and malnourished, his father gorged on blood.

His blood.

The victims he took and drained were wasted. His father only played with them and left a small amount for Dorian to feed on. But every week, just as Dorian would start to feel less groggy, his father would force him down and drain him. A king with a feast, while his servant starved.

"Did you forget your functions, boy?"

"N-no father."

"Stop stuttering or I'll break your jaw. That'll certainly keep you silent for a time."

Dorian's small fangs cut into his lip when he bit down. The piercing pain was sharp and too brief, it didn't overshadow the sting on his cheek from his father's slap like he hoped. If only he was bigger, stronger, smarter, he could stand up to his father and stop this madness from continuing.

But he couldn't.

He refused to drink willingly from the victims his father took. And, for whatever gluttonous reason, his father kept him drained each day. Even if his father had to vomit his meal to make room in his belly to drink from Dorian, he did it.

Why?

To keep him wasted and puny. Weak and brittle. Why? If he wanted Dorian to be like him, why wouldn't he allow Dorian the chance to

140

strengthen?

Because his father knew if Dorian had the chance, he'd –

"Cleaver!" his father shouted. "NOW!"

Dorian slowly rose to his feet and walked over to the wall of dulled, rusted, filthy weapons. Snatching the cleaver from its hook, his gaze shifted to a small paring knife and he swiftly snagged it as well. Keeping the cleaver within his father's sight, Dorian tucked the tiny paring knife into the waistline of his stained, torn breeches and made his way back over to his father's workstation.

"Drink her while I cut."

Dorian vomited in his mouth at the thought. He refused. It was always this same song and dance. His father would command him, Dorian would refuse, then his father left him no choice.

"Do it or I'll make it worse for her." The cleaver hovered over the woman's naked breasts. "It's up to you how she dies, boy. Swiftly or mercilessly. Now drink."

The woman was out cold, and Dorian prayed she stayed unconscious. This wasn't going to end well for anyone. It never did. His father was getting more and more creative with his punishments lately – both for his victims and Dorian.

"I'm not hungry," he mumbled.

Dropping the cleaver, his father's hand slammed down on Dorian's shoulder, the other wrapped around the nape of Dorian's neck. "Feed or I'll gut you."

Then gut me, *he wanted to say. But he was too chicken shit to let those words tumble from his cracked lips. He didn't want to die. He just wanted out of this life. Away from this terror. If he were stronger, he could run faster. He saw how quick his father was. He wanted to be the same.*

"Drink, son. I'll not tell you again."

Dorian's eyes squeezed shut and he bent over the woman's neck. His father's forceful hands shoved him down, forcing him to either feed or die. What Dorian chose would determine this woman's final fate – let her be hacked into pieces or go easily in her unconscious state.

Mercy sometimes looked like murder.

And he was so hungry. He hadn't eaten a bite of food in four days and water wasn't enough to satisfy his thirst. His fangs throbbed. Tears stung his eyes as he opened his mouth and clamped down on the woman's neck. I'm so sorry, *he screamed in his head.* I don't know how to get us out of this!

The woman jerked beneath his fangs. Her blood rushed into his mouth when his teeth tore her skin.

She's awake! No! *Dorian drew back — and though his hunger demanded he keep drinking, he refused to give into it.* "Run!" *he screamed. Pulling the paring knife out, he spun around, ready to strike his father.*

But it didn't happen.

Instead, his father cracked the cleaver down on the woman's right leg, severing it. "Yes, dear, run. Run fast before I cut your other leg off as well."

The woman's mouth opened in a silent scream. Her eyes bugged out of her head as the puncture wounds in her neck poured blood.

Dorian puked. Backing up, he panicked and couldn't figure out which way to run. Palming his tiny blade, he knew he'd never be able to kill his father with something so small. But that didn't mean he wouldn't try. Better to die fighting than live like this another day.

Dorian attacked.

"You stupid fool!" *His father bit down on Dorian's arm, taking a chunk of meat with him. Dorian screamed. His father raised his cleaver and swung down hard.*

Dorian moved out of the way just in the nick of time. The blade only cut instead of cleaved. The sudden pain of both wounds made Dorian's senses sharpen. He rolled out of his father's reach as the cleaver fell again. It cut into the wooden floorboards of their shack.

"You can't outrun me, boy."

Good. Because Dorian didn't want to outrun him. He wanted to kill him.

His father lunged and managed to sink his massive teeth into Dorian's right thigh. Dorian punched his father's head. His father took another hunk out of his sunken in torso. Dorian's voice broke with his next scream. He snagged the well bucket — the only thing in his reach — and smashed it against his father's head until it busted and crumbled to pieces. It did nothing but make the old monster laugh.

"Let's play a game, Dorian." *His father rose to his full height and glared down at him with blood all over his chin and cheeks.* "Hide and Seek. Remember how I taught you to play it? Run, Dorian. Run for your life and hide. Pray I don't find you."

Dorian didn't want to run. He knew he couldn't hide. His father would find him, come hell or highwater. That bastard loved the hunt and chase. He was a master at it.

The woman on the table screamed and thrashed about. Dorian's father dashed to her as fast as a lightning strike and broke her neck. Dorian scrambled out of the house and headed into the woods. Blood poured from his wounds. He was disoriented and numb.

Bumbling through the forest, he spun around, unsure which direction to go. If he headed left, he'd end up in a village and there was no way he was willing to lure his father towards more people to prey on.

Something hit his back. Dorian pitched forward and slammed on the ground. Scrambling on all fours, he winced at the fresh pain and scuttled behind a tree. Panting, he reached back —

An arrow protruded just under his shoulder blade. Biting his lip, he squeezed his eyes shut and tried to snap the shaft. He was too chicken to pull it all the way out right now. Dizziness made him sway. His stomach lurched and he dry heaved.

"Come now, boy. I taught you better than this. You're not even trying."

His father rounded the bend, holding his ancient bow and pulled a fresh arrow from his quiver. He'd seen his father hit a cardinal in mid-air at thirty yards away once. Dorian was a much bigger target. He wasn't going to get out of this alive.

Dashing back towards the house, his brain checked out. He just wanted to be home. This was the safest place for his father to be trapped anyway, and the woman was already dead. She couldn't be saved. None of them could.

With his father's laughter ringing in his ears, Dorian ran into their little shack and started tipping everything over. The animal grease used for cooking. The hay beds. The wooden spoons and plates. They didn't have much, but it was all flammable.

Dorian picked up the rickety stool he was forced to always sit in to watch his father work, and he smashed it on the floor. Splintered pieces flew everywhere just as his father kicked down the door.

"You weak little shit." He stormed over and grabbed Dorian's arm, forcing him to drop the wooden leg with the sharp, splintered end. "Look at the mess you've made."

Dorian raised his other hand, and swung down, piercing his father's jugular with the paring knife. His father roared in fury and let go. Yanking the knife out of his neck, his father's laugh rumbled the termite infested shack. "You'll have to play with bigger weapons if you want to kill a beast like me."

He lunged forward. Dorian dodged him. For once, his puny size was a plus. Dorian kicked a few embers still sparking in their small hearth and it caught some of the hay on fire.

His father stomped forward, hands out and claws sharp. He swiped across Dorian's chest and did it again on his back when he spun out to run. The grease caught on fire. It had been splashed everywhere and flames caught quickly.

Smoke filled the shack. His father's blood loss slowed him down just enough for Dorian to make it to the other side of the burning shack. He grabbed blade after blade, tossing them at his father. Some struck home, others missed their mark. His father roared and broke through the growing smoke.

For as small as their shack was, it now felt too big. It should be burning faster than this.

Dorian's legs were knocked out from under him, and he went airborne. Slamming on his back, the arrow shoved in deeper, snapping the shaft, and he smacked his head hard enough to blackout for a second. His father's hands clamped down on his ankles and every single uneven floorboard hammered his spine while he was dragged to the center of the room.

His father was a bloodied mess, his eyes blackened with rage. Slamming his fists down, he broke several of Dorian's ribs at once.

He'd have howled in agony if he could breathe.

Smoke thickened. Flames ate the walls and spilled across the floor, consuming everything it touched. Like a ravenous monster, the fire devoured the bed, the furniture...

The evidence.

Dorian's fate became crystal clear in that moment. If he distracted his father long enough, he'd burn. His father was compulsive. He could get so fixated on one thing he'd let the world around him fade out of existence. That's how he worked. One-track mind. Devoted obsession...

But in order to keep his father here, Dorian had to stay too. He had to burn with his father...

Dorian coughed and gagged against the smoke that no longer filled his lungs. The water in the shower had turned to ice again. On his hands and knees, water still spraying down his back, he heaved and sucked in hot, steamy air and water. "I should have burned..."

Turning his gaze upwards, he stared at Lena and wished fate wasn't such a cruel bitch. Lena deserved better than him. She shouldn't be here. But... he couldn't let her go. It was impossible to even consider it now.

Just like his father... he now had a one-track mind. *Lena.* The rest of the world faded into nothingness. *Lena.* She was his new obsession and Dorian was devoted, one-hundred and ten percent. *Lena.*

"I am my father's son," he whispered before passing out.

CHAPTER 21

Lena's hands wouldn't stop shaking. After Dorian rambled on and on about his father — who had to be the devil — and victims and arson, he collapsed and had remained that way for the past ten minutes.

Once Lucian carried him out of the shower, sopping wet, and stripped him out of his clothes, Lena watched from a safe distance while Lucian dropped Dorian onto his bed. Sighing, the vampire ran a hand down his face and took one last look at Dorian before gesturing to Lena that they should leave the room.

"Is that all true? Did he murder someone?'

"It's not how you think," Lucian blew out a big exhale and pointed towards the kitchen. "You want some coffee?"

"I want answers." She crossed her arms over her chest. "If all of this is real, and I'm not even saying I believe it is, but if it is, then I need to know what I'm getting into with Dorian. No," she said, waving her hand in the air, "I *deserve* to know."

"You're right." Lucian cocked his head to the side. "Soooo we're gonna need something stronger than coffee for this."

Lena's hand instinctively went up to her neck to protect it.

"Relax." Lucian chuckled. "I meant hot chocolate."

"Hot chocolate?" What the hell?

"I'd prefer whisky, but Dorian doesn't drink. He doesn't have any booze in this house, so hot chocolate it is."

"Vampires drink hot chocolate?"

"Vampires, werewolves, humans, we all like a lot of the same things, Lena. Vampires drink blood to survive. No one," he said, pulling a saucepan out of a cupboard, "drinks hot chocolate to survive. We just like to indulge ourselves, am I right?"

For all the intense mess Dorian was, Lucian was the exact opposite. While Dorian oozed aggression, Lucian exuded controlled confidence. Dorian's gaze was tempered and dark, Lucian's was playful and curious. She suddenly wondered who would win a fight between them.

Lucian poured milk into the saucepan. His broad shoulders filled out his t-shirt nicely. His profile looked like cut perfection—slender nose, sharp jawline, plush mouth.

"We're designed to lure you in," he said in a deep, quiet voice. "If you catch yourself staring, don't be ashamed. You'll get used to our appearances eventually and pay us no mind."

Lena looked away. The silence grew awkward and uncomfortable.

"What do you feel when you look at Dorian?" Lucian swirled the pot of simmering milk.

"I... I'm not sure exactly."

"Yes, you are." He turned off the burner.

"I just met him."

"Doesn't matter." He grabbed chocolate from another cabinet and poured it in. Lazily, he swirled the pot with a wooden spoon. "What do you feel, Lena?"

She blew out a long exhale. "I feel safe." That's the worst part of this whole thing. She should feel the opposite of that with a train wreck like him, right? But she didn't. Lena also felt somehow responsible for his current condition, which absolutely made no sense.

It was the way he'd screamed her name at the mansion earlier. That sound did something dangerous to her. It made her feel wanted and cherished. Needed.

Ugh, she was pathetic.

"You should feel safe with him." Lucian licked the spoon before dropping it in the sink. "He'll never hurt you. In fact, he'd raze this world if he thought that's what it took to protect you." He handed her a mug of hot chocolate. "No marshmallows, I'm afraid."

Lena almost laughed. "I don't like them anyways."

"Neither does he." Lucian took a sip from his mug and eyed her closely while she did the same. Then he dragged his tongue

147

over the tip of one of his canines. "You didn't seem too frightened when Malachi drank from me."

She didn't want to respond to that.

"We can smell you, Lena. Keep that in mind. Your mouth can lie, but your body can't. We all smelled the lust in that room."

"Oh Jesus Christ." She turned away and sat her mug down, then braced herself against the counter.

"That's a good thing," Lucian leaned next to her, flashing his fangs with a big grin. "It means you're accepting of how we are. A good deal of lust goes into a blood exchange like that." He frowned and put his hand up, "Wait. I mean *usually*. The King and I aren't like that." He shivered and added, "Holy Hell, I wouldn't want to be his bottom. He'd annihilate my ass. The King has a serious weapon of ass destruction, I can't imagine what it would take to—"

Lena burst out laughing. "Wow. Do you say everything you think?"

"Try to." He shrugged.

"No wonder Dorian likes you." She crossed her arms and grinned. "You probably balance each other out. He seems a little closed off and you're like a megaphone."

"The yin to his yang." Lucian bowed. "I'm the yin. Totally the yin."

"Does it matter?"

"Only if one thinks it does." He took another sip of his hot chocolate. "And Dorian's an open book. Always has been. Ask him anything and he'll tell you the truth. I don't think he has the capacity to lie. He's not built that way." Leaning against the counter he crossed one foot over the other and stared at her for a long minute. His brow furrowed. "Help us save him, Lena."

"I'm not even sure what you're asking me to do. I don't understand how I'm supposed to save someone I don't even know."

"Yes, you do. The King already told you. If Dorian doesn't bond and mate with you, he *will* die. And... it's going to happen soon."

Her heart clogged her throat. "How do you know that for sure?"

"I've seen it," he said quietly. "And I hope I never see it happen again. A vampire's curse is the cruelest of them all. And Dorian's got double the battle to fight because some piece of him

148

believes he deserves this death... even though his soul cries out for you to save it."

Holy Hell, how did we go from hot chocolate to soul saving? Lena's throat tightened, and tears stung her eyes. The mere mention of Dorian in need like that was...

Wow, she couldn't put words to it. Devastating? Gut-wrenching? Confusing? All of the above.

"How does all this work?"

Lucian's eyes brightened. "You're going to do it?"

She put her hands up. "I'm asking how all this works. I'm still processing."

"But you're willing to consider it?"

Damn her soul, but she nodded back at him. "I... the King said some things that struck a chord. Plus, seeing Dorian's reactions to me." She tossed her hands up and said, "I swear I've never been saner and crazier at the same time. This is nuts."

"I'll help you however I can," Lucian straightened up and closed the space between them.

"So how does this work?"

He licked his lips and stared at her, contemplating. "You want the long version or a summary?"

"Somewhere in the middle? I don't know how long we have before Dorian wakes up."

Lucian grinned, "Okay, vampires and Lycan are blood cursed."

"There's werewolves too?"

"Try to keep up," Lucian teased. "There's a lot to cover here."

Lena crossed her arms over her chest again. Werewolves... of course there would also be werewolves.

"We're blood cursed. Way back, like wayyyyy back, a woman had been seduced by two charming suitors. One," he said, holding one finger up, "came to see her by day. The other," he added, holding up a second finger, "by night."

"Lucky girl."

"You'd think, right?" Lucian leaned against the counter again. "The one who came by day was the vampire."

"I thought vampires couldn't —"

"Shhh! Save your questions for the end." Lucian cleared his throat. "As I was saying. The vampire and Lycan species were in danger of dying out. The *Savag-Ri* had hunted them down to near extinction. These two males were both, unbeknownst to the other, drawn to the same woman. Both seduced and bedded her. Both got her pregnant around the exact same time. The phenomenon's known as superfecundation twins. Neither father knew about the other. When the woman's condition was exposed, she was forced into confinement and went through the pregnancy alone. She longed to see either of her lovers, though neither ever came to her — not by day or night. No matter how many letters she wrote, they didn't answer them. She spent her pregnancy longing for the men she loved and grew spiteful and hateful that they hadn't returned. Then, when she delivered the babies, they both arrived for the birth of their sons. When they realized they both bedded the same woman for the same reason, they fought outside the birthing chambers. Meanwhile, she hemorrhaged out and cursed both of their bloodlines in the process. The vampire and Lycan would live forever longing for the love that would never come to them. Just like she'd longed for them to return to her all those months."

Lena's mouth dropped open.

"But," Lucian said, wagging his finger, "because she still loved her children and wasn't a total bitch, her curse could be lifted *only* if they found their mates in time. Until then, vampires would remain cursed with constant longing, any satisfaction they find would be painfully temporary, and their souls forever tortured and hollow without their true mate."

"Because both the vampire and Lycan had been too late in coming back to her, but *had* come at the bitter end instead of never at all?"

"Yup." Lucian turned around and started washing the dishes. "She really was a horrible bitch now that I'm rethinking this whole story. It sounded more romantic when I was younger."

"What happened after she died?"

"The vampire was enraged. Grew bitter. Raped and killed with a fevered starvation and sired many, many more bastard children. He couldn't bear to look at his own reflection anymore, so he banned all mirrors in his home, not knowing reflections were the key to helping his children find their fated mates. His eldest son — the one who started the curse's cycle — had one day seen a reflection of a woman in the bottom of a well but didn't understand what it

150

meant. He never searched for her but told his brothers about what he'd seen. Thought it was a ghost, I guess. Over the next few weeks, he grew more feral and aggressive. Started killing everyone in villages below theirs. A mob came after him and brought him to the center of town. Tied him up to burn him at the stake. A girl approached as he was set on fire. It was the girl from the vision in the well. He was fixated by it. His compelling powers lured her into the flames, and he bit her. Shit got crazy after that."

"I can imagine."

"The Lycan had a different outcome. The father bayed at the moon, crying his apology and regret to the woman's soul. He raised his son and wooed many women, promising to care for and do better than he had with the mother of his first born. He never succeeded. There was no love in his heart anymore. Maybe there never had been to begin with. Hell, if I know." Lucian blew out a big exhale. "His son fell in love with a girl, married her, naturally, and kept his wolf form a secret. He sired several children, all of them Lycan, but when another woman was brought into their clan and paired with one of the hunters, he felt protective and possessive of her, but stayed faithful to his wife. He drank heavily to dull his instincts and also started chugging a form of liquid silver since manmade booze burns fast with their metabolism. Rumor has it, he began dreaming of the other woman every night and it drove him wild and restless. Guilty too. As the full moon grew closer, his desires for her got stronger. He was undeniably drawn to this other woman."

"That's awkward."

"Awkward enough to drive his wife to commit murder." Lucian said with a frown.

"She killed her competition."

Lucian nodded. "Soon after that, on the night of the next full moon, he turned into a wolf and stayed in his animal form forever. He never saw his sons again. That's how they found out the fate of a Lycan who didn't claim their mate in time."

"Holy Hell."

"Right?" Lucian dried the saucepan and put it back in the cupboard. "The blood curse makes it so once we see our *alakhai*, we are on borrowed time unless we find, bond, turn and mate with them. While we search for our mate, our bodies begin to deteriorate.

We've always been able to walk in the sun, but it does burn hotter on our skin. We get slower. Color fades. Taste dies out. Hearing loss, weight loss, sanity goes out the window. Until… poof!" He made explosion hands. "We turn to ash."

"You burn?"

"Like tissue paper in a bonfire."

Lena had to sit down.

"Hey, whoa, hold up." Lucian grabbed her arm and helped her to the couch in the living room. "Better?"

"No."

He sat next to her and frowned. "I'm not telling you all this to freak you out, I'm just keeping things honest and open between us. Dorian's likely not going to say a word of this."

"Why?" she whispered, still trying to grasp this whole curse thing.

"He's stayed clear of anything that even remotely had the possibility of showing a reflection. So long as a vampire doesn't see it, they're safe."

"So, the second he saw me in a mirror, that's when his life was in danger."

"I mean, yes but no. No, because Dorian's life would continue just fine if he never saw you. Yes, because our enemies would love his fangs on their trophy wall, so he's always had to watch his back. Not that anyone stands a chance against a vampire of his caliber."

Lena connected more dots. "But he has a mirror in the bathroom." *And more mounted in the living room.*

"All this," he said, pointing around, "was installed just after he saw your reflection. In fact, he obsessed over another chance to see you until it happened."

She felt a little warm in the belly over that. Oh geez. "Who's your enemy?"

"*Savag-Ri* mostly, but Lycan too. We blame each other for what happened with the woman and her two lovers."

"And what's a *Savag-Ri?*"

"Creatures who've killed our kind long before the blood curse ever did. It's how the Lycan and vampire species almost went extinct in the first place."

"Why do they hunt you?"

"They deem us abominations and their only purpose on this

earth is to rid the world of us. Anything less is likely an embarrassment and stain on their bloodlines."

"Wow." Lena rubbed her temples. "I'm sorry, I just... this is fucking crazy."

"I know it seems that way, but—" Lucian shrugged and scrubbed his face with both hands. "I'm not pulling your chain, Lena. This is serious. I can't lose Dorian. He's my best friend and I've already lost one brother to this curse. Call me selfish, but I can't bear to watch Dorian die."

"I don't want him to die either."

He grabbed her hand and squeezed, "Then help me help him. Do this. He'll spend his whole life making you happy. You have no clue how devoted vampires are."

"So devoted they abandon their pregnant lover?"

"That was different," he argued. "And a long time ago. Don't blame us for the sins of our ancestors and don't think we haven't evolved and learned from their mistakes."

"Why not?" Dorian growled from the archway and broke the conversation. "She's right to do so."

Lucian let go of Lena's hand and stood up. "Don't fucking start this again, Dorian."

Lena wasn't sure if she should jump between them or run for cover. The aggression in the room was thick enough to cut with a knife.

"Lena," Dorian held his hand out and she came to him willingly. He pulled her close to his chest and inhaled deeply. "What did you tell her, Lucian?"

"Only about the curse."

"Which one?"

"There's more than one?" Lena was gonna need a notebook for all this shit.

"There's *only* one," Lucian pressed. "Don't let him make you think otherwise."

"Get out."

"Dorian, I—"

"Get. Out!"

Lucian looked like he'd just been kicked in the balls. With his brow pinched, eyes pained, he licked his lips and nodded slowly. "Fine, Reaper. Dig your own goddamn grave." He marched out and slammed the front door shut.

Lena's fingers curled around Dorian's and she turned to look at him. "I think—"

He crushed his mouth to hers and burned all thoughts from her mind.

CHAPTER 22

He shouldn't be kissing her. It was the best and worst idea all wrapped up in firm muscles, soft skin, and a sigh that lingered on the tip of her tongue, which Dorian happily worshipped with his mouth. Kissing this woman was like driving a stake through his own shriveled heart. It was freeing and aching at the same time.

A fire blazed in his veins, consuming him entirely. He deepened their kiss, starved for more of her.

When he'd woken in his room earlier and heard Lucian and Lena talking, he had tried putting his head back together. Get his priorities straight. Attempt to collect his mangled morals and make some sense of this mess. He failed miserably.

All Dorian wanted was to get his hands on her again. Smell her scent. See her face. Feel her skin just to confirm this wasn't some grand nightmare sent by the universe to destroy him.

But devastation had more than one clever game to play. What hadn't killed him as a child, surely left him ruined as a grown male. He spilled some of his story to her in that shower earlier. Lost in a foggy, fevered trance, he'd told her a little of his life back then.

But she needed to know more of it. All of it.

"Dorian," Lena whispered, cupping his face and pulling back from his mouth.

He wasn't ready yet. "No." He crushed his mouth to hers again and ate her next moan. *Please give me this*, he silently begged.

She owed him nothing, he knew that, but it didn't matter. He was a depraved bastard who lived in the gutters too long to climb out of them now. Knowing he would drag her down with him, selfish though it was, he desperately wanted just one fucking evening of pure bliss.

"One night," he pleaded against her lips. "One night with you and I'll die knowing I attempted to claim some small bit of happiness with you before accepting defeat." He sounded pathetic and didn't care. He needed this too badly to care.

And if she didn't want to kiss him, fine, he could put his mouth to use on other parts of her body.

Lena pulled away from him again. "Lucian said—"

Dorian hissed against her collarbone. "Don't say his name right now." The only name on her lips should be his.

"*Dorian.*" She sighed when he kissed across her throat column and licked the vein in her neck.

He wanted to sink his teeth into her so badly, his teeth hurt. "I want to taste you."

She placed her hand on the nape of his neck and he froze. The feel of her hand there…. The sensation of someone forcing his head where they wanted it to go, made his instincts flare with aggression. Dorian squeezed his eyes shut and focused on exactly *who* had control of him right now.

Himself… and ultimately Lena.

No one else. No ghost. No memory. No one.

She squeezed the back of his neck and tipped her head, rubbing her cheek against his. "How is this possible?" she whispered. "How can I feel this way when I don't—"

He kissed her again, this time grabbing her ass, hauling her up and carrying her back to his bedroom. She'd just seen him at his lowest point. His worst. Dorian wanted to show her his best before it was too late.

"Our curse makes it so we're in constant longing," he said against her mouth. Letting her feet gently hit the floor, he kept his gaze locked on hers, "Fuck, how I've longed for you, Lena." He reached behind her back and unzipped her red dress. Her skin felt like fire and he wanted to burn.

Lena stared up at him, bewildered. "How is this possible?"

He didn't know, nor did he fucking care. He'd fought this exact thing for as long as he'd drawn breath and now, facing his doom, Dorian wanted to live a thousand lives with her in one evening. Leave his mark on her so no one dared touch her even after he no longer prowled this earth.

For if he must, he'd find a way to crawl back to her even from his hellish grave and protect her even in death. No grave, or ash, could keep him away from her even in death. He'd find a way back to Lena... and maybe then, he'd be worthy of her.

"One night," he said as he slipped her dress down her shoulders and kissed the dip in her throat. "That's all I'll beg for, even though I don't deserve it."

"I'm owed three." Her lips quirked into a playful smile. "As my host from The Wicked Garden, I'm owed three nights."

I might not have three nights left in me, he thought. But he would try. Damn him, he'd fucking try. Flicking his wrist, candles ignited around his room. Lena gasped.

"Parlor tricks," he shrugged.

"What else can you do?"

Kill, maim, dismember. "I'm not a host there. I've no talents in pleasuring a woman the way they do at The Wicked Garden."

Lena pulled back from him and he got a good look at the lacey number she wore under her red dress. Holy Hell, she was so beautifully built. Sinful, scrumptious, and sweet.

"How do you know what kind of pleasure I enjoy, Dorian?" Her dark brow arched. Damn, how he loved that challenging glare on her. "You never did read my file."

He bit the inside of his lip and let blood rush into his mouth. Swallowing, he said, "Are those bruises from a lover?"

"No." She ran her hands down her breasts and traced the lace around to her back. Unhooking her bra, the pathetic covering dropped to the floor between them. "I like to hit things."

"Hit things?" He pressed into her, letting her feel how hard he was. "Things that hit back, I presume."

"Only if I haven't knocked them out first." She reached up and nipped his earlobe. "Don't worry, I win more than I lose."

But he *was* worried. Who the hell was she fighting against? Who could hurt her in so many places and she not mind? He wanted to rip the arms off whoever made those marks on her. "Who?" Or *what*?

"Can you keep a secret?" she whispered.

Dorian clenched his jaw and nodded.

"Me too." Lena eased back on the bed and spread her thighs,

not giving him the answer he wanted.

His gaze deadlocked on the wet spot in her panties.

"You like pain with your pleasure?" Dorian dropped to his knees and crawled over to her.

"That's what I came here to find out."

Fuuuuck. That she hadn't experienced such things before him, cranked his ass up to dangerous heat levels. His dick twitched and mouth watered. Snagging a blade from his bedside table—he kept weapons everywhere—Dorian dragged the edge across his pec. He showed her exactly what pain did for him by grabbing his hard cock and stroking it through his pants.

Her lust smothered the damn air. If Dorian had any reservations about how dark to go with her, they just disintegrated. "You can have your way with me. I don't care what you want to do. Do it and I'll fucking come so hard I'll likely hit the ceiling with the mess I make."

Lena's eyes widened. Then her mouth formed an adorable o-shape. Then she laughed. "Have you no shame?"

"None." He dropped the blade and pressed his chest against her hand. His wound sealed immediately and he loved how her eyelashes fluttered while she watched his body mend itself. Next, she ran her finger in his blood, smearing it across his skin. A shaky breath escaped her lips. "This is crazy."

Their eyes met. The world fell away. Their next kiss was ravenous. Tongues dueling for dominance. Hands clawing, gripping, squeezing everything they could touch on each other. He'd changed into a pair of gym shorts after waking earlier, which were easy enough to take off.

Her fingers grazed every inch of his body she could get her greedy little hands on. It set him on fire—each scratch she made, the dig of her nails, her grip on his arms.

It was torture. Raw and real and undeniable torture.

Dropping down, he grazed her hardened nipple with his fangs.

"Ohhhh shiiiit." Lena arched into him. "Bite me... please fucking bite me."

Dorian's eyes narrowed on her pulse. Her veins rose to the surface of her skin. He backed off immediately and sucked in a few ragged breaths. "I can't." He hated denying her. "If I taste your blood... it'll make us one step closer to bonding."

She wilted on the spot. "I thought that was the plan. You... you said I'm your mate."

"You are, but..." Fuck, how was he supposed to explain any of his feelings to her? Dorian sucked at feelings. He was better at executions. That wouldn't impress her though, it would likely drive her further away from him—something he didn't want tonight. Not yet...

"I'm not good enough." Lena put distance between them, suddenly furious. "I'm never good enough, this is just perfect. *Perfect!*" She snagged her bra from the floor.

Dorian slammed her against the wall. "You are too good for me," he snarled. "And you will learn that soon enough, Lena. When you do, it's over." He grabbed her throat and held her still—not choking her, but definitely making it clear who was in charge. "I don't want to ever hear those ugly words come out of your pretty fucking mouth again. We clear?"

Her lust kicked into the air like hot steam in a bath house. Dorian remained steadfast and didn't let his elation show when he growled, "Get back on that bed."

Lena didn't budge.

"You're killing me." He spun her around and slammed her hands against the wall. Running his hands down her back, he scraped his fingers down her sweet skin and squatted so her ass was in his face. He nipped her right cheek before standing again and kicking her legs out further. He rubbed her ass cheeks, greedily. Then he hooked his fingers under her lacy panties and ripped the damn things off.

"Bed. Now."

She still didn't move. The vein in her neck fluttered wildly. He closed his eyes and locked his needs down tight. Tonight was all about her.

Backing up, Dorian snagged another blade from his stash, ignoring how many weapons he kept at arm's length in his house. Pressing the tip of the blade to her spine, he carefully applied pressure and slid it down to her ass crack.

Lena trembled, her ass cheeks flexing as she tensed.

He wasn't going to cut her. No way did he have it in him for that. But he could sense she wanted him to do something bordering on violent.

Bite me… please, fucking bite me.

"You're mine," he said while running the flattened blade across her waist.

"Prove it," she moaned.

He nearly died hearing that. Dorian swept his fingers across her wet slit, groaning at how slick she was already. He toyed with her. "Is this what you want, Lena?" He dipped his finger into her pussy and kept her pinned and facing the wall. "No one goes to The Wicked Garden for a finger fuck." He shoved another digit inside her pussy. "Say it."

"I can't… I…." She grunted when he quickened his pace.

Her thighs shook. Hands clawed the wall paint. "I can't…"

"Can't what?" He knew the answer but wanted to hear her say it.

"I can't come," she whimpered. "Please… oh my g—"

Dorian worked her into a tight ball and burst with passion when she gushed around his fingers. Her body clamped down, pulsing, milking him. He pulled out and sucked his fingers clean. Sweet mercy, she was delicious.

Spinning her around to face him, he cupped her pussy, rubbing his thumb mercilessly on her swollen clit. Lena's mouth opened in a silent roar, and she detonated again. Dorian lifted his hand and dragged his long tongue from the heel of his palm to the tip of his middle finger. He cocked his eyebrow at her. "You were saying?"

Lena's knees buckled. "How did… how…"

"Would you prefer I take you on your knees next?" He spun her around again and dropped down behind her to grip her hips, positioning her into a bent position with her ass out and face pressed against the wall. Spreading her ass cheeks, he feasted like a man on death row with his last goddamn meal. Lena's body flushed with heat. He spun her around again, like she was his personal little toy to play with and looked up at her with a hungry gaze. Her jaw was slack, eyes heavy and cheeks red. Dorian dragged his tongue across his teeth, making her tremble with her next exhale.

Next, Dorian leaned in and licked her cunt with a slow drag of his hot tongue. Lena grunted and shoved her pussy further onto his face. He licked at her. Sucked and nipped. Shoving his finger back inside, he hit her g-spot and didn't stop until she exploded again. He watched her unravel and melt while he feasted.

She slid down to the floor, no longer able to hold herself up.

"Oh God, Dorian," she cried out and tried to crawl away from him.

"Where are you going?" He grabbed her ankles and flipped her around. If she really wanted to get away, she wouldn't have spread her thighs as an invitation for him right then. Fuck, she was stunning. Biting back the urge to take her on the floor, Dorian picked Lena up and carried her to the edge of the bed. Forcing her backwards, Dorian kissed her hard and fingered her again, easily coaxing one more orgasm to blast through her starved body. She scratched his arms and back, his body flexed, and goosebumps erupted along his arms while she came again.

"Draw blood next time," he growled and sucked his fingers clean again.

Lena let out a half-moan, half-growl, and she somehow managed to flip them over and reverse positions. "Careful, Reaper, only one of us is in charge in this position," she cupped his balls and caressed his cock. "And it isn't you."

His laugh quickly turned to a hiss when she sailed down his torso, grabbed his cock, and sucked the tip. "Jesus, woman."

"Fuck my mouth, Dorian." She wrapped her lips around his head again, and his goddamn brain glitched. He gripped a handful of her hair and thrust his hips, fucking her pretty mouth and hitting the back of her throat. She gagged and he loved it. When he pulled back, she grazed his length with her teeth and his balls tightened. Lena looked up at him, and he swore she was more animal than he was with that predator's gaze she shot him with. Flattening her tongue, she took more of him down her throat.

He nearly came at the sight of being devoured like that.

But he wasn't fast with things he enjoyed. No, no, no, Dorian took his time.

Sliding his hand under her chin, he said, "Lick me, don't suck." He popped out of her mouth, and he watched her pink tongue twirl playfully along his shaft.

He groaned as she scraped her teeth along his cock again when he slid out of her mouth. "Get up here and ride my face."

Her round ass was going to wear his handprints before the

night was over. Her pussy glistened in the candlelight, all puffy and swollen with need as she crawled up his body shamelessly flushed and eager to obey. Her thighs were thick and muscular. Back toned. His mouth watered while his tongue snaked out to lick her cunt while she sucked him off.

Lena lost her rhythm long before he did. She pitched forward, releasing his cock from her mouth and screamed. Dorian held her steady and gripped both her hips while he feasted on her climax. He maneuvered her around and flipped her over. She was breathless and spent, and they only just started.

"How long since you've come?" He dragged his tongue over his mouth to savor every drop. This was nothing but an appetizer. "How long?"

"Months," she gasped with agony lacing her voice.

"Do you know why?"

"I can't ever get out of my head," she rasped. "I can't make myself come. I can't ever—"

"*I'm* the only one who can satisfy you," he growled against her ear.

It was the truth. When a mate was on the cusp of transition—prime and ripe for turning by their mate—they lost the ability of self-satisfaction. They'd seek some form of release, but it was never between their legs.

Dorian was caught between pity and elation for her. To not be able to reach that sweet climax on her own, or by another's passionate touch, was a gruesome level of agony.

His beastly side purred with pride and possession. She was his. *His.* Her orgasms, her cries, her soul, her blood all belonged to him.

Lena. Belonged. To. Him.

For one night, Dorian was going to bask in this victory.

He pressed her head down, "Ass up, Lena. Spread your thighs wider for me."

Her obedience and trust made him nearly lose control of his impending orgasm. Sliding two fingers into her slick heat, Dorian pumped, hitting that notorious spot to make her scream his name until she ran out of breath again.

It didn't take long for her thighs to start quivering. At this angle, behind her, he was able to focus on her body and not her veins — the saving grace of this whole operation — and Dorian pulled his fingers out just as her inner walls clamped down.

Lena screamed bloody murder and clawed the sheets. He plunged back in and said, "Don't you dare come from my hand again. You cream on my cock and nothing else."

Even his tongue would have to wait for another turn.

Lena tensed, her breathing labored, and he felt her inner walls tense again. He pulled out before she could come.

She asked for edging in that club, and he hadn't forgotten it.

"Dorian, please!" Lena was now sweating and shaking.

She asked for this. Not him.

He was merely her servant tonight.

"Dorian, please!" Lena unraveled in his bed and clawed the sheets. She dug her fingers into his pillow when he said, "Hold still," and braced herself.

The bed shifted, his weight no longer causing the mattress to dip.

Cool air hit her ass and damned if she didn't almost start crying. This wasn't what she expected to have happen between them. Not his forceful commands. Not his dominating grip. And not his —

She whimpered incoherent pleas into the pillow when Dorian shoved an ice cube inside her.

"Stay. Still," he ordered again.

She tried. Damnit, she tried, but then his mouth latched onto her pussy and he *sucked*. Her clit was already a throbbing, sensitive time bomb and when used his wicked tongue on her, Lena felt another glorious orgasm barrel down the tracks to run her over.

He pulled back *again* and she heard the ice cube crush in his mouth as he ate it. *No, no, no!* Lena felt unraveled and completely out of control. A hot ache seared her core. Tears streamed down her face. She needed another release so bad, her head spun with the desperation for it.

Was this... was this even a smidgeon of what Dorian's blood curse was like? To long for something so fiercely and not find it. To have a temporary satisfaction that did nothing to truly soothe the ache in his soul? This seemed like a piss poor comparison, but it hit home for her. Lena lifted from the mattress, obeying the whims of her lover's touch. "Dorian." She swiped her tears away. "Please... let me fall."

He'd had her on the cliff of pleasure so long now, it was starting to hurt. This was exactly like how every night had been by herself, alone with her fingers and desperate attempts to find release. So close and yet... nothing.

She'd sell her soul to get this release.

"You asked for this." He rolled her hips back, so her ass was in the air again. "You wanted to be edged."

She did. He was right.

"I need you," she said without thought.

Dorian froze... "It'll pass."

The coldness in his tone was lined with a razor-sharp edge to it. He was giving her a taste of what a night would be like with a mate. It made this feel too final, too fast, too frightening. Lena refused to acknowledge the instincts in her gut. *This can't end. This can't be all there is.*

"I want to bury myself inside you." He licked up her spine, making her arch from the trail-blazing heat of his tongue.

"Do it." Her heart was a wild thing in her body, clashing everywhere. "Take me Dorian. Even... even if you won't keep me. Take me tonight."

He made a strained sound in response. She shivered when he caressed her sides. She couldn't feel her bruises anymore. Couldn't feel anything but Dorian. Then he grabbed her hair and twisted it into a rope around his hand. His gaze was pure fire. "Are you sure?"

Tears stung the backs of her eyes because this torment was going to linger in her, soul-deep, and would hurt like hell later. How long had she searched for her place in this world? How long had she hunted acceptance? The darker her days became, the more violent her nights.

Was she going to forever be in a state of lonely suspense?

Her thoughts shattered when the blunt tip of Dorian's cock rubbed against her clit. "Answer me, Lena. I need to hear you say it. Are you sure you want this?"

"Yes," she groaned.

Then her mouth opened in a silent scream as he pressed the head of his cock to her opening and began pushing his way inside. "So wet." He pushed a little more, retreating then pushing more inside each time. "That's it... fuck, you're tight." He bottomed out and Lena gasped. He filled her, stretched, and stroked her.

She nearly came again at the thought. Greedy, Lena tried to shove backwards to make him move.

"Easy." He held her hips steady. "We need to go slow until you adjust to my size. I don't want to hurt you."

"But I want that pain." She trembled against him. "Please. I need to check out."

Dorian was eerily still for a moment and growled low in his chest. Then he slammed into her, going balls deep, and Lena roared with how much he filled her. He hadn't been all the way before... now he was. Huge difference.

Massive.

The sting and ache quickly soothed away to a glorious friction.

"Fuck, Lena. I can't believe how perfect you are."

Perfect was one thing she most certainly was not. Lena made that clear when she ground her ass into him, forcing Dorian to rail her harder and she said, "Spank me. Put your handprints on me."

She wanted to be owned. Marked. Spent and adored. And damnit she wanted his teeth to sink into her too. All while he took her from behind. Whether this was real or not, fantasy or fucked up, she wanted to be ridden hard and made boneless. She wanted to drip in come, sweat, and blood.

Dorian's grip tightened. "Stop talking or I won't be able to control myself."

Lena hadn't realized she'd confessed those things out loud. With a wild grin she kicked backwards and nailed Dorian in the leg with her heel. He reeled back as she scrambled up the bed. "If I wanted a man with control, I'd have stayed at home instead of coming to New Orleans, Dorian."

He swept his hand across his mouth. His eyes glowed in the dim candlelight. His fangs gleamed when he licked his canines. Perched at the foot of the bed, cock hard and glistening, Dorian snarled at her. "You don't know what you're playing with, Lena."

She slid off the bed and sashayed her hips as she backed away from him. Dorian ran his palms along his thighs, as if his hands itched to touch her again. He looked poised to attack her. Their gazes remained deadlocked as she said, "I came here looking for danger."

"You found him." Dorian lunged off the bed and pinned her to the ground.

Lena's heart leapt in her throat when he spread her thighs with his knee, at the same time he kissed the breath out of her. "I'm not good for you." He centered the head of his cock to her opening again.

"I don't believe that," she said, wrapping her legs around his waist and raised her hips. He thrust into her, making them both groan. "No one bad can feel this good." Lena threaded her fingers through his curly hair and gripped the nape of his neck again. "Fuck, you feel incredible."

His teeth grazed her neck, and she tilted her head, silently begging him to go all the way and sink his fangs in. Her desire to be bitten before was nothing compared to the blaze of desperation burning in her body now.

"Please!" she cried out.

Dorian's voice cracked as he thrust into her harder. "I can't do this to you." Yet his speed picked up. His force. His tension.

Lena lost her patience and slapped him.

Dorian stopped moving immediately. Poised above her, his cock still buried in her body, Dorian's gaze went from stunned to savage. Lena's heart galloped around, looking for a place to hide. His gaze darkened, pupils blowing wide. Dorian's body tensed on top of hers. His lips curled back, fangs sharp and glinting.

Damn if she didn't strike him again.

Or... she tried. Dorian caught her hand and pinned it above her head. Then he fucked her so hard, Lena couldn't do anything but bear down and take his fury.

It felt amazing. Too amazing. *Soooo amazing.* Dorian held her throat, forcing her to look at him. *"Lena."* His voice was deeper, darker...

It set her off like a rocket. She clamped down on him and screamed through a violent orgasm. It was endless, and with each thrust he made, sliding them across his bedroom floor, she relished in the rug burn on her back and the sting of his grip. Dorian's head tipped back, and he roared. His cock twitched and jerked inside her and an ungodly heat filled her up as he came.

Dorian braced himself to keep from collapsing on top of her. He fought to catch his breath. Trembling, he dipped his head down and his curly hair fell forward to hide his eyes.

"Dorian," she unlocked her legs from around his waist.

He pulled out, but still wouldn't look at her. A chill swept over her skin as she reached out to touch his arm. His hand whipped out and caught her wrist, keeping her from touching him.

"*Dorian.*" This time her tone was more severe.

"I almost... I almost..." He rocked back on his heels and stood. His body nothing short of chiseled perfection. His golden skin coated in a sheen of sweat, his muscles rippling with each breath he tried to suck in. Running a hand through his hair, Dorian pivoted, then swung back and let his gaze roam her body. "Are you hurt?"

Lena didn't realize she was crying.

He scooped her into his arms and laid her on the bed, checking out every place he'd touched her. "I should cut my hands off for marking you like this," he growled.

"That's dumb." She wiped her tears away.

"It's deserved."

"Well, if you do that, how else will you be able to do this to me again?"

Dorian sat on the side of the bed. He was trembling something fierce.

"Hey." She leaned forward. "I'm fine." Lena was more than fine. Her tears weren't because he hurt her. He'd done no such thing. She was crying because—

"One night," his voice cracked in the darkness. "I said I wanted one night with you then I'd die knowing I attempted to love." Dorian swept the hair from his face and glared at her. "I don't want you for one night." He started to choke up. "I want you for forever."

It would have been such a romantic moment if his window hadn't shattered when a Molotov cocktail crashed through it and burst on the floor. Flames erupted. Lena screamed.

"Get down!" Dorian threw a blanket over her head and carried her out of the bedroom.

CHAPTER 23

Torn between getting Lena to safety and putting out the fire in his bedroom, it was a no brainer. Dorian chose Lena. His house could burn, nothing mattered but her. Slinging her over his shoulder, Dorian ran out of the bedroom with her wrapped in a blanket. Once he got Lena someplace safe, he would hunt down the fucker who did this. No one threatened him, or her, and got away with it.

Swinging open his front door, he ran smack into Lucian. Thankfully, that vampire hadn't actually left. Dorian knew he'd stay close, even after his attitude earlier. Lucian must have stayed to guard them for the night. He was gracious like that.

"Motherfucker!" Lucian snarled. "I didn't see them. By the time I heard the crash, they were already gone. I have no clue how they got past me without me sensing them."

"No scent?"

Lucian looked a little ashamed. "None I could catch in time."

"Take Lena for me." Dorian placed her down on the ground and swiftly rearranged the blanket to fully cover her and cupped her face. "Are you okay?"

"I'm fine."

Dorian shoved a finger at Lucian, "Guard her with your life, understand me?"

"I've got her. Go!"

Dorian ran back inside the house. He needed to grab Lena's things before they burned—if it wasn't already too late. The fire wasn't spreading fast. It was partially because he didn't have much

168

in his home to catch fire. His bed, however, was already a massive torch. His clothes would be next.

Grabbing her dress from the floor, he pressed the fabric to his face to filter the air. Then he ran into the kitchen, and, in a last-ditch effort to save what little he had, grabbed the fire extinguisher from under his sink. Running back in, he sprayed everything.

The fire died out and the air remained smokey. Furious, he glanced around, relieved the damage wasn't worse.

"Dorian!" Lena yelled.

At the sound of her voice, he turned just as she ran back into his bedroom. He dropped the fire extinguisher with a clank and stormed over to her. "I said to stay out!" But his anger went MIA once he pressed his lips to hers. "I have to get you someplace safe."

"I'm not going anywhere." She pushed away from him to look at the damage from the fire and all the shattered glass on the floor.

Dorian yanked her back. "There's too much glass everywhere. You'll cut yourself."

Not only did he not want her hurt, but if she cut her feet, the scent of her blood would have him undone. He couldn't afford to lose what little bit of clarity he'd somehow gained tonight.

Lena's brow furrowed. "Who did this? Do you have any idea?"

"The property's clear," Lucian huffed from the doorway.

"I told you to keep her safe, Lucian."

"Yeah, well," he stopped to catch his breath. "There's no stopping her from getting to you, man. She nearly took my nuts off just now."

Dorian faced Lena and grabbed her shoulders. "You can't be here."

"I'm not leaving."

He noticed she was holding one of his weapons in her hand. She must have snagged it from his counter on the way back inside. Why did that have to stir need in him right now when he had prey to hunt down and kill?

"This world's too dangerous for you," he growled.

"And I'm not easy to spook. I go with you. This was just as much an attack on me as it was on you." She jabbed the business end of the knife at the broken window. "Whoever did this, watched us, Dorian. They specifically chose your bedroom at this exact time. That's not a coincidence. I refuse to believe otherwise."

She was right. He didn't want to point that out to her, but it's exactly what he'd been thinking too. A possessive growl ripped out of his throat. The idea of someone peeping through his window and seeing Lena naked made his blood boil. He whirled around and went to his closet. Nearly ripping the door off its hinges, he searched for something better than a blanket to cover her with.

Tossing her a black t-shirt and a pair of his sweatpants, he swallowed around the lump in his throat. "Put these on." He swiftly got dressed.

Lucian kept watch in the doorway, his back respectfully turned to them. "This is a major slap in the face, Dorian."

"I know."

"No one's been bold enough to attack like this before. And with *fire*. Fuck that."

"I know."

"Maybe it was someone just being an asshole?" Lena buttoned her shirt. "Just a... human?"

"No human is that foolish. I've lived here a long time. No one fucks with me like this." It was a deliberate move by an enemy.

"We need to run another perimeter check." Lucian played with his blade. "Something's off about this entire attack. Why go for just one blaze? If they wanted your house to burn, they could have been way more thorough."

"My thoughts exactly. This was just to smoke us out. Why?" Dorian yanked on a pair of pants and zippered them up. "I'm just glad I got Lena out in time."

"There wasn't much damage," Lena frowned, pulling on the pair of pants he gave her.

"No, but what if some of that fuel splashed onto you and burned you?" He stared at her. "I... shit, I can't even let my head go there." He finished putting on his clothes and went back into his closet again. Snagging a box from the back, he punched in the codes and yanked out a gun.

"You have stabby shit all over your house, but you lock up your gun?" Lena grabbed a particularly sexy blade and palmed the handle, testing it out. "You make no sense."

"This isn't a regular gun," Dorian answered cautiously.

Holding up a bullet, he let her see the glowing purple killing juice inside it. "These are specifically for *Savag-Ri*. It's got a poison in it that can slow them down."

"Not kill them?"

"It can definitely kill them," Dorian said as his smile went predatory. "But I enjoy taking that pleasure myself with a little more intimacy." Like his hands and teeth.

Lena let out a trembling puff of air. "This is nuts."

Dorian grabbed her hand and started leading her outside the bedroom again with Lucian behind them. "Which part? That you're stuck in this shitshow or what I just admitted about myself to you?"

Because both made him feel horrible.

"I'd rather not answer right now." Lena held the blade between her teeth while she pulled her hair back and tied it in a knot.

Dorian's heart clenched over her refusing to answer his question. But honestly, he didn't think he could stand hearing what she had to say. He knew he was deranged. He knew it was all his fault that she was roped into this nightmare.

Lucian halted in the living room and put his hand up, stopping everyone. Silently, he turned his head to look at Dorian and then pointed up.

Someone was on the roof.

Dorian glanced at Lena and put his finger to his lips, "Shhh" he told her without making a sound.

Lena nodded and gripped her blade tighter, spreading her feet about shoulder width apart, like she planned to attack the intruder should they fall though the damned ceiling. Lucian moved with speed and dashed outside. Dorian tipped his head and focused on the movements of whoever was above them.

At least his hearing had improved. Was it the king's blood or Lena's closeness making him stronger?

Or was it something else?

A loud thump raised Dorian's hackles. Lucian hollered from outside and Dorian ran towards the front door, only to find Lena already beating him to the chase.

Shit, was he slowing down, or had she sped up?

What the fuck was going on here?

"Down there!" Lucian roared. "The other went this way!" He

started running in the opposite direction.

The sun would be rising soon, the streets were beginning to lighten. They needed to catch this bastard and kill him before they had witnesses waking up to make their coffee and go on their morning walks.

Dorian couldn't run with Lena trying to keep up. And he couldn't leave her at the house unguarded. While he tripped over his conscience, Lena dashed down the road. Dorian sped up and stopped her. "Take the car and go," he ordered. "Now, Lena."

"Key?"

"Already in there. Center console" Lucian always left a spare fob in the car in case of something like this.

Dorian watched her jump into Lucian's car, and he let out a sigh of relief when the engine roared to life.

"Go! Go!" She peeled wheels, leaving Dorian to run after this bastard on his own.

Dorian picked up speed and ran down the street, cutting through yards, eagerly trying to catch a scent trail. Only he couldn't find one that marked it as a *Savag-Ri*.

To his left, one block up, wheels screeched. Dorian's breath caught. Cutting across the street, he saw Lucian's car parked in the middle of the street, the driver's side door open.

No Lena.

With a loud, animalistic roar, Dorian kicked into high gear and followed her scent. She went south, towards the main road. Lucian was hot on his heels—his speed far superior than Dorian's right now. Blades out and ready, the two vampires beat feet across the yards with enough speed to go undetected by humans. "Over there!" Dorian hollered.

Lena was on the ground, fighting against someone nearly twice her size.

Dorian. Saw. Red.

The attacker's hooded head popped up just as Dorian and Lucian closed in on him. He yanked Lena by her hair and held a blade to her neck. Dorian couldn't move without risk of this fucker slicing her throat wide open.

It was a sacrifice he couldn't make, even after Lena yelled, "Do it!"

Dorian hesitated. But when the bastard's blade began to slide across her neck and Lena's eyes squeezed shut, Dorian dropped his blade and pulled out his gun. Popping off every round in his chamber, he blasted the attacker's face into ground meat. The headless sonofabitch shook and convulsed on the street then caught fire, leaving nothing of his remains but ash and smoke.

Vampire.

Dorian's heart slammed into his throat, mortified. He grabbed Lena to get her away from the remains. Holy shit, how was this possible?

Lucian rushed to their side and skidded to a halt. "A *vampire* did this?" His words were laced with venom.

No sense in answering, they both knew what they were looking at. Since Dorian had used the *Savag-Ri* specific ammo on the cocksucker, his ashes swiftly melted into sticky goo on the street, making him completely unidentifiable. They had nothing to go on.

Lucian swiped a hand over his mouth before saying, "I couldn't catch the other one. They got away."

"Any scent?"

"None I recognized."

"This could be Marius's doing," Dorian growled. He didn't want to assume the old king would go this far, but, "He's gunning for me and I have no idea why. Those guys were strong enough to flash, that's why you couldn't catch them."

"Then why didn't they flash completely away from us instead of hanging back?"

"No clue." Dorian thought of how some Lycan loved to fuck with their prey. How they loved to watch it struggle and trip up before corning them and going for the kill.

Could it be a Lycan?

No. Impossible. Besides, their scent would be everywhere, and it was too distinct to miss.

Then who? And why?

Lucian tipped his boot in the sludge. "We need to go back to the mansion and report this."

"I'm not taking Lena near another of our kind. Not until..." Dorian bit back the rest of his words. Until what? He died? He sorted this out? He turned her? None of those sounded best for Lena. "She can't go back there with us."

"Then where?" Lucian argued. "Your house is compromised."

"I'm taking her home." Dorian held Lena tighter, concerned over her silence.

Lucian cocked his brow. "Home as in *pack* land?"

"Yeah." He kissed the top of his mate's head and ignored the fact that she wasn't talking, or even shaking—regardless of being attacked, held at knife point, and just had bullets whizzing past her face. Going by the scent rolling off her sweet skin...

She *liked* it.

CHAPTER 24

Lena replayed the last ten minutes in her head while remaining completely silent all the way back to Dorian's house. In the background she could hear Dorian and Lucian talking about stuff, but she wasn't in the state of mind to focus on them. She was too busy rehashing Dorian's fatal move on that guy who'd held a knife to her neck.

"*Do it.*" She'd screamed. What a fucked-up thing to say. It was too loaded of a request. Do it. *Slice my neck so I bleed for Dorian.* Do it. *Shoot this guy and save me.* Do it. *Kill him.* She exhaled a shaky sigh and clenched her fists in her lap as they pulled up to Dorian's house. After he opened the door for her, she slid out of the back seat, still unable to speak.

His face, she thought. The razor-sharp edge of his clenched jaw, those needle-sharp canines showing as he hissed, the deep lines set in his brow when he ran up on her and her attacker. Dorian was terrifying. Fierce. Confident and savage.

Hot. As. Hell.

And when that asshole held the knife across her neck? Dorian pulled the trigger. Emptied his chamber without blinking. Without remorse.

Was it too soon to say she was madly in love?

Probably. Yeah, no, definitely.

His eyes. Lena sucked in a deep breath and let it out nice and slow. Dorian's eyes had been swallowed in blackness and his body looked so tense, it was a miracle he was able move at all. Not to romanticize him blasting some dude's head clean off, because killing was bad and blah, blah, blah. But… there was a primal, feral and dangerous quality to Dorian she sensed just under the surface, and now she had proof of his ferociousness.

"I came here looking for danger."

"You found him."

He hadn't lied about that.

"I'm never going to lie to you." Dorian didn't hide his true nature from her either. He told her the truth, no matter how crazy it sounded. The clencher was how easily she kept accepting his stories. She trusted him. Lena never trusted anyone she just met, yet here she was. Breaking her own damn rules.

It was instinct to do so.

"He'll never hurt you. In fact, he'd raze this world if he thought that's what it took to protect you."

Or blow the bastard's head clean off.

"Hey," Dorian tipped her chin up and stared at her with a frown on his handsome face. "Did you hear what I just said?"

Nope. Lena gulped and her gaze roamed across his features. His eyes were back to green. His hair, a riot of curls, fell into his eyes again. He clenched his jaw and she knew, *just knew,* he'd bitten the inside of his lip and drawn blood. How could she know that? "I'm sorry, no."

"She's in shock," Lucian leaned in to look at her. "You need to sit down?"

"I'm fine," she said quietly.

This was going to take time to process. She was far from fine, but what made her fearful wasn't what happened. It was what was *going* to happen. Lena slammed her heart into a box and followed them into Dorian's house. Fine, white powder coated everything. The smell of chemicals from the fire extinguisher and the remaining smoke knocked her out of her stupor, so she grabbed her purse and went over to Dorian's line up of killer toys.

"Take your pick." Dorian squeezed her shoulders, lightly massaging them. "You won't need them on pack land, but if you'd feel safer loaded, then by all means, take anything of mine you see."

Pack land. What the hell was that? "Where are we going?"

And why was she so willing to leave? Lena didn't back down from anyone, ever. No matter how scary a situation got, Lena didn't back down. She embraced it. Sometimes almost hadn't survived it.

"I'm taking you someplace safe."

"You said the mansion was safe. The Wicked Garden, was supposed to be safe. This house, was supposed to be safe." Lena turned around and shoved her finger in his chest. "Nowhere is safe, Dorian. We can't run forever."

"I don't have forever," he said quietly. "And if it's all the same to you, I'd rather know you're safe so I can—"

"Die in peace?" Lena rounded on him again and shoved her finger back in his face. "You bring me into this life and then have the balls to abandon me to wolves?"

She didn't know then, how very accurate that accusation was. But she was about to find out.

Dorian strangled the steering wheel and kept his gaze on the road. He refused to let Lena drive. So long as he had his vision, he was going to take control and cling to it for however long he had left. Lena kept quiet for the past three hours. Every once in a while, he caught her swiping her cheeks and smelled her salty tears.

He couldn't do a damned thing to console her.

She was right. Dorian was taking her onto Lycan territory and hoped like hell they showed her the same grace and mercy they once showed him when he stumbled into their lives half-dead and in dire need of help.

Lucian had headed back to the mansion to do damage control. Again. Holy Hell, he owed Lucian so much and now there was no time to repay that vampire for all his devotion. Dorian looked behind him again, feeling like an asshole for not having a rearview mirror in his car.

"It would help if your fancy car came with mirrors," Lena crossed her arms and rested her head against the window.

"I made it a habit to stay clear of them."

"Until me."

Dorian swallowed around the lump in his throat. She probably felt rejected and used and he didn't blame her for it. "It's complicated."

"It's life or death. I get the complication. But it didn't save you, did it?"

Her tone drove him to the brink of madness. He wished he could kiss the pain out of her voice. Soothe her worried mind. Fuck the anger and resentment out of her body. But he couldn't. What happened was a mistake on his part.

All of this was a big mistake on his part.

"I'm sorry," he said for the billionth time.

Lena's sadness dripped in her voice when she replied, "Me too."

Lena fell asleep and when she woke, there was no way of telling where they were or how far they'd gone. She really didn't care either. Going by the sunlight, it was past lunchtime though. With all that had happened, she wasn't even hungry. As they headed toward "pack land" she went from hurt, to angry, to depressed, to salty.

The car was too silent. Lena hated it.

"My parents hated me." She pressed herself against the passenger side door as if the more space she put between her and Dorian, the less she'd want to touch him.

"I'm... sorry. That must have been hell."

"They died in a plane crash on their way home from a business venture in Sweden." Lena was nineteen at the time. "They left me a small fortune, but I guess you knew about that when you stalked me."

"Lucian said you were the heir to the McKay fortune, but I didn't know what that meant. He and I don't run in the same social circles."

Lena bit her lip and tried to figure out what that was supposed to mean. Dorian and Lucian looked like well-dressed models who just stepped out of a magazine. But clothes didn't make the man. Attitude did. Lena wondered if they would've run into each other somewhere along the way even if he hadn't seen her in the mirror.

"Anyway, I invested most of my inheritance in small business ventures, stocks, and scholarship funds."

"Vampire Tacos lady?"

"Count Tacola," Lena grinned. "Yeah. Her name's Carmen."

"Is she a close friend?"

"No," Lena admitted. "But she helped me once and I never forgot it. This was a way for me to pay her back."

Dorian pulled onto an exit. "You have a big heart."

"I just have deep pockets and guilt. Imposter syndrome is also a bitch."

"You're not an imposter if you own your truths. You're an heiress and a philanthropist. Nothing wrong with that."

"It feels wrong to have inherited the money." She blew out a big breath. "I wasn't exactly the poster child for the perfect daughter."

"Perfection's rarely seen in the mirror," Dorian said. A smile spread across his face, though he kept his eyes on the road. "That is until I saw you in the mirror."

She rolled her eyes. "Lame."

He laughed and it was the first time she heard it. It surprised her. Warmed her. Made her smile.

"What about you? Where did you grow up, Transylvania?"

"Not quite." He grinned as they pulled onto a dirt road. Dorian slowed to a stop. "Are you ready to meet my family?"

The sound of ATVs roared up ahead with howls riding on the wind.

CHAPTER 25

"Well look who finally came back for a visit!" Emerick hopped off his ATV and clasped Dorian's arm. "Just in time for the ceremony. Damn, brother, never thought you'd come for one of them. Did Emily talk you into it?"

Shit, the ceremony. Dorian had completely forgotten about it. And Emily. Shit, she was going to think he was a hypocrite once she met Lena.

"She might have mentioned it," Dorian said quietly.

"She's been a total bugaboo lately. The girl's wound tight and being pent up on pack land isn't helping." Emerick's golden gaze swung to Lena. "And who's this slice of paradise?"

"This is Lena McKay." Dorian pulled her into his arms, automatically getting way too protective and possessive of her again. He knew no one here was a threat, but he couldn't stop himself. His instincts screamed to keep her close and safe at all times.

Mark her. Turn her. Bond.

He saw the realization dawn on Emerick. The shifter's eyes peeled wide, and he stood stock-still while staring at Dorian. "Hoolllyyyy shiiiit, brother." Emerick's gaze snapped to Lena again and his playful nature dropped as he bowed his head low, "I'm Emerick Woods. First son of Alistair. Beta."

"Lena." She held her hand out for him to shake. "Just Lena."

Emerick's gaze lingered on her face before issuing a quick survey of the rest of her. "Nice clothes," he said with a big grin. "Reaper's wardrobe suits you."

Dorian thought so too, but only because he enjoyed her wearing his possessions for other reasons. His scent would be all over her, offering one more layer of protection. Those who knew Dorian well enough didn't fuck with him or anyone who belonged to him. Those who did seek him harm, would soon be killed anyway. It was just a bonus that her sweet skin would be saturated in his scent for his own selfish reasons.

Emerick cleared his throat. "Let's get you up to the house. Emily's gonna wanna see this, and I'm making popcorn for it." He smacked Dorian's arm and added, "Mom's making a big dinner for tonight. She's going to shit a brick when she sees you."

Mom. Dorian's heart swelled at the mere thought of Marie. She'd been a mother to him when no one else would bother to look in his direction let alone show him kindness or offer a warm meal. She and Alistair took Dorian in the night he nearly died escaping his father and raised him as one of their own.

He rarely visited pack land anymore. The more dirty work he did for the House of Death, the less worthy he felt of being on pack land. But that was on him, not them. They never made him feel like a monster. Wolves were understanding killers themselves.

"Come on." Dorian's voice was low and gravelly. He ran the back of his hand against Lena's arm and offered her a smile. "I want you to meet the rest of my family."

As they hopped onto Emerick's ATV, Dorian's heart sluggishly pounded in his chest. It tripped up and struggled to find its rhythm again. Dorian's vision blackened. He slumped over the handlebars.

"Dorian?" Lena's hand pressed against his spine. "Are you okay?"

He inhaled forest air while his heart managed to get back with the regularly scheduled program. "I'm fine." He hoped. Dorian caught Emerick watching from the edge of the woods and saw him mouth the word *Fuck.* Then Emerick shifted into his wolf form, shredding his clothes in the process, and howled to let the others know company was coming.

"Oh my God," Lena gasped. "Did he just—"

"Yeah." Dorian managed to smile. "Welcome to pack land."

Dorian's body was hot to the touch, even with the wind blasting them as they headed up the dirt road on the ATV. Lena's mind raced. A vampire raised by werewolves? But didn't Lucian tell her something about werewolves and vampires hating each other?

Someone didn't have their stories right.

That dissection could be left for another day. Right now, Lena's adrenaline was spiking again with the rush of everything around her. Pack land. Werewolves. Vampires. Ceremony. What's the ceremony? Oh no, she hoped it wasn't some kind of human sacrifice.

Wait. They usually had to be virgins, right? *Phew!* She was safe then.

Up ahead, a huge log cabin with smoke piping through the chimney lay nestled in the thick woods. The wrap around porch, firewood stacked off to the side, chimes hanging in the trees, and a hammock that had seen better days, made the place look enchanting.

The front door swung open and a giant stepped out wiping his hands with a towel. "Dorian." His smile was toothy like a predator's.

Dorian climbed off the ATV with Lena and made his way over to the big man. "Been a while. Sorry."

"Never be sorry, son. You're busy protecting your own. No apologies for that." The gigantic man turned his attention to Lena. "Well, I'll be damned."

He didn't look happy to see her. He looked scared shitless.

"I'm Alistair." He shoved his humongous hand out.

"Lena."

"Lena, what a beautiful name for such a miraculous creature." He brought her hand up and kissed her knuckles. "You look like you've been to war, child. What's going on?"

"Dorian!" Shouted a female from inside the house. The door swung open again and a young gorgeous black-haired beauty came dashing out. She halted the second she saw Lena.

It made the hair on Lena's arms stand on end. "Hi," she said with a wave. "I'm Lena." She really needed to come up with a better way to introduce herself. Especially after Emerick's big intro.

182

"Emily," Alistair barked, "Get your mother out here. Now."

Emily didn't budge. She was staring at Dorian, her face six shades of red.

"Now, Emily!"

"We'll go inside," Dorian said. "No need to drag Marie out of her natural habitat."

Alistair huffed a small laugh and put his arm around Dorian's shoulder. "I'm glad you came." He kissed Dorian's curly head. "Jesus Christ, we're gonna need booze for all this."

Lena's fingers linked with Dorian's and the contact made her feel warm and confident. She didn't like Emily's reaction to seeing her and Dorian. She didn't look jealous... she looked betrayed. Why?

Emerick popped out from a shed and was fully dressed in different clothes. He jogged up behind them, and his weight rocked the porch as he bounded up the steps. "This is gonna be fun."

"Shut up," Alistair growled.

The second Lena entered the house, her chest made a strange vibration. Like a weird flutter in her lungs with each breath she took.

"The sensation will pass," Dorian squeezed her hand. "Just give it a minute."

How'd he know what she was feeling? Was that a vampire thing or did he feel it too?

Music blasted from the kitchen and Alistair was the first to go in, followed by everyone else. "Look what Emerick found lurking at the bottom of the road."

"It better not be another baby skunk. I'm not taking care of anymore of those damned —"

She spun around with a spatula in her hand and dropped it the second she saw Dorian. Pure elation swarmed her features and she rushed to him, wrapping her arms around him in a huge hug. "Oh! I was beginning to think I'd never see you again! You've stayed away so long." She clasped his cheeks. "Let me look at you."

Her face fell immediately. The joy died and was replaced with something else. Then her gaze sailed over to Lena.

Let's face it, Lena was practically shrinking back at this point. Everyone kept having the same reaction. Happiness then dread.

It was directed at Dorian but meant for Lena. She could feel it.

Read it in their body language. It made her feel like an asshole and this wasn't her fault.

Instead of Marie holding her hand out, she swept Lena into a crushing embrace. "I can't believe this." When she pulled back, tears were already spilling. "Oh." She wiped them away, "Where are my manners? I'm Marie, Alistair's better half. Alpha female."

"Lena." She grinned. "Dorian's most likely crazier half. Human."

Several booming laughs rocked the kitchen. Dorian, however, didn't find it as funny as they did. He looked like he was about to keel over.

"Holy fuckballs," said a raspy deep voice. "I knew tonight was gonna be lit, never thought we'd have this much action during the pregame though."

Lena's mouth dropped when she saw who strolled into the kitchen wearing a pair of tight jeans and a Henley. Her heart literally leapt out of her. "Bane!" Without thinking, she ran at him and jumped into his arms.

She never felt so shocked or relieved to see that sonofabitch. "I can't believe this!" Several emotions swarmed her at once. The aftershocks of the past couple of days, the fear, elation, exhaustion, and tension... it poured out of her in tears. Seeing Bane, a familiar face in a sea of total strangers, made this more bearable.

More believable.

"Uhhhh." Bane continued holding her but pulled his head back to frown at her. "I'm not Bane. I'm Bowen."

Lena stiffened immediately and pushed away. "What?"

"Lena?" Another voice interrupted from the back door in the kitchen.

She looked over her shoulder and it was like having double vision. "Bane?"

Bane looked at Dorian, then Lena, then Dorian, then Lena. His hand went up to his mouth as if stifling a sound rising from his throat. His eyes widened. The backdoor slammed shut on his ass. Then he came at her, nearly taking two kitchen chairs out when he stormed across the kitchen and lifted her into his arms. "I can't believe you're actually standing in my mother's kitchen."

Lena clung to Bane and cried even harder because this guy was *definitely* the right one. He smelled like Bane. Hugged like Bane.

Felt like Bane.

She started rambling incoherent words against his shoulder and he rocked her saying, "Shhhhh, it's gonna be fine. Damn, girl, don't do this. It's gonna be fine. You're safe."

"How do you two know each other?" Dorian's voice was laced with aggression.

Bane peeled Lena off of him on that note. "We fight in a club together."

Dorian's jaw clenched. His eyes sailed over her face again. "That's how you got all those bruises?"

She didn't know what to say. Was he going to laugh at her for fighting? Be angry? Want to know more? The only way to belong to that fight ring was to never breathe a word about it. But if Bane admitted this much, maybe she could too?

"I told you I earned and asked for them." Did they think she was crazy for fighting all the time? Well, tough shit. She liked it and had no plans of getting a different hobby. Still, their unwavering gazes were a little heavy on her confidence and she dropped her gaze to the floor.

Dorian placed his finger under her chin and tipped her head back up. "Never drop your gaze, Lena. Not with me. Not with any of us."

She rounded her shoulders, figuring she might as well confess more about herself. "I'm one of the reigning champions in an underground fight club and the only female. I've been in it for close to three years now."

She could have heard a pin drop. Even the music stopped playing.

Dorian's eyes darkened. "And you fight with *Bane*?"

"Had my ass kicked by her twice."

"He held back." Lena narrowed her gaze at Bane. "*Clearly.*"

Dorian wheeled around and slammed Bane against a wall. "You hit my mate for fun?"

"Relax, brother." Bane put his hands up, even while Dorian choked him. "She holds her own. She's fearless. No shifters or vampires are allowed to use their extra abilities in a fight. We go as humans and fight like them."

The air whooshed out of Lena and she rocked back on her heels. "How many of you are there in the club?" She had no clue she went up against werewolves and vampires. For some reason, it made her feel a little betrayed. She'd been duped. It also made her confidence skyrocket because if she could handle them in a bare-knuckle fight, she could handle anything else they tried on her now. Dorian didn't have to worry so much.

"A bunch," Bane shrugged. "You gonna let me go or are you gonna continuing pinning me, Reaper? Cause if we're gonna be here a while, I'd like some pie. You can spoon feed it to me while you lightly choke me and tell me I'm pretty."

Dorian, surprisingly, chuckled and let him go.

Bane tugged on his shirt and cracked his neck. "I love you, man."

Lena was back to feeling confused and lost. She wanted Dorian to look at her and he wasn't. She wanted to say something more to him but couldn't.

Did he think she was crazy for fighting? Was it because she was a woman? Was it because she and Bane had a history, and he didn't like that?

Well tough shit.

"How about we get you some new clothes," Marie said sweetly. "You look like you could use a little freshening up."

Now Lena was insulted. Regardless of whether Marie was right or not, Lena didn't need it pointed out that she looked like a train wreck in men's clothing. But she also didn't want to stay in the kitchen with Dorian and everyone else if they were going to continue acting like she was a plague or something.

"Yes, that would be great." Lena finally said, her gaze penetrating Dorian. She wanted him to look at her, and say something, *anything*. But he didn't. His shoulders slumped and his head bowed, fists remaining clenched at his side. She shoved past him, knocking into him as she left the kitchen.

Dorian wasn't the only dangerous one in their fated relationship.

Maybe it was giving him second thoughts?

CHAPTER 26

"You found the perfect girl." Bane dropped his ass into a chair and pulled an entire pie over to him. Snagging a fork, he dug in. "Why do you look like you've just been told your puppy died?"

"I'm not turning and mating her," Dorian confessed. He, Emerick, Alistair, Bane, and Bowen all sat at the table just like old times. Emily was MIA. "I can't do that to her."

"You can't do what?" Bane shoved a heap of apple pie into his mouth and talked while chewing. "You can't give her a better life? Love her endlessly? Have your soul set free?"

Was that bitterness in his tone? You better believe it. Dorian didn't blame him for the attitude. "She deserves a lot better than me."

"Fate doesn't think so," Bowen said from Dorian's right. "Clearly."

"When I first met Lena, I thought she was a vampire already," Bane shoved another forkful into his mouth. "I was shocked as shit when I discovered she was just human. Her speed and agility have heightened over the years."

"Because she's prime for transitioning."

"That's what I suspected." He wiped his mouth with a napkin and leaned back in his chair. It creaked with his weight. "I'm the one who told her about The Wicked Garden."

Dorian glowered. "You allowed her to be food for my kind?"

"She needed to be food. She wants to be food."

Dorian shot out of his seat, lunging to attack him again. If Alistair hadn't held him back, he would have leapt across the goddamn kitchen table. "Easy, son. Your instincts are riding you too hard and it's unnecessary here."

He knew Alistair was right. No one here was a threat. In fact, if Bane hadn't told Lena about the kink club, there may have never been another chance of seeing her again since Dorian had backed out of even knocking on her door before that.

"I'd hoped she'd have made it to the third visit. Had every confidence she would. And, from there, maybe one of the vamps could help her out. Her taste for violence is impressive. And terrifying."

"You make her sound psychotic." Something Dorian didn't appreciate.

"I make her sound accurate for who she is." Bane took another bite of pie. "She's incredible. Strong, resilient."

Dorian didn't need any of Lena's qualities pointed out to him. He knew all that already from the little bit of time he'd spent with her.

"Mate her, Dorian."

He jerked his head to the side and clenched his jaw.

"You're willing to die instead of love her forever? That must really make her feel fucking special." Bane shoved away from the table, grabbed his pie, and went out the backdoor.

Dorian stared at the now vacant chair and didn't say a word.

"He's right," Alistair said. "Boys, why don't you leave us for a minute?"

Emerick and Bowen stood, their chairs noisy as they slid across the wooden floor. They left the kitchen and Dorian buried his head in his hands. "I'm no good for her."

"You're no good for yourself with that attitude." Alistair turned in his chair to face him. "If you were a monster, do you think I'd have ever taken you into my home, son?"

"You didn't know it then." But he found out soon afterwards when Dorian killed a man in front of all of them.

"That day you killed the man in the woods, do you even remember why you did it?"

Dorian tensed. He never forgot. "He was attacking Emily. He was going to rape her."

Fuuuuck. Just saying those words made Dorian want to set the world on fire. His body tensed to the point that he started trembling with pent up fury.

"You cried for two weeks afterwards. Remember?"

"I don't recall that."

"You don't recall many things." Alistair frowned. "I think some of it is because of the trauma you went through, but I also..." His mouth turned down in a frown.

"Also, what?" His voice was strangely deep. The colors in the kitchen had started fading about ten minutes ago, and now his stomach was cramping.

"Your mother and I have always wondered if your memories were erased by that bastard vampire."

"You mean the monster who sired me." He never called him father in front of Alistair. It would be an insult too huge to forgive.

"Yes," Alistair growled.

"If that's the case," Dorian said, easing back in his chair. "I wouldn't remember my time with him. And I remember every second of it... with perfect clarity."

"But you still don't recall anything before him, correct? Not even much about your mother?"

Dorian's jaw clenched. He shook his head.

No, he couldn't remember his mother at all. He only knew she had curly hair and that was because his sire always remarked about it when he shaved Dorian's head. And none of the victims ever had curly hair — something his sire was particular about. Dorian excused it as his sire missing Dorian's mother so much, he couldn't bear to kill anyone who even remotely looked like her.

That strange delusion was something Dorian cradled in his mind on dark, stormy nights when his father would go hunting. Somehow, to think his sire still longed for his mother even after her death, made him... tolerable. His madness excusable. At least the monster never turned a human into a vampire. That would have been... shit, Dorian couldn't even imagine such a gruesome outcome.

People talk about how you couldn't pick your family, and perhaps that was true. But Dorian was given a second family the day he knocked on Alistair's door and he chose to love and protect them, and they returned the devotion ten-fold.

Alistair scratched the stubble on his cheek. "Our kind and yours have always suffered this blood curse. It'll never go away. I felt unworthy of Marie when I first saw her."

"What did you do about it?"

"Proved my worth," he said with a shrug. "Still do, to this day. Even though she says it's entirely unnecessary."

"The difference between us is you're a good man. I'm not."

"Neither of us are men, Dorian. We're both savages who would gladly tear the throats out of anyone who dares to come for us and what belongs to us."

He wasn't wrong there.

"And that's what our mates deserve. Beasts who would shred the world down to its bones to keep them safe. Beasts who sink their teeth into the souls of their mate and never let go. Beasts who, each night, will curl against the love of their lives and hold them fiercely while their hearts beat as one."

Dorian didn't want to be reminded of what he was giving up. He pushed away from the table. "I can't do this."

"Then why did you come at all?" Alistair snarled.

"Because she's in danger, and I have no place to take her."

The shifter leaned back in his chair his brows furrowed. "You've never been fearful of anyone in your entire life, Dorian. It's not like you to run and hide."

"I'm not running. I plan to go back to the House in the morning."

"So, you're abandoning her with us?"

"Only until I..." Dorian didn't even know what he was about to say. *Until I die? Until I take care of this little problem of someone fucking with me?* "I just need to know she's safe while I handle some things."

"A girl who fights bare-knuckled with shifters and vampires is not the one who needs protecting."

Dorian didn't even want to think about that. Imagining Lena in a fight against anyone—let alone a male, and especially someone like Bane—did questionable things to him.

Great, he was getting a hard-on.

Alistair's laugh was cold. "I can't believe you're going to waste this gift." He shoved away from the table and left, but not before he added, "I raised you better than this, son."

190

Emily handed Lena a stack of clothing. "These should fit you."

"I'll lay out some towels in the bathroom." Marie smiled.

"This really isn't necessary. I don't mind wearing Dorian's things." She didn't miss the look on Emily's face. "If you have a problem with me, just say it. Don't give me your clothes and pretend you don't mind. I hate fake."

Gee, she was really pissy, huh? Lena closed her eyes and blew out a puff of air. "Sorry. I don't mean to be a bitch."

"We're all bitches here." Emily flashed her a sarcastic smile.

Marie rolled her eyes and pretended to straighten up the room.

"I'm just shocked this is happening, that's all." Emily plopped down on the bed that must have been hers at some point. It was girly but with a flare of punk rocker. Exactly how Emily looked dressed in a black t-shirt, skinny jeans, and hot pink fingernails. "Dorian and I just had a conversation about this only a few days ago."

Lena's jaw clenched. "And?"

"Better to live a half-life alone than chase after destiny and be killed by fate," Emily said.

Marie leaned back on the dresser, clutching her chest. "Emily."

"It's true." She crossed her arms over her chest. "He and I have always felt that way. When we lost Killian, it made Dorian's creed make all the more sense. I don't want to turn out like that."

Lena saw them both wipe away tears.

"No one wants that fate," Marie said. "But you shouldn't have to live alone. Our existence is so long. Why spend it alone?"

"I don't have to have a soulmate to be loved," Emily argued. "Neither does Dorian."

Lena got pissed. "But if someone could love you, wouldn't you want to let them?"

"Loving and mating aren't the same," Emily argued. "And both come with repercussions."

"Like?"

"Dorian's *dying*." Emily studied Lena's reaction. Her eyes widened. "Holy shit, you knew that already, didn't you?" She shot up on her feet and shook with rage. "You're just going to let him *die*? What kind of heartless bitch are you?" Her voice rose with each word she spat out.

Lena dropped the clothes on the bed and got nose-to-nose with her. "I'm not the one rejecting this whole mate thing. *Dorian's* refusing."

The truth smashed Emily far more effectively than Lena's fist ever could. Emily backed up, shaking her head, and left the room.

Marie quietly shut the door and wiped more tears from her face. "We were afraid of this. Alistair and I. Dorian's past is ugly, and it's clouded his vision of himself."

Lena crossed her arms and looked out the window. She saw Emily run out of the house and across the yard towards a barn. She also saw Dorian was already at the barn's entrance. He turned around just before he got slammed by her. He embraced her, much like Bane had Lena.

She didn't know how to feel about it, but again it wasn't jealousy. It was something else. "Can you fall in love with someone who's not your mate?"

"Yes, but it's more damning in the end. At least, I'd assume that's the case for vampires. Wolves only see their mate when they drink a specific liquid form of silver. Vampires, unless they manage to go their entire lives without seeing a single reflection, can't escape their fate so easily. But in both cases, the longing grows the longer one lives without their mate. For vampires, they're called *alakhai*. For us, it's *Deesha*."

"Are you saying Dorian could live forever had he not seen me at all?"

"As long as he wasn't killed out in the field, yes. But I fear his soul would become more hollow. His humanity could wane. He'd likely end up..."

"A monster anyway."

"Maybe." Marie sniffled. "I don't like to think of any of my children like that."

"How did Dorian come to live with werewolves? Where are his parents?" Lena rethought her question. "Or can your kind mix breeds? Can you have Lycan and vampires from the same union?"

"No," Marie lightly laughed. "Lycan only breed Lycan. No crossbreeding allowed. Especially after the curse's legend. Honestly,

I don't even think it's possible. We aren't exactly friendly with each other, so I don't think the theory has ever been tested."

"Lycan and vampires hate each other... except for you guys and Dorian."

"He was an exception. But no Lycan would ever bed him or another of his kind. Once he was old enough and had finally come to his full power and maturity, we knew we had to get him into a vampire House. Alistair made some calls and Malachi jumped on the opportunity to meet him. Dorian chose the House of Death, King Malachi's House, and we moved here and took over this territory to stay a little closer to him. Alistair insisted."

Wait a second. "How old is Dorian?"

"Over three-hundred. We have no idea of his exact birthday because he didn't know it, or how old he was, when he came to us. But I'd say around three-hundred and twenty, give or take. He looked like a child when he arrived on our doorstep, but that changed swiftly once we got him healthier."

Wow. This was just... yeah, wow. Lena chewed on her bottom lip and let all this sink in. "Someone's after him. Us. I don't exactly understand it."

"I'm sure he has a lot of enemies, the *Savag-Ri* not included. Dorian's made a name for himself among the vampires."

"As an executioner."

"As a *protector*. A hunter." Marie licked her lips and cringed a little, "I think being raised by Lycan works against him. He's had to fight twice as hard as any other of his kind to get to where he is now. And his past doesn't paint him in a pretty light either. His father was a brutal and cruel bastard."

Lena wished to ask more about it but wanted to hear that story from Dorian. She heard plenty about his father during Dorian's episode in the shower. "I don't want to lose him," she said quietly.

"Neither do we," Marie whispered.

"How do we stop him from dying?"

Marie stood up and looked out the window with Lena. "Dorian's never run from danger before," she said thoughtfully. "I can't believe he would do so now."

"It's my fault. He's hellbent on protecting me, even though I'm perfectly capable of doing that myself."

193

"I have no doubt." Marie smiled. "Especially hearing that you and Bane run in the same circles. That's impressive."

Lena rubbed the back of her neck. "I'm violent and unapologetic. Dorian should probably bear that in mind."

"You two are cut from the same cloth then." Marie tapped her chin and continued looking out the window. "I think I have a plan."

CHAPTER 27

Dorian leaned against the side of the doorjamb, instantly enthralled with his view.

Lena stood in front of a mirror braiding her hair.

Against his better judgment, he imagined this being their life. Him waiting for her to get dressed for an evening out on the town. Her fussing over her hair and him saying she looks perfect no matter what style she chose to twist it in. He gifted himself the image of running her bubble baths each night and reading to her by candlelight. Making dinners together. Drinking from each other while they made love. Then he'd go off to work, hunt, and chop the heads off *Savag-Ri* and send their bones to be ground to dust and used as a ward.

Yeah, that last bit wrecked his whole fantasy.

She couldn't be happy being mated to a killer like Dorian. He took tremendous pleasure in torturing, gutting, and beheading things. His own mother couldn't stomach being mated to a monster like that. She died to get away from him in the end.

Dorian couldn't stomach the thought of Lena choosing death over a life with him. Ironic he was making that same decision himself now.

"There you go again." Lena spoke calmly, her gaze meeting his in the mirror.

"What do you mean?" He covered the distance between them in just a few strides of his long gait. Standing behind her, they looked at each other in the reflection of the mirror.

"You go from having this beautiful face to a nauseous one

every time to you stare at me too long. Everyone here seems to have that response to me. Am I that repulsive?"

"It's not what you think."

"Oh boy, now we're going with the 'it's not you it's me' speech? Save your breath." She pulled away from him and he hated it.

"I'm sorry."

"You keep saying that, too." Lena crossed her arms over her ample chest.

"Only because it's true."

"Why did you bring me here, Dorian?"

"To keep you safe."

"And when you die, am I supposed to live here afterwards? Alone, or should I run to Bane? At least he enjoys spending time with me."

Dorian hissed and his fangs ached against his gums. "Bane?" Not likely.

"You have no say in my future if you choose to die instead of love me."

Was she trying to pick a fight with him, or make him feel like utter shit? She was succeeding at both right now.

But she had a point.

"How about this?" Lena dropped her arms and swept one in the direction of the window. "I'll keep Bane's bed warm, and you can keep Emily's nice and cozy."

That was too far. He backed her up against the wall, pinning her in place. His nostrils flared, and he smelled her lust kick into the air. "What the hell is your problem?"

Her words and body were contradicting each other.

"What's yours?" She twisted her arms and broke out of his hold with little to no effort. It made his cock hard and blood heat. "Dorian, I'm so twisted over this, I can't breathe!"

That makes two of us, he thought.

"You act like I'm all that matters to you, yet you're literally letting yourself die in front of me." She waved her hand up and down at him.

Dorian looked at himself in the mirror and saw what she meant. His eyes were bloodshot. Tiny capillaries in his cheeks stood out against the scruff of his whiskers. His hair was limp, no longer full-bodied and lush. And his skin looked sallow.

He was disgusting.

Closing his eyes, he backed up slowly. "I want better for you."

"And what about what I want, you jackass?"

She was right. He hadn't cared to ask. He was making this decision for them both, without her input. But he had good motherfucking reasons, damnit!

"Marie said you came to them half-chewed on, beaten, burned, starved, with an arrow embedded in your back."

Dorian's knees almost buckled. Was it his weakened system crapping out on him, or had she just knocked the pride clean out of his body with those words?

"Is that true?"

"It is." He swayed and sat down before he collapsed. The room was starting to spin. "My father and I had a... disagreement."

"Tell me more." Lena dropped down on her knees before him, resting her hands on his thighs. "Please, Dorian."

Maybe if he explained things, she'd understand why he refused to mate her. If she knew his truth, she would run far away from him and then his death would be all the more swift and easier to accept.

"My father," he stopped talking and bit the inside of his cheek to let a little blood well up, then he swallowed it along with some of his pride. "Was a murderer. A psychopath and serial killer. I didn't know any better. I was... little. My mother died and he raised me alone. We were dirt poor, living in a shack." Dorian huffed at the memory. "I didn't even know there were other vampires in existence, let alone know anything about *Savag-Ri*, or vampire Houses. I only knew humans and a little about Lycan."

Lena remained silent with her brown eyes locked on his. No emotion showed on her face. Not even as he continued with his saga.

"He'd drain me," he said. "Kept me constantly weak. I wasn't allowed to leave our property ever." When Dorian was a kid, he thought it was for his safety. As an adult, he wondered if it was because of something else. "He gorged on me to keep himself alive and left me with nothing but a few drops of human blood, forcing me to take from his victims. If I refused, I was beaten. The few times I stood at death's door, he'd prick his finger, but barely allowed me a few drops to lick off his crusty, dirty finger. He always insisted I feed on the humans he brought."

As if the memory conjured the scent, Dorian could still smell the smoke of the fires as they burned the carcasses while he told her all this.

"Blood carries power—human or otherwise. My father was obsessed with blood and the energy it could carry. It wasn't about our blood curse for him. It was something more sinister than that. Humans held a fascination for him I never understood. He tortured his victims, taught me what to do, what pieces to cut and how deep, which veins to keep intact until the end..." He was going to puke. Swallowing the bile rising in his throat, he hated the sensation of his sweat trickling down his back. But he had to keep going. She needed to know why he wasn't good for her. "I couldn't do anything but follow his orders. No matter how hard I tried, I couldn't disobey."

That particular weakness he bore the most shame about.

"Before the victim's heart stopped, he'd force me to drink from them. Place his big hand on my shoulder, the other at the back of my head, and shove me into their necks." Dorian's fangs cut his tongue when he licked his lips. "He wanted me to taste fear, to use the tainted blood as a source of power. I never tasted that though. I only guzzled down hate. And hate is what fuels me even to this day."

It's what tainted him most.

Lena's steady hands remained on his knees, her thumb rubbing across his thigh, soothing him as he continued.

"One night, my father grabbed another woman and... I'd had enough. Years spent watching him do this to innocent humans made me desperate to get away. The woman died before I could help her. I tried to fight him but was still too weak and brittle. My father was a massive man. Or at least he was to me. I later found out my growth had been severely stunted because of how he'd neglected and abused my body."

Dorian stretched in height and bulked up with muscle within two years of living among the Lycan. It's incredible what three-square meals and a safe, warm bed to sleep in each night could do for a kid.

"What happened next?" she whispered.

"I attacked him. More like set him off. He bit me, tore chunks of my flesh away. Shot me in the back with an arrow when I tried to run. Crushed my windpipe when I tried to scream. He broke me."

"Did he?" Lena's brow cocked, challenging his remark.

How she could look at him right now with pride in her eyes was beyond him.

"He did," Dorian admitted. "I ran but knew I couldn't escape him. He was an obsessive creature. He excelled at hunting, tracking, capturing." Dorian ran a hand through his hair. "I ended up doubling back to our shack. We kept plenty of flammable liquid to burn the bodies of his victims, so I doused the shack in it. Then set it on fire with myself inside, knowing his obsessive nature would demand he go in after me."

"You were going to sacrifice yourself to kill him."

"That was the plan. But I chickened out. My arm caught on fire, and it spiked my survival instincts. I didn't want to burn. I didn't want to die. I just wanted to get away from him and make it so he couldn't kill anymore."

A tear fell down Lena's cheek then. The only sign of emotion she allowed him to see. He focused on that tiny detail. Narrowed in on that pathetic tear because it meant she felt sorry for him. Pity was for weaklings.

He cupped her cheek and swiped it away with his thumb.

"I was able to use a splintered stool leg to club him in the head. It didn't knock him out but gave me a chance to wiggle out from under his tremendous weight. Flames ate our shack in no time, so much of it was rotten to begin with, and our hay beds went up like kindling. The roof started to give way. I grabbed a cleaver and a hammer and whacked him as much as I could until the roof collapsed. I dropped my weapons and dodged the only beam that held our house together. It slammed onto him and I tore out of the house with my clothes on fire. Rolled around in the grass. It was raining..." His vision wavered, and he had to take another deep breath. "It always rained on his killing nights."

He closed his eyes until his vertigo faded.

"Anyway," he bristled, "I ended up running through the woods, away from the nearest village, fell into a river, and nearly drowned. Decided I really didn't want to be fish food, crawled out of the current and made my way to a tiny cabin in the middle of nowhere. I banged on the door and Alistair answered." Dorian's mouth curved into a smile at the memory. "Marie was pregnant with the twins then." His eyes popped open. "They took me in, fed and clothed me, raised me even though all the Lycan in their clan and others rejected and tried to kill me."

"They tried to kill you too?"

"When I say I have enemies, Lena, I'm not saying it to sound badass. I mean it. Lycan mostly hate vampires. Alistair and Marie ended up being abandoned by their clan, though some decided to come back after I left to join the House of Death."

Lena stood slowly and pulled him up along with her. "I'm so sorry," she said while cupping his face.

"It's nothing for you to be sorry for. It is what it is."

He loved the feel of her hands on him. Loved that her brown eyes had little specks of amber and gold. Loved how her lip quivered a little bit. Another tear fell down her cheek. He wanted to lick it away. Instead, Dorian let it fall for them both.

He never shed a tear in his life. Maybe he wasn't capable of it. Maybe that, too, had been drained out of him by his cruel sire.

"You fought hard to have a better life," she said quietly.

Fucking right he had.

"And now you're willing to let all that go to waste because of me?"

"What?" His heart seized. "No!"

"Yes!" She started crying in earnest. "How could you go through all this and at the grand finale not want victory?"

"It's not *victory* if it means tying you to something like me. Doing so makes me no better than my father was. My mother *died* to get away from him, Lena." Dorian started shutting down and putting his walls up. "I'd rather die myself than find you've committed suicide to escape a life with me."

She slapped him. Hard. "Fuck you if you think I'd be so weak."

"It's not weak if it's the only way you see an exit."

She slapped him again. "Fuck you for thinking I'd want an exit!"

"You want to live with enemies at your door, day and night, Lena? Because what's mine *will* be yours if I turn you and we mate for life. Every bastard I've ever pissed off, the *Savag-Ri,* hell, even

Lycan, will be gunning for you. Is that the future you always envisioned for yourself?"

Damn his soul, because, deep down, he wanted her to say yes. If she did, it meant that no matter how bad it was, she still wanted to be with him. That she wanted his bite, their bond, and would trust him to protect her, no matter what. Forever. Fucking hell, he wanted to hear her say yes so badly, his head spun.

Lena got all in his face as she said, "When that asshole set your house on fire, did I run and hide? No. What did I do, Dorian?"

She hopped in a car and chased the fucker down... *after* checking on Dorian's safety.

"I don't run from a fight. I relish the chance to show my opponent exactly how big a mistake they made by going after me."

"This isn't a fight club."

"And this isn't only *your* choice." She shoved him.

"What if," he jabbed his finger at his temple angrily, "*What if?* That's all I keep asking myself. What if she dies? What if someone takes her? What if a *Savag-Ri* finds her? What if I'm not there in time to stop them?" He sucked back a ragged breath. "Jesus fucking Christ woman, I can't even bear the fact that I hadn't been there in time to stop that vampire from ripping you out of the car last night and holding you at knife point!"

Lena's head tipped back, and she laughed—all out *laughed* like this was a joke.

"It's not funny!" he roared in her face.

She kept laughing, and it was laced with anger. "Is that what you think happened, Dorian? That I was driving around searching for an arsonist and he somehow stopped my car and dragged me out of it?"

What else could have happened if not that? It was a vampire who attacked her. They had abilities no human could measure up to.

"Oh honey," her sarcastic tone paired nicely with the sway in her hips as she backed up. "I hit him with the car on purpose, then I hopped out and chased after him."

Annnnd caught him. That's what she hadn't tacked on. She chased after a *vampire*. What kind of person did that?

A fearless one.

Or a human with a death wish.

Dorian's ears began ringing. He was going to pass out. Clamping down on his focus, he tried to hold his shit together for as long as possible. If he dusted right now, it would really piss him off.

"Fighting off an attack isn't the same as what I do, Lena."

"Yes, you also blow their brains out and turn them into sludge."

She wasn't taking this seriously. "I'm the House executioner. The Reaper. I torture for a living. Kill them slowly most times." He canted forward and made sure his fangs showed as his confession dropped to a dangerous tone. *"And I fucking like it."*

Lena leaned right back into him and didn't skip a beat when matching his tone. *"As well you should."*

He reared back. "You're crazy."

"Takes one to know one." Lena glowered unapologetically. "So maybe you're trying to cut and run, now, because *you* don't want to be the one looking for an exit later. Maybe this *I must die to save my mate from a lifetime of being with a monster* is really the other way around. *You're* trying to leave *me* now before you're officially committed to eternity with my crazy ass."

Dorian was flabbergasted. "Never," his voice cracked. "I... no... that's not it."

"You know what Marie told me? She said you've spent your whole life protecting those you love. Even those in your House. She said the only ones you kill are sworn enemies and those so violent, they threaten the existence of Lycan and vampire. She said you've never laid an angry hand on an innocent. She said you keep to yourself and always come when one of the Lycan need you. Same for vampires."

Dorian's eyes narrowed. "Marie talks too much."

Knowing her, Marie was probably concocting some crazy plan to force Dorian and Lena together one way or another. Damn, he loved the woman who stepped in and took over the role as his mother when the rest of his world turned dark. But he wasn't happy that she went and told Lena as much as she had.

Then again, Lena should know all the good and the bad about Dorian, right? She needed to make her own decision based on all the facts before surrendering her mortality.

He ground his molars together while he came up with something else to say. "She makes me sound like a hero when I'm anything but."

"Was she lying?"

"No." The one-word truth flew out of his mouth before he had a chance to eat it. "But I assume she failed to tell you how depraved and violent I can be too."

Lena swallowed hard. "I joined that underground fight ring looking for more than an adrenaline rush, and I came to New Orleans looking for something more than a hot fuck. I've searched in the darkest corners for something that could make me feel like I belong, because I know I'm not meant for sunshine and rainbows. I prefer violence and danger."

He could relate.

"And now that I've found exactly what I've always wanted," she said, her voice rose with her temper, "you're denying me. For one who runs when someone needs them, Dorian, you're doing the opposite with the only one who's fated to matter to you. *Some mate you'd make.*" She turned to walk away from him.

Dorian snatched her by the waist and wheeled her around until her ass hit the dresser. His breath came out in punches. "You're right," he growled. "You're fucking right."

"Then don't die," she pleaded. "Give us a chance."

"What if you hate me later for this? If I'm too much monster for you to suffer?"

"I'll kill you myself."

His heart clenched. That she said such a thing without hesitation did unspeakable things to him. "Holy Hell, this is so messed up."

"That's how I know it's right." Lena broke out of his hold again and gripped his face. "If I'm really your *alakhai*, Dorian, why deny us? Why walk away from something that could be glorious?"

His body trembled with emotions too strong to unleash. "What if—"

"No more what ifs," she demanded. "I'm not saying I'm in love with you yet, but I'm willing to admit that I can't pull myself away from you. When you came into my room at The Wicked Garden, I felt a thud in my chest." She tapped her breastbone. "Then I heard your voice and it pounded even deeper within me. And when we fucked at your house, the only thing running through my head was for you to bite me, and it had *nothing* to do with a

203

kink. It was something far more damning than that."

Damning. What an accurate word for it.

"When you took off to chase that vampire down, all I thought was *I need to kill him before he hurts Dorian*. I've never felt a level of protectiveness like that for anything in my life. I'd kill for you, I realized. I'd take a life to protect yours. When he got the upper hand on me, and I saw your face, I knew that fear and possession and anger in your eyes, because I also felt it in my goddamn bones. That blade he held to my throat?" She leaned in with a vicious glare and whispered heatedly. "I *wanted* him to use it, Dorian. I *wanted* him to spill my blood if only to make *you* drink it. But you popped his damn head off with those weird bullets, and that was when I realized you'd kill for me too."

"I'd do worse for you, Lena."

"And I you," she leveled him with her stare.

There was a strange silence between them for a minute. He wanted to say something but fuck if he had any words that would help. What might soothe her? What could make up for all this? Not a damned thing.

Lena sucked in her bottom lip and held it between her teeth. Her eyes softened. "I can't feel this much in me for no good reason. Even psychos have a limit, but I seem to have none where you're concerned."

Fate is a twisted and savage beauty. For destiny to give him a woman so fierce was one thing. But for her to most likely match his thirst for darkness was more than he'd ever have the courage to wish for.

Yet here she was.

It scared the piss out of him to take a leap like this. His fears of turning into his father were still prominent in his mind. He refused to forget whose blood coursed through his veins. Staring at Lena, however, made him hopeful that he wasn't a complete lost cause. No beast could feel this tender for another creature without having some goodness in him.

"Would you really kill me?" He bumped his body against hers.

"Would you really want me to?"

"Is it fucked up if I say yes?"

"Is if fucked up if I promise?"

Dorian laughed at that. It was hard to tell if either of them was being serious about that last bit or not... but part of him hoped so, because if this didn't work out, he'd need to be put out of his misery because failing her as a mate was a Hell far more gruesome than the one he let burn down in that shack three centuries ago.

CHAPTER 28

Lena focused on Dorian's green eyes, then let her gaze linger on his slender nose, and finally land on his mouth. His lips were slightly parted, and she could see the tips of his fangs. Tingly sparks of lust trickled down her spine and straight to the joining of her thighs.

Dorian was built like a weapon. He was a killer. If they were a true match, she figured his brutality was merciless. He'd fight to the death and make sure he always won. That much potential danger, all wrapped in a stunning package of toned muscle and seduction, made him incredibly alluring.

"We're designed to lure you in." That's what Lucian explained to her. Looking at Dorian now, she felt drugged by his sensual mouth and charming eyes. His thick, curly hair was chaotic perfection. His jawline? Razor sharp. Even the way his Adam's apple bobbed when he swallowed was sexy.

Swallow. Lena was weakened by that word. Empowered by it too.

Would her blood sustain him? Would he enjoy pulling from her vein? Would she somehow boost his abilities? She wanted to find out. Now. "Are we doing this or what?" She tempted him, tilting her head to the left to expose her throat.

Dorian's gaze deadlocked on her jugular. She watched his pupils blow wide, until his eyes were solid black. More heat pooled between her legs. This man... no, this vampire, was deadly.

"What's running through your head right now, Lena?" His voice was pure sin. Deep, gravelly - like he swallowed a bucket of fiberglass and lead. The bass of his tone rumbled through her ears, down her spine, and made her nipples hard.

When he wrapped his hand gently around her neck and rubbed his thumb along her pulse point, she was undone.

"I'm thinking about how dangerous you are, but also that you'd likely saw your own arms off before laying a violent hand on me."

"Fucking right, I would." Dorian smothered her with his body, taking up all the space in the room, and stealing the air straight from her lungs. "I'm glad you understand that."

"I'm glad you understand that too." Her gaze fell back on his mouth again. "Bite me?"

She was part begging, part praying.

Lena saw the trepidation in his eyes even though his sexy mouth turned upwards into a wicked smile. "This isn't going to turn you, but it is the next step."

Her disappointment must have shown. Dorian's gaze softened, "There's still time," he whispered. Collaring her neck with his hand, he rubbed his thumb up and down, over and over her pulse, until he lulled her into a hazy headspace. "Do you want it to hurt a little?"

"Would you judge me if I said yes?"

Dorian shook his head, his smile widening. "Close your eyes," he said softly.

She didn't.

"Close your eyes," he repeated with his ungodly deep voice raised a little more.

Lena obeyed and bit her lip, bracing herself. Dorian slid his hand around her neck to cradle the back of her head. "Breathe in, breathe out," he said calmly. "I won't take your vein if you're afraid."

"I'm not afraid."

His grip tightened a little. More lust shot down her body, heating her skin. Dorian leaned in and inhaled. "I can smell how turned on you are already."

"Then rest easy knowing I'm not afraid of you."

"Your heart beating like a jackrabbit tells me otherwise." He dipped his head down and licked her neck.

"That's the sound of impatience."

His grumbling laugh made the apex of her thighs swell with need. The hair on the back of her neck stood on end. Her nipples were so hard, they hurt. Were they going to stand here all day or was he going to finally —

His mouth sealed on her skin, the swipe of his tongue, hot and promising. Lena gripped his shirt, fisting the fabric to hold steady for him. He didn't bite her. His mouth remained right on top of her vein, but his hands skated down her back, sending little tingles shooting over her. Lena gasped. Her eyes rolled back as her body melted into his arms a little more. He grabbed her hands, pulling her off him and laced their fingers together. Then he pressed his body flush against hers and kept her arms pinned down to her sides with his.

Dorian's heart slammed wildly against his chest. Hers was just as frantic.

Lena's mouth dried up. She discovered, too late, what he was doing.

He lured her in…

No fantasy compared to the real deal. A guttural groan ripped out of her when his fangs pierced her skin. Lust flooded her system. Had he not held her so fiercely, she would have collapsed. The sting of his fangs hurt just enough to bring tears to her eyes, and it felt so good she cried out.

Dorian's body tensed. Then she heard him swallow.

Another moan slipped out then, and her brows pinched as he drank from her. His hands tightened around hers. Lena's world tipped over. The pumping of her feral heart forced her blood up and into his mouth. She untangled their fingers and clasped the nape of his neck to keep him in place.

He tensed.

She knew this was hard for him on many levels. But instead of freaking out, Dorian groaned and pulled harder from her vein.

Her mouth parted, his name on the tip of her tongue.

It felt like he was inside her while he drank. Sensations overwhelmed her — all of them more sensual than the next. His hands threaded into her braid as he kept drinking. His hips rocked, rubbing his arousal against her. Dorian's hands were hot on her skin when he slipped them under her shirt. She jerked a little as he roughly pulled down her pants next.

Lena moaned when he cupped her pussy. It cracked a dam between her thighs. She heard him swallow more. Her eyes fluttered shut.

Lena was either going to come or pass out. Maybe both. "Keep going. Don't stop."

Her eyelids grew heavy. Her pussy swelled. Her arms erupted in goosebumps. The floor fell out from under her. Lena was floating. Stars twinkled in her vision, the edges of the room darkening and closing in. More heat pooled between her thighs.

Overstimulated and half-drugged in lust, she came under his touch. How many times, she lost count. Her eyes crossed and muscles melted.

Dorian's grip tightened around her to keep her upright when he unlatched from her vein. His eyes blazed with lust as he looked at her. His lips were stained red.

"Keep going," he purred. "Let it go, Lena."

Let what go? She wasn't holding anything.

Dorian dipped back down and struck her vein again. She cried out. She focused on the rhythm of her heartbeat matching his throat muscles working to drink her down. *Boom, boom.* Swallow. *Boom, boom.* Swallow.

The instinct to free fall was suddenly all she knew. *Let go.*

Lena closed her eyes, letting her body do whatever it wanted. An orgasm tore through her with such force, she lost her voice when she screamed. Sparks of electricity bit her skin. She was a live wire, a lightning bolt streaking across a night sky. Crackling. Sizzling. Burning.

More pleasure. More pain. More free falling.

There was no end to it. Her mind hit some kind of subspace, and it was dark and endless and peaceful.

Another orgasm ripped through her. She screamed again. Her voice broke and something heavy landed on her mouth to stifle her sounds. Tightness clamped around her throat. A burn seared her neck.

Cold ice slid down her spine.

Another orgasm began to build. Holy shit, she didn't think she could take much more. Tears stung her eyes. She wanted to say something but didn't have the capacity to make words. She panicked. Grappling for something to hang on to.

209

Hot flesh gave way under her fingernails. Her grip tightened. She heard a roar.

She roared right back.

Light bloomed in her eyes, and the darkness receded. It was like her soul catapulted out of her body, only to now fall back down into it by gravity and madness. The room exploded in color, her pussy clenched as she came again, and every inch of her body blazed with lust.

She couldn't catch her breath. Dorian's hand remained on her throat as he made a long drag of his hot tongue against the puncture wounds to close them. She could feel her skin pull tight around the wounds he made.

His fingers slid back down over her pulse point again. Dorian leaned back and locked gazes with her. Licking the corner of his mouth, he reminded her of a wolf more than a vampire. But the tips of his fangs were a stark reminder of exactly what he was—a predator no matter what name he went by.

He said something but no sound came forth. All Lena saw was his mouth moving, then his eyebrows pinching together with concern. Lena blinked slowly. He said something again, but she still couldn't make it out.

"I can't hear you."

Dorian cupped her cheeks and dipped his head, so their gazes locked again. "Can you hear my voice now?"

Relief flooded her. She sagged with her exhale. "Yes." The ringing in her ears died immediately. The tingles across her body receded. She was disoriented as a barrage of emotions swarmed her, making it hard to pick one to embrace.

"Aww fuck." Dorian picked her up and cradled her in his arms. Bringing her over to the bed, he laid her down and crawled in with her. Keeping her tight against his chest, he rubbed her back in small circles and cooed sweet words of comfort.

Lena bawled her eyes out for no reason. "Why am I doing this?" she sobbed. "I don't know how to make this stop!"

"You're dropping." He kissed her head and continued touching her. "Damn, you're so strong, Lena. So brave and fierce."

His words contradicted how she felt, which made her more scatterbrained. Crying pissed her off but she couldn't stop it. It got ugly. Really ugly. Now she was nauseous. Confused. Lethargic.

"This is my fault," he whispered. "I wasn't thinking straight. I pulled back too fast from you."

"I don't know what that means," she hiccupped.

"It means I'll do better next time. Now that I know… I'll never let this happen again."

Lena's tears went into overtime. She didn't want him to never let this happen again. She loved what he did, even if her reaction afterwards didn't show it. But she couldn't explain herself. Lena couldn't even keep her eyes open. With her next exhale, she passed out.

Dorian held Lena while she came down from her subspace.

What an asshole he was. Dorian thought he was doing something she wanted. Giving her the next thing on her list of desires. In The Wicked Garden, she'd specifically said *"I want to be railed hard enough so that I go into some kind of subspace. I want to float and fly apart. Scream, cry, sweat, and lose myself."* Even when they fucked at his house, she said she wanted pain with her pleasure because she wanted to *check out*.

He gave her what she asked for but slipped up. Drunk on her blood, he let her fly apart and forgot the higher the float, the harder the drop. Vampires were notorious for sending their lovers into euphoria. It's why The Wicked Garden had a three-visit cap, and afterwards the minds of the guests were erased.

This level of seduction was dangerous, addicting, and came at a price.

Dorian foolishly assumed she'd done this kind of thing before with a human Dom. Her confidence was so fucking believable, he never gave it a second thought. Dorian delivered what she asked for.

But with a vampire twist.

He longed for someone like Lena more than he cared to admit. To have a mate. A lover who trusted him implicitly and whom he didn't have to dull his sharp edges for. Lena was a razor blade. He was a scythe. Together they would make blood run.

He barely took enough of her vein to form a connection to her. So focused on giving her pleasure, Dorian put her needs before his own—as any worthy mate would. Taking from her vein just now wasn't going to turn her but should start the bonding process if he was lucky.

With everything that's happened, he didn't want to go too fast with this commitment. What Lena thought she wanted now, could change later when the adrenaline wore off. He wanted her to see the ceremony tonight before pulling from her vein again and start the true process of making her his vampire mate. Once they did that, there was no going back.

Her blood felt like bubbles in his system. Lively, fragile, excited. He didn't trust those to be her true feelings though. They were most likely from the thrill of victory. He caught that wild gleam in her eyes when he conceded to her earlier—she loved playing with danger. She was a junkie for it.

Dorian refused to be her drug right now.

He also couldn't deny that he'd longed for a woman like Lena. To have a female regard him with such fearless adoration. He wanted to have her look at him that way forever. But he wasn't selfish enough to make it happen now by turning her too soon.

Since this was their first time, Dorian wanted to give her the gift of her desires instead. To pleasure her beyond reason. Fling her into that glorious headspace between numbness and electrified intensity. While sipping from her, Dorian suspended her in euphoria for as long as he could, relishing how she screamed his name while coming undone from his touch. Fuck, how he loved feeling her tremble against his hardened body.

She'd played with an animal and became one.

As he drank from her vein, Lena hissed, bit, clawed and roared while he brought her to orgasm over and over. Did she remember any of it? Doubtful. That was okay, Dorian committed every second of it to memory. How her body undulated, skin blushed. Her sweet mouth opening and slender fingers biting into his arms as she clung to him.

Clung. Like he was her lifeline while her soul scattered into space.

He wanted always to be that for her. A line she could wrap her hands around and tug when she needed backup or a boost. Pride swelled in his chest. The taste of her blood lingered on his tongue, making his dick rock hard. He wanted to fuck her so badly while he took her vein, but she'd exploded long before he could get his pants down.

Lena probably thought he drank her blood for hours. In reality, he'd barely pulled from her vein, too worried he'd go too far in his current state. Gorging on her blood could kill her, and he wasn't about to let that happen. He would rather starve than risk it.

So he took a sip of her life source, and gave her a feast of sensations. Just before sinking his teeth in, Dorian wished he had the ability to make her immobile. He imagined her standing stock still, unable to wiggle away from him. It wasn't because he wanted to cheat or take her freedom away, it was because he was scared with that much temptation spread before him, he'd hurt her when he pierced her vein. If she'd jerked even a little, it could have torn her skin unnecessarily and Dorian didn't want that to happen.

To his astonishment, she stiffened beneath him the instant his hand gently wrapped around her throat. Lena stayed perfectly still under his mouth once his lips touched her skin. He'd punctured her vein without any accidents.

Holy Hell, she was a magnificent creature. And she was all his. How phenomenal was that?

Dorian smiled when her body slackened in his embrace. Her light snoring made him feel like a king. She trusted him. Gave him the greatest, most precious gift in all the world. He didn't deserve her. He knew that, but he was still going to keep her.

Cherish every motherfucking minute they had together.

Next time he took her vein, he'd go slower on the seduction lift and make sure the aftercare was exactly how she needed it to be, so the drop wouldn't be so severe. For now, Dorian held her close and whispered a thousand loving promises to her...

And ignored the burn blazing down his back.

A soft knock snapped him out of his enthrallment of watching Lena sleep. Slipping off the mattress, his movements were sluggish. *Weird.* He cracked the door open.

"Dinner is being served," Alistair said softly. "I brought you two a plate."

"Thanks." Dorian flashed a quick, appreciative smile. He never ate at the large ceremony dinners. No Lycan other than the Woods family would suffer sharing a meal with him because of what he was. What his father had been. Dorian never blamed them or took offense by it. Lycan and vampires never got along, the anomaly, of course, being Alistair and Marie and their kids with Dorian.

"Will you be watching?" Alistair's deep voice remained quiet. With his keen shifter hearing, he most likely knew Lena was asleep by the sound of her deep, steady breathing. He probably also knew what Dorian just did to her. If her screams of ecstasy hadn't tipped them off, the scent of her blood on his breath would.

"Yeah. I want her to see the ceremony. She needs to understand the severity of this decision." The blood curse on Lycan was different than the vampires but damning just the same. He swallowed around the tightness in his throat. "Is Emily going to do it?"

Alistair shrugged and only said, "I'm glad you came, son." He placed a hand on his shoulder and squeezed. "You make us proud, you know that?"

He couldn't help but cringe. "I'm a killer."

"Aren't we all?" Alistair turned and walked away, never answering the question about Emily.

Holding the plates of food, Dorian willed the door shut with his mind and sat at the foot of the bed. His veins burned as though the fizzy bubbles he felt earlier had turned to acid and were eating him from the inside out. It hurt like hell.

He'd tolerate it.

Looking over his shoulder, Lena's eyes locked on his instantly. She reminded him of a cougar just awoken from her nap. He stood up, and Lena tracked his movements. It cranked Dorian's lust up to dangerous levels. He was a sucker for a predator.

"You need food," he said cautiously. He might not have taken much blood from her, but he couldn't recall having seen her eat a damned thing in... too long.

They both sat across from each other on the bed. Dorian held a plate in one hand, a fork in the other. "If I may?"

Cliché or not, he wanted to feed her. She just gave him the greatest meal of his sorry life, the least he could do was this tiny act of providing for her. The roast beef smelled heavenly. Marie was an amazing cook. Dorian cut a small chunk of meat off with the side of his fork and swirled it in the gravy. "Open."

Lena obeyed. Her little pink mouth parting, widening for him.

His hand shook as he brought the fork to her lips. Her teeth scraped the tines as she pulled her bite off and chewed it.

"You'll hurt your teeth like that," he reprimanded, playfully.

"Bad habit." Lena started to blush. "I scrape my teeth on utensils and chew straws."

"Mmph." He cringed. Then Dorian broke her off another piece of meat and added a tiny bit of carrot with it. His hand trembled so much, the food fell off the fork and plopped back onto the plate.

Dorian stared at it, unable to focus on what just happened. Then he exhaled slowly, concentrated, and tried again. He managed to get the fork halfway to her when Lena grabbed his arm, and gently braced it so he could feed her.

Her teeth scraped the tines again. Neither mentioned that he could barely hold the utensil at all. She allowed him to feed her the entire meal this way. It was humbling, too.

"You're not going to eat?" She dabbed her mouth with a napkin. "Or... sorry, that was dumb."

"Vampires do eat food. It helps with our muscle mass." He placed the plates on the dresser and leaned back with his arms crossed. "But my hunger is sated, thanks to you."

Damn, he loved how her cheeks turned pink.

"If that's true, why are you shaking so badly?"

"I'm not entirely sure." He didn't want to think about it.

"Am I not enough? Is my blood no good?"

"What? No!" Jesus how could she even think such a thing?

Out of nowhere, a sharp pain slammed into Dorian's gut. Grunting, he doubled over. Then slammed to his knees. The pain stole the breath from his lungs. *Shit! What is this?* Dorian rocked back on his haunches, head down, body wracked with tremors. He couldn't breathe, he couldn't... he couldn't fucking breathe!

"Dorian!"

He shot his hand out to stop Lena from getting closer. Inwardly, he cringed. Outwardly, he hissed. Alarm bells rang loud in his mind. Lena dropped down to be at his level on the floor. *Don't*, he wanted to warn her. *Stay back!*

Those warnings never had a chance to leave his tongue. She grabbed him by the throat and spoke in low tones. "Do it."

Could she sense his desperation? See the starvation in his

dark gaze? Feel the need to make her his in every way possible? Her blood finally hit his system and mixed with his. The result was a raw, primal, deadly perversion that stormed over his walls and dropped him into a deeper level of deterioration.

If he didn't act fast, he was going to lose her... and himself.

"Do it," she urged him again.

He wanted to spread her legs, impale her, drink her, mark her, turn her, own her.

Dorian clenched his jaw to keep from using his fangs on her sweet flesh. At this point, he'd hurt her and would never forgive himself if that happened. He let out a warning growl. Knew saliva dripped off his canines as he hissed at her.

She didn't back down.

Were her survival instincts busted? Didn't she see how dangerous he was?

Pushing her down onto her back, Dorian crawled on top of her. She spread her thighs, giving him an invitation. His mind screamed to *back down! Gain control!*

His dick and fangs had other plans.

His nails elongated, sharpening to talons which he used to claw the floorboards. It felt good to dig his claws into something that could handle his level of aggression.

Lena wouldn't be able to. She was human.

Precious. Fragile. Breakable.

Killable.

Dorian pushed off her immediately. He couldn't do this. He might kill her by accident. Gripping the sides of his head, he squeezed his eyes shut as a flurry of terrifying images crashed into him. *Lena bloody on the ground. Cuts, deep and fatal all over. Knives lined along the table. Chains. Rope.*

Cleaver.

"Nooooo!" Dorian thundered. Pure fear struck and he heaved backwards, slamming into the dresser and rocking the solid piece of furniture.

"Dorian!" Lena hollered, but he no long heard her voice.

He heard his father's.

"Fetch me the bucket, boy."

"Drink her, son."

"You're a waste of spunk."

The shack, wood, fire, screaming...

Shaking his head, Dorian scrambled to get out of his own head. He jerked as a fresh wave of pain attacked him from all angles. His arms and back sizzled and pure fear struck his heart. He was burning. *He was fucking burning!*

"Lena!" Eyes widening, he reached out, desperate to cling to the one thing worth living for.

And vanished with Lena still screaming his name.

CHAPTER 29

Lena scrambled across the floor and over to the dresser where Dorian had just been. *"Dorian!"*

The bedroom door crashed open. Lena kept screaming. Alistair and Bane rushed in. Bane grabbed Lena from the floor and caged her in his thick arms, driving her backwards. Alistair kneeled, spreading his hand flat on the floorboards.

"No ash." Glancing back at Bane and Lena, the terror in his eyes melted into relief. "No ash. He's not dead."

Lena's knees buckled and down she went.

"Whoa, shit," Bane scooped her up and sat down on the bed, putting her on his lap. "We got you," he said soothingly. "He's okay. He's okay, Lena."

He wasn't okay, he was gone! GONE! Her head and heart couldn't catch up with each other. "I just watched him sizzle into nothing!" She was going to puke.

"He must have flashed," Alistair stalked around the room, scenting the air. He stopped and scrubbed his face with both hands. "Christ, I'm gonna hurl my meal."

"Don't blow chunks on Emily's bed. Mom will have a fit."

Alistair braced himself against the dresser, his broad shoulders testing the limits of his cotton t-shirt. His muscles bulged each time his chest expanded and contracted. Several more footsteps raced up the stairs. Emily dashed in first, followed by Marie. Then Bowen and Emerick.

It was a goddamn party in here.

"What happened?" Emily blanched. "Where's Dorian?"

"Flashed," Alistair sighed. "He's only flashed."

"He can't *flash*," Emily argued.

"Well, he *did*," Bane snapped back.

Marie pressed her hand to her mouth and walked around the room carefully. "You're sure?"

"It's the only explanation. There's no ash, Marie." Alistair gripped his mate, and she wrapped her arms around him, then started crying with relief.

Lena realized how very loved Dorian was here. For a child who didn't belong to them, or even their species, they made him part of their family as if he was of their own blood.

Emily stood in front of Lena. "Are you okay? That had to have been terrifying."

"I... I don't know what I am." Lena pulled herself off Bane's lap and swiped the tears from her face. Her throat was sore from screaming so loud. Her head throbbed. "I don't understand what just happened. I thought he was going to k—" She stopped right there. The words kiss and kill both fought to come out first. To make it worse, Lena wasn't sure which she wanted to say.

Dorian's actions contradicted everything his gaze reflected. He wanted her to stay away, yet his black eyes begged her to come closer. He shoved her down on the ground, and she welcomed everything his body promised to deliver. Yet his hissing and growling were clear warnings to get up and run.

Dorian...

She closed her eyes, concentrating on his name.

Dorian...

Who knows what the hell she expected to have happen? It's not like she could summon him back to her. She didn't even know where he would have gone. *But he's not ash.* That's all her brain could compute.

There was still time to save him.

Oh hell no. Not here. Dorian had reformed in a place he never wanted to step foot in again. He recognized his old home immediately—the atmosphere held the energy of his past and it made him want to scream in terror as he stood on the ground that once took part in shaping him into the monster he was now. Even though the shack had burned long ago, with everything including his father in it, the land remembered. As if even fire couldn't purify and absolve this place of all the sins committed here.

How the hell had he flashed here? Flashing was never a gift of his. Not all vampires were built the same, but anyone who could flash had royal blood in them. Oh. Wait. This must be residue leftover from taking Malachi's vein. Yeah, that made sense.

How long will the power last in his system?

It was a convenient skill. One he understood the gist of from other vampires. All one had to do was think of a destination and *go*. Never thought he'd get the chance to try it though. And why, of all places, would he have come here? It made no sense.

Unless his subconscious was messing with him? All this talk of the past had clearly rattled his brain and glitched his circuits.

He needed to get out of here and go back to Lena. Yet his feet remained rooted to the spot.

His nostrils flared. Turning slowly, he took in his surroundings. It was fitting that he landed right here of all places. The shack was long gone, but the footprint was still there. He could feel it, like hallowed ground—or more like haunted territory. A slight breeze blew through his hair, forcing some of his hair to fall into his eyes. He was colder than usual. Sick. Twisted up.

Biting his inner lip, Dorian let that sweet release of pain and blood ground him as he swallowed the blood welling in his mouth. He knew why he was here.

To remember.

Crouching, Dorian touched the forest floor where once a table and stools had been. If he closed his eyes, his memory could fill in all the gaps, erecting the walls of his old, dilapidated shack, the hay beds, and even that mildew coated well bucket.

His eyes flicked to the right. A squirrel skittered up a tree. These woods were now protected land. No one could build on it and by the looks of things, no one came this deep into the woods still. It was completely untouched. Dorian might have laughed if it hadn't been the exact reason his disgusting father chose this particular spot to set up shop. No one ever came this deep into the forest. Into the mouth of the beast…

His gaze swung to the left and Dorian's heart seized when he saw all the flowers. It made his skin crawl and stomach twist. Those blooms grew because of the fertilizer scattered on that side of the property. Fertilizer, like the ashes of his father's victims.

When Dorian was a kid, he plucked seed pods in the woods as he foraged and scattered them along the mounds of the dead — his pathetic way to cover up what his father had done.

No... what *they* had done.

Dorian's guilt for being a part of his father's murders would forever plague him. It didn't matter how weak Dorian was back then. How frail or helpless he was. It didn't matter that he'd been forced and beaten to near death if he didn't obey. It. Didn't. Matter.

Because he should have used that knife sooner to pierce his father's neck. He should have set fire to that shack long before those victims were dragged into it and tortured. Before they were drained. He should have—

Dorian squeezed his eyes shut and took a breather. He could smell his father's rancid odor. Hear his deep growl. Smell the dried blood on all the tools that bastard used on those humans.

Bile rose in his throat, but he didn't dare give it another inch. Fuck that.

He let his father have power over him when he was a kid, and that tight leash never really disappeared. Everything Dorian did now, was because of his father in some way. Even the way he killed … it was fashioned from the way his father had taught him to do it.

But instead of for fun, Dorian killed on behalf of his king. He did it to protect his race...

Still made him a monster though. A murderer.

Damnit. Dorian was never going to escape this doom. Maybe he deserved to be stuck with it. If he'd had more courage when he was a kid, maybe he'd have more dignity now.

"I hope you're rotting in Hell, you fucking bastard." Dorian stepped back from his old stomping grounds and flashed back to Lena before he finished the job he started three centuries ago and set his sorry ass on fire once and for all.

He might die today from his curse, but he'd be damned if he was going to burn to ashes here among the ghosts of his past.

CHAPTER 30

Dorian landed back in the bedroom he left Lena in.

"Oh my God!" She screeched and ran at him. He caught her in his arms and stumbled back. Still dizzy from his flash, he clung to her tightly, as if she could help keep his scattered ass tethered to solid ground. "I'm so sorry if that scared you."

Whatever feral, possessive, visceral energy rode him so hard earlier fizzled out. So had the pain. Dorian figured it was a combo of his need to turn and mate his *alakhai*, and the king's pure blood in Dorian's system now mingling with Lena's.

That's some powerful stuff right there.

"I thought we lost you!" She nearly choked him with how hard she squeezed.

"I thought we lost me too." He half-chuckled and looked over to see Emily scowling at him. "Seems I learned a new trick."

Emily frowned back. "Where'd you land?"

"The old place."

Emily's eyes widened. She knew where he was talking about. "On *purpose*?"

"Not sure. I had too much roaring in me with Lena and then I felt this burning and panicked. Next thing I know, I'm standing where the shack used to be."

Emily stuffed her hands in her back pockets. "You're full of surprises lately, Reaper."

Dorian set Lena down and kissed her forehead before turning to Emily. "I can't help any of this, Em. You know I—"

"I know," she said, cutting him off. Glancing at Lena, Emily gave her a once over before saying, "I'm going to hang with the others tonight and give you two privacy. Do me a favor, Dorian." She squeezed her eyes shut and exhaled angrily, "Don't scare us like that again. Turn her, mate her... whatever it is you vamps do for your *mates*, do it so we don't have another heart attack thinking you turned to ashes next time, okay, asshole?" She shoved past them, knocking Dorian on the shoulder as she left.

Lena's chin trembled. "She was just as scared as I was. I think she's in love with you."

"She's just lonely and confused right now. Tonight's festivities aren't helping her mood."

Lena wasn't buying it. "Do you love her?"

"As a sister," he admitted. "We were never romantic. I can't even imagine how that would have gone over if we even tried to be lovers." He visibly shivered. "Emily just gets like this every time there's a ceremony. She debated on doing it this time. Talked to me about it last week to see if I'd come support her." He saw jealousy burning in Lena's eyes. The last thing Dorian wanted was for them to not get along. Emily was precious to him and Lena was too. Dorian didn't know what he'd do if they weren't friends. "She and I have always followed the same motto... No soul mates."

"Ever?"

He shook his head. Damn, he was such a hypocrite right now. But it couldn't be helped.

"Marie wants her to settle down and have kids, but she won't."

"Wouldn't she need to find her mate first before all that?"

"In a perfect world, sure." Dorian shrugged. "But our world is far from perfect. She can love anyone. Have kids with another Lycan. But..."

"If she found her mate later, her husband would be kicked to the side."

"Yeah. That wouldn't be fair to anyone."

Lena let that sink in for a minute. "And... what about vampires? Same rules?"

"Mmm hmm. But we're colder creatures. We'd rather have pleasure than partnership."

"Makes sense," she whispered. "Being tied to someone for all eternity is a big commitment. Being tied to someone else out of obligation is just as big a move."

Move or mistake? Sometimes there wasn't a difference. Dorian was glad to see she was finally understanding the level of seriousness this was.

Turning vampire wasn't like it was in the movies. Neither was immortality how it was in books. Everything about Lycan and vampire was dangerous—their love, their passion, their enemies, their powers.

Commitments this huge needed to be considered carefully.

"What—" Lena cleared her throat and tried again. "Dorian, what the hell just happened. I mean… before the flashy thing."

"I think my survival instincts are getting more feral." Shame landed in his belly like a rock.

"Then do something to stop this." She grabbed his shirt and shook him. "I don't understand your hesitation."

Because you don't know what you're getting into, he thought. He wasn't prolonging this transition because he was a coward, he was doing it to give Lena the best possible chance of success.

"It's not that easy." He pulled her hands off his shirt and kissed her knuckles.

"Yes, it is."

Dorian dismissed her persuasive gaze and pulled away from her. The struggle was real. He knew it was foolish to prolong the turning but rushing it could kill her too. It was a delicate thing and needed to be handled cautiously.

Blood curses came in a variety of ways. That's why Rogues were dangerous. If a vampire, in the wrong headspace, bit and turned a human, it could damage the mixture of saliva, blood, and intention. It could destroy the one they bit.

What if Dorian fucked Lena up? What if he wasn't pure enough to turn her safely? He needed to make sure they could both do this, which meant moving slower than she liked, and faster than he was ready for.

That fear rocked his ass earlier when shit got real, and he'd clawed the floorboards. This level of aggression could taint their blood bond and turn her into a monster like him. He didn't want her changed in any way.

"Was it my blood?" She crossed her arms. "It's not as good as you hoped or something?"

"What?" He must be losing his hearing again. No way did she just say that. He closed the gap between them, "Your blood's incredible." What a lame ass answer to pop out of his mouth. "I've never tasted anything so divine."

Jesus. Roosevelt. Christ. Just kill him now.

Lena's jealousy skyrocketed. "Do you drink from others often?"

"No." Dorian got seriously agitated. "I barely take a vein, and only when it's absolutely necessary." He tipped her chin up so she met his gaze. "Does that bother you?"

"I know it shouldn't," her lips tightened into a thin line. "It would be like you getting mad at me for having a hamburger."

"That's right." His aggression rose as if competing with hers. *What's happening now, damnit?*

Lena's next statement dropped like a bomb. "But it pisses me off, Dorian. I can't stand the thought of your mouth on someone else. I don't give a shit if that's how you live or what you need to survive."

A smile spread across his face and the tips of his fangs peeked out.

She looked positively delectable when she said, "The thought of anyone else giving you what you need makes me murderous."

Music to his ears.

Dorian dipped his head down until they were almost touching noses. "That's because as my mate, your instinct is to feed only me." He leaned forward and clipped her earlobe with his teeth. The tiny prick would send shivers of desire all over her. "Does it ease your jealousy if I say no one's ever fed from me since I was taken in by these Lycan nearly three centuries ago?"

Lena leaned back, eyes narrowing. Suspicion looked adorable on her.

"I'll never lie to you, Lena. No one's taken my vein since I was a child." His father was the only vampire to ever tap Dorian's blood, between that, and Dorian getting raised by Lycan, no one in the vampire community would drink from him during a blood exchange. They considered him tainted and disgusting.

Ruined.

"Apart from one time with the King, the only vampire I've ever fed from is Lucian." Dorian's guilt for that never relented. An aristocrat like Lucian, feeding a low life like him was unacceptable in Dorian's eyes. Even though Lucian willingly and honorably opened his vein anytime Dorian asked, he couldn't shake his shame. "I don't do it often, only when I must."

He was used to going on so little, Dorian's body was accustomed to starvation. For better or worse, that never changed. Even while he lived with the Woods family, he never drank from anyone's vein. Dorian supplemented however he could, but in the end, had to join a vampire House, which turned out to be the best thing for everyone.

Having the King's blood in his veins now was a game changer for Dorian. A gift he didn't plan to let go to waste if he could put it to use and finish making a bond with Lena.

Turning her was another hurdle he'd save for later.

"Come on." He coaxed Lena towards the door. "We have a ceremony to watch."

Once outside, a cacophony of voices rose from all directions in the woods and surrounded them. ATV engines roared in the distance. Howls erupted. Lycan prowled the property in small groups, howling and hollering at one another. Escorted in on four wheelers or shifting and running through the woods in wolf form, all guests finally gathered, and the ceremony could officially begin.

Before Dorian lived with the Lycan, most everyone here was part of the Woods clan. But when Dorian was adopted, the other shifters nearly went to war with Alistair over it.

His adopted family chose Dorian over them. That decision cost the Woods family a lot.

It was one more hunk of guilt Dorian carried on his shoulders over the years. He had no clue what he would have done if Alistair hadn't taken him in. Back then, Dorian knew nothing of vampire Houses, let alone how to interact with someone. He went into shock the first time he was given a hot meal.

These Lycan taught him how to hunt, how to read, how to write and play…

They gave him everything, and it cost them everything.

Most who left eventually returned once Dorian joined a

vampire House and left the Woods family. Not that Alistair ever forgave them for their initial abandonment. The entire Lycan community was shaken by Alistair's devotion to Dorian. Some admired him for it, but most were disgusted by it. His children were constantly judged for having an adopted vampire brother too. Not that they ever let another Lycan's opinion get to them.

But it definitely got to Dorian.

He smelled the wood smoke from the massive bonfire burning on the other side of the barn. Okay, *barn* wasn't a good word for this structure. It was more like a massive extended dining room with a retractable wall that opened up to the massive bonfire lit for the ceremony.

"Once I came to live with them," Dorian said as he escorted Lena around to the right of the barn. "The pack broke away and left."

"Alistair must have felt betrayed."

"I'm sure he did, but he never said it. Not around me at least." They got closer to the fire. "They eventually came back, but Alistair makes them work for the invitation to join the ceremonies."

"That's generous of him."

Dorian thought so too.

"I smell vampire," snarled a Lycan about fifteen feet away.

"My son is here visiting," Alistair explained, then steered the Lycan away from where Dorian and Lena stood.

"We can watch the ceremony from here," he whispered against her ear. The night was young, and clouds covered most of the dark sky. The smell of pine and smoke wafted into his nose. It fucked with his head.

Lena frowned. "We're not allowed to be down with the rest of them?"

"My kind doesn't practice these rituals. I don't want to intrude." Dorian's heart sank a little. "Alistair's youngest, Killian, did this ceremony two years ago. He didn't find his mate in time."

Lena's gaze sailed to the half-circle of Lycan handing out vials of a watery liquid silver. "He turned?"

"Yes. And he stayed a wolf. He's lost forever to his animal." *And will eventually be hunted and put down.* Dorian couldn't bring himself to say that part. His heart couldn't take it.

Seeking comfort, he wrapped his arms around Lena's waist

and inhaled her cherry blossom scent.

"So those men... Lycan over there. They're all going to risk their lives to find their mate?"

"Mmm hmm."

"And they have until the next full moon?"

"Mmm hmm."

"What happens if their mate hasn't been born yet?"

Good question. "I believe their longing intensifies as their *Deesha* draws closer to being primed to turn Lycan. It's just a theory, but it's solid. A Lycan's soul would reach a fever-pitch with its need to be completed by a mate's bond. If they feel ready, then it's time to drink the silver water because their *Deesha* is out there already. If not..." he shrugged, "I suppose they just stay suspended in longing, as if its a chronic ailment, until the degree of emptiness they feel deepens."

Lena swallowed hard. "What happens if they find their mate on the last day?"

He didn't want to answer. The brutal truth wasn't something he was willing to unleash. But she got it. He watched her face pale and mouth slacken as the progression of events pieced together for her. It was life or death. A lifetime of joy or torment.

If it got down to the last day, there was no time to court or explain or coerce. It was bite or run. Sacrifice or surrender.

Dorian might not know when he'd burn to ashes, but he was giving Lena a chance to run. Pushing the limits of his curse to allow her time to make an educated decision. Lycan normally had a similar luxury. Their time on earth ticked down to a predetermined endgame. The shifters knew exactly how long they had, from the second they saw the vision of their mate, to the night the next full moon swung into that fatal position in the sky.

Tonight, five Lycan from the surrounding area were taking the leap.

Protectively, Dorian pulled Lena back to cover them in shadows. "Can you hear it?" he whispered against the shell of her ear. "Life, fear, hope—it's everywhere in these woods tonight."

Animals scurried. Fire crackled and popped. Those prepared to drink the liquid silver closed into a tight circle, praying for fate to guide them safely towards their mate, their *Deesha*. The rest of the Lycan? Well...

Dorian tucked his hand under Lena's chin and turned her head towards the direction of three Lycan fucking under a tree. He loved her gasp. Enjoyed how her pulse sped up. "Our curse is to always be in constant longing, remember?" His hands fell to skim along the sides of her breasts. "The satisfaction is temporary without a true mate."

But damned if Lycan and vampires alike didn't chase those little moments like a pack of ferocious beasts.

Dorian nipped under her ear and pressed his body flush against her back. She leaned into him, eager for what he had to offer. Savoring this tension, he ran his fingers across her belly in light strokes, relishing her fluttering muscles. "So responsive," he growled.

"Your hands are shaking," she whispered.

He didn't want to think about that right now. All he wanted was to be inside her in every way possible. Unhooking her bra clasp, Dorian ran his thumb across one of her hardened nipples and pinched it.

"Mmm." Lena's head hit his chest and she ground her ass against him. Fevered, he clamped both of her nipples this time and gave a twist. Then a tug. She let out a half-cry, half-grunt that got him ten kinds of worked up. "Are you going to turn me here?"

"I'm going to *fuck* you here." He maneuvered to block the view of the threesome behind him. "Turning will still take time."

"Time is something we don't have."

"Then stop wasting what's left of it." He playfully tugged the button on her jeans and unzipped them. Dropping down on his knees, he peeled her pants off slowly, then buried his face in her pussy. "No panties," he growled. "Are you trying to kill me, woman?"

"I wanted the friction," she confessed while threading her hand in his hair, guiding him back towards the joining of her thighs. At the last second, he turned his head and nipped her inner thigh playfully. "I want to drink from you again."

"Will I turn vampire this time when you do?"

He hated how she kept pushing this. "No. You'll need to drink from me for that to happen." Dorian peppered her skin with kisses. "I need to be in a better mindset before I turn you or I could damage your transition. I'm being careful so I don't destroy you,

229

Lena. I just want to offer you what I can for now." He coaxed her body to melt under his touch easily. Her thighs were already quivering. Damn, how he wanted to bite her again.

"Do it," she begged. "Do whatever it is you want to me."

Those were dangerous words.

"I want this." He scraped one of his fangs against the tender flesh of her inner thigh. "Say yes to me, Lena. Tell me I can taste you again."

Her grip tightened on his hair. "Will it feel like it did the last time?"

"Do you want it to?" Running his hands up and down her thighs and cupping her ass, he waited for her answer.

"Not this time. No."

He pushed his hair away from his eyes and looked up at her. Holy Hell, what a vision she was. Completely unabashed. "What would you like from me, Lena? Say the word and it's yours."

"I want to be turned."

"Soon," he growled, and kissed her thigh again. "I promise."

Around them, moans, howls, and laughter filled the air. He could hear the rushing sounds of the river about a quarter mile away. Smelled wood burning. Heard metal lids twist off mason jars filled with moonshine. Scents of fear, lust, and anger mixed in the air.

The word *vampire* kept getting thrown around. The moans behind them grew louder. Someone said, *Shhhh.* Twigs snapped as boots pounded along the forest floor. Wolves growled, completely out of sight. More Lycan were shifting.

His hackles raised. Dorian clenched his jaw and scanned the woods.

A hiss slipped from between his teeth.

Dorian suddenly second-guessed the safety of all this. He was out-numbered here. The most Lycan he ever fought at one time was seven. There were nearly ten times that many here tonight. Not that he wanted to fight but aggression pulsed in his veins again. Loud and fierce.

Something was wrong.

Really wrong.

Growls resonated in his ears. His senses were heightened somehow. *Pop, snap, crack!* The fire spat out embers. A female Lycan laughed. Bane and Bowen were talking in hushed voices. Footsteps dashed across the forest ground.

A branch snapped.

Dorian yanked Lena's jeans back over her ass. "Come with me." He ducked down and guided her closer to the house.

"What's happening? What's wrong?"

"I don't know," he admitted. "I don't feel right."

Dorian's grip tightened on Lena. He pulled her along, the instinct to get her back to the house driving him over the edge of paranoia and straight into panic territory. *Get her safe. Get her safe. Get her safe.* They were in danger. It made no sense, but Dorian knew it with every fiber of his being.

Howls erupted from all angles, and someone screamed.

Dread hit Dorian like a battering ram to the gut. *"Emily!"*

CHAPTER 31

Animals dashed through the woods, running far faster than Dorian could with Lena in tow. She yanked out of his hold, "Lead and I'll follow."

Damnit, if she was really going to be part of his world, threats weren't something she could run from. He couldn't hide her forever either. Taking her to the house wouldn't save her. Whatever was in these woods could easily break into the house next.

Dorian absolutely hated this with every fiber of his doomed being.

He wanted Lena to understand what she was getting into? Well, here was his chance.

"Stay behind me," he said and took off.

At the top of a hill, his curse kicked him in the balls. Vertigo flipped his ass upside down and he stumbled forward, tripping on a root and pinwheeling his arms to balance himself. Sucking in a harsh breath, he cursed. This was his own damn fault. His speed and fine-tuned senses were deteriorating because he hadn't turned Lena yet.

And here she was, right by his side, running into danger instead of away from it.

All because she was willing, didn't mean she should. He hated how his heart was cut in half right now—part of it scared shitless for Emily, and part of it thumped with relief to have Lena with him.

How sick was that?

Was it possible to fall in love with someone in a moment like

232

this? Yup. Sure was.

"I can't smell anything but you," he admitted. Dorian's gaze darted all over the woods. "I can't see anything clearly."

Lena tried to scan the area, but she didn't know what to look for.

Lycan zipped past them—stealthy and swift. Someone hollered. An animal yipped. Dorian's head jerked in the direction of those sounds and he took off again with Lena hot on his heels. The scent of freshly spilled blood hit his nose and Dorian's fangs grew a fucking pulse.

He followed it, crashing through thorn bushes, small trees, and brush.

Diabolical rage ignited in his gut.

"Oh my God." Lena gasped.

Hanging from a tree was a mutilated wolf. Emily stood below it, fisting the fur, trying to yank the dead animal down. She wouldn't stop yanking. Her hands, all the way up to her elbows, were covered in blood.

Dorian shielded Lena with his body. Not from the grotesque carnage, but from the Lycan now circling them. Under this level of threat, there was no telling what the Lycan might do to outsiders.

"Was it a *Savag-Ri*?"

The air crackled and thickened around them. Dorian's lungs tightened with dread he'd not suffered for centuries. "No."

This wasn't the work of a *Savag-Ri*. They never wasted time on an animal kill. Nor would they take a risk of this magnitude just to make a statement. They'd kill a Lycan and keep going, making sure nothing was left as evidence.

This? This was a show. A message.

But why? For who?

"A vampire did this," a Lycan growled. "I can smell its stench."

Dorian's nostrils flared. He couldn't smell anything but blood and a little of Lena's signature cherry blossom scent. The combo did awful things to his instincts. His body hardened. His possessiveness flared. His aggression turned him savage.

The angry Lycan faced Dorian, his golden gaze raking down his body in complete disgust. "Look at him," the Lycan seethed. "Bet he's got a hard-on for this." He spat in Dorian's direction, "You make me sick, you nasty piece of shit."

Dorian breathed through his mouth and tried to calm the fuck down before he leveled the Lycan or did worse to him. He was outnumbered here, and he had Lena to protect. This might be his family's property, but the Lycan clans who gathered for tonight's ceremony weren't his family or his friends. Dorian was only tolerated as a courtesy and only if he stayed a respectful distance from them.

He didn't want to cause trouble for the Woods family. They'd done so much for him over the years, he would never jeopardize his adopted family by attacking a Lycan on their land.

"Emily." His voice held all the control his temper lacked. "Step away from it."

Emily only wailed louder. "I can't tell," she sobbed. "I can't tell if it's Killian!" She kept yanking on the wolf while it dangled from a rope.

Alistair broke through the wall of Lycan and stumbled to a stop when he saw the animal and his daughter. "Emily," he barked at her. "Back away from it."

Marie showed up and cupped her mouth with both hands. "No."

Emily refused to stop pulling on the dead animal. "Is it Killian?" she screamed. "*Is it Killian!*"

Bowen picked Emily up, dragged her back. "Bane, get him down."

His twin climbed the tree, pulled out a blade, and sliced the rope. The wolf's body fell into a heap of fur and meat and splintered bones.

Dorian was going to fucking lose it.

Those bones. Those cuts. That —

"It's not him," Bane's voice cracked. "It's not Killian. It's just a wolf."

Marie fell to her knees and started sobbing. Dorian wanted to reach out to her and Emily, but if he budged, it could be misinterpreted as an attack. No Lycan outside the Woods family trusted Dorian. And they were all watching him now.

Blaming him.

"I didn't do this," Dorian snarled. "I was in the woods just beyond the barn all night."

It was wasted air. His reputation alone made him a suspect. His past was no secret, nor was his current position in the House of Death.

Dorian's gaze dragged back to the wolf on the ground with its dead eyes and mouth open, tongue lolling out. It made him want to puke. The cuts, the position of the bones. It was too familiar and yet strangely displaced.

He couldn't speak a word as several Lycan dropped to the ground while Dorian stood there like a shield for Lena. Everyone around them was scenting and confirming the same thing.

Vampire.

The word was released over and over, like a quiver of arrows aimed right at Dorian.

Bowen knelt and pulled something small from the wolf's crooked jaw. A piece of cardboard. Bowen's face paled once he read it, and his gaze snapped to Dorian.

"What does is say, son?" Alistair shoved forward. "Read it."

"Never forget, Fear Eater." Bowen handed the note to the first Lycan who reached for it. Then he wiped his hand on his pants as if the very cardboard was tainted and toxic. All eyes spun to Dorian.

Fear Eater.

That name would be the final nail in his goddamn coffin.

"Never forget," another Lycan snarled. "No, I don't think we ever will." He growled at Dorian, his lips peeling back to reveal teeth already sharpening as he started to shift.

Dorian's sick and twisted past wasn't a secret. He told Alistair and Marie everything when he first came to them a bleeding, broken bag of bones. As if confessing all the crimes committed, all the horrors witnessed, would bring him absolution and forgiveness. As if, in being openly honest—no matter how gruesome his stories—they would trust him because he hadn't lied.

He'd done the same thing once he joined the House of Death. Told Malachi everything.

Truthfully, he feared the monster he'd been carved into was a risk to any who took him in. He *wanted* the Woods family to know what they invited into their home, so he never hid his past, thoughts, or cravings. They took him in regardless of his warnings. Loved him like one of their own. Even asked permission to share his story with others. Dorian said yes, of course. Word spread and turned to warnings which turned to fear which turned to hate and disgust. All directed at Dorian.

Rumors of the Fear Eater spread across continents. The vampire child raised by a monster, forced to suck dry the veins of victims at their highest terror-point.

Fear Eater. The name was spat at him by countless Lycan and vampire over the centuries. It was the curse he could never break.

"Do you think this is funny, Fear Eater?" a furious Lycan named Derek growled. "What have you done, *Reaper*?"

"He didn't do this!" Lena roared.

Dorian squeezed his eyes shut and clenched his jaw. As much as he appreciated the back up, he didn't want Lena making this worse.

"Alistair." Derek went after the Alpha of this territory. "You open your home to this vampire and his little fang fucker, allow them to witness our most sacred ceremony, and look at what it's cost you. What it's cost *us.* How many times will you cough up the payment for this creature's sins?"

Alistair wasn't intimidated in the slightest. "If Dorian says he didn't do it, he didn't do it. This violence isn't his style."

Derek huffed a cold-hearted chuckle. "No, the Reaper's style is more dignified now, isn't it? He decapitates, tortures, disembowels, and does who knows what else with his victims. Just like his sire did before him." Derek had the nerve to touch the toe of his boot to the opened ribcage of this animal. "Didn't your sire do this to some of his favored ones? Is that how you learned to perfect cuts this clean?"

"Enough." Alistair growled.

Derek licked his lips with a smug look on his face. "Never. Forget. *Fear Eater.*" His gaze raked reproachfully down Dorian. "No, we never will forget the terrors you wrought."

Dorian's carefully constructed control fractured. He took a step forward, envisioning tackling this Lycan to the ground. Fury made his blood boil. Contempt killed his conscience. His fangs extended, making his gums bleed thanks to his curse. He wanted to rip this motherfucker's head off. Drink, drink, drink until he choked on Lycan blood. Tear this cocksucker limb from limb and scream at how wrong he was.

But Derek was right. Nothing the Lycan said was out of line.

Dorian had gone out of his way to become infamous for his execution style. He told everyone about his past and thus, his father's heinous acts.

"*How dare you*, Derek." Emily ripped out of Bowen's hold and ran at him. "You can fuck right off. Dorian would *never* do this!"

"Emily." Dorian didn't want her in the middle of this either. She had to live with these packs, not him. She couldn't afford to make enemies like Derek and the other Alphas here tonight. They were all watching her and the Woods family closely, biding their time until they challenged Alistair or Emerick for this territory.

Alistair turned to Dorian, his expression grave. Dorian knew that look. *Leave.* That's what he was silently pleading Dorian to do.

Leave.

If he stayed like he wanted, and helped search for the vampire who did this, it wouldn't go well because no one would believe the culprit acted without Dorian's knowledge. Or worse, consent. It could, and most likely would, start a war between these Lycan and the House of Death. Dorian needed to protect more than his mate and his position right now. He had a king to protect too, and a lot of vampires. Alistair needed to do the same for his kind.

"I'll escort them out," Emerick said and grabbed Dorian's arm. "Let's go." His voice was a warped growl. He was close to shifting.

With Lena by his side, Dorian could feel everyone's eyes on his back like a thousand daggers — stabbing, twisting, draining him down to a hollow shell.

"I didn't do this," he whispered.

"I know." Emerick ground his teeth and kept his gaze forward. "We'll take care of it."

He hated this. The Woods family always sided with him, which he appreciated, but at what cost to them? They'd lost so much already.

"I'd get that little fang fucker a metal collar!" Derek shouted. "Wouldn't want her pretty little neck to be ravaged and eaten off next."

Every molecule Dorian possessed turned to electricity. Emerick squeezed his arm, "*Don't.*"

They kept walking. Derek kept talking. "Hey sweetie, when you're done sucking off the psycho, be sure to get tested for STDs.

He probably humps his prey while he kills it. Can't imagine what's coating that filthy cock you like to suck on."

Emerick growled, most likely knowing that was the final straw.

Dorian stopped dead in his tracks. Rage burst out of him. Spinning to attack, Emerick's hold tightened around Dorian's bicep. He barely felt it. "Don't let him get under your skin, man. Derek's trying to prove to the rest that you're exactly what they fear."

"No one talks to Lena like that and lives."

Emerick doubled down. As strong as the Lycan was, he struggled to hold Dorian back so Alistair stepped in and helped.

"That's right!" Derek called out with a shit-eating grin. "Let Daddy Wolf and big brother take care of you. Maybe you should put a choke collar on your pet, Alistair."

Dorian wrenched free and Bane and Bowen blocked him from attacking Derek. It was maddening. Bowen said in a low tone, "*Don't* take his bait, Dorian. He's trying to get into your head. Don't let him."

If Dorian attacked, it would start a war between the House of Death and the Lycan. He didn't have time for that bullshit. But not retaliating in some way, went against Dorian's deranged moral code.

"Don't do it," Emerick warned.

He didn't.

But Lena did.

She calmly turned around and swaggered back to the crowd.

"Aww *shit*," Alistair groaned.

Aww shit was right. There was a sway to her hips, a grace in her stride. Marie walked with the same swagger whenever she was about to knock someone on their ass. Lena approached Derek, assessing him with disdain written all over her face. Dorian held his breath. She didn't say a word to Derek or the others. Didn't lose her composure one bit. Dorian's heart slammed in his chest with panic.

If Derek hits her, he dies.

Hell, if anyone touched his mate, they would die.

Everyone watched with bated breath. Dorian tried to reach for his blade, but Alistair's grip tightened around him arms. "Don't," he warned again.

Dorian wasn't going to fight the man who sheltered and loved him. But he couldn't stand there and let Lena go head-to-head with a shifter either.

It was maddening.

"What?" Derek smirked down at Lena like she couldn't do shit about what he'd just said.

Quick as a flash, Lena boxed his ears and punched him in the throat. Two strikes and *bam!* the Lycan went down on his knees instantly.

Bane half-chuckled. "I taught her that," he said, puffing with pride. "She how fast her reflexes are? She's prime for transitioning, Reaper."

Alistair barked, making him shut up.

Lena looked around at everyone else. "I'd happily stay to help you fight whatever vampire did this tragic and disgusting act to that wolf, but not at the expense of my mate. If you know his history already, then you know he's not a liar. What would be the point in hiding his truth now? If he said he didn't do it, why wouldn't you believe him and move forward and work together?"

"You know nothing of Lycan or vampires, girl."

Lena turned to the shifter snarling at her and she said, "I know of the blood curse on both your species. I know why you drink liquid silver, and why vampires stare at reflections. I know about the *Savag-Ri.*"

"Then you know too much, human."

Lena wasn't done. "I also know animal cruelty is unforgivable. I know you're all scared and hurt and pissed off. I am too."

Derek waved her off. "Get her out of here, Emerick. We don't need a tiny human whore acting like she's even *close* to our caliber."

"I just proved I was," Lena growled. Stalking over to the biggest Lycan—next to Alistair—she tipped her head back and glared at him. "Want me to drop you in three seconds too? Because I will."

"Watch yourself, girl." Derek shivered and snarled, then shifted into an explosion of black fur and vicious teeth. In human form, he was a foot taller than her, and a hundred pounds heavier, at least. In wolf form? Shit, even on all fours he came up to Lena's chest. Derek was an Alpha and built for fighting.

Lena didn't even flinch.

As if sensing Dorian already running towards her, she flicked her hand in the air, telling him to back off. His body obeyed her, though he didn't know how it was possible.

"Careful, Derek," Lena cautioned, staring the wolf directly in the eyes. "I might not be able to shift, but I've got my own set of claws and teeth, and I've been dying for a chance to use them."

Derek gnashed his teeth at her. Saliva dripped down the corners of his mouth as the fur on his back stood on end.

He attacked. Dorian's heart seized. With lightning speed, Lena screamed as she flipped on top of the wolf and slammed his muzzle shut.

"Holy shit," someone said from the sidelines. "That's..."

"Impressive. Necessary. Slightly scary," Bane said with a smile.

Lena squeezed Derek's snout. "Who needs the muzzle and choke collar here, asshole?"

"Damn," Bane said. "Someone just got a lesson in manners."

"Shut up, Bane," Alistair growled.

Unfazed and fearless, Lena climbed off the wolf and stabbed her finger in the air at him. "Don't ever try to make Dorian feel less than what he is again, or I'll wipe the goddamn floor with you."

Derek actually backed down and shifted into his human form again. Crouched on the ground, naked, he tossed her a smile that was one part hate, two parts humiliation, and three parts impressed.

"Apologize," Alistair barked at Derek.

He looked like he'd rather eat a broken glass sandwich, but said, "Sorry. I stepped out of line."

Dorian's eyes widened with shock. Derek's never apologized to anyone for anything. He was an alpha for fuck's sake, and alphas don't like being brought to heel. Although Dorian was impressed, he was also worried about the Lycan taking revenge for this humiliation.

Was Derek dumb enough to try?

Probably.

"Damn, Lena." Emerick regarded her like she was a masterpiece as she marched over to them. "Welcome to the family, woman."

She swept the hair out of her eyes, and Dorian saw that she

was trembling.

"Sorry," she said to everyone. "I'm..." her brow pinched as she tried to explain herself.

"No explanation needed, Lena." Dorian cupped her face and pressed his forehead to hers. He wanted to kiss her, mate her, and worship her for what she'd just done. Hell, he wanted to do it no matter what.

Dorian's heart swelled at the sight of her flushed cheeks and fiery gaze. It sparked a heat in his soul that scorched his heart and strangled his senses.

He had no idea love could pack a punch like that.

CHAPTER 32

Lena felt bad about the dead wolf. Animal cruelty was never okay, and the note left in its mouth didn't make a lick of sense to her, but it was clear it did for Dorian and some of the others.

Emerick rubbed the back of his neck as they walked towards the car. "I'll handle things and call you when we find something."

Not if, *when.*

"I'll make the execution worthy of the crime," Dorian promised.

He swayed on his feet, his face ashen and sweaty.

"Jesus, Dorian." Emerick got him into the car and handed Lena the keys. "Get him..." his voice died off.

"I'll take care of him," she said.

Emerick nodded and marched off, stripping out of his clothes as he went, then burst into his wolf form and took off.

Lena drove out of the Woods' property, with Dorian quietly sitting in the passenger seat. He didn't look well. He looked downright murderous.

She made it about an hour down the road until her nerves started to get the better of her. "Someone's after you," she said out loud. Lena suspected that the dead wolf and note, just like the Molotov cocktail before that, were meant for Dorian.

It made her feel protective of him. She needed to get him to safety. "Damnit." She kept glancing in the rearview mirror that wasn't there. The sideview mirrors had been removed too. She bit her lip and thought about how much trouble Dorian went through to live with no reflections. No risk of ever finding her and having his life cut short.

"No matter what happens," she said nervously, "I want to be turned."

Was that selfish to say? She didn't care. Her life was on the line now too and seeing what she was up against between vampires and Lycan, staying human made her inadequate. This was an unfair match for a fight.

Because she was in a fight, whether Dorian wanted her to be in one or not.

Lena raced down the road, hellbent to get them both to safety. All the while praying Dorian lasted long enough to get home.

She was going to be sick. Torn between anger and worry, she almost pulled over on the side of the road and forced him to turn her in a gutter. Time was ticking and making her panic.

"Hurry home." His voice was deep and groggy. "Can't... stay out... in open."

Home. She wasn't going to take him back to the House of Death. It was too far, so she decided to take him back to her house in Georgia. Lena craved the safety and comfort of familiar surroundings.

"Talk..." Dorian's head dropped back on the headrest, eyes heavy with exhaustion. "Tell me something."

Lena's heart cracked in half. She didn't have a clue what to talk about.

"Mmph." Dorian's head lolled, and he smacked it against the window.

"Don't die on me," she pleaded. "Please don't die on me, Dorian." She slammed down on the gas and pushed the limits of his car. Worried it might already be too late, she shoved her arm in his face, "Drink."

Please, please, please...

What more could she do? Why was he dropping so fast? Was this how vampire curse deaths happened? Fast and without much warning?

She was going to puke. "*Drink!*"

He shoved her arm down and held it with both his hands. "Please... Lena...talk."

Talk about what? Her shitty childhood? Her fucked up life? The weather?

Swallowing the lump in her throat, she decided giving him fluff stories would be a disservice. Dorian had showed her all his ugliness. Exposed every truth he had. She needed to do the same with him.

"My parents had me later in life. I think they did it because they wanted to leave their wealth and legacy in the family. I spent my entire childhood in my own personal Hell."

Dorian let go of her arm, and his fists clenched in his lap.

Gripping the wheel with both hands she said, "They dressed me like a doll. Made me take etiquette and dancing classes. I was groomed to please and curtsy and charm. As a made-up doll, I felt like I had no say. I was just a puppet who wasn't allowed to speak up for myself or feel things. Just do as I was told." Up ahead was the exit she needed to head home. Lena flicked her blinker, habitually looked behind her, and frowned because the damn mirrors weren't there. "I hated every second of my childhood— from the parties to the nannies, to the private school system and later… the match making."

A guy in a navy-blue hoodie was walking along the side of the road. She sped past him, veering into the opposite lane, then looped onto the ramp and hopped on the highway.

"The more my parents pushed me—when they were around to actually do it themselves—the more I rebelled. I remember my first fight. It was with this asshole my senior year in high school. He would pull my hair all the time in the hallway. He'd done it for three years, every day. My mother taught me to be tolerant. 'It's nothing more than harmless flirting,' she'd say. But I hated it. So, this one day, just after English, we were switching classes and I see his smug face come straight at me from the opposite end of the hall. I didn't wait for him to reach out and yank my hair. Instead, I dropped everything except my heaviest book, and I clubbed him upside the head with it."

She smiled at the memory.

"That smack of the book on his face was music to my ears. He careened, holding his face. Then his temper rose and fists closed." Lena's pulse sped up. "He tried to intimidate me. Pressed me against the lockers. Shoved his hand on my chest to pin me while he called me names and chewed me out for what I did."

A terrifying growl rumbled out of Dorian's chest, but his gaze remained fixed on the road.

"I slapped him as hard as I could. But it was weak. So damn weak. Then I pushed against him, but he had about six inches and fifty pounds on me so that wasn't helpful. He slammed me against the lockers again, and I cracked the back of my head. Then I saw red. Everyone was watching, he was laughing at me, then he pulled my hair hard enough to rip some of it out. I jabbed my fist into his nose and broke it. Broke my thumb too because I didn't have a clue how to make a proper fist. They don't teach you that stuff in etiquette class. Then teachers interfered, and I was suspended for two weeks."

Best two weeks of her adolescence too. Her parents were so disgusted by her behavior, they wouldn't even look at her, so she had time to herself with no parties, dinners, or snobby match ups with other pompous assholes her age.

"The rush of swinging my fist and not taking his shit anymore was worth the price of my broken thumb."

But that wasn't all...

"I'd finally stood up for myself." Her stomach clenched because she was about to tell him something she hadn't thought about for a long time. "Before that fight..." She gulped down her nerves, "I'd been attacked by someone else."

Dorian's next growl was stronger. She took that as a sign that he was maybe getting better again.

"My parents were in the middle of a big property deal. The guy who owned the land they wanted in Vermont said he'd only sell them the property if he got to fuck me."

She was sixteen at the time.

"I didn't know it, but when my mom picked out this ridiculous dress and told me I had to wear a set of blue lace lingerie under it... I started asking questions. She said I was to just have dinner with the guy. Alone." She gripped the wheel tighter. "It was almost too late when I realized I was the dinner."

Dorian let out a vicious hiss.

"I froze," she admitted. "He paid our bill and then said he was going to drive me home. He didn't. We sat in a parking lot and he put his hand in between my thighs. I was so scared and mad and hurt because when I threatened to tell my parents what he was doing, he laughed in my face and slapped me. He told me this was

245

part of their negotiation. My untouched body for sixteen-hundred acres containing six of the largest interconnecting mountain peaks for another ski resort. My parents sold my virginity to grow their portfolio. Then he told me he'd bought the dress and underwear and gave it to my mother to dress me in for that night. He called me his pretty little doll. His pretty little fuck doll."

Dorian slammed his fist into the dashboard. Another horribly vicious noise ripped out of him. Was it terrible that she liked his reaction? Was it twisted that his violent outburst made her feel safe?

Lena kept talking. If making him mad and furious, triggering his protective instincts, igniting passion of any level kept him going right now, she would happily confess her whole life story to him.

"He smacked me a couple more times when I started crying. So, I stopped. Then he unzipped his pants and pulled his dick out. I was terrified of what he was going to make me do. I pushed myself against the door to put as much space between the two of us as possible. He made me flash him my panties while he jerked himself off in the driver's seat and told me to watch." She'd been scared to death. "I didn't know how to get out of it, so I—" She blew out a puff of air. "I did all the things my mother pressed upon me. I was tolerant. Complacent… obedient."

Dorian made a strangled noise.

"He didn't touch me, even after he came all over his slacks and hand," she said, now worried Dorian would shred the car in a fit of rage. "I managed to talk him into taking me to a hotel. I told him if I was going to give him my virginity, I wanted to be treated like a spoiled fuck doll, not a cheap one. He let me pick the hotel. When he pulled up to the valet, I got out first and sprinted into the lobby, screaming my head off. The concierge knew me, my parents always ate dinner in their restaurant. He kept me hidden in the back and called the cops."

Her parents hated her for that. The lawyers, the press, the truth—it cost them bank to keep it all quiet. And they lost the deal on the property. Her mother was furious. Her father never spoke another word to her after that.

"So back to the hair pulling asshole," she said, smiling. "I was thrilled to have finally found my voice. If it was violent, so be it. I'd been tolerant long enough with him too, so when I got suspended for two weeks, I signed up for boxing lessons. That dickwad never

246

pulled my hair again. And I stopped being a complacent, fearful little mouse in a den of lions."

She kept talking and talking, trying to fill the empty space between them the whole way home. Lena bit her lip and sped faster, hating that she kept looking in her rearview and it wasn't there.

"I trained with this one guy," she jabbered on. "His name was Mick. You would have liked him. He taught me most of what I know now. Then one day he asks me if I want to get my hands dirty and fight with some big boys. I was all for it, so he brought me to my first underground fight as a spectator. No gloves. No protection. No mercy. Just sweat and raw aggression with a lot of pounding. I was like an addict after that. The entire time I trained in the boxing ring, I burned my anger off with the punching bag, or Mick, since he was the only one who gave me the time of day there. I convinced him to finally let me into my first fight. When I hopped into the circle with sweat, piss, blood, and men screaming and cheering over each other surrounding me? Something clicked into place in my heart. I had to prove myself first, of course." She pulled off on an exit to fill up their gas tank on that note. Dorian still hadn't said a word, but that was okay. His color looked better at least. And they were almost home.

Hopping back inside, she strapped her seatbelt back on and looked over at Dorian. Sweat trickled down his temples and his jaw clenched, making the lines of his profile sharper. Lena started the car up and headed out again. She looked back and cursed the fact that she kept trying to use a mirror that wasn't there.

A figure ran past her on the right. A guy in a blue hoodie. The same guy she saw earlier. Wait... what? No. By the time her head caught up with her body, she looked again, and the guy was gone.

Okay, wow, stress really did awful things to a person's mind.

Lena wasn't mentioning it to Dorian. Not without knowing for sure it wasn't just a trick of her exhausted mind. He had too much on his plate as it was. But she needed to keep on guard for both their sakes.

She eyed the blade strapped to Dorian's hip and wished she had one too.

Maybe she should say something?

Nope. They were both wiped out and shit kept getting worse.

Dorian could likely die if they went hunting for a vanishing hoodie guy she may or may not have hallucinated because she was up to her neck with stress too.

Her priority was Dorian right now. Saving him was all that mattered to her.

"Anyway," she said, picking up where she left off. "Mick died of a heart attack before I made a real name for myself with the guys in that fight club. I met Bane a couple years ago and he started giving me pointers."

She flicked her gaze towards him and frowned. "Are you okay? Should I stop talking?"

Dorian's nostrils flared. He didn't say a word.

Lena drove the rest of the way home—her home—in complete silence. Then she began questioning everything.

Was this the right thing to do? Should she force herself on Dorian and make him turn her? Was he second guessing being tied to someone like her?

The instant she saw her house come into view Lena nearly burst into tears. The relief of being home, in her familiar space, was overwhelming. She pulled into her driveway, numb and blurry-eyed. It hadn't occurred to her how much she needed to be home until she was on her soil.

Hopping out, she silently helped Dorian out of the car. He looked like he was knocking on death's door even though he tried to say he would be fine. As he followed her up the steps, a flurry of emotions whirled around her at once. Resentment, fury, sadness, loneliness, fear, worry.

How much happened in the past twenty-four hours?

Too much. Looking over at Dorian, she realized also not enough.

Pulling her attention off the swaying vampire at her side, Lena stared at her front door for a minute and panicked. She didn't have her keys. They were… hell, they were all the way back in New Orleans in her hotel room! Pressing her hand to the door, she almost started to cry. Okay, she really needed to get it together. Now wasn't the time for tears. Bristling, she remembered her spare key under the flowerpot.

So cliché, but this neighborhood and her life were safe and quiet.

Until now.

The realization of her current situation hadn't really settled in until just this moment. No number of locks could keep this new danger out. Planting petunias and hanging ferns off the porch wouldn't ward away enemies. Philanthropy wasn't going to buy her a damned thing in this new life.

She was no safer here than at The Wicked Garden, the mansion, or on pack land.

Safety was an illusion.

CHAPTER 33

Dorian had spent the entire ride focusing on the sound of Lena's voice. The more she talked, the easier it was for him to breathe past the ache in his chest. He clutched every word, every syllable, that flowed from her sweet lips. And her scent. As bad as he'd wanted to roll the windows down and get fresh air, there was no goddamn way he was willing to trade a whiff of her for anything so meaningless as air.

Incapable of driving and unwilling to risk getting into an accident and Lena getting hurt just so he could have control behind the wheel he'd sat in the passenger seat and focused on not dying.

He begged her to talk. Her voice the balm to soothe his burn. Not once did he imagine she'd confess those horror stories. Each bit of her past fueled his ass to live long enough to destroy the bastards who hurt her.

Hey, everyone has goals in life, right?

Damn, his woman was fearsome. To know how terrified she must have been back then and how bold she was now? It was mind-blowing and humbling to have Lena in his life.

Once Dorian stepped foot on her porch, deja vu ran his ass over. The last time he stood in this very spot, he'd been willing to give her up and die without ever having seen her face or touched her body. Now? He was a very different creature.

Jamming her key in, Lena unlocked and opened things up. He was blasted in the face with the heady scent of his mate and his body responded... *intensely*.

"Do you need to be invited in since you're a v—"

He crushed his mouth to hers and gobbled up her moans. Fuck, she felt good. It was as if just touching her surged power into him. For Lena to have such an affect on him was incredible. Undeniable. He pulled back and inhaled her sweet cherry scent again.

Lena looked flushed. "Are you going to stand outside all night, or come in?"

Dorian made no move to do so. "You invite a monster into your house."

"Ever consider a monster just lured you into her lair?"

Touché. He stepped into Lena's home and his world fell off its axis. Everything about this place was his mate. The colors, the scent, the sounds. He was starstruck by it. Breathing in through his nose, he filled his body with new life, relishing how his senses had returned to him. He looked around and his heart melted a little. He guessed it, little colorful throw pillows on her couch.

"I'll just be a minute. Make yourself at home." Lena ducked away and went upstairs.

While he waited, Dorian looked around her first floor. Thankfully, his vision cleared again. He'd gone blind on the ride home and didn't want to freak her out with the news. They were the longest moments of his life. Dorian kept running over threats in his mind. If someone attacked them on the road, he'd be useless. Sloppy.

But it wouldn't have stopped him.

He was grateful they got here safely and without incident. He'd walked carefully up her driveway, hellbent on not letting her find out how messed up he was. Then she was in front of him, opening the door and he could see her silhouette. Once Lena opened things up, it was like the sun blazed into his soul and his vision returned. It wasn't perfect, but it was enough. More than enough for now.

Dorian ran his hand across the back of her sofa. It was soft and cream colored. Her walls were a pale gray. Maybe. It was hard to make out colors just yet. He went into the kitchen next, his nostrils flaring. This was the strangest thing—to scan for threats and be consumed by the love of your life's very existence at the same time.

He smiled at a pile of lemons in a bowl. *I knew it*. The counter and cabinets were white. Sleek stainless appliances and a large stove range. Cautiously, slowly, he prowled around the first floor, taking in everything, constantly sweeping the area for lurking threats.

He was going to turn her tonight. If he could get his ass back in gear and head on straight, he was turning Lena. He wanted a life with her. Immortality with her. He just needed to get his head in the game.

His body and soul were already there.

His ears perked up to the faintest sound of a kitten mewling. Dorian listened closely. Aww hell, it wasn't a kitten.

It was Lena.

His heart seized and he took the steps, two at a time. "Lena?" No answer. "*Lena?*" Still no answer. He tracked that godawful sound all the way through her bedroom and into her bathroom. He pushed the door open...

"I'm sorry." She sniffled on the side of her tub. "I'm—"

Dorian lowered between her legs. "It's me who should be apologizing. I've drug you into a mess."

"No." Lena wiped her nose with the back of her hand. "I'm just tired and confused."

He looked around for a towel to dry her eyes with but ended up cupping her face and wiping her cheeks with his thumbs. He wanted to lick those salty tears away. He wanted to lick every inch of her. The longer he held her, the closer he drew near, the clearer his senses became.

"Is this a spell?" she blurted out. "Is this some kind of compulsion I'm under?"

It's me who's spelled and beguiled, he wanted to say. *It's me who's under your thrall.* "I don't have that skill set," he said cautiously. "Nor would I ever use such a thing on you."

"I can't tell what's real anymore," she whispered. "Everything feels weird. I don't understand what's happening now." She started sobbing and he figured recent events had finally caught up with her. Now that she was back in *her* safe space, she was allowing herself to fall apart.

Christ, he was an asshole for all of this. He made her this way. He was the reason for her tears.

Like he needed another reason to hate himself?

"Why do you feel spelled?" Call him paranoid, but part of him feared she was under someone else's enthrallment, though the possibility was practically zilch. Still...

"I don't understand why I feel this drawn to someone I barely even know. Why I feel this possessive and protective of you." She sniffled again. "And my feelings are getting worse."

Worse, or stronger?

He swallowed the lump in his throat. It was most likely getting worse because *he* was getting worse.

"You're tired," he said quietly, scooping her into his arms and carrying her to bed. "You need rest. I'll stay close, but you have to get some sleep." He laid Lena gently in her fluffy bed with more pillows on it than made sense. Then he doubled back to get her some water and pain reliever meds because she had to have a raging headache at this point. He sure as shit did.

Dorian slipped back into her bathroom to look for medicine. Her cabinets were filled with bandages, creams, splints. He gawked at the amount of first aid she had. Holy... shit. This was all for when she came back from a fight?

His heart perked up at the fact that his mate was such a fearless fighter. Not many women were built like Lena... in fact, he was certain she broke the mold the day she was created.

And she's created for me... as I am for her.

Dorian grabbed a bottle of pain relievers from a bin under her sink and went down to the kitchen for a glass of ice water. "I'll be back with something for you to drink." He doubted she even heard him, he moved so fast.

Skidding down the steps, he stopped long enough to lock her front door, then made his way into the kitchen. Yanking the fridge open, he snagged a bottle of water and slammed it shut. He caught movement outside her window. "The fuck?" He peered outside, arm already reaching into the knife block, fingers wrapping around the first thing they touched as he looked out into her sunny backyard.

A cluster of birds flew out of a tree and landed on the ground, pecking, and hopping around before scattering to the sky. Narrowing his eyes, he scanned the yard again just in case, but it was hard to tell what was what. His vision was depleting again because he was too far from Lena.

Backing up, he smacked into her kitchen island. A butcher block and cleaver lay on the counter, next to the bowl of lemons. Dorian's lips curled at the sight of that blade. He tucked the damned thing under a small dishtowel and headed back upstairs to take care of his mate.

Lena was passed out on the bed, her hair a mess of wisps and tiny knots around her face. Dorian smoothed her hair away and kissed the top of her head. Then her temple. Then her cheek. Her jaw. He got as far as under her ear before stopping himself. His fangs throbbed and his cock hardened. He drew back before he went too far.

Sitting on the edge of the bed, Dorian studied Lena while she slept… all the while planning what he needed to do in order to keep her forever.

CHAPTER 34

Dorian held Lena in his arms, cherishing even her breathing rhythm, when a terrible, familiar sensation blazed down his spine. It was the same one he felt when he'd flashed. *Shit, shit, shit!* He had no control over this!

Suddenly, he was standing in the heart of the House of Death, breathless and disoriented. Malachi sat in his massive chair in front of his big ass mirror. Lucian stood at the other end of the table, pouring blood into a wine glass for their king. He took one look at Dorian's sudden appearance and dropped the crystal. It shattered, spilling blood all over the floor. "Holy shit."

Dorian gasped to catch his breath.

"You've fed." Malachi didn't bother looking over at him. *"Good."*

"What's—" Dorian held his arms out and stared at them. They felt like a million ants were nibbling on his skin. "What's going on? How the hell did I just flash here? I wasn't thinking of this place at all."

"How did you flash *at all*?" Lucian gawked. He knew Dorian didn't have that ability before now. Not all vampires were built the same, and anyone who could flash usually had royal blood in them.

"I called my blood in you." Malachi's brow arched.

Dorian heard the King had that power, but as far as he knew, Malachi never used it. Probably because he never fed anyone in the House. The idea that he could force Dorian to come when called didn't sit well with him. It made him feel too out of control of his own body.

"Relax," Malachi grumbled. "I can only do it once."

So, the fear was evident in Dorian and the king saw it. Great. Now he felt exposed.

Why was everything making him feel vulnerable? *Because I am vulnerable until this curse it dealt with.* "I need to get back to Lena."

"Not yet," Malachi said. "We have a problem."

Lucian was still stuck on Dorian flashing. "His new power is from *you*, Malachi?" When the king didn't respond, Lucian approached Dorian with his eyes still wide in shock. "You *fed* from our King?"

"I'm not losing my Reaper." Malachi growled. "Nor am I the only one he's fed from. But it wasn't enough. Not nearly enough. Sit, Dorian."

A chair skidded back from the large table and Dorian's ass slammed down on it. He wasn't in control of his body. "Sire?" Dorian's panic rose.

Malachi put a finger up, his gold ring glinting in the candlelight. His gaze remained fixed on the huge, gilded mirror, even as Marius stormed into the room with an entourage parading behind him.

"I demand answers!" Marius thundered.

"And I demand you keep your voice at a reasonable volume," Malachi growled. "Lest I rip your throat out to force your silence, you ill-bred imp."

What. The fuck. Was happening. Dorian and Lucian both looked at each other for a heartbeat before Lucian snapped into guard mode. Dorian, however, remained in his seat. He couldn't move a muscle beyond leaning forward or leaning back. It was like being in some kind of invisible straight jacket. This was the king's doing, but why? It felt violating. Scratch that, it *was* violating. It brought out the bad pieces of Dorian he wished would stay buried.

"Another of my men has gone missing." Marius slammed his fist upon the large table.

"And this is our problem, how?" Lucian's entire demeanor morphed into a cold, calm, aloofness that was sure to push all of Marius's buttons.

"He was last seen here," Marius accused, jabbing his jeweled finger on the table, "in *your* territory."

"We're not babysitters." Lucian shrugged. "If you can't keep track of those in your service, that's not our issue."

"He was important," Marius growled. "He was a *weaver*."

That got everyone's attention. A weaver was a gifted vampire who could turn the bones of *Savag-Ri* into the enchanted dust they used to keep them away from vampire property. It worked the same way salt warded against evil in some forms of witchcraft. Basically like how brick dust was used to protect and repel negative energy in other practices.

"If he was so important, surely he would have had an escort with him. Start there." Lucian's jaw locked after that. As in locked and wouldn't reopen voluntarily.

"He was my son's lover," Marius said with great distaste. He pulled a photo out of his breast pocket and slammed it on the table. "I demanded they break up about a year ago. Stryx was... unforgiving about it."

Which would explain why the young vampire might have run away.

It made more sense now. Marius couldn't afford to lose his son over something this foolish. Stryx was, after all, the heir to the House of Bone and a pure-blooded vampire.

Malachi didn't bother looking at the photo. "Do you think this one went looking for Stryx, or might they have run off together?"

"I don't know." Marius sagged into a chair. "I only want my boy back. I can't sleep knowing he's out there unprotected. He's too young, too foolish for this world. If they've run off together, I must find them. I can't lose my son over a romantic tragedy. I refuse to accept that. And Bram's a naïve idiot."

Marius slid the picture across the table, and Lucian picked it up to study it first. His mouth twitched. Then he handed the photo over to Dorian without making eye contact.

One glance at the photo and Dorian knew why too.

"Bram's dead." Dorian dropped the picture on the table like it was dipped in poison.

Malachi blindly reached out for his glass of blood and took a sip. "How do you know this, Reaper?

"Because I blew his fucking head off myself. With *Savag-Ri* ammo."

Bram was the one who set fire to Dorian's house. The one who Lena fought in the middle of the street with.

"How dare you!" Marius bolted from his seat and flashed to him. Lucian beat him there. "He attacked Dorian's house, Marius. Set the thing on fire with Dorian still in it. We were within our rights to punish him."

"*Punish*," Marius seethed. "Not annihilate!"

"No." Dorian leaned back in his chair. "He earned death the second he put a blade to my *mate's* throat."

Silence fell like a heavy blanket over them.

"Bullshit." Marius raked an angry gaze over Dorian. "You have no mate."

Dorian bit down and let his fangs pierce his inner lip. The slight tang of his blood tasted different now. Different... because he had Lena in him.

"I demand to see her. I want *proof!*" Marius, King of the House of Bone, looked around the room and tossed his arms in the air. "Where is she then, Reaper?"

He didn't trust Marius at all. Or the sleezy entourage accompanying him. For all he knew, this was one massive set up to make Dorian look even worse so the House of Bone could wage war and demand custody of Dorian as retribution for killing royalty or a royal's property without a proper trial. If they already sacrificed a weaver, and were also using the king's son for this charade, how far would they really go to get Dorian in their House? Or worse... have him executed for attacking their sacred members? Marius wanted the House of Death's fighters. That was well-known. He hated Malachi — another truth that was universally known. But why drag Dorian into this? It made zero sense.

Stryx was still out there. Was he going to attack? When, where, why? Did Stryx even have the balls to attack? Most royals were pampered pussies, Dorian couldn't imagine the prince going assassin on anyone.

No, something wasn't right about this.

"I want to see your so-called *mate*," Marius insisted. "I want to hear her spit out this preposterous lie herself."

Dorian knew why and the reason infuriated him. If Lena lied to Marius, he'd be within his rights to punish her for it. Humans were food and entertainment for most vampires. Unless Dorian could turn her, she'd fall under a different set of House rules — fated or not.

But it wasn't a lie. Lena was his mate. That didn't mean Marius wouldn't try to trap her in another falsehood just to take her away from him and set a war into motion. For that's exactly what he'd get if this asshole tried to come for Lena. Fuck territories. Fuck kings. Fuck laws. And fuck this.

The longer he stayed here, the longer Lena remained vulnerable and unprotected in her house.

He couldn't stand this.

"Dorian will bring her here shortly." Malachi's empty wine glass thudded on the table. "You're welcome to remain as guests of my House until that time, Marius. But if you treat my men the way you treat your own, I will escort you outside myself and drain you dry."

Marius glowered, his jaw flexing as he clenched his teeth over and over.

One of Marius's escorts whispered, "He's *lying* about Bram, sire. The executioner would never use a gun. You know this. He only ever uses blades and teeth."

"I made an exception," Dorian said calmly. "Don't presume you know all my methods of killing, asshole. I've got tricks that will make your blood scream before it drains from your bony little body."

Marius tensed. "You're up to something, Reaper. You're *all* up to something."

"Funny, we were just thinking the same about you." Lucian poured his king another glass of wine and handed it to him without looking.

Marius's eyes narrowed and he jabbed a finger at Dorian. "Have you turned her?"

"Why are you so fixated on his mate?" Lucian snarled.

"Answer the question, Reaper."

Dorian did no such thing.

"That's a no then." Marius smiled wickedly. "Good to know."

Dorian tried to leap from the table and couldn't move. His instinct was to rip the vampire's head from his shoulders for that mild threat, yet he sat still as a statue, looking the epitome of calm. His vision darkened until he went completely blind again.

"If you try to harm her, Marius," Dorian seethed from his seat, "I'll personally tear you in half. Starting with that tight ass of

259

yours, and ripping you clean up to that fat mouth you like to use so much."

"I'm royalty!"

As if that mattered?

"Yeah, a royal pain in our ass." Lucian chuckled. "And you're nothing but a guest on our territory. We have our own set of House rules, just like you. You have no power here, Marius. Remember that."

Dorian leaned in and glared at the furious vampire king, praying his gaze landed on its mark. "I get why you're emotional over your son, but that doesn't mean you can stomp in here with your parade of asslickers and think we'll bend over for you. And if you threaten my mate in anyway..." His nostrils flared as he sucked in a breath. "You so much as make a shit remark about the hair on her head, I'll eat your tongue out for the insult and let her finish you off. And she will. My *alakhai* is as savage as the devil himself."

"Well, you would know," Marius seethed. "You're so well acquainted with monsters and barbarians."

"Keep talking," Dorian purred, "while you still can."

Marius looked around at each of them, disgusted and frazzled. "You're all animals here."

Lucian blew him a kiss. Malachi didn't break his stare from the mirror.

"Then I'd tread carefully if I were you." Dorian flashed a toothy smile. "Animals like us eat prey like you for a snack. And, dare I say, my King is famished. Aren't you, sire?"

"Beyond reason," Malachi purred.

The instant Marius and his band of merry motherfuckers left the room, Dorian regained movement.

"Forgive the intrusion," Malachi said from his seat. "I know how you abhor control being taken away, Dorian. But I also know that you're not in your right mind yet. Cutting you loose could have done more damage than I'm prepared to suffer today."

Dorian wanted to roar over the violation of losing control of his body, but the king was right. He'd have murdered Marius the instant he tried to threaten Lena. That death could wait for another day. Any energy spent now, was less energy saved for Lena later. He had a lot left to take care of with her.

"I brought her to my family."

"Nice," Lucian said with a grin. "How'd she like it?"

"Good until a wolf was found dead and strung up with a note shoved in its mouth," Dorian rubbed his forehead. "Oh, and Lena dropped a Lycan with two hits."

Lucian's mouth fell open. "No shit?"

"Your mate is built for this lifestyle," Malachi noted. "She'll be an asset to us."

Oh hell no. "She's not to be used for anything." Dorian's hands tightened into fists.

"That's her decision, don't you think?" Malachi paused before adding, "I doubt your mate likes being told what to do or how to live."

Dorian stared in Malachi's direction. All he saw was black, black and more black. A few tiny twinkles of the occasional star or blob. He wanted to bark back at his king but couldn't. Malachi was right. Lena had spent her life being shaped into what someone else wanted and she'd hated every bit of it. Rebelled against it. If Dorian brought her into this life and made her a member of the House of Death, he couldn't force her into a safe role if she didn't want it. Nor would he.

"Forgive me, Reaper. I wouldn't have torn you from her if I'd known you hadn't turned her by now. But House business is still Reaper business."

Which meant this was Dorian's final warning to get his shit together.

"Jesus." He gripped the sides of his head. "I can't bear to think of her turning into something like me."

"Damnit, Dorian!" Lucian slammed his fist on the table. "For the love of all that's unholy, please stop hating yourself for things you couldn't control!"

He sat at the table, speechless. They didn't get it. No one did.

"We're made however we're made," Lucian went on. "I'm sorry your father did so much wrong, but you've more than made up for it your entire life!"

"You mean I've carried on and continued his cycle."

"Is that what you think?" Lucian gripped Dorian's shirt. "That you've continued the cycle of killing innocents?"

No... "I'm saying all I've done is put more men in body bags."

"Rephrase," Malachi commanded.

"I've put more *Savag-Ri* in body bags..." Not innocents. Never innocents.

"That's right. You've protected our House since day one of your arrival." Lucian let go of his shirt and Dorian didn't even have the heart to straighten it out and smooth away any wrinkles. "You deny yourself any joy," he fumed. "You refuse to live in the House with the rest of us, refuse to be part of anything other than our hunts and executions. Jesus, have you ever even come to a dinner?"

The answer was no. He wasn't worthy. Dorian kept hunting and killing on behalf of the greater good because that was all he knew to do. The only way he could say thank you for accepting him.

Welcoming him.

Holy Hell, why hadn't he realized his hang-ups sooner? They accepted him when he pledged fealty to Malachi, and still he pushed them all away or, at the very least, kept them at arm's length. Victoria, Reys, Lucian, and Xin were the only ones who never took offense to his introverted ways. Same for the king.

He'd blown it. Ruined his whole life by keeping everyone away because he feared himself.

No, that wasn't right either. He *hated* himself. Hated what he might one day turn into—his father. A monster.

Fear Eater. But fear was never what he tasted in those victims. It was hate. And his father forced him to drink so much... it made Dorian hate himself. "You'll never be him," Lucian's voice cracked. "Jesus, Dorian, when are you going to understand that?"

Probably never. Not entirely. But he was starting to.

"The Lycan have shaken you." Malachi's deep voice softened.

The Lycan hadn't, it was that damned note. "There was a piece of cardboard in the wolf's mouth that said, *Never forget, Fear Eater.*" Dorian dropped his hands. "The beast was splayed in an old-fashioned wing job."

They knew what that meant. All vampires eventually learned of Dorian's father's practices. The "old-fashioned wing job" was taken from ancient practices of torture. Dorian never dared to do it

262

because no one and nothing deserved that level of pain and torment.

Do you think they can fly, son? His father would ask. *If I gave them wings, would they beat the air as furiously as their heart beats blood?*

"Someone had to have followed you up to pack land." Malachi growled. "They're doing this as a means to shake you."

Lucian sighed somewhere to Dorian's left. "Think it's the House of Bone? They certainly have been persistent lately. Like a toe fungus."

"Perhaps," Malachi rubbed his chin.

"I'm not worth this much effort." Dorian couldn't be convinced otherwise. "It makes zero sense."

"You don't know your worth," Malachi growled. "Remedy that immediately, Reaper."

"Maybe a Lycan did it," Lucian cut in. "It's not like they haven't fucked with us a gazillion other times to spark a new battle between House and Clan."

"This was during their sacred ceremony," Dorian argued. "They'd never bring impurity to their rituals. And *never* would they sacrifice one of their own."

"Was it a lost Lycan?" Lucian asked.

"No." But wolves, even the regular variety, were one of their own. "They said they smelled vampire."

"And naturally, blamed you." Lucian groaned. "Assholes."

"They have a right to suspect me, given who I am."

Malachi hissed.

"What did you smell there?" Lucian was closer to Dorian now. "Could you verify the scent? Was it truly a vampire?"

"I couldn't smell anything except Lena by the time we found the wolf. She's all I know, smell, taste... see." He turned his head in Lucian's direction and had no way of confirming if he was meeting his friend's eyes or not.

"Shit."

That's all he needed to hear to know he'd missed his mark. Dorian rose to his feet. "I have to get back to her."

"Turn her, Reaper. By the looks of things, your time is near."

Yeah, he didn't need the king's reminder. He could feel the blisters forming on his back already.

CHAPTER 35

Lena rarely dreamed, and when she did, they were always weird. Like she was two different people, split and floating above everyone—including herself—she watched things unfold like a movie.

The Lena before her wore a pale pink gown and perfectly manicured nails. Her hair was pinned into a cascade of curls down her back. She drank from one of her mother's antique teacups—a collector's gem Lena was never allowed to touch from the cabinet in their outrageously large dining room.

Inside the cup wasn't tea. It was deep, thick red liquid that coated the rim. She took a sip and tasted nothing. She never tasted anything in her dreams.

"Lena."

She turned around and saw a blurry faced woman come towards her and knew it was her mother. "What are you doing, girl?"

"Drinking." Lena took another sip. Swallowed.

"I didn't raise you to be so…"

"So, *what*, mother?" Strong? Independent?

Violent?

"So disappointing."

Though she couldn't see her mother's face, Lena knew damn well the woman was rolling her eyes and her painted red lips would be set in a thin line of disgust. Her mother always looked that way. "You must like being punished, Lena. You do everything you can to embarrass me and make me punish you."

"I've done nothing wrong."

"You breathe, that's enough."

Lena's sadness washed over her like a tidal wave. It arrested her heart and caused her grip to loosen on the teacup. The porcelain fell, in slow motion, to the floor and shattered. Blood splattered everywhere.

"Now look at what you did." Her mother's tone cut into her spine and made it soften.

"I'm sorry."

"You're always sorry. I wish we never had you. So much trouble for so little reward. You cost us billions."

"I didn't ask to be born."

"We made a mistake having you. You bring shame to our name."

"I've built your legacy into something better!" And Lena had. She invested all the money she could into people who were following their dreams. Making ripples, movements, shaping communities and bettering life for others. Scholarships, small businesses, community centers... "I made your name worth something more than a ski slope."

Silence rang in her ears. Tears spilled down her cheeks, hot and angry.

She wasn't worthless, but her mother never saw it that way after she'd lost her family that property in Vermont. They had a child for the wrong reasons. Maybe her mother was right... she should have never been born.

Her mother vanished.

"I want one person to love me as I am," she said into the void. "I'm not a teacup. I'm not delicate and fancy. You can't paint flowers on me and call me something else." Her throat tightened. She stared at her feet. Porcelain fragments lay scattered across the floor in blood. "I'm too strong for your world..." She slowly lowered to the ground. "I don't even want to be in your world." She wasn't even sure who she was talking to at this point. Her mother? Herself? Someone else?

It didn't matter. Lena dropped down and braced herself on hands and knees. She stared at the blood on the floor, a terrible desire rising out of her. Everything fell away except for the red on the ground. Lena leaned down and froze.

Her heart hammered. Her emotions ran amok.

Then, the two Lena's fused together. The one floating and watching fell into the other on all fours. She sucked in a deep breath and smelled...

Dorian.

His name was a balm to her aching heart. "Dorian." On all fours, in her ruined pink dress, Lena lowered her face down to the floor and licked the blood, not giving a shit about anything else. Not the shards of porcelain, not the opinions of others, not her past, not her present. Nothing mattered except getting exactly what she wanted.

That. Blood.

She dragged her tongue across the floor, letting the spilled blood coat her tongue. Sitting back on her haunches, she ran her fingers through the puddle and made lines across the pristine white floor. Her dress soaked it up like a sponge, turning from pale pink to a deep crimson.

Dorian.

She tipped her head up, expecting the sun to hit her face. "Dorian?" she called out into the nothingness.

Heat bloomed in her center and spread through her body. An aching hollowness was carved into her heart. She clasped her chest and whimpered with longing. Rising, she had to find a way out. "I don't belong here anymore." Lena stumbled away from the broken cup and her broken past, searching the void for a way out.

"Dorian," she cried. "Where are you?"

Surrounded in silence, Lena didn't know how to get out.

"*Lena,*" a deep voice stole the air from her lungs. A mirror appeared in front of her. Dashing towards it, she saw she was no longer wearing a blood-stained pink dress, but a black gown of pure lace which hugged every curve she possessed. A deep, plunging neckline showed off her breasts. The flare of her hips was enhanced. Her hair spilled in waves around her face, dark and thick.

"*Lena.*" The voice haunted her. Echoed in her bones.

"Where are you?" She braced her hands against the mirror's frame. Her eyes glowed. Lips full and blood red. "I can't find you." Her heart lost its beat, tormented and aching. "Where are you?"

"Find me," the voice purred. "Find me now..."

Ripped from her dream, Lena's eyes popped open, and she sucked in a ragged breath, preparing to scream.

"Hey, hey!" Dorian was perched on top of her, cupping her face. "You were having a nightmare."

Holy crap, that was terrifying. Lena clutched her chest, still feeling the echo of aching longing. Tears sprung from her eyes. She really needed to get a grip on herself, this was starting to wear her down.

"I lost you." She gripped Dorian's arms. And.... Ohhh God, he looked so scared for her.

"I couldn't wake you," he said. "You kept screaming my name, but I couldn't wake you."

He kissed her hand and placed it over his frantically beating heart. "It just about gave me a damn heart attack." Dorian wrapped his arms around her and clutched her so tight, she lost breath.

Lena started crying again. That dream was her wake up call. It was frighteningly accurate and real. That hollowness. That torment. That emptiness from a loveless void chilled the marrow in her bones. And the mirror... the flare of hope when she looked into that stupid mirror...

Was that what it was like for vampires who hadn't found their mate? A constant emptiness, an agonizingly cold longing for someone you weren't even sure existed? To think Dorian went his whole life feeling that way broke her heart.

For all the agony of longing she suffered, there was also a rush of excitement and hope when she heard his voice. Warmth filled her belly and spread down her limbs. It was incredible. Was that what it felt like to find your missing piece? Was that what turning into a vampire would be like? Was that what having a fated mate meant? Two broken people with their pieces in mid-air, mid-explosion, halted and reformed into an unbreakable force? No... Dorian was already an unbreakable force.

Her gaze sailed across Dorian's features.

"Talk to me," he whispered. "You're thinking so loud, my bones rattle with it, but I can't hear what your mind is screaming. I can't help you if I don't know what you need help with."

"Kiss me?"

He didn't hesitate. Sealing his mouth over hers his kiss burrowed into her soul, giving her warmth and strength. He took his time with it. Deepened it a little more with every stroke of his tongue.

Cradling the back of her head, he held her captive. Her body homed in on the fierceness with which he cherished her. He was hurting, too. Always had been. His father had butchered his soul down to slivers of what he might have been. Would she feel this in love with Dorian if he was any other way?

No… she didn't think she would.

Lena couldn't imagine feeling this way for anyone other than this man, the way he was now, just as he was now. Whatever made him the Reaper, whatever shaped him into a deadly force to be reckoned with… she didn't disparage it. She was grateful instead. She loved Dorian from the tip of his blade to the bottoms of his boots. If that made her sick and twisted, so be it. She loved Dorian just as he was — sharp edges, haunted soul, and all.

CHAPTER 36

Dorian flashed back to Lena and spent nearly six hours holding her in his arms while she'd slept. It was the greatest six hours of his life except when she twitched, whimpered, then all out screamed his name. Dorian unraveled.

If he had the skill of dream-walking, he could have plunged into her dreamscape to save her from whatever made her so terrified she called out for his help.

Such longing in her voice. Such devastation in each tremble she made against his embrace.

He knew that pain. That torment. Spent his existence suspended in such paralyzing ache.

If he could slay the beasts haunting her nightmares, he would in a heartbeat. Any beasts that came after her in reality, Dorian already considered dead men walking. Thankfully, he was able to wake her up.

But now she was crying her eyes out and he had no clue how to fix it.

"There's nothing I wouldn't do for you," he said against her mouth. "*Nothing*, Lena." He'd shred the skin from his own body, down to the bone, if it spared her a second of pain. He'd burn the world to the ground for her. Walk through Hellfire for a chance to caress her sweet skin. It would be worth it. She was worth anything, *everything*...

He confessed all of that and more to her while kissing every inch of her body, slipping her clothes off, and crawling on top to kiss her hot, silken mouth again.

"Turn me," she insisted.

Dorian hovered above her, his hands bracketing, caging her beneath his hard, frazzled body.

"If you'd do anything for me... prove it. Turn me. Now, Dorian."

Aww hell.

"Actions speak louder than pretty words." Lena wrapped her hand around his neck. "I don't want you to put yourself in danger for me. I don't want you to fight my nightmares, lay waste to lands, or sell your soul. I want you to give me yourself. Give me life with you."

His heart bucked like a panicked stallion — kicking and wishing to bolt out of confinement.

"Live for me." She squeezed the back of his neck, her eyes pleading. "Don't abandon me when I've finally found you."

He couldn't take it. Not her tone, her words, the look in her eyes. She wasn't asking for him to turn her for immortality's sake. She was begging him to turn her so *he* survived.

"I love you." Her tears fell. He licked them away, unable to speak the words etched into his dark soul.

Lena was right. Words were weak.

Dorian wasn't fucking weak.

Hadn't he spent his life proving that? The only one who didn't believe it was him.

"There's no going back," he warned. "You don't have to stay with me, but there's no going back once this is done. You'll be forever changed. You will no longer be human at all."

"I think I've been waiting my whole life for this moment, Dorian." She steadied herself under him. "I've been waiting my whole life for *you*."

His heart exploded hearing her say that. She was killing him.

"I'm not sure what the transition will be like for you," he warned. "It's different for every human who turns." It also depended on the mental state and blood power of the vampire turning them.

"I don't want to go over the possibilities. No more *what ifs*, remember? I'd rather just do it and find out."

He respected that. "Do you want pain with it?" he asked in a shaky voice.

She blushed. "I want pain and pleasure."

Damn, he loved her so much.

"I can do that." Hell yes, he was all about that. Pain and pleasure he could totally do. Yup. Dorian unsheathed his favorite blade, a karambit, and tossed it aside so it would be within reach in a minute. Next, he tugged on his belt and shimmied out of his clothes. Even his fingers trembled. Lena hissed when she saw his body.

"Don't look at it," he said quickly.

"What happened?"

The burn blisters were spreading.

"I'm burning." He leaned down and pressed his mouth to hers. "For you."

She shoved him off and frowned. "You're close. I'm close to losing you, aren't I?"

It didn't matter anymore because his fangs throbbed and elongated. He was done talking. Done trying to make sorry ass excuses and finished with punishing himself. He nudged her thighs wider to make room. "I won't be able to control myself."

"Then don't even try." She wrapped her legs around his waist and grabbed his cock.

He groaned loudly when she rubbed the head of his dick against her soaked pussy. She was swollen. Wet. Full of need and want for him.

"I ache for you." She arched her body. "Make it stop."

Holy Hell, he was a goner on those words. Dorian pushed into her and came undone when he bottomed out. "I love you." *Thrust.* "I never thought I deserved a mate." *Thrust.* "Didn't think fate would ever gift me someone as strong and perfect as you." *Thrust.* "And here you are." *Thrust.* "In my grasp." *Thrust.* "I had no idea I've been suffocating my entire life until you became the air I breathe."

Lena held on tightly to his neck and shoulder while he drove them up the bed. "God, Dorian."

"You're incredible." He ground his hips and hit her pleasure points. "And so fucking tight." He loved how her thighs quivered against him as she rolled her hips in time with his harsh thrusts.

"Take me," she urged. "Drink me."

Dorian kissed her one last time and gathered what was left of his strength, then he broke away from her lips. With a ferocious hiss, he sank his fangs into her neck.

Lena tensed and cried out. He bit down harder. Swirling his hips, he pleasured his mate until she melted into a puddle of lust beneath him.

Sweet mother of all things unholy, Lena's blood tasted incredible. Even headier than before. He drew hard, filling his throat with her taste. He clutched her, fucked her, swallowed her.

His body burned. His bones ached like he'd run a hundred miles through the desert. His vision danced, stars bursting in his eyes. He pulled off her vein just long enough to reposition Lena onto his lap and groaned as she sank down on his cock. Gripping her hips, they worked together to make her detonate. He watched the blood from his bite trickle down her neck and licked it.

Her inner walls clamped down on his dick and pulsed with her orgasm.

It was time.

Dorian grabbed his karambit. Bringing the tip of the blade to his neck, he made a sharp, quick slice. The pain didn't register at all. Not with so much pleasure rocking his system right now.

Lena didn't need instruction. Her instincts and desires ran the show now. Dorian tensed the instant her mouth latched onto him. With a roar, he exploded in divine pleasure as she swallowed him down.

Holy. Fuuuuuck.

Dorian scratched down her back before grabbing her hips to rock Lena back and forth on his cock while they took from each other. She started making mewling noises. Pulled from his vein harder. Gulped all she could.

He was never going to get enough of this.

With one final pull from her vein, Dorian licked her wounds closed and kept rocking her back and forth while she continued drinking from him.

This was… indescribable.

There was nothing like it in all the world.

"That's it. Take from me," he coaxed her. "Let me sustain you. Let me be all you need." He cradled the back of her head, holding her close to him and flipped her onto her back. With short, quick thrusts, he made her come three more times.

Because it wasn't enough to just give her immortality.

She wrapped her body around him and pulled mouthfuls of blood from his body. He stood up and carried her over to the wall to rail her harder. Her teeth sank into his flesh, her tongue lapping at him. The combination made Dorian roar and set his veins ablaze. He rocked against her harder, using his body to find both pleasure and completion for her sex and her hunger.

Her inner walls tightened more and more.

Lena broke off his neck, tipped her head back, and screamed. Their skin slapped together as their pants grew louder. A picture fell off the wall. He put a dent in the drywall.

"Keep going." Holding her, Dorian tilted her hips and forced her to slam down on him, over and over and over again.

"Yes, Dorian!"

Sweat soaked tendrils stuck to her forehead and cheeks. Her eyes were alight, cheeks flushed. But he knew her hunger, her desperate desire to explode. She wanted more and he was there for it.

With a guttural noise, Dorian pulled her off his cock, dropped her onto the floor, and slammed into her from behind. Angling her hips, he drove himself balls deep into her wet heat, turning into a merciless monster starved for her pleasure.

His cock was covered in her cream. His nostrils flared with her cherry blossom scent. His mouth still savored the taste of her blood. He was close… so close to coming now.

Dorian caged her in with his arms and bit down on the back of her shoulder. Not to drink, just to pin.

"Fuck! Yes!" She cried out. "Oh my God, oh my God, *ohmygodohmygod.*" Lena clawed the floor, her sharper nails digging into the hardwood. He slammed into her hard enough for both of them to see stars. "Come for me," she gasped. "Come inside me again. I want to feel you inside me every way I can. Fill me."

Dorian was all too happy to grant her wish. Grinding his cock, swirling his hips, and slamming into her one, two, three more times, he roared as he came inside his mate. His cock pumped so much cum into her, it dripped out of her pussy, between her thighs and all over him.

He lost his breath at the sight of her. Swollen, wet, messy. Blood was everywhere.

273

Wait…

He touched his neck to make sure the wound had closed. It hadn't. No big deal. His body just needed a little more time. Hell, he just depleted himself in every way for his mate just now. He might need a minute. Plus, he was more worried about Lena. "Are you okay?" Holy Hell, his voice didn't even sound like his own. It was deeper and coarser than usual.

Lena lay on her belly still gasping for breath.

"Hang on." He slipped out of her slick heat and stumbled to the bathroom. Yeah, woah, she must have really taken her fill if he was too weak to even stand right now. Dorian didn't mind though. She could suck him down to a husk and he'd soar with delight about it. Snagging a towel from a rack, he staggered back to the bed and attempted to clean her off a little.

"Turn over for me." He coaxed and caressed her ass. "Let me clean you up a little more."

Lena rolled over, her breaths shallower and faster now. She shuddered when he swiped between her thighs. Groaned when he pressed a kiss to her belly. He crawled up her body and peppered kisses all over her sweet face. She curled into a ball and whimpered.

"I'm so sorry," he whispered. "It'll be over soon."

Dorian braced himself, pinned his mate down, and screamed right along with Lena as her transformation began.

CHAPTER 37

How could someone go from soaring in bliss to dropping into Hellfire in one fell swoop?

It hurt like a bitch, and Lena relished every bit of it.

Her body cycled through waves of ice and heat. Her veins coursed in different directions. Her blood was icy hot. Electricity skated under her skin - zipping and biting, warming and melting her. She had no idea how long this state lasted, but the next one was much worse.

Her lungs slammed shut. Her skin grew taut across her bones, shrinking, cracking, stretching.

Clawing at the air, her body bowed. She screamed. The pain was paralyzing. She went into sensory overload.

"Let go." Dorian's fingers laced with hers as he pinned her down. "Let it go, Lena."

His thighs bracketed her hips. Holy shit, her heart pounded so fast it ran out of steam and stopped. She sucked in air to scream with and bucked on the floor. Her teeth ached, and gums split. Her lungs burned. Biting down on her bottom lip, she winced as her new fangs pierced her mouth and blood rushed onto her tongue. The sensation and taste had her reeling.

Everything hurt. Agony of this magnitude shouldn't exist.

Shit! Even the tips of her fingers stung!

"I can't!"

She couldn't take much more of this. It was too much. Too extreme.

"You're strong, Lena. Fight for your power. Let go of your old self."

A rolling heat wave smashed her next. The apex of her thighs swelled. Her nipples hardened to the point of pain. Her back cracked. She jolted and cried out.

Dorian's grip tightened even more on her. Lena curled her fingers around his and squeezed back with equal strength.

Gasping for air, she coughed and cried out again.

"That's it." His voice cracked. "Keep going. Oh fuck, you're almost there, Lena."

Too many noises rushed into her ears at once. She heard everything from Dorian's voice to the pounding of his pulse, to the air conditioner running to the bugs crawling across the blades of grass outside. It was too much. Way too much.

Overwhelmed, she squeezed her eyes shut and grunted, shaking her head wildly as if to rattle the sounds out of her head.

"Easy," Dorian barely whispered. "Easy, Lena. Don't focus on any one thing. Let it wash over you. Ride the current."

Ride the current? There was no current! It was like a tsunami, and she was drowning in too many things slamming into her at once.

"Breathe in," he whispered. "Breathe out."

That sounded great if she could just... Take. A. Breath. But she couldn't! Her lungs froze. If she inhaled, they'd shatter, and she'd die.

"Trust me," he said. "Breathe with me."

Lena shook her head violently.

"Trust me," he said, swiping her face. "Trust me. Just breathe and ride the current." He'd never give her bad advice. He'd never tell her do to something that would jeopardize her safety. Lena sucked in a small bit of air and let it out. Each time, she increased the amount of air.

The noises died down to a reasonable volume. Her skin stopped burning.

"I can't see," she whimpered. "I'm blind."

"Breathe." He readjusted and brushed her ribcage with the back of his hand. "Can you feel me?"

"Yes," she groaned.

"Good. Focus on my touch and the sound of my voice. You'll regain everything you've lost soon. Just hang on a little bit longer."

Lena nodded, her heart fluttering in her throat. "I'm thirsty." Her mouth was dry. Someone replaced her tongue with a strip of sandpaper.

Dorian deeply chuckled. "You can drink soon, just concentrate on my voice and my touch."

She expected him to run his hands all over her body. Kiss and suckle on her. Fuck her maybe. But Dorian didn't do any of that. He continued to hold her wrists with one hand, and ran his thumb along her bottom right rib, making tiny circles.

Round and round and round his thumb went with a featherlight touch. She narrowed her focus on that single sensation while the rest of her body was at war with itself. The pain was agonizing. She cried and convulsed, unable to do anything but breathe through it.

Dorian didn't relent his constant rub against her rib, nor did he let go of her hands.

"Breathe," he reminded her. "You're so damn strong. You're almost through. Good girl, breathe. Keep breathing."

She had no idea how long she lasted in this state. It felt like an eternity. Dorian's thumb kept circling, she kept breathing, her veins kept burning, her body kept aching. All her focus narrowed down to that tiny touch of his.

Finally, the pain lessened to the point where it barely registered. The buzz in her ears died down after that. Part of her wondered if she was stuck in another dream, one where she was lost in a vast space with no direction to run to. She was floating, drifting, coasting along. Her vision sharpened and things slowly came back into focus.

There's the ceiling fan, the wall...

Dorian.

Her voice cracked as she said, "I found you."

He looked like he'd just been to war too. Scratches covered his face and torso. His left eye was swollen. Blood trickled out of the corner of his mouth.

Lena's protective instincts roared to life. "What happened to you?"

"You," he answered. And he *smiled* about this.

She didn't have the capacity to ask how, because a hunger the likes of which she'd never known roared within her. Dorian's body stiffened in response, his eyes darkened, and fangs elongated.

He looked like a demon — dark and deadly, riding on the shadows of wickedness. "Tell me what you need." He stared at her like she was the prettiest little monster he'd ever seen in his life.

She lured him closer to her mouth. "I'm so thirsty,"

Dorian tilted his head, "Take your fill." His warped voice rumbled the marrow in her bones.

Lena bit down and pierced his neck. A rush of heat flowed into her mouth. She drank greedily. The world spun and the air shifted. She vaguely noticed Dorian was carrying her into the bathroom.

Placing her on the counter, he thrust into her. The more violent his movements, the harder she bit down on his skin. Sucking, fucking, climaxing, it was a trifecta of chaos she'd gladly keep in circulation for all eternity. Fevered with these new sensations, she clamped down harder on his neck. Dorian hissed when she accidentally ripped his skin. The instant it happened she drew back. "I'm sorry."

"Don't be." He kissed her. "We're unapologetic with each other in all things. Take more, Lena. Take whatever you need from me."

That offer was a dangerous one. Especially with how starved she still was.

His neck looked ravaged. Holy Hell, was she a vampire or a shark?

The fact that she caused him damage was the only thing keeping her from chomping down on him again. Well, that and the exquisite bliss he was coaxing out of her body. Between Dorian's blood in her system and cock in her pussy, Lena's eyes rolled back, and she absolutely rode this current without fighting it.

Her body tensed and tightened. She was close. So, so close.

Dorian slipped his thumb along her clit and rubbed it while he thrust. She didn't last long with him working her body so well. She detonated with a wild scream. Her mate turned animal and pounded into her, chasing his own release. Dorian pulled out and yanked her off the counter, forcing her to her knees. "Suck me," he hissed, "Fucking suck me, now."

Lena took him into her mouth and deep-throated him. She didn't even know she was capable of it, but her gag reflex was completely gone. Dorian's grunts turned to pants, and he fucked her mouth relentlessly. Then he roared as warm jets of his cum poured down her throat.

With a grunt, he eased out of her mouth and she grazed his dick with her teeth just to hear him hiss with pleasure. "Holy fuck, woman." His chest heaved. "This... this is gonna be dangerous between us."

She grazed her nails down his torso. "Scared?"

"A little." He grinned.

Lena licked her lips, savoring his taste. Then she flinched when she cut her tongue on her own fangs.

"They're sharp." Dorian tilted her chin up, inspecting them. "I didn't think it was possible for you to get any hotter. Yet here we are." He spun Lena around so she could see herself in the mirror. "Look at your reflection. See yourself now."

Lena's breath hitched. She was the same, but not. All her features were just a little enhanced.

"Damn, Lena. Where did you come from?"

"Hell," she whispered as happy tears sprung from her eyes. "Or... my version of it."

And now she was in Heaven. With Dorian. Immortal and strong and fierce as ever.

Dorian kissed the back of her shoulder, his gaze locked on hers in the mirror. "This Hell is no better than the one you just left."

"At least these monsters won't pretend to be my friends and family. This Hell —
if that's what you want to call it—is unapologetic about its savagery. I'd say that sounds like heaven to me." She turned around to cup his face. "*You're* heaven to me."

"Damn... Lena." Dorian searched her face for a moment, looking for signs of regret or fear or she didn't even know what before he crushed his mouth to hers and picked her up again. Carrying her into the shower, he let her feet touch the tiled floor.

"I can stand on my own."

"Let me hold you. If I don't, I won't think you're real." He flicked the water on. "I have no idea why fate would give me such a precious gift," he murmured against her skin before suckling on her breast.

She threaded her fingers into his hair and arched into his

279

mouth more. His fangs scraped her tender skin. He smelled incredible. Her teeth throbbed. Mouth watered.

"I'm thirsty." Now she felt guilty. Dorian could only have so much blood in his body, and she was going to kill him draining him. Yet she couldn't stop herself from latching on his chest and biting down around his nipple, drawing his flesh and blood into her mouth at once.

"That's it, Lena." He cradled the back of her head. "Take all you need."

But I'm going to kill you, she thought while swallowing.

Her body roared. Chaos closed in on her, threatening to consume her.

"Breathe." His hands fell to her hips. "Breathe, Lena. Ride the current, don't fight it."

She was fighting it.

"Come on, open for me. Let me... there we go. Ride that." He pumped his fingers into her pussy. "Come for me. Come on my hand while you drink."

Her bones turned to rubber with her next orgasm. It happened so fast it wasn't even fair. She relaxed into a strange subspace as she pulled away from him and licked her mouth. "Dorian." She clutched his shoulders, and he took all her weight.

"Ride and breathe."

She inhaled Dorian's intoxicating scent. Let it fill her while he fingered her, pumping and coaxing an orgasm from her body.

Lena was a puppet. An insatiable, horny, bloodthirsty puppet.

He deepened his thrusts and hooked his finger to hit her g-spot.

"Don't stop."

With a throaty chuckle, Dorian gently leaned until her back hit the wall. The sudden coldness of the tiles sent shivers down her body and hardened her nipples. Her hair was plastered to her face and back. Dorian sank to his knees and lifted her leg to rest on his shoulder. Kissing the inside of her thigh, he pumped his fingers in and out, hooking and hitting that spot deep within her over and over. Lena quivered. Holy shit, this felt good.

His pace quickened.

Her breaths became shallow.

A few more flicks and Lena exploded in a soundless cry that

had her straining. She came violently. Endlessly. Dorian fused his mouth to her core, attacking her clit with no mercy, and her orgasm doubled down.

Her knees gave out and he caught her before she fell.

"Good girl." He licked her cream off his mouth and tongued one of his fangs playfully. "I think I found a new way for you to come."

"Or die," she said breathlessly. "Holy shit, what did you do to me?"

"Worshipped you... as is my honor as your mate."

Once she could stand on her own again, Dorian washed her hair and took his good old time sudsing up her body. She could do nothing but stand with her face buried in his chest, inhaling his scent like he was the only air her lungs would allow in.

"You're incredible," he said while rinsing her hair one last time.

She tipped her head back to look at him. His bruises and cuts had finally disappeared. It made her feel more at ease because seeing him hurt, for any reason, made her feel murderous. Smiling, he trailed his middle finger along the underside of her breasts, lazily, playfully. Then he brought his wrist up to his mouth and bit down, piercing his skin and opening a vein. The act sent a shiver down her back.

"Drink," he said, his eyes black as coals again. "Don't stop until I say so."

With the water turning cold, she latched onto his wrist and drank deeply until the world, the room, Dorian, and herself fell away into darkness.

CHAPTER 38

Lying face down on the floor, Dorian cracked his eyes open and groaned. Holy shit, had he been hit by a semi? Christ, his fangs throbbed. He must have fallen off the bed at some point after crashing in euphoric bliss and blood loss. Bracing his arms, he —

Nope, he couldn't even move his arms let alone use them to push up. What the hell? Did he have six-hundred-pound weights strapped to his limbs or something? He sucked in a couple deep breaths and tried once more, with feeling.

Grunting and groaning, Dorian was able to lift his torso up enough to see Lena's ankle dangling off the bed. He pulled his sore ass up on all fours and crawled over to her. She was lightly snoring and perfectly at peace. Boy, did that light his ass up with bliss.

For fate to gift him something this spectacular, this damn precious and perfect? *Holy shit.* He gently ran his hand through her hair, swiping it back from her face. Climbing into the bed with her, Dorian carefully got into a better position to hold her while she slept off the last bit of her big change.

Lena went through her transition like a warrior. He knew she would, but watching her go through the phases of morphing from human to full-fledged vampire was remarkable. Even when she thrashed around, swung her fists, kicked her legs, clawed and bitten him in the very beginning, he was enraptured and more madly in love than he thought was possible.

He encouraged her to keep swinging, keep going. Embrace those emotions and let them embed in her new body. That fight in her? That savage violence was a survival skill. He wanted her to have as much of it as possible. Dorian took her pounding and coaxed as much violence out of her as he could. She'd held back, he knew that, but what she dished out was plenty.

Blood curses and blood gifts were tricky. Whatever emotions Dorian harbored, any amount of toxicity he carried, could filter into Lena's system, and change her during her transition. Turning someone was a delicate and precarious thing.

So, when he turned her, Dorian made sure his intentions and heart were the purest they'd ever been. He gave her only love, protection, adoration, and boundless loyalty. Trust and encouragement. Strength. The rest that came after? That violence? That hunger? That insatiable need for both pleasure and pain at once? That was all Lena. Those were gifts already pumping in her veins - her inner strength, her secret desires - all Dorian did was invite them to come out and play. He only fortified what she already was.

His perfect mate. His *alakhai*. Lena was built for him and his world.

"Dorian," her sultry, sleepy voice gave him an instant hard-on.

"I'm here." Holy shit, his throat ached like he had shards of glass jammed in it. "I'm right here."

"I'm thirsty," she mumbled into her pillow.

Holy Hell, he didn't think he had any blood left to give her, but what he had was all hers. The mating thread between them was like a constant tug on his instincts. As if his very existence was to serve her, and it would be his honor to do so for the rest of his life. He was the luckiest son-of-a-bitch in the whole wide world.

"Here," he said, rolling over and brought his arm up to his mouth to bite and break his skin for her.

She lashed out with lightning speed and stopped him. "Water," she purred. "I need water, Dorian."

He blinked slowly, "Hang on." He groaned as his bones cracked.

Lena shot straight up, eyes wide with terror. "Holy shit," she squeaked. "What's... what's all over you?"

Welts, bites, bruises, deep cuts, scratches. The answer depended on where you looked.

"It's okay." He dragged himself off the bed and collapsed

onto the floor.

Shit, yeah, maybe he just needed to lay here a minute longer. Catch his breath. Find his spine.

"Dorian!" Lena ran towards him so fast, he wondered if she'd flashed. "I can't believe I did all this." Her gaze flickered all over him. "I can't believe you *let* me do all this."

"Hmmph." He grinned, even as his head lolled to the side.

"Oh my God!" She grabbed his shoulders and propped his sorry ass against her bed.

"Just give me a minute. I'll be fine." He'd been drained down like this many times before by his—

No. Not going there. Never going there again. His past had no place in his future. Life with Lena was a different atmosphere. The air up here was clean and fresh. He was done living in his Hell.

Lena straddled his lap and clasped her hands to his face. Dorian's brow pinched together. If she needed to be fucked again, he'd happily do so, but, "I need a minute." His words slurred now. "One sec—"

His eyes drifted closed. Sleep started dragging him down. *Crack!* A sting burst across his face. His eyes snapped open, and he hissed.

Then his eyes fluttered shut again.

Okay, shit, she might have taken a little too much, he vaguely thought. He wasn't going to be able to pull out of this quite as fast as he thought.

"Dorian!" *Crack!*

He smiled with his eyes closed. Or... at least he thought he was smiling.

Dorian's head lolled back, and he couldn't find the strength to open his eyes. Lena smelled so good sitting on his lap. He focused on that as he drifted off.

"Dorian!" *Crack!*

The sting barely registered. Something thin and sharp pried his mouth open. Hot liquid poured onto his tongue.

Feed. His body clung to that instinct. His mouth latched onto the offered source. His eyes opened to slits and he deadlocked on Lena while he drank. Liquid steel poured down his throat. Pure, intoxicating, exotic nourishment.

He pulled deeply. *Just a little more.* Then he broke away and licked her wounds to seal them.

"More," she urged, shoving her arm in his face. "You need a lot more."

"I assure you I don't." He was stronger already. Her vampire blood was so new, so fresh and potent, a few drops went a long way.

His wounds healed and disappeared entirely. His heart found a healthy rhythm again. Holding her hips, he enjoyed the weight of his mate on his lap. Damn did she feel wonderful. But he needed to get up and stretch his limbs a little. They were too stiff. But first, he pressed a gentle kiss on her jaw, "You're divine."

"Please don't be romantic right now." She climbed off him and he was able to stand without collapsing. Hurray for small victories.

Lena tucked her hair behind her ears. "I'm so sorry."

"Don't say that word ever again to me." He swept his thumb across her bottom lip. "No apologies. Ever."

"But I—"

"You did exactly what you were supposed to do. As did I, as your mate."

She cringed. "You were going to let me drain you dry?"

"If you needed me to. Yes."

Lena blanched and recoiled. He gripped her chin, "Hey, look at me." He forced her head to tilt up. "You'd have done the same for me. Search your soul and tell me that's not true."

"Of course, I would," she said without sparing a second to think it over. "But—"

"That's what a mate does, Lena. We'd die to give the other life." He pressed his forehead to hers and threaded his fingers through her thickened hair. "I will always do this. It won't be the last time you need so much, and it's my honor to give you all I have."

"I could *kill* you."

"I know." He flashed her an adoringly warm smile and kissed her again. "But you won't." Even if she did, he'd die happy knowing it was to strengthen her. To save her. "You'll learn limits. Control. When to let go. When to feed."

He'd learned those limits himself once he matured into a full-powered vampire. If he could do it, Dorian knew Lena would have no problem. Right now, it was all too new for her. The hunger would likely ride her hard for a little while. That was okay. He just needed to remember to guide her through it better next time, for both their sakes. The last thing he wanted was to remain weakened while she was new. It was a vulnerable time for both of them.

And predators loved defenseless prey.

They took another shower before Dorian stripped Lena's bed. "Just burn the sheets," she chirped, bringing over a fresh set. "I don't think any amount of bleach is going to get all that blood out."

Dorian agreed and tossed them into a pile. He couldn't keep his eyes off his mate. She was so spectacular. Lena even looked seductive while she tucked in the fitted sheet and started making her side of the bed.

Her side.

His heart swelled at the thought of sharing not just a bed, but the rest of his life with her. To think he'd almost lost this. Had wanted to give it up. Dorian had a feeling death without Lena would be even worse than life without her had been.

Her tits jiggled under her tank top. The muscles in her shoulders were toned and taut.

"You keep staring." She put her hands on her hips. "Is... am I..."

Her cheeks reddened. It was endearing how she had insecurities that made her blush. There was nothing for her to be insecure about — not that she'd ever believe him.

"I didn't think it was possible for you to be more stunning than you were the first night I saw you," he said.

Now her cheeks got redder. He ate that up, too.

"I'm glad I don't disappoint."

Dorian tensed. *Disappoint?* Like that was even possible? "Never," he growled. Prowling around to her side of the bed, he got all in her space and nipped her neck. She sighed and leaned into him, already playing with the waistline of his pants.

"Is it always going to be this way?"

"Define *it*." His hands sailed down her back to grab her ass while he kept nibbling on her neck.

"This," she groaned. "I feel like I can't get enough of you. Your scent. Your touch. Your taste."

"Yes." he smiled against her collarbone. "And I'm going to fully admit that I'm excited to be obsessed with you for the rest of my days. And just as thrilled you'll be the same way about me."

He never thought he'd have someone like Lena in his life. Never thought he was worthy enough to have a gift like her.

Dorian's cell went off, the specific ringtone was set only for one person. "I have to get that."

Lena backed away and Dorian rummaged through the pile of clothes they'd yet to pick up from the floor. Where the hell was his damn cell? He snagged it from under her bra and hit accept, "Emerick."

"We couldn't find the vampire," the Lycan said. "Whoever this is, they're excellent at covering their tracks."

There was something to Emerick's tone that made Dorian suspect there was something he was holding back. "What else did you find?" His hand squeezed his cell tighter. "Was anyone else hurt?"

Emerick was quiet for a minute. "No. No one was hurt."

"Then what?" Dorian's voice deepened. "Just tell me."

"We found a cleaver."

Those four words slammed down on Dorian's gut like an anchor hitting the bottom of the ocean. His voice dropped to a dangerous level. "Where?"

"Embedded in a tree on the south side of the property. It was covered in wolf's blood."

So that was the weapon used to torture that poor animal. Dorian figured as much. "Anything else?"

"Nothing."

"How's the rest of the family?"

"Dad's taking care of things."

Closing his eyes, Dorian let guilt wash over him, "I'm so sorry I brought this to you guys."

"You didn't bring shit to us, Dorian."

"Yes, I did." He felt responsible for everyone in his life. The Woods family, Lena, the king, Lucian, the list could go on and on. "Tell Alistair and the others I'll get to the bottom of this myself. When I find who did this, do you want first choice?"

Emerick was quiet on the other end again. So quiet, Dorian thought he might have hung up. "Hello?"

"No," he said. "I think you need to keep this within the House of Death's realm. If possible, record it. If not, your word is enough for us."

"My word doesn't mean shit to any other Lycan."

"It doesn't matter, Dorian. Whether you take this asshole out in front of all our clans or not, they'll still never accept you as we do. Just... do it for us... and we'll handle the rest on our end."

"I can't let a war start." His words were a harsh whisper. "I can't allow your family to stick your necks out for me again. If you want this kill, it's yours. I'll hand deliver this bastard to you. My King will understand."

"It's not your King who worries us."

Dorian tensed. "What aren't you telling me, Emerick?"

"One of the younger Lycan said they recognized the scent of the vampire. He's insisting he knows who it is."

"Then tell me, and I'll take care of it."

"He might be wrong. We have no way to verify without bringing you or another trusted vampire back here to confirm, and that can't happen right now."

Dorian's gut eased with the mention of "trusted vampire". To know the Woods clan still had Dorian's back even though all signs pointed to him, or one of his kind, as the monster who desecrated such a sacred animal, twisted Dorian's heart all up. He needed to fix this. End it. If they had a clue, a lead, no matter how shaky it might be, Dorian wanted to know it. "Whose scent was on the weapon, Emerick?"

"Stryx, the House of Bone's precious prince. The shifter won't say more. His clan's furious that he's been in contact with a vampire at all."

Stryx. Marius's son.

How did Marius not have knowledge about any of this? Was he that skilled of an actor that not even Lucian could detect his lies? Or was Dorian right all along about Stryx going Rogue?

At this point, the answer didn't matter. Stryx was a dead vampire walking.

Dorian detached from all warmth and comfort. There was no panic in his mind. No uneasy frazzle. Just a coldness surrounding him like a weighted blanket. This was the mindset he fell into when he was about to make a kill. This frozen, isolated room in his subconsciousness.

"I'll take care of it." Dorian hung up.

CHAPTER 39

"*Alakhai,*" Lena murmured thoughtfully. "What's that mean?"

Dorian sat across from her in the House of Death's private jet and smiled. "It's an ancient word that, in our old language, means the 'All Key'."

They were flying back to New Orleans. After Emerick's call, Dorian reported his findings directly to Malachi, and Lucian got the jet lined up to bring them back. Lena's parents once had a plane. Much smaller than this one. She used to fear they'd crash in it. Turns out she was right about the crash, wrong about which mode of transportation.

Planes, trains, automobiles. They were all potential coffin makers.

She refocused. *Alakhai.* Chewing on her bottom lip, she let the word sway like a blood-drunk lover dancing in her head. As if the very word had a form to it — graceful, solid, confident, and serenely content. *Alakhai.* Those ribbons were back… fluttering and swaying in the back of her mind.

"What's the *All Key* and why is it stuck in my head?"

Dorian looked like Hell again and it was all her fault. She drank him down to his last pint, several times. Ashamed that she had zero control over her thirst yet, she bit her bottom lip, accidentally piercing herself and wincing. *Ouch!* Damn, these fangs were sharp as needles.

But the blood welling in her mouth tasted so good. It tasted a lot like Dorian. Maybe she could suck on herself for a little? Was that weird? That's weird, right?

Dorian shifted in his seat. He looked like sex dipped in danger. Lena's mouth watered.

"Remember the blood curse?" Dorian leaned forward to rest his elbows on his knees, hiding his erection. "The All Key, *alakhai*, is the one who cures the longing."

Lena's mouth went slack. She remembered vividly that supreme hollowness she had in her dream. Remembered wondering if that was the emptiness vampires experienced before they found a mate.

"*Mate* sounds less significant for some reason," Dorian leaned back in his seat again, his erection back in full display. "But the word *alakhai* puts pressure on fated ones, so no one uses the term much anymore."

"So, you no longer feel the longing?" The jet rocked as it hit a bit of turbulence. Lena's stomach clenched. She really hated flying.

"Hey," he said softly, and reached over to rub her thighs. "You're okay. It's just a little turbulence."

"I know, I'm just..." Dorian stared at her with the same look he had on his face when he'd turned her. Like he was enraptured by her. It made Lena all squishy and self-conscious.

Apart from the veins still spiderwebbing around his eyes, the greens of his iris had darkened to a reddish black, and the veins in his neck were protruding and pulsing under his paler skin, he looked ravishing. Strong.

Mesmerized by her.

"I still feel longing." He gracefully dropped out of his chair, sinking down onto his knees before her. Lena's legs opened for him and she cursed the jeans she wore. "I don't think I'll ever be able to stop longing for you." He brought her hand to his lips and kissed her fingertips, one by one.

The ribbons in her head danced—all shadows and sensuality.

"I see ribbons in my head. Dancing or something. Is that normal?" Of all the changes she'd just experienced, from the crystal-clear eyesight, brightness in colors, loudness of noises, over-the-top sensitivity of her skin, this was the one thing that concerned her?

She needed a priority check, ASAP.

"The spirit of an *alakhai* is different for everyone." Dorian slipped her shoes off and ran his hands up her calves. "They usually involve the color red and a binding symbol."

"Do you have it too?"

"No, but I'm a born vampire. Only an *alakhai* would have something like that. But, when I was maturing, I had this vision of a river current that would make a strong, steady whirring noise in the back of my head."

"Do you still hear it?"

"Yes, sometimes. It's loudest when I'm killing."

Her lust spiked at the mention of him slaying something.

Dorian eyes widened with surprise. He must have sensed her getting turned on. "Let's see if we can't alleviate some of that tension." He unhooked her fly and pulled her jeans down.

Lena bit her lip again and winced. Damnit, she needed to stop that! It fucking hurt!

Chuckling, Dorian leaned in and captured her mouth with his. His kiss was languorous and deep. It set her loins ablaze. "You'll get used to your fangs," he promised.

"I'm looking forward to getting used to yours."

He chuckled deeply. "You're killing me." Then he lowered his head between her thighs and ripped her panties off with his teeth.

"I liked those."

"I'll buy you more. Then tear those with my teeth too." He buried his face in her pussy and rendered Lena speechless for a solid twenty minutes. Three mind-blowing orgasms later, he pulled away and she moaned at the sheen of her lust smeared across his mouth.

He licked his lips and smiled. "Delicious."

Lena eagerly grabbed him by the belt and started unlatching the buckle.

"No," he said. "I need to stay this way for a while."

"Why?"

"I need that edge for what we're about to do."

Lena wished she could argue, but she got it. Really, she did.

Dorian's gaze flicked to the pilot's door then back to her. "We'll be landing soon."

She better get dressed.

As Lena bent down to get her jeans, Dorian grabbed them before she could. "Not these," he said. "I had Lucian pick you up something else."

Lena was stunned speechless when Dorian stood up and went to the back of the jet. In a storage compartment, he pulled out a garment bag. "I hope it fits okay."

She unzipped the bag and, "Wow."

Wow didn't cover it.

Lena's cheeks tingled as she pulled the dress out of the bag. It was stunning.

And eerily familiar.

The black lace number hit the floor and she nearly fainted. It was the exact dress she wore when staring at herself in the mirror in her weird, crazy ass blood dream. She didn't know what to say.

"Do you hate it?" Dorian grabbed the other end of the material. "Shit, I... I should have asked what you liked. I just wanted to get something nice for you to have your debut in."

"Debut?"

"With the House of Death. I... Jesus I'm an idiot." He speared his hair with his hands. "I got a thing about this. I'll work on it. It's not important I just..."

She shut him up with a kiss that she hoped would make him surrender all his worries to her. "I love it."

Dorian wasn't buying it but seeing how he went from ten to zero on the confidence meter had shaken her. Why did it matter what she wore to see the king? They'd already met. Debut. She looked back at the dress and clung tightly to the lace. This didn't feel like a debut. This dress said way more than "Hey guys, wuussupp, I'm a vampire like you now." It meant something more.

Especially if this was the dress she dreamed about.

"Are premonitions common with *alakhai*?"

"Rarely," he rubbed the back of his neck. "Why?"

Lena bit her lip. If premonitions were a rarity... was seeing things one minute that were gone the next a rarity too, or just a hallucination brought on by stress and fatigue?

"Lucian picked out the dress," Dorian babbled. "I told him your measurements and what I wanted, but if you hate it, don't wear it. It's not important."

"Yes, it is," she whispered. Dragging her gaze up to meet his, Lena knew why Dorian always dressed to the nines. Same as why everything had to be clean. It was his way of covering up the filthy horrors of his past, his fight against where he'd once been trapped.

"You're not a doll," he blurted. "Holy Hell." He gripped his head. "I'm an idiot. I'm such an idiot. I didn't think when I asked for that dress. I didn't—

Lena pressed a finger to his lips and shut him up. "Stop overthinking and letting our pasts haunt you, Reaper."

His gaze darkened.

"It's stunning and I love it," she went on to say. "I'd be honored to be presented as your mate in this gown."

He made a small choking sound in response. "I'm so sorry." His lips brushed against her finger.

"No apologies between us, remember?"

Stripping out of her clothes, she shimmied into the dress and let Dorian help her. His hands shook terribly. His jaw clenched shut. She needed to do something to make this less awkward. "How do I look?" she spun in a tight circle knowing exactly how she looked. This dress fit like a second skin and was absolutely stunning.

"G-good," he stuttered. He actually stuttered. Dorian wiped his mouth and took a step back to admire the view.

"I dreamed of this dress," Lena finally said. "Just before you turned me... I was wearing this dress in a dream." She didn't tell him about the first part involving the teacup and her mother. That shit didn't matter. The only important thing right now was Dorian, herself, and their future together.

"Do I look like a Reaper too?" She wiggled her ass.

He choke-laughed. "I don't look that edible in a dress."

"I'd like to form my own opinion on that," she teased.

"Come here." He yanked her arm and crushed his mouth to hers, nearly eating her alive with his kiss. It was a wonder her dress hadn't gone up in flames from the heat levels rising between them.

Ding-ding, the pilot's intercom chimed. "We'll be landing in about fifteen minutes, Reaper."

Dorian cursed and reluctantly pulled away from her. "There's not enough time to worship you properly."

"We have all of eternity."

"Still not long enough."

Dorian went into the back bedroom on the jet and came back out in a fresh suit. It was criminal how ravishing he looked in everything he wore.

"I think I saw someone follow us home," she blurted. Total

mood killer, yes. But her instinct was to tell him so…

Dorian's brow cocked. "When?"

"As I was driving us back to my house from the ceremony."

His eyes widened. "Why didn't you tell me?"

"I…" Lena had to gather her thoughts. He looked arresting in his ensemble and it made her hungry.

He snapped his fingers. "Focus, Lena."

She bristled and climbed out of her lust-induced mind trip. "You weren't speaking and I knew you already had a lot to deal with. Besides, I didn't think I really saw it. I shrugged it off as a delusion brought on from all the stress and exhaustion. But I… I'm pretty sure I saw someone in a navy-blue hoodie. Twice."

Dorian rocked on his heels and then slid back to his seat. Scrubbing his face, he was deadly quiet as the pilot announced, "Ten minutes, Reaper."

"I'm sorry?" she cringed.

"What did I tell you about that word?"

To never use it between them. But she'd gone her whole life saying sorry for her actions because they'd disappointed someone else. Like her mother…

"I might not have seen anything," she said, backtracking. "I mean, it was like I thought I saw someone on the road, then they were gone. Or they were actually a pole or tree or something."

"Or they'd flashed once you got close enough to see them."

He was right.

Dorian clenched his jaw for a few heartbeats. "Did you see anything we could use to identify them again?"

"Short of the hoodie? No. And really, I might not have seen anything at all."

The look on Dorian's face made her feel worse for not saying something sooner.

"If that was Stryx following us," he said, tapping his knee, "why wouldn't he have attacked when we were both at our most vulnerable?"

Hell if she knew. "Maybe it wasn't him? Maybe I'm right and it was just a figment of my imagination." Now she felt terrible bringing it up. "I should have told you what I saw, even if it turned out to be nothing. My only priority was getting you home. Fuck all else."

The jet began its descent.

Dorian scrubbed his face with both hands. "I should have put dust around your house. I should have protected us better."

"Don't take blame and responsibility for this, Dorian."

"You *are* my responsibility," his voice rose with anger. "I *am* to blame for this. I know the dangers, and I got sloppy."

She disagreed. "If anything, I'm to blame. You told me to take us home and I took you to *my* house. Not yours."

"And I was too far gone by that point to correct your course," Dorian seethed. "What kind of mate let's himself get so low he can't even protect his woman?"

"Stop," she jabbed her finger at him. "Don't do that, Dorian. You were suffering and couldn't do anything but—"

"Couldn't do *anything*," he said, latching onto those words. "That's all that matters, Lena. I couldn't do anything because I'd waited too long."

The plane landed with a few small bounces.

If she wasn't allowed to say *I'm sorry*, he didn't get a free pass either. For crying out loud! She still wasn't convinced what she saw was real back there. Besides, Dorian's curse no longer jeopardized what they had so it was a moot point now. "Doesn't matter. It's over and done with."

"It's not over," Dorian stood and stepped away.

Lena followed him. The instant the jet door opened the hot, southern humidity blasted them in the face. They both climbed out of the plane, Lena first. "What did you say?"

"I said, it's not over."

They reached the bottom step and Lena snagged Dorian's arm. "What do you mean? I've turned. We're together. I know we'll have threats left and right, but at least you're not going to die from the curse." Tears stung her eyes because he looked absolutely crestfallen. "Dorian, it's *done*. Your curse ended."

He winced before looking away from her and ran a hand through his hair, destroying its neatness.

Lena's hackles went up. "What aren't you telling me?"

He looked back at her and ran a featherlight touch across her brow, sweeping stray hairs from her face. "My body is still blistering and I'm feeling weaker. My curse didn't lift."

CHAPTER 40

He'd lasted this long, here's hoping he kept going long enough to see Lena come into her full power... first they needed to get this shit with Stryx squared away.

Dorian wished like hell he hadn't had to tell her about his curse not lifting, but he wasn't going to lie to her. He also didn't want her to worry about anything but herself. As a newly made vampire, Lena was still adjusting. Her human side died the instant her vampire life stepped into creation. It was, by far, the fastest turn he'd ever heard of. Almost as if her body had been waiting for it, primed and poised to make the transition. But she still needed time to acclimate.

His smile tightened. He felt like shit. No, he felt cheated. He'd done everything he was supposed to and the curse hadn't lifted.

"It'll be fine," he tried to reassure her.

Dorian had managed to keep his focus locked on Lena and her needs the whole plane ride, but now their little bubble burst. Back home, in vampire territory, with a stalker to go after, it was time the Reaper went to work.

And with Lena safely turned, she would be better equipped to handle anything that came after them. That was at least one bonus for now. Besides, maybe this was a temporary setback because she drained him so much. Maybe this was just par for the course and his curse lifted, it was just taking its good old time fizzling out of his depleted system. His heart latched onto that pathetic splinter of hope. The alternative was too devastating to think about.

Aww hell. Deep down he knew the truth. His curse stuck. He

was doomed to die.

What a joke. What a goddamn disaster. He plucked an innocent woman out of her safe life and tossed her into a jungle with predators far older and stronger than she. Now what? He'd soon turn into a crispy Cajun fried pile of useless ash?

Fuck this curse. Fuck this life. Fuck Stryx. Fuck everyone. Fuck everything.

At least he had all his senses back. That was probably the best and worst part. He could protect his mate with all pistons firing, no problem. But he was closer to combusting and instead of frying and dusting out of this existence, blind, deaf, and numb, he'd likely burst into flame with perfect clarity and feel every ounce of agony his curse pelted him with.

How poetic, right?

Like most of the victims from his childhood, Dorian would die acutely aware and helpless to stop it.

The familiar vision in the back of his mind was no longer a river current. It was a tumultuous, unforgiving clash of rapids. The whirring noise he was accustomed to hearing was now a riotous roar.

With the little bit of time he had left, he would arm Lena to her teeth. Teach her everything including getting back up to takeover when he was no longer capable.

Holy Hell, Dorian froze. His heart thundered at the possibility of someone else protecting Lena until she was a full-blown vampire. It made Dorian see red.

She'd want sex. She'd want blood. She'd need those things, there was no compromise. Someone else would have to service her... then she would what? Join the House of Death? Fall in love with some other vampire who wasn't her mate?

Dorian would be ashes by then. Gone. There was nothing he could do...

Another thought formed, and it was a thousand times worse. Would Lena die with him because she was his *alakhai* and maybe once fate sank its teeth into a set of mates, they'd both survive or both die?

It didn't seem likely, but he wasn't hopeful enough to rule it out. All because that hadn't happened before with other vampires didn't mean it couldn't happen now.

Dorian's heart stumbled to a halt. "She can't die," he said under his breath. Sweet mercy, please don't let his mate die over his mistake. Whatever he did wrong, let him be the only one to pay the price.

"You're scaring me," Lena said with a shaky voice.

Dorian sucked back his emotions and boxed them up nice and neat and shoved them in a dark closet. Inhaling deeply, he kept his eyes fixed on the waiting car up ahead. Reaching for Lena's hand, he squeezed her just enough to say, *It's going to be fine*, because there was no way he'd allow that lie to leave his tongue. He could only hope the strength of his touch would offer her a boost of confidence. She was going to need it. They both would.

Walking over to the parked car, Dorian noticed some of the tension had left Lena's shoulders and she smiled at Lucian.

The blond vampire dipped his sunglasses further down his nose and whistled at Lena. "Dayem, you are stunning." He waggled his brows. "Black lace and vampirism look good on you, girl."

Dorian growled, possessively.

Lucian tossed his hands in the air and chuckled. "Hey man, I'm just—" The smile fell off his face.

"Let's go." Dorian opened the car door and helped Lena get inside. "Drive us home, Lucian."

"You look like shit, man," Lucian grabbed Dorian's arm. "What the hell happened?"

"Get us to the King."

Lucian stopped him from climbing in the car, his gaze fiercely concerned. "I thought you turned her."

"I did."

"Then why are you still afflicted?"

"I don't know." Dorian slipped into the backseat with Lena and slammed the door shut.

They drove to the House of Death, hoping they'd find the answer before it was too late.

CHAPTER 41

Dorian squeezed Lena's hand, "You ready for a supreme game of hide and seek?"

"What are you talking about?"

"We're going out for a hunt." Dorian explained. "Once we meet with the King, you and I are going to arm up and hit the streets. If Stryx is tailing us, he'll show himself eventually and we'll catch him."

"I really don't give a rat's ass about Stryx right now."

"You need to," he frowned.

"I only care about *you*. What will it take to save *you*? That's what I want to hunt down."

Lucian made a small, choked noise in the front seat, but other than that, he didn't make a peep. Good thing, Dorian didn't need them to gang up on him about this.

"I'm the last one you need to worry about." He brought her hand to his mouth and kissed her knuckles.

"Why are you acting like the world isn't ending," she whispered, her teary eyes pleading with him to drop the act.

"I'm not dead yet. There's still some fight left in me."

She pulled her hand out of his and closed it into a fist in her lap. "How did everything go from amazing to dismal in the blink of an eye?" she choked. "I can't lose you, Dorian. Not now. Not after everything. Maybe I lack something in my blood that's supposed to save you?"

"Don't." He gritted his teeth. "We can't think about this right now."

He put his walls up, regardless if that made him an asshole or not. It was the only way he would make it home without screaming.

"Stryx needs to be taken down immediately." Dorian said loud enough for Lucian to hear.

"Damnit, Dorian!" Lena smacked her thigh, "Why are so fixated on him?"

Because I can be obsessive over a target just like my father. "Because if what you think you saw is true, it means Stryx already knows where you live. He knows your scent. Your appearance." Dorian's brow pinched and he sat forward. "Holy shit... the sonofabitch was in your backyard. I didn't think—"

The fleeting memory of when he thought he saw something out on her lawn when those birds scattered and flew away. Aw hell, even that cleaver on the counter. He knew it was out of place.

Then the wolf, the cleaver there, the note, the name Fear Eater...

Stryx was taunting Dorian with all his worst memories. Why?

They pulled into the House of Death's front circle and Dorian bit back a groan as he exited the car. Holding his hand out for Lena, he glanced at her.

She was thirsty again. Her eyes were darker, the veins in her neck pulsing wildly. He'd remedy that issue after he spoke to Malachi and got her into a private room.

They stormed through the front doors and the place was practically buzzing with anticipation.

"Holy shit, where have you been, Reaper?" Xin hissed from the balcony. "Whoa."

"Yeah, whoa and wow," Victoria grinned like a Cheshire cat. "Oh, and hell yes, too." She stared directly at Lena. "And probably 'Can I get an amen?' for good measure." She swaggered over to Lena and walked a slow circle around her. "Nice work."

Dorian didn't say a word. He wanted Lena to have this moment.

"I'll be damned," said Reys. "You look absolutely ravishing, *Cherry.*" He kissed the back of her hand and Dorian let out a small warning growl.

"We have to meet with the King." Lena went right into business mode.

Xin cracked a laugh, "She's just like you, man. Workaholic."

Dorian flipped him the bird and smiled. More and more vampires came out to see their newest addition.

"*Reaper.*"

At the sound of Marius's pompous tone, Dorian rolled his shoulders back and glowered at the sonofabitch.

"It's about time you showed up." The House of Bone's pain in the ass king swaggered right over. "My, my." He walked circles around the two of them, slowly. "She's not what I imagined."

"I don't give a shit what you imagined. If I were you, I'd keep my mate out of your imagination." Dorian leaned in and unsheathed his karambit. "Unless you'd like to also see what I use *my* imagination for." He held the blade to Marius's throat and pressed forward, causing Marius to take a few steps back. "You will not come within fifteen feet of my *alakhai* again."

"Dorian!" Malachi thundered from his private quarters upstairs.

Shoving his blade further into Marius's neck, Dorian hissed, "Lucian, escort my girl upstairs."

"Jesus fucking Christ," Lucian grumbled. "Come on, Lena."

"I'm not going anywhere without Dorian."

Damn, he loved how she said that.

Lucian cocked a brow at Dorian, waiting for him to act like a gentleman instead of an overprotective psycho. Easing back from Marius, Dorian tugged his sleeves down and pulled his shit together. "Come on," he said briskly, grabbing Lena's hand. They headed for the stairs with Lucian at their backs.

"You're going to start a war today," Lucian hissed behind them.

Dorian looked over his shoulder. "Stryx's scent was all over the dead wolf. We suspect he also followed us to Lena's. He was in her home, and mine."

Lena jerked out of Dorian's hold. "Wait, what? You never said you found someone in my house."

"I didn't," Dorian snarled as they hit the top step. "But I thought I saw something in the backyard while I was in your kitchen and your cleaver was out on the chopping block when nothing else was out of place."

"I... I don't own a cleaver."

Well shit.

"Come on," Lucian stormed down the hall. "Let's get this over with. Marius needs to leave… preferably with his son in a pine box." He grabbed the double door handles and ripped them open.

Malachi was dead ahead.

"Come here, Lena. Let me look at you."

She practically marched over to him. Dorian bit his lip, falling deeper in love with her with every angry step she took towards the king. "What have I done wrong?"

Dorian was gob smacked. He started forward, but Lucian stopped him.

"What makes you think you've done anything wrong?" the king purred.

"He's not cured." She went down on her knees. "Please… what more do we do? How can I save him?"

Dorian wiped his mouth to stifle his groan. His heart dragged itself into a hole and cried. The sight of his mate on her knees, begging the king to save him was too much to bear.

"Do you pledge fealty to the House of Death, Lena?" Malachi's tone was all business. "If so, give me your arm."

Lucian slammed his hands down on Dorian, holding him back. His protective instincts weren't triggered, his possessive one ruled the roost now. An uncontrolled hiss tore from his teeth when the king bit into her skin and drank from her.

Between the fierce burn under his skin, the ache in his chest, and the sight of his woman in the arms of another male vampire, Dorian unraveled. He fought to get to her, forcing Lucian to use every ounce of strength he possessed to hold him back.

The king pulled away from her arm and licked his wound closed with a flick of his tongue. "It is an honor to have you as one of our own." Malachi looked at Dorian's reflection. "It's time to hunt," he said cautiously. "Come find me once you've secured Stryx."

Lena slammed her palm on her thigh. "Tell me how to save him!" she screamed.

"That's an order, Lena. I'll not repeat myself."

Lucian let go of Dorian on that note. He stormed over to be closer to her. "Come on." He kissed her forehead. "This ends now." The kings bite marks had vanished from her arm already, which was a relief. Dorian didn't think he could stand seeing another male's teeth marks on his mate–for any reason.

She didn't say another word until they left the mansion and drove back to Dorian's house. Before they left, Victoria handed Lena a duffel bag, "These are about your size. Keep them till we go shopping."

Lena snagged the damn thing and mumbled a thank you.

She didn't get it, Dorian realized. Lena had her own set of priorities, but once a vampire is in a House, those things get rearranged. Even with Dorian close to death, House business came first. Finding Stryx took precedence over Dorian.

It might as well though, right? One could be handled, the other just had to ride its course.

They pulled up to Dorian's house and the instant he went through his front door, he could finally breathe again. He might not have cushions and colors and bowls of fruit, but it was loaded to the brim with weapons. This was his safe space. His comfort zone.

He easily ignored the lingering scents of burnt fabric and tinge of chemicals leftover from the fire.

"Stay outside," he ordered Lucian, Victoria, and Xin, who'd followed behind him in a second vehicle.

While those three stayed outside, protecting his house, Dorian strapped Lena with enough blades to arm a colony of heathens.

"This is a little overkill, don't you think?" She looked down at her torso. He'd strapped a variety of weapons. "If we're going after a vampire, don't we just need a wooden stake?"

Dorian laughed. "It takes more than an impalement to kill one of us. A stake through the heart just slows us down. And the stronger we are, the less impact it has. Besides, we're going after more than just a vampire, the *Savag-Ri* are out there too. If they find us, they'll attack. You need to be prepared for anything."

She was going on this hunt with him. She was going to have her first taste of their world from Dorian's side of the battle lines. If they were lucky, they'd find Stryx and be done with him. No one had told Marius what they'd learned, and Dorian planned to keep it that way for now.

Punishment would be delivered accordingly.

He was looking forward to it.

"What are you smiling about?" Her attitude was getting meaner. No doubt due to the fact that her heart was crushed for

Dorian's sake.

He couldn't go there right now. Of all things to be thinking about, it was, "I'm imagining your first time seeing a *Savag-Ri* and how you'll react."

"Accordingly." Her sharp tone was razorblades on his skin. "Same for anyone else who threatens to take you from me."

Be still his doomed, black heart. He cupped her chin. "I love you."

She pulled away from him. "We need to go."

Lena was putting walls up now. He let her because doing otherwise made him a hypocrite.

Was it strange that he was looking forward to so much bloodshed? Nope, it was typical. This was Dorian's life. He spent his whole existence killing. Now he had a partner in crime.

Would she enjoy seeing how he killed *Savag-Ri* or traitorous vampires? Or would she be repulsed by his methods?

He was about to find out.

"Feed." It wasn't a lover's request. Dorian pierced his neck with the sharp tip of a push dagger before tucking the blade into his harness.

"I can't," Lena said, though her eyes latched onto the blood oozing from his wound and her eyes flashed black. "Dorian, I...."

He coaxed her into his arms, angling himself so she could latch on good and proper. She sucked hard and it made his toes curl. "Pull back when you first think it." He held her to him, ignoring how rock hard his cock was, and held back the groan clawing up his throat.

Lena gripped his shoulders, going up on her toes for a better reach. He winced when she bit down a little too hard. Her aggressiveness was appreciated and adored. He wanted to tear her hunting clothes to shreds with his knives. Bend her over his kitchen counter and fuck her senseless.

But that would have to wait...

Lena pulled back with a tiny grunt. Her fingers dug into his shoulders.

"Lick it closed for me." He loved being the one to teach her how to be a vampire.

Lena dragged her hot velvet tongue along his neck, and it made his eyes roll in ecstasy. He stayed still while she watched her magic go to work. Their saliva had healing properties in it. That, coupled with their generally speedy healing, made the puncture wound close and disappear in less than three seconds.

"That's incredible," she probed his throat gently.

"Are you ready to walk our streets as a predator, Lena?"

She was strapped down with enough blades to look like a wet dream.

"What was I before today?"

Dorian nipped her bottom lip, "Prey. You were our prey."

CHAPTER 42

"I need pussy," Xin grumbled as they headed towards Bourbon Street. "I hate hunting with a hard dick. It's uncomfortable."

"Will you shut up." Victoria swaggered down the road, twirling a throwing star. "Your voice annoys me."

"Everything annoys you, Vic. You need to get laid."

"You offering?"

"You wish you could handle this." Xin blew her a kiss.

Victoria chuckled. "I think I handled you just fine the other night."

"I'm glad my theatrics worked."

"Says the vampire who wore the French maid outfit last night."

Dorian and Lena both looked back at the same time. "That's kind of hot, actually," Lena said, grinning.

"Right? I rocked it." Xin made a chef's kiss.

"Shut up and hunt," Lucian snarled.

Of all people to not contribute to this playful conversation, Lucian was the last one Dorian suspected. But that guy was worried sick, and it showed from his walk to his talk, and especially his intensive glowering. Jesus, even his gait looked furious. The bunched-up lines between his eyebrows aged him a few centuries. Not even his scowl was a normal one. That vampire was wound up tighter than a drum.

Dorian was the pot to Lucian's kettle.

Thankfully, the others were trying to lighten the load for

Lena's sake, even if it was annoying as hell.

"Smell that?" Lucian halted. "What is that?"

"Smells like charred pork." Victoria shrugged and kept walking.

The scent was more distinct though. Dorian knew what it was. "Someone's being burned," he growled. He was well accustomed to what charred flesh and melting body fat smelled like.

"Over there." Lucian beat feet and Dorian was right there with him. They stopped in an alleyway behind a theatre. The stench was awful. The person crawled out from behind a dumpster, gasping for air, half their body blackened.

"What. The. Fuck." Victoria hissed as she snagged the victim by the hair and callously tipped their head back. "You see what I see here?"

The *Savag-Ri* roared and stabbed Victoria in her calf. "Oomph!" She kicked him in the jaw hard enough to flip him over.

Dorian halted Vic for a second. This was going to be a teaching moment. "Come," he said to Lena. Then he brought her closer to the *Savag-Ri*, taking over where Victoria left off. Immobilizing the enemy in a tight hold, Dorian said, "I want you to get a good look at what our sworn enemy looks like."

She squatted down.

"Look at his eyes," he said calmly.

He loved how she had already unsheathed a blade, prepared to use the damned thing.

"See the cross? All *Savag-Ri* have a crisscross in their eyes." The single mark cut through their irises and was the trademark of the vampire and Lycan's biggest predator. "We've hunted each other for so long, I doubt anyone remembers the original motive of our war."

"Then why are you still fighting at all?" Lena asked.

"Because you exist," the *Savag-Ri* spat in response. "You're disgusting parasites."

Dorian smashed the heel of his palm into the bastard's nose. "Mind. Your. Manners. She wasn't talking to you."

Xin picked up a zippo and bottle of lighter fluid from behind the dumpster. Waving them in the air, he rolled his eyes. "Could be self-inflicted for show."

Dorian jerked the asshole's head back. "Did you set yourself on fire?"

"Fuck you."

"Answer the Reaper, cocksucker." Lucian smashed his boot on the *Savag-Ri's* back. "Was this self-inflicted or not?"

"Go to Hell."

Victoria licked her weapon like a lollypop. "Last chance."

"No," the *Savag-Ri* grunted. "Vampires did this."

"Who?" Victoria squatted down. "Give us a name."

"Don't... know. One had a fucked-up face."

When Dorian let him go, the *Savag-Ri* pulled himself up, his burns already healing though his clothes were ruined.

He lunged right at Lena. Just as he expected the piece of shit to do. Dorian's heart thudded in his ears. Standing back to let Lena handle this was hell on his instincts. It went against every molecule he possessed.

The rest of the crew spread out because *Savag-Ri* rarely came out alone. Just like Vampires and Lycan, they, too, hunted in groups.

Lena's reflexes were quick enough to dodge and weave. The guy was sloppy for a *Savag-Ri*. He couldn't catch her for shit. With swift agility, Lena swept her leg out and knocked him on his ass.

"He's not human," Dorian called out. "It'll take more than that to knock him down and keep him there."

Nodding, Lena didn't pull her gaze from her target. Her cheeks were red and flushed from adrenaline. Her body poised. She was enjoying this.

Annnnnd there went his heart swelling so big it barely fit in his chest. Dorian kept close, knife in each hand, ready to strike should she need him to jump in.

But Lena didn't need his assistance. Not after she tested a few more blows and watched them heal immediately on her opponent. *She's playing with him*, he realized. His smile was so big, his cheeks might split.

"What do I do now?" her voice trembled.

"*FINISH HIM*," Xin hollered in his best Mortal Kombat impersonation.

"How do I do that?" She dodged another of his attacks.

Dorian silently sliced a finger across his neck to her.

Lena's eyes widened. He wanted to help her with this, but she needed to do it alone. Needed this experience. No way would she be the kind of mate who stayed home and baked cookies. She was too bloodthirsty and violent. He just needed to test how violent.

"You fang whore," the *Savag-Ri* flicked his blade into the air, fast as lightning. The tip of it struck Lena in her torso, right between her ribs. She hollered in pain. Dorian roared with rage.

He didn't realize he'd flashed until he was behind the *Savag-Ri*, slicing his neck deep enough to nearly decapitate the motherfucker. Then he reached in through the neck cavity and went elbow deep, groping for what he wanted most.

That sonofabitch's heart.

Lena gawked and took several steps back as she watched her mate turn savage. The *Savag-Ri* was dead, but that wasn't good enough for Dorian. No one threatened his mate and got off so easy. With a roar, he ripped the still beating heart from the carcass and crushed it to a pulp in his hands. Throwing it on the asphalt, it made a sticky splat then sizzled until it bubbled and thickened to a molasses like substance.

Next, he ran to Lena. She had pulled the blade out of her ribs already and held it out, terrified. "I can't believe I just got stabbed!" The standard ka-bar was nothing too extraordinary, yet she shook violently, pale and rattled by the weapon covered in her blood. "Great. Just great. My first day out and this happens."

"Congrats, your cherry just got popped," Victoria said. "We've all been clipped millions of times. These guys are just as quick and skilled as we are."

"Makes the hunt more fun," Xin said with a shit-eating grin.

Lena's eyes rounded. "Do they poison their blades?" She looked at Dorian, eyes wide in terror. "Is it coated in something that'll kill us like your bullets for *Savag-Ri*?"

Dorian crushed her to him, "No, no, no. Nothing works like that on us," he kissed her head, working to get ahold of the fact that she wasn't upset over the attack or being wounded, but at possibly of losing her new life with one stab. She would soon learn she was way more indestructible now. "Can you breathe?" He needed to make sure her lung hadn't been punctured.

Mental Note: order mate a bullet proof vest and helmet.

He wanted her out in the field with him, but not at this cost. Fuck that bullshit, he was buying bubble wrap for her too. And a shield. And a tank.

"I'm okay," she winced as she pulled up her shirt. "I barely felt it."

"Atta girl," Lucian clapped. "She's tough stuff, Reaper."

"Bet she gets tougher as her power forms," Victoria winked at Dorian, "That'll be fun in the bedroom."

Hell yeah.

"So, I'm still not a full-blown vampire?" Lena frowned at Dorian. "What happened, did I mess it up?"

"Not at all."

"It takes a little while for you to completely bloom." Lucian beamed her a warm smile.

"How long?"

"Sometimes a few years." Lucian shrugged. "Maybe less, maybe more. You transitioned super-fast, so I guess we'll just have to wait and see."

"Years?" she whispered in terror. Swinging her gaze back to Dorian, her brow furrowed. "You don't have that kind of time."

"It'll be okay," he said, because right now wasn't the time to discuss it.

Lucian snapped his fingers. "Bonding." He shoved a finger at Dorian. "That's it. You didn't fully *bond*. That's what's wrong with you."

"We *did* bond!" Lena raised her voice, completely insulted.

"Nope," Lucian tucked his second blade away and walked off. "Chop, chop. Let's see this done so Dorian can practice a little more follow through on his mating journey."

Lena stayed back and took up the rear with Dorian. They walked slower than the rest on purpose to steal a moment for themselves. "How does he know so much about mates when he's single?"

"He's been obsessed with the blood curse for a long time." Dorian said with a frown. "And now that Luke has died, I think he's only going to get worse about it."

"Who's Luke?"

"That was his brother."

"I sense something up ahead!" Xin called out. "Never mind, false alarm."

"Spread out," Lucian ordered. He turned to Dorian. "You

good on your own back here?"

"Yeah." Dorian said, unsure how true that really was. He felt like shit, but at least he had his focus and complete control. Everything just hurt and burned. Maybe his body was at a standstill with the curse?

Or maybe this was the calm before the storm.

Either way, "Do a quick check of the block and meet us at the next intersection."

"Got it!" Lucian hollered back.

They watched as the other three vampires disappeared around the corner.

"I hate what this blood curse has done," Lena whispered sadly.

Dorian didn't bother to say there were worse curses. He was living proof of that.

"Fear Eater."

Dorian froze at the sound of that tone.

"*Fear Eater.*"

The hair rose on his arms. "Get armed," he snarled.

"Already am," Lena bounced on the balls of her feet, her back pressed to his.

A frail-framed silhouette stepped around the corner and headed right for them. From the opposite direction, Lucian, Victoria, and Xin had headed in.

Stryx flashed right in front of Lena. "Found you."

Dorian lunged at Stryx. He flashed out of reach and reformed ten feet away. "You can't catch me, Reaper. Stop trying."

Dorian released three throwing stars in quick succession, missing the mark two out of three times. But that third one? It struck Stryx right between the eyes. The vampire's head tipped back, and he grunted from the force.

"Get behind me," he ordered Lena.

The young vampire's face went blank for a second. Dorian used the time to yank two bigger blades out of his arsenal. He threw them both, but Stryx evaded them with ease.

Shit, this kid was fast. It made Dorian wonder if he was about to mature into his full power. He was certainly the age for it. The kid must be about twenty years old now. Or maybe it already happened, and this was the result? If so, Stryx was spindly for his age. Royalty liked to be thin, but this was a little too bony to be considered healthy, and his skin was sallow.

Stryx flashed in front of Dorian, gulping for air. "Help," he said in a different tone. His voice sounded smaller. Squeakier. With stiff, choppy movements, he reached out to them. "Help me, Reaper." He stumbled forward and caught himself. Grunting, his back bowed and then he straightened his spine as a long hiss slipped from his thin lips. He started marching forward with his head down, fangs out, an ugly grin spread across his face, contorting his features even further.

What the hell?

Stryx flashed to Lena and pulled her into his chest. Then he yanked her hair hard. "I can't wait to taste you."

Lena slammed her fist back and broke his nose just before Dorian tackled him to the ground. But the bastard flashed out of his hold. *FUCK!*

Lena cried out again. Dorian spun around.

No, no, no!

Fear paralyzed him. Unable to scream, fight, or attack, he remained frozen in place. Something sharp pierced his thigh. He couldn't even look down to see what it was. An icy sensation flooded his veins, almost cooling his constant burn. Rendered helpless, Dorian was wracked with unholy terror. Something hard and cold pressed against the side of his head next.

"What next, father?" Stryx said eagerly from behind him, holding a gun to Dorian's temple.

In front of him, Lena was in a choke hold, fighting like a wild animal to free herself from the bastard who'd caught her. Dorian's heart and soul crashed, robbing him of clarity.

Stryx shoved a knife into Dorian's back, digging it deep enough to hit bone... and a nerve. It was a well-placed puncture. A familiar, well-placed puncture.

No. no, no no.

The man fighting Lena was too big to be Marius.

"Dorian!" Lena screamed.

He couldn't move. Not yet...

"Stop fighting me, girl." His grip tightened and he swung her around, finally giving Dorian a good look at him. "You'll only make this worse for yourself. Isn't that right, Reaper?"

That voice. That face. That tone. That smell....

Dorian gagged at the sight of his nightmare come to life.

"We have to go!" Stryx urged. "The others are coming back."

"Then get moving, son."

Son.... Dorian's mind reeled and stomach lurched. Behind him, Stryx made a strangled noise — something close to a whispered scream. It was so out of place and yet unbearably familiar...

For a second, Dorian thought he was having some kind of out-of-body experience in a supremely fucked up dream. Stryx's movements behind him, the knife in his back, the gun to his head, his mate standing across from him and completely out of his reach. The scent of burnt flesh was fresh in Dorian's nose.

This can't be happening. No, no, no, no....

The one holding Lena started laughing. The sound hooked Dorian's soul and sent him careening back into his skin. With a roar, he threw his head back and cracked Stryx in the face. *Boom!* Stryx pulled the trigger. The bullet grazed past the bridge of Dorian's nose as he twisted and rolled away before the blade in his back could cut into his spinal column next. Without wasting another precious second, he attacked not Stryx...

But his father.

CHAPTER 43

A chemical taste bloomed on Lena's tongue. Her head thumped. The house, if it could be called that, was completely empty and chewed away by nature, time, and decay. It smelled like a sewer but way worse. Dangling from a set of chains attached to an eyehook in the ceiling, she swung like a side of beef.

How the hell had this happened?

One minute she was fighting a deranged animal, then blackness.

Looking around, she noticed her weapons laying on the countertop with a roach crawling across a few discarded darts. Were those animal tranquilizers?

Lovely.

Dizziness threatened to make her vomit, but she wouldn't allow it. *Dorian.* Where was Dorian? Had they taken him too? Were they keeping him separate? Was he dead?

Nope, she couldn't think like that.

Piecing together what happened, she tried to put the events in order. *Savag-Ri* on fire, Stryx's attack, scarred man grabbing her.

Dorian was frozen for the entire last half of that shitshow. She didn't think that was possible. Dorian. Her Reaper. The Fear Eater... was scared shitless.

That couldn't be good. In fact, she couldn't think of anything worse than that. If this guy scared Dorian that much, he must be the devil incarnate.

Dorian warned her a thousand times that this life was dangerous. Made it clear he had enemies at every corner. But she didn't care because all that mattered was life with him. Danger she could face.

But a life without Dorian?

Holy Hell, she couldn't even bring herself to think about it. Rejected the possibility with every molecule she owned.

"Lena."

Her heart leapt at the groggy voice coming from the second floor of the shithole house. "Dorian?"

"Are you hurt?"

"No."

She heard him exhale in relief. And then she heard the rattle in his lungs.

He was deteriorating faster.

The front door swung open and a light flicked on, illuminating exactly what kind of place this was. Oh hellllll no. Lena's gaze couldn't latch onto any one thing at once. Bile rose in her throat and she gagged.

Curtains made of skin and human hair covered the windows. Dried blood crusted the rotten, wooden floorboards. The kitchen, or what once was the kitchen of this little house of horrors, had doorless cabinets with different body parts in various stages of decay.

White powder coated the floor and boot prints were all over the place in a circle around where she dangled.

Hand-to-the-man, if she heard a chainsaw start up, she was going to piss herself.

Panicked, she started hyperventilating and kicking her feet to swing herself around on the hook. She sensed someone watching her. Sucking in fetid air, her eyes watered. Throat tightened. Thighs clenched.

Her shoulders were going to pop out of their joints if she thrashed about too much, but the need to get out of there overrode all her other instincts.

"Dorian!" she cried out.

He responded in a flat tone, "You're a doll, Lena,"

What the hell?

"My you are a pretty one," purred the vampire somewhere behind her. Lena tensed when his rough finger slid down her spine. "It's no wonder my son chose you to play with."

316

Above her, dust and ash fell from the ceiling as Dorian thrashed around upstairs, roaring and fighting to get to her.

All it took was this man's voice to set Dorian off. First with unbridled fear, now with white-hot fury.

Oh shit. She knew who this was. And knew what he was capable of.

You're a doll, Lena.

Dolls were complacent. Obedient. Tolerant.

Dolls also had no real emotion.

Dolls... had no fear.

Dorian was giving her a way to get out of this alive. If this vampire enjoyed torture and coaxing fear from his victims, she'd make sure to show him nothing at all. *I'm a doll. I'm a doll. I'm a doll.*

This wasn't going to work. Nope. Nope. Nope. Lena's stomach roiled when the bastard ran his hand along her ass. The sensation was vile and disgusting and Lena clamped down on her emotions and attempted to give him nothing. Not a whimper. Not a gasp. Not a twitch.

Above her, Dorian fought for his life. Each grunt and slam she heard made her shudder. More of the ceiling crumbled down around her.

"Bring him down!" the cruel vampire hollered.

Dorian was right, this guy was a monster. Burn scars puckered across his face, over most of his balding skull. More scarring disappeared into his t-shirt. His cargo pants were filthy and tattered. His jagged fingernails were long and blackened with fungus. One of his eyes could barely open from heavy lacerations that never healed right.

He stared up at the ceiling. The fight was getting worse up there, and Lena put her money on Dorian having the upper hand. The ceiling crumbled, wood cracked, then *BAM!* Dorian and Stryx fell through and slammed onto the ground in a twist of limbs and fists and teeth.

"Enough!" the scarred one hollered. "You can both take turns. Stryx, Dorian, play nice."

Dorian grappled for a piece of broken wood to use on Stryx but the other vampire kicked it away before he could reach it.

"Damnit, Dorian." The monster stormed behind Lena and the next thing she saw was three daggers go flying. At such a short

317

distance, they each hit their marks and did unholy damage. Dorian and Stryx both howled in pain. Smoke rose from Dorian's body and he dropped to his hands and knees. Stryx scrambled away.

"Father," Dorian's chest heaved as he struggled for breath. Blood poured out of his wounds. Free flowing. Those knives hit vital organs. "Father, *don't.*"

Something sharp scratched down her skin and she clamped down on her courage, holding onto it for dear life.

"So pretty," the monster said behind her. "If I give her wings, Dorian, do you think she would fly?"

CHAPTER 44

Dorian burned in furious agony. He sucked down oxygen and the taste of rotten air seized his lungs, setting them alight. He had no clue how this was happening. How this was possible. But fear gripped him and when those daggers flew into his body, he was a small boy again. A small boy in a fight for his life against a monster with more tricks up his sleeves than the devil himself.

If there was truly a Hell, Satan must have spat this beast out and forbid him to ever return. That's the only possible reason his father could still be alive.

"So pretty." His father ignored him and took his time inspecting Lena from tip to toes. "If I give her wings, do you think she would fly?"

Stryx cried out as he ripped the dagger from his shoulder.

"Stop whining, son." The monster tsked. "I taught you better than that. Now, get over here."

Son. Dorian kept his gaze locked on the monster, but when Stryx came forward, hobbling and panting, he noticed things he hadn't earlier.

Stryx was nothing more than bones and skin. During their beatdown upstairs, Dorian managed to rip Stryx's hoodie and shirt to shreds. Beat his face in a good bit too. But he was slower because he was dying... and by the look of Stryx's chewed up, bruised body, he wasn't much better.

His father was abusing Stryx the way he used to abuse Dorian. He was also calling him son.

Lena swayed, suspended in the air with chains. Her eyes were dead as she stared straight ahead and offered the monster nothing. No fear. *Good girl.* He prayed she stayed strong until he got them out of this nightmare.

"Let me," Dorian hauled his tired, drained, dying ass up and stumbled forward. He slipped on his own blood and crashed to his knees again.

"You'll get your turn," his father purred. "When I say you get your turn."

Lena sucked in air through her nostrils. She was starting to panic, and Dorian couldn't make her stop. Not from this level of uselessness. His gaze darted around the delipidated house. It was set up similarly to what he grew up in.

Old habits die hard...

"If she flies, I want to be the one to give her wings." The words flew out of his mouth, but it felt like someone else saying it. Dorian was floating again. Detached and cold. Numb and emotionless.

His father chuckled, deep and bubbly. "I should think you would since you are so fond of her."

"I don't care about her," Dorian lied. "She's just a whore I've been feeding from."

"Your heartbeat betrays you when you lie, son. Did you know that?"

Yes, he did. *Shit.* "I have no heartbeat, father. Nor a soul."

"I dare say, you seem to be knocking on death's door." His father wouldn't come closer to Dorian, he realized. He was keeping his distance. That made him smile on the inside. His father was afraid of him, as well he fucking should be.

"Teach me how to cheat death then, father." Dorian hobbled closer to test his theory, and hope flared in his chest when he saw his father take a step further away. They could play ring around the motherfucking rosy in this tiny house all night long, Dorian was still going to catch him.

"Careful, son. You're losing blood faster than you can make it."

Dorian didn't care. He just needed to get this bastard away from Lena so she wasn't caught in the bloodbath Dorian was about to start.

In his peripheral vision, he saw Stryx dart forward, his

breathing labored. He was going for Lena. Dorian turned his focus on him, because the little shit just picked something up from the counter. Dorian didn't need to look to know that counter would be loaded with tools to use on a woman's body. He darted forward, still too weak to flash.

"Stay!" his father commanded.

Dorian obeyed.

He tried to move. Tried to fight. Tried to break free.

But his boots remained pinned to the ground.

Lena took lessons in self-defense. She was also a damned good boxer. When she started kickboxing and judo, her mind became a vault of defense moves. Bane being one of her teachers, she had a few tricks up her sleeve too. All she needed to do was figure out how to use those lessons from this position.

And keep her fear locked down tight.

The thing in her head, those twisted ribbons taking up residence in some bizarre part of her brain, weren't dancing at all, she realized. They never had been. Those ribbons moved in a series of exercises she'd learned over the years, only they jumbled and knotted all together.

Ignoring Dorian and the monster talking to each other, she narrowed her focus on those damned ribbons. Tilting her head up, she calculated how much force it would take to yank the eyehook from the ceiling.

This place was broken and weak.

She wasn't.

"I dare say, you seem to be knocking on death's door." The monster teased, bringing Lena's attention back to her mate. Dorian was bleeding out, fresh blisters exploded down his arms. His face was drained of color.

If she could reach him, feed him somehow, he'd be strong enough to beat this guy.

Although, by the burning fury in Dorian's eyes, she knew he'd beat this guy anyway. If he didn't combust first.

Panic built momentum in her. She yanked on her chains with no success.

"Teach me how to cheat death then, father."

Lena's suspicions were just confirmed. *Father*. The burn marks, the shack, Dorian's reactions... the monster from Dorian's past had come back to devour him.

This vampire was the one who tortured and abused him. The one who made Dorian think he was a monster too. That alone made Lena want to kill the bastard. But this wasn't her fight. It was Dorian's and she couldn't do much anyway since she was hanging like a punching bag.

"Careful, son. You're losing blood faster than you can make it."

Stryx had hobbled around the side of the house and disappeared behind Lena. Dorian's eyes were black coals and he hissed as he attacked and his father yelled, "Stay!"

Dorian froze in place.

Lena's heart shattered when she realized Dorian was compelled. It was just like what Malachi did to Lena when they'd met.

Stryx gripped her hip. "I'm hungry, father," he whined.

The vampire in charge broke his gaze from Dorian and focused on Stryx. Lena watched Dorian's knee bend as he shifted his weight. His gaze snapped to hers. Quick as a flash, he looked up at the chains, then back to her again.

She... she wasn't sure she understood what he was getting at, but a plan formed in her mind. Dorian's boot dragged another inch. She licked her cracked lips and prepared herself.

"Have a taste," Lena said with a sultry tone. "I don't mind."

Stryx groaned and it wasn't a pleasant sound. It was strangled. Pained. Scared.

"Not yet," growled the scarred vampire, reaching for a weapon. A cleaver. "I need to season your blood before I'll allow him to feed."

She dared not look at Dorian now, though. But boy did she want to, if only to draw courage from him.

Fear Eater.

Lena knew what needed to be done. Here's hoping she could actually pull it off.

CHAPTER 45

Dorian had one shot. One chance to get this right. He played the part as well as his instincts allowed without losing himself to bloodthirst, desperation, and wrath. He pretended to be compelled by his father, to give that fucker a false sense of control.

He prayed Lena understood that. If she was scared, it didn't show, and he needed her to keep it that way.

"Have a taste," Lena said with a sultry tone. "I don't mind."

"Not yet. I need to season your blood before I'll allow him to feed."

So, the old man hadn't changed his ways one bit. Good to know.

"I know how to spike her adrenaline." Stryx needled. Then he pulled out his gun and aimed it at Dorian.

Buckling down, Dorian flashed just as the trigger was pulled. He reformed behind Stryx and disarmed him before he could fire again.

At that same moment, Lena lifted herself into a mid-suspension and clamped her legs around his father's neck. The monster stumbled in surprise and dropped the cleaver. Jerking and thrashing to free himself, Lena doubled down and didn't let go.

Dorian wrestled Stryx to the ground and grabbed the gun, firing it into Stryx, who flashed before the bullet found its mark.

Damnit!

Lena twisted and hollered as Dorian's father tried to bite into her. Stryx reformed, hanging upside down on the ceiling, hissing. Dorian pulled the trigger and shot him in the chest. He fell to the

323

ground and flashed out of sight again.

"Let go!" Dorian screamed at Lena and barreled into his father, tackling him to the ground. The cleaver skidded across the floor. He tried to grab it, missed, and got clocked in the face by a familiar left hook. Dorian's head snapped back and stars burst in his vision. Blood poured from his nose.

He slammed into his father, dragging him back before he could reach the cleaver. "Kick free!" he shouted at Lena. He couldn't help her and kill his father at the same time.

Lena flipped herself until her feet hit the ceiling and started smashing her heels into the wood around the eyehook. The wood splintered and cracked. Lena screamed with frustration.

Dorian's father snagged the cleaver. *Shit!*

"You never learn, son." He swung out and managed to cut into Dorian's thigh.

Fresh pain assaulted him.

The ceiling cracked.

Lena fell.

"Run!" Dorian roared a second before he was smashed in the head with something big. The crack of his skull echoed in his ears. He slammed down on the ground, too weak to flash or fight any harder.

Wheezing, he struggled to gain control. His skin crackled like logs on a fire. The scent of burning flesh wafted into his nose. His body - blistered, bruised, cut, and bleeding - was finally giving out on him.

"Run!" he hissed as he crawled to the first thing he could use to fight with.

Lena didn't run. She was dragged away instead.

Stryx had her by the ankles and hauled her ass out of the house while she screamed Dorian's name.

"Let her run." His father staggered while laughing. "We're in the bayou. She has no chance of surviving. I've got the entire area rigged with traps, and that's only if the snakes and gators don't get a piece of her first." He held his side and sucked in another ragged breath. "Playing hide and seek just got more interesting, boy." Hobbling over to Dorian, he said, "Too bad you aren't going to live long enough to see her fly."

He swung the cleaver down and Dorian's world went black.

Stryx dragged Lena out of the house with her screaming and thrashing about. She wasn't leaving Dorian in there with that animal. She wasn't leaving this place without Dorian, period.

The chains were still attached to her. They rattled and clanked as Stryx pulled her further and further away from the cabin. He looked at her with blood-shot eyes and said, "Get help! C-c-c-can you f-f-f-flash home?"

Lena didn't answer and just kept fighting to get out of his hold. He didn't let go of her.

"K-k-keep still," he jumped onto her and they wrestled across the ground. He wrapped his legs around her middle and squeezed the air from her lungs as his fingers dug into her arms.

Her heels and elbows dug into the wet ground.

They were in a swamp.

She had no idea what he was going to do to her out here in the position he held her in, but when the chains rattled and the weight lifted, she twisted furiously, screaming and gnashing her teeth, until Stryx flashed out of her reach.

Lena scrambled to get up and noticed her chains had been removed.

"Run!" Stryx hollered from twenty feet up in a tree. "Run, girl! You have to r-r-run!" He doubled over, groaning in pain and fell off the limb he'd perched in.

A bear trap clamped onto his leg and he screamed.

Wide-eyed, Lena scanned the ground, terrified of what else lay nestled in the grass. Carefully turning, she couldn't see anything but *swamp, trees, tall grass*. Hard to say what hid in all that.

Stryx yanked on the beartrap, trying to free his leg. Blood was everywhere. The scent filled Lena's nostrils, making her thirsty. *Fast movement in the grass to her left*. She pivoted. Was it a gator? A rat? Another vampire? A Lycan? A *Savag-Ri*?

Rolling her shoulders back, Lena clenched her fists and quieted her mind. *Detach, detach, detach. Focus on one target at a time.*

Stryx panicked as she cautiously slid past him, hellbent on getting back to the shack.

"No, don't!" he screamed as he tried to catch her. The

beartrap prevented him from getting anywhere.

"I'll come back for you," she said without looking at him.

To kill him or free him, she wasn't sure yet. That would be Dorian's call.

Serial Killer Pro Tip: When staring death down, keep your cool. Show no fear. If not, it only made the process more pleasant for the one doing the killing. When Dorian saw the cleaver come at his face, he thundered with rage and felt himself combust.

Or... rather flash in an awful, painful way.

It wasn't far enough away from the cleaver's strike but at least his face didn't take the hit.

His arm had. Nearly severed at the elbow, Dorian's forearm dangled like a useless accessory as he stood up and swayed on shaky legs. He wasn't going to die on his back like a wounded animal.

He staggered forward, headed straight for his father.

Fuck cleavers. Fuck weapons. He'd kill this monster with his bare hands and teeth.

His father kicked him back, sending him sailing into the countertop and part of his spine snapped, making his legs go numb.

Damn his blood curse. Damn his father. Damn himself.

He wasn't making it out of here. "Lena," Dorian wheezed.

Fight off Stryx and get to safety.

Swaying, he was just about to give in when two bodies crashed through the already broken windows on either side of the cabin. Going into shock, Dorian stood rooted to the spot.

Xin... Lucian.

A third person kicked down the door.

Victoria.

How had they found him?

"What the hell kinda b-rated horror movie stunt double mayhem you get us into, man?" Xin stalked right over to Dorian's father and cold-cocked the bastard. "Jesus, you're an ugly one."

While they started fighting, Lena ran over and grabbed Dorian by the back of his neck, helping him sit up. "Drink." She bit into her wrist and held it up to his mouth. "Drink, hurry!"

But he couldn't. Not now. Probably never again. Dorian couldn't move his jaw to even open it. Teeth clenched, he focused only on his father. The monster was going head-to-head with both Lucian and Xin.

Die.

His father needed to die.

In the distant parts of his mind, Dorian heard Lena's pleading, muffled voice urging him to drink from her. He was vaguely aware of his skin sizzling as he began to incinerate. Tears welled in his eyes. He wasn't getting a pardon from this death sentence.

His curse would kill him before he kissed his *alakhai* again... or before he could slay the monster who never died all those years ago.

I'm so sorry.

If he had to chose one over the other, then he'd go to his grave with this one regret. But choosing his father was the only way to keep Lena safe from him once Dorian died.

He shoved himself off the floor and staggered across broken glass and splintered wood. Picking up a piece of the broken beam, he stumbled forward hellbent on ending this. His heart barely beat anymore. His face tingled. The high-pitched ringing in his ears was awful.

Dorian crashed, desperate for this all to end — his torment, pain, regrets and hate. All the things laced in the blood of those victims now burned and set him in motion.

Lena kept screaming his name.

Dorian closed his eyes, wishing her screams wouldn't be the last thing he heard before he burned alive.

Xin and Lucian held his father down. They both understood how important it was to Dorian that he be the one to kill him.

"Do it!" Lucian shouted.

Sucking in a breath, Dorian thrust his hand out, driving the stake into his father's chest. It barely penetrated.

The monster's scarred face twisted with laughter. "You can't, son."

He was right. Dorian might as well have tried shoving a toothpick through concrete. He couldn't do it. He was too depleted and caught up in the anguish of knowing he was going to leave everything he loved behind and this monster would survive long enough to destroy it after Dorian died.

"No." He refused to accept defeat. Refused to fail killing this monster twice. Steadfast, Dorian used his body weight and one good arm to push the stake deeper into his father's chest. He looked down at the impalement. Blinked slowly. It wasn't enough. He couldn't do it. He had no strength left.

A second set of hands wrapped around his. *Lena.*

Soundlessly, she helped him shove the stake further into his father's chest, impaling him right through his heart - if the monster even possessed such a thing.

"Not enough." Dorian's tongue burned and blistered. His saliva boiled in his mouth.

With a gurgling grunt, his father fell to his knees and Dorian went down with him. They were face-to-face, both monsters to the bitter fucking end.

"You've done me proud," his father sputtered as blood welled in his mouth. "I've trained you well, son."

Dorian's heart sank to his boots.

"You're just like me." He said, smiling with a mouthful of rotten, chipped teeth.

While on his knees, bloody, burning, and broken, Dorian remembered moments like this back when he was kid. Reminisced about their shack where his father took people against their will and made sure they never got out alive. Rehashed how he was forced to watch innocents live through horrors, just so his father could coax their fears forward. The rotten piece of shit played with them like toys. Discarded them like trash. Didn't care about anything other than the high he caught while killing, and the pleasure of Dorian's anguish when he'd cry over their dead bodies while they burned.

Dorian's death count was different. Murder might be murder, but the ones he killed were sanctioned and necessary to secure the safety of their race. He never raised an angry hand to an innocent. Never forced someone to do something against their will. He was the exact opposite of this monstrosity before him.

"I'm *nothing* like you."

He looked beyond his retched father and locked eyes on Lena. She held a huge, curved blade in her hand, and silently held it out to him. He reached for it, wrapping his hand over hers as she brought the blade to the monster's neck. Lena drove her knee into the vampire's back, forcing him to bow, then shoved his head, tipping and holding it against her stomach.

She exposed his throat.

Her gaze remained on Dorian.

Holding that blade together, they sliced that monster's neck wide-the-fuck-open.

Lena showed no fear. Blood sprayed, releasing Dorian from countless shackles, regrets, and remorse.

Closing his eyes, he exhaled the breath he'd been holding for a lifetime.

CHAPTER 46

Dorian was a child, running and giggling. He brushed his fingers along the perfectly box-shaped shrubs and squealed when he was caught...

He shot up gasping.

I'm alive.

Chest heaving, he looked down at his arms. Not a single blister. Not an ounce of pain.

"You're awake!" Lena's relief made him feel ten kinds of ways, none of which he could put a finger on.

He blinked fast and licked his dry, cracked lips.

"He's awake!" Lena yelled.

Lucian popped his head into the room. "It's about time. I was starting to feel like a permanent piece of furniture in the hall."

Dorian huffed a laugh and winced. Shit that hurt.

But the pain was good. The pain meant he wasn't dead.

"How long have I been out?" He sat up in the bed and scrubbed his face with both hands. Oh hey, what do you know, his arm was reattached.

"About two weeks," Lena said. "I think. I don't even know. I've lost track of time."

"Sixteen days," Lucian said quietly as he sat down in a chair by the vanity. "Your mate hasn't left your side for a second. Stood guard by your bed the whole time."

Dorian noticed Lena had lost a little weight. Her hair was pulled back in a braid that had seen better days too. In her hand was his favorite karambit. He arched his brow, "What do you plan to do with that?"

She shrugged nonchalantly. "I can be creative."

He chuckled.

"She threatened to use it on the next person who knocked on the door to check on you. The whole House has been worried for you."

Dorian didn't know how to feel about that. He honestly didn't think anyone in the House of Death, besides a handful of vampires, even cared whether he lived or died. It was kind of nice to learn that wasn't the truth. He lived to protect each being here, so a little compassion in return was nice.

"How do you feel?" Lucian hedged.

"Different." And that was the honest truth. He didn't know what changed, but something had. Maybe it was the rush of cheating death? Maybe it was the final piece of his curse lifting?

"You bonded," Lucian smiled. "It saved your ass in the literal last minute, man."

Dorian's brow furrowed. He shook his head, "What do you mean?"

"In the act of killing your father," Lena said, "the last piece of the *alakhai* bond clicked into place."

"Slaying your biggest and fiercest demon," Lucian added, "unlocked your blood curse and saved your sorry ass from incinerating."

"He's dead?" Dorian needed to know for sure. He wasn't going to believe it if he didn't see it himself.

"Torn to pieces, burned to ashes, dusted in the humid, mosquito infested swamp breeze." Lucian gave him a minute to grab onto all that. "I'd have saved you the proof, but we didn't leave anything of that mongrel behind. He's gone, Dorian. I swear it."

He trusted Lucian enough to believe him.

Dorian leaned back on his pillow with a sigh. He felt like shit for failing to kill that monster the first time around. How many innocent lives had his father claimed over the years? He couldn't bring himself to make those calculations.

His head started banging. Wincing, he gripped his head and swallowed the bile rising in his throat. Visions flashed in his mind, all wild and vaguely familiar.

Wait... what?

He shook his head. Blinked. Still saw them.

"Memories." His concentration was shot to shit. He doubled down on catching the visions from his dream.

Running and laughing, touching the shrubbery...

"What do you remember?" Lucian asked cautiously.

"What happened after I passed out?"

"You mean almost bursting into flames and ash?" Lucian sat back in his chair. "Or after we brought you home, a ravenous wreck of a vampire?"

"I only remember cutting my father's throat." He looked up at Lena and smiled. "With your help."

His mate actually *blushed* over him talking about beheading someone together. Holy Hell, where had this woman come from?

Lucian nodded. "How about the part where his head rolled off his shoulders?"

Dorian's brow pinched as he tried to summon the memory.

"Damn, Reaper, you're gonna have smoke coming out of your ears again if you keep thinking that hard." Lucian pushed out of his chair and swaggered closer. "Short version or long?"

"Short," Dorian and Lena said at the same time.

Dorian's smile widened. "He talks too much, doesn't he?"

"Yes! And exaggerates."

"Whoa! Hey! I do not exaggerate, I just give a little flare when needed." Lucian flipped Dorian the bird. "Okay." He clapped his hands and rubbed them together. "Here it goes."

Dorian kept his gaze locked on Lena and held her hand while Lucian prattled.

"Your father survived the fire you set when you were a kid, clearly. No idea where he went to, but he bided his time to come after you, according to Stryx."

"Stryx?"

"I'm telling the story, please save all questions for the end." Lucian inhaled dramatically, "Where was I? Oh yeah, so anyway, your father isn't your sire."

Lena's hand tightened on Dorian's.

He stiffened. "Repeat that?"

"He was never your real father," Lucian said more seriously. "I was hoping to skate over that with a little more finesse. Missed the mark, huh?"

"Are you being serious?" Because if so, then what Dorian's mind was filled with could be—

Nope, not going there. Miracles never came in threes.

"He kidnapped you, Dorian. Killed your father and kept your mother for a little while before killing her too. He erased your memories leading up to that point. Replaced them with lies. Kept you drained and used your blood against you, to enslave you." Lucian's tone darkened with vengeance and fangs extended while he continued. "You're royalty," he said. "You're Malachi's great nephew."

Dorian shook his head. "That can't be right."

"It is," Lucian pushed. "You've had the power to flash, compel, and who knows how many other things. You just never thought to use those powers because you didn't have a clue... the memories were either repressed or taken. And you've been holding yourself back for fear of what you might be capable of because of that asshole."

"Then how has that all changed now?"

"Lena." Lucian tipped his head towards her. "She was the one thing you'd do anything for. The impossible made possible. She was what you thought was worth living for. Because let's face it, man, you haven't lived. And you definitely haven't thrived. You've just been a weapon doing the King's bidding on behalf of the House of Death. You harbor more guilt than a pack of convicts at the pearly gates."

Dorian's throat tightened.

Then the visions he just had were memories.

Dorian closed his eyes and recalled them with perfect clarity: *Running down a hallway lined with the finest cobalt blue rugs, dipping his finger in a bowl of cake batter, music playing, his mother and father laughing while they danced in a kitchen three times the size of the house Dorian now lived in.*

He'd been tucked into bed once. Fed homecooked meals. Played hide and seek in the lavish hedge garden out back of their estate.

"The hedge garden," he murmured.

"That's where you were kidnapped," Lucian confirmed. "And you weren't the first, but certainly the one who lasted the longest according to Malachi."

"He knew?"

Lucian sobered. "Yeah. But you not remembering anything about your kidnapping or much about your real mother made him hesitate to reveal it until now. He didn't tell me until last week. No one else knows yet. We figured you could tell them yourself or keep it your secret."

Dorian lived his life, or so he thought, with no secrets at all. "What about Stryx?"

Lucian groaned. "Skipping ahead." He rotated his finger in a fast-forward motion. "Stryx and his boy toy, Bram, had run off like Marius thought. But they got separated. The Rogue, which, by the way, was what that whacko actually was, took Stryx and then Bram. Thought he'd got a two-for-one special, is my bet. A royal and a weaver."

Lena's lips pursed, "What's a weaver again?"

"One who can spell *Savag-Ri* bone dust for us to use as protection against them. They're rare and having one enslaved would be a major boon for that whack job and would have put a crippling dent in our armor."

"Was that the powder all over the floor in his cabin?"

"That was almost all lime, sweetheart." Lucian's nose crinkled. "It did nothing to keep the rancid stench down in there either."

Dorian's head started throbbing again. "Where's Stryx now?"

"Reunited with Marius. He'd been altered like you. His memories wiped clean of anything before the Rogue took him."

Even now, his fath... no, not father, *the monster*, had no name.

"A Rogue?" Made sense considering they lived without a House. He'd never thought about that until now.

"He was most likely the longest living one in our history. You have no idea how lucky you are to have survived so long in his clutches."

Yes, he did.

"Once the Rogue died, your altered memories should have restored. That's how it works."

Dorian nodded. He knew how it worked. He stayed clear of creatures with that gift and never gave anyone reason to use that violating trick on him.

"So back to Stryx," Lucian cleared his throat. "You gotta stop derailing my story, man. You're fucking it all up and I practiced my delivery countless times this week."

"Forgive me."

"Forgiven. Now shut up." Lucian started pacing. "The Rogue was compelling Stryx. But since the young prince was twenty-two, he was so close to maturity *and* was also a pure-blooded royal, his higher-level instincts kicked in at some point recently. The Rogue wasn't able to keep him compelled as long as he could a younger vampire... say, someone around the age of ten or so."

About the age Dorian had been when he was abducted then.

He thought he'd been with that animal for two decades, when it had only been one. It felt like a hundred.

Lucian sighed. "Bram was a pawn the same way your mother had been. He was used to keep Stryx in line. Only you blasted his head off, which cut the game short."

Well, shit. Dorian felt a little sorry about that now since Bram was most likely being compelled too.

"Stryx was forced to follow you and report back to the Rogue. Apparently, the old vampire was obsessed with reminding you of where you came from but wouldn't come close to you. He even had Stryx convinced you were his long-lost brother." Lucian rubbed the back of his neck, "That Rogue did fucked up shit to Stryx's head."

That vampire did fucked up shit, *period*.

"The dead wolf was the Rogue's work. Stryx had nothing to do with it." Lucian went on. "Apparently, the bastard had also become fixated on Emily."

Dorian's lips peeled into a snarl as he growled viciously.

"Trust me, you aren't the only one who had that reaction, man. I've already spoken with the Woods family about all this."

"Good thing this guy's dead." Lena sighed. "He's made a mess."

"You have no idea, Lena," Lucian's eyes burned with rage. "You two saved four species from a killer who seemed to defy all odds. A fact Malachi is making all Houses *and* Lycan clans aware of even as we speak."

"He never used reflections either," Dorian murmured, no longer paying attention to Lucian. "My fa—" Shit, he couldn't get used it, "that *Rogue* would coat his blades in blood or grease to keep them from showing a reflection. And I was the one who always had to get water from the river or well. It most likely helped him prolong his life... and spurred his madness."

Lucian's shoulders slumped. "I'm so sorry for all this. I spent two minutes with the guy, and he made my balls wanna do the tuck and run. I can't imagine what it must have been like for you."

"It's done," Lena bristled. "It's over."

Dorian's brow furrowed. "How did you even find us?"

"Malachi," Lucian sighed. "He was able to get a bead on Lena since her blood was still fresh in his veins. Called me on my cell while we were doing that perimeter search. We'd have gotten there faster if we hadn't been ambushed by six *Savag-Ri* who saw us running and decided to jump off a roof to attack us."

Talk about perfect timing. He knew Malachi could trace the ones in his House during their first days of pledging fealty to him. Never thought it would come in handy though.

"I owe you guys," Dorian winced as he tried to sit up straighter. "If you and Xin hadn't held him back to give me a chance to kill him, I might not be here right now."

Never mind the fact that Lena had helped him make the final cut.

That was just.... Yeah. Whoa.

Lucian waved him off. "You don't owe us a damned thing."

The vampire had always been his friend and gave him what he needed when he needed it. That included blood from his vein and the courage to go after Lena.

"You might have to kiss Victoria's ass for a little bit," Lucian's brow raised to his hair line, "She controlled Stryx long enough to get him home and yada, yada, yada. I think she kept the bear trap as a souvenir. Crazy bitch."

Dorian chuckled. *Ouch.* "Why do I feel like I've been hit by a train?"

"Your body's still healing from the curse. That's going to take time. How you were able to stave off the final burn is beyond me. I just about pissed myself when I saw your skin sizzle."

"Sheer stubbornness." Dorian puffed.

"And grit," Lena bent down and kissed him. Their mouths fused together.

Pretty sure he just caught fire again.

"Annnnd on that note, I'm out of here." Lucian headed for the door and neither of them stopped him.

The door clicked shut, and Dorian smiled against Lena's mouth. "Get over here so I can ravage you."

"Is that a promise or a threat?" She crawled over to straddle him on the bed.

"Think Malachi would get pissed if we broke this headboard?"

"Only one way to find out."

Dorian's soul set ablaze for his mate. Threading his fingers through Lena's hair, he unbound her braid and rolled her over. Nestled between her thighs, he nipped her bottom lip. "You're overdressed." He yanked her shirt, tearing it down the middle. Her shorts didn't stand a chance of survival either.

"Better?" She cocked a brow at him.

"Significantly."

He kissed her slowly, savoring every stroke of her tongue and brush of her lips. "You killed for me."

"You lived for me."

He nudged her thighs open a little wider and ran his fingers along her pussy. "So wet."

"I've been on guard duty, watching over a killer vampire. It makes me hot. And thirsty." She hooked her legs around his waist and his eyes rolled back when she sank her fangs into his neck. He thrust into her, one inch at a time, as she drank from him.

His soul went up in flames like a set of curtains next to a bonfire.

His pace turned vicious. Her kisses deepened. They clutched, bit, clamped, sucked, and clung to one another.

"I love you, Dorian." She brushed the hair from his face as they continued to worship each other straight through the night. "I love you in a way I didn't understand was possible."

"Love is a terribly weak word for what I feel for you," he said against the shell of her ear. "I've been set alight by you."

Lena gripped his shoulders as he took them both closer to that perilous current of ecstasy.

"Burn, baby, burn."

EPILOGUE

Dorian canted forward in his seat, eyes pinned between Lena and her opponent. It took tremendous control to watch her fight without intervening. He didn't like the idea of someone getting a hit on his mate, but seeing her face light up? Those flushed cheeks? The bounce in her body as she weaved, ducked, and went in for another strike? That was fire.

"Ooph!" Bane winced next to him. "That had to hurt."

Dorian's smile widened, and his fangs pierced his bottom lip. "Bet it did."

"You teach her that move?"

"What do you think?" His heart cheered when Lena got in another six quick jabs and finally slammed her opponent on the ground. Some dude named Jackhammer got his ass handed to him by none other than the sweetest, most savage, seductive opponent of his fucking life. Lucky sonofabitch.

Dorian couldn't wait to get out of here and give her a victory fuck.

His hard-on raged in his slacks. He always had this level of arousal watching Lena move like a predator. She tossed her hands up in the air with victory lighting up her face. She had some cuts and bruises, but they were healing fast, thanks to the constant blood exchange she and Dorian made.

Leaping out of his seat, he was at her in four strides, kissing her in front of everyone before dragging her into a shadowed corner of the abandoned warehouse they were using tonight.

"How'd I do?" Lena sucked in air and wiped the sweat from

her brow.

"Spectacular." He wiped her hair back and out of her face. "Hurt anywhere?"

"Not really." She twisted her torso and looked down. "He got a nice one on me here. I thought I saw God for about two seconds when that happened."

"We'll work on that then." Because if they weren't hunting or making violent, wild love, Dorian was teaching her new ways to fight the creatures who went bump in the night. He made sure his woman was equipped to fight them all and always win. If she came close to losing, he'd jump in and help. Fuck the rules. Lena came first.

Her independence was important to her. Her safety was paramount to him.

"I want you inside me. Now." She dragged him by his crisp, white shirt and kissed him with the ferocity that made his toes curl and dick harden to the point of pain.

He loved how hot and bothered she got after a fight. And before one.

Actually, she was always hot and bothered and he relished every second of it. "I'm needed at the Kill Box in two hours. Then we have dinner at the mansion at nine."

They'd been having dinner with the rest of the House twice a week. It was amazing. Dorian finally felt worthy to be among his kind instead of just serving them.

He didn't tell anyone about him being royalty. It wasn't necessarily a secret. Just a fact that didn't matter in the grand scheme of things. He was still executioner. Still protector of his House. That's all. Bloodlines didn't play a factor in his honor at all.

They had, however, redecorated Dorian's old house. He had cushions galore. And apples in a bowl. Bananas too. Lena made his house a home and gave him a life worth living for.

"Backseat?" She was already tugging him out of the warehouse.

"No way. If someone sees your fine ass through the window, I'll have to gouge their eyes out."

"Hmmm, hotel?"

He held the keycard up, way ahead of her.

She squealed and raced to the car and they arrived at the hotel within twenty minutes. Damn traffic. He'd flash to work from here and Lena could take the car and meet him at the mansion later. She still hadn't been able to flash yet, but he suspected it was coming. His blood flowed through her system, so his skills should blend into her natural ones.

Heaven help them all when Lena's power fully bloomed. She was already a force of nature. Once her powers amplified, Dorian figured she'd be legendary.

And he was the lucky sonofabitch who got to spend eternity with her.

They tossed the keys to the valet guy, and she started ripping his clothes off while they were in the elevator.

"Easy, I only have the one shirt."

With a cocky grin, she ripped the damn thing, sending the buttons flying.

Dorian growled as he pinned her against the wall. "You're killing me."

She laughed just to set him on fire, like always, and he ate that magic up. Capturing her mouth with his, he carried her into their hotel room, slammed the door, and wrecked the room worshipping her on every surface.

They could send him a damage bill later.

For information on this book and other future releases, please visit my website: **www.BrianaMichaels.com**

If you liked this book, please help spread the word by leaving a review on the site you purchased your copy, or on a reader site such as Goodreads.

I'd love to hear from readers too, so feel free to send me an email at: sinsofthesidhe@gmail.com or visit me on Facebook: www.facebook.com/BrianaMichaelsAuthor

Thank you!

ABOUT THE AUTHOR

Briana Michaels grew up and still lives on the East Coast. When taking a break from the crazy adventures in her head, she enjoys running around with her two children. If there is time to spare, she loves to read, cook, hike in the woods, and sit outside by a roaring fire. She does all of this with the love and support of her amazing husband who always has her back, encouraging her to go for her dreams.

Printed in Great Britain
by Amazon

18283386R00203